MW01166690

TALES OF HEROES, GODS & MONSTERS

CHINESE

MYTHS & LEGENDS

FLAME TREE PUBLISHING
6 Melbray Mews, Fulham,
London SW6 3NS, United Kingdom
www.flametreepublishing.com

First published and copyright © 2024
Flame Tree Publishing Ltd

24 26 28 27 25
1 3 5 7 9 10 8 6 4 2

ISBN: 978-1-80417-806-5

Cover and pattern art was created by Flame Tree Studio, with elements courtesy of the
Metropolitan Museum of Art, New York, www.metmuseum.org (*Guan Yu*, unidentified
artist, *c.* 1700, Purchase, The B.Y. Lam Fund and Friends of Asian Art Gifts, in honor of
Douglas Dillon, 2001) and Shutterstock.com/gorozhinak/chasiki/svekloid.
Additional interior decoration courtesy Shutterstock.com/grmarc.

Judith John (Glossary) is a writer and editor specializing in literature and history. A
former secondary school English Language and Literature teacher, she has subsequently
worked as an editor on major educational projects, including *English A: Literature* for
the Pearson International Baccalaureate series. Judith's major research interests include
Romantic and Gothic literature, and Renaissance drama.

Sources and contributors for the tales in this book include *Myths & Legends of China* by
E.T.C. Werner, 1922, *The Chinese Fairy Book*, Ed. Dr. R. Wilhelm, Trans. Frederick H.
Martens, 1921, O.B. Duane and N. Hutchison. With thanks to Hin Ming Frankie Chik
for the conversion of spellings within the stories to Pinyin.

A copy of the CIP data for this book is available
from the British Library.

Designed and created in the UK | Printed and bound in China

COLLECTOR'S EDITIONS

TALES OF HEROES, GODS & MONSTERS

CHINESE

MYTHS & LEGENDS

Reading List & Glossary of Terms
with a New Introduction by
HIN MING FRANKIE CHIK

FLAME TREE PUBLISHING

CONTENTS

4

TALES OF HEROES, GODS & MONSTERS

CHINESE

MYTHS & LEGENDS

SERIES FOREWORD

Stretching back to the oral traditions of thousands of years ago, tales of heroes and disaster, creation and conquest have been told by many different civilizations in many different ways. Their impact sits deep within our culture even though the detail in the tales themselves are a loose mix of historical record, transformed narrative and the distortions of hundreds of storytellers.

Today the language of mythology lives with us: our mood is jovial, our countenance is saturnine, we are narcissistic and our modern life is hermetically sealed from others. The nuances of myths and legends form part of our daily routines and help us navigate the world around us, with its half truths and biased reported facts.

The nature of a myth is that its story is already known by most of those who hear it, or read it. Every generation brings a new emphasis, but the fundamentals remain the same: a desire to understand and describe the events and relationships of the world. Many of the great stories are archetypes that help us find our own place, equipping us with tools for self-understanding, both individually and as part of a broader culture.

For Western societies it is Greek mythology that speaks to us most clearly. It greatly influenced the mythological heritage of the ancient Roman civilization and is the lens through which we still see the Celts, the Norse and many of the other great peoples and religions. The Greeks themselves learned much from their neighbours, the Egyptians, an older culture that became weak with age and incestuous leadership.

It is important to understand that what we perceive now as mythology had its own origins in perceptions of the divine and the rituals of the sacred. The earliest civilizations, in the crucible of the Middle East, in the Sumer of the third millennium BCE, are the source to which many of the mythic archetypes can be traced. As humankind collected together in cities for the first time, developed writing and industrial scale agriculture, started to irrigate the rivers and attempted to control rather than be at the mercy of its environment, humanity began to write down its tentative explanations of natural events, of floods and plagues, of disease.

Early stories tell of Gods (or god-like animals in the case of tribal societies such as African, Native American or Aboriginal cultures) who are crafty and use their wits to survive, and it is reasonable to suggest that these were the first rulers of the gathering peoples of the earth, later elevated to god-like status with the distance of time. Such tales became more political as cities vied with each other for supremacy, creating new Gods, new hierarchies for their pantheons. The older Gods took on primordial roles and became the preserve of creation and destruction, leaving the new gods to deal with more current, everyday affairs. Empires rose and fell, with Babylon assuming the mantle from Sumeria in the 1800s BCE, then in turn to be swept away by the Assyrians of the 1200s BCE; then the Assyrians and the Egyptians were subjugated by the Greeks, the Greeks by the Romans and so on, leading to the spread and assimilation of common themes, ideas and stories throughout the world.

The survival of history is dependent on the telling of good tales, but each one must have the 'feeling' of truth, otherwise it will be ignored. Around the firesides, or embedded in a book or a computer, the myths and legends of the past are still the living materials of retold myth, not restricted to an exploration of origins. Now we have devices and global communications that give us unparalleled access to a diversity of traditions. We can find out about Native American, Indian, Chinese and tribal African mythology in a way that was denied to our ancestors, we can find connections, match the archaeology, religion and the mythologies of the world to build a comprehensive image of the human experience that is endlessly fascinating.

The stories in this book provide an introduction to the themes and concerns of the myths and legends of their respective cultures, with a short introduction to provide a linguistic, geographic and political context. This is where the myths have arrived today, but undoubtedly over the next millennia, they will transform again whilst retaining their essential truths and signs.

Jake Jackson
General Editor

TALES OF HEROES, GODS & MONSTERS

CHINESE

MYTHS & LEGENDS

INTRODUCTION
& FURTHER READING

A NEW INTRODUCTION TO CHINESE MYTHS & LEGENDS

WHAT IS CHINESE MYTH?

The assertion that China has a history spanning 5,000 years has long served as a political slogan by the Chinese government. However, nearly 1,500 of these 5,000 years stem from fantastical accounts recorded by later generations. Myths in China have played a crucial role in tracing the origins of human civilization and are present across various texts. The Chinese term for myth, *shenhua*, directly translates to 'sayings about gods'. Yuan Ke (1916–2001), a distinguished scholar of Chinese mythology, categorized Chinese myths into 'mythology', 'legends' and 'fairy tales'. Of these, 'mythology' primarily explores the relationship between humans and nature, while 'legends' focus upon individuals with exaggerated abilities and achievements. 'Fairy tales', evolving from 'mythology' and imbued with Daoist influences, delve into the concept of immortality, detailing the lives and ascension of immortals. This introduction aims to highlight key aspects of Chinese myths, offering insights into ancient Chinese perceptions of the world and their place within it.

OUR SOURCES

Chinese myths pervade numerous sources, spanning different genres and visual mediums. Early Chinese thinkers often employed myths to bolster their arguments, leaving abundant records of their visions of a distant past. Archaeological finds, such as lacquer and silk paintings and shamanic effigies, provide intriguing insights into ancient mythologies and the societies that sustained them. Historical texts also recount tales now categorized as myths. The *Records of the Grand Historian*, China's inaugural official history, incorporates mythical and legendary narratives from the pre-dynastic era, suggesting that its author considered these myths an integral part of human history. During the middle period (*c.* 100–1500 CE), compilations of uncanny tales, for example *In Search of the Spirits*, which explored spiritual and supernatural realms, were classified as part of 'miscellaneous history' rather than as literary fiction.

Given the widespread circulation of mythical stories across different epochs and regions, many have multiple versions. Such variations not only reflect shifts in cultural tastes but also reveal the 'plasticity' of these tales, allowing for adaptation to the storyteller's needs. For instance, the *Story of the White Maiden*, with its myriad iterations since the Tang dynasty – ranging from novels to opera performances – continues to be reimagined to suit contemporary preferences, underscoring its enduring appeal among Chinese audiences. Myths were thus omnipresent in pre-modern China, making it remarkably easy to encounter mythical narratives.

CHINESE MYTHS AND RELIGIONS

In pre-modern China, the religious lives of the elite were dominated by three major institutional religions: Confucianism, Daoism and Buddhism. Confucianism, with Confucius (c. 551–479 BCE) as its founder, places benevolence at the heart of its ethical philosophy, aiming to establish a society in which individuals understand and fulfil their societal roles. Daoism, recognizing Laozi as its patriarch, distinguishes itself by a focus on ontological inquiries in its philosophical form and on deities, rituals and religious practices in its religious form. Buddhism, originating from India and introduced to China in the second century CE, subsequently underwent Sinicization, becoming a significant religion in China and East Asia.

Despite their doctrinal differences, which sometimes led to conflicts over orthodoxy, it was not uncommon for political and cultural elites to adhere to more than one of these traditions. This syncretism was even more prevalent among commoners, typically not affiliated with any religious community or organization. These three religions, integral to Chinese folk religions or 'diffused religions', were accepted by ordinary people as long as their teachings were seen as beneficial or provided inner peace. Such flexibility allowed a harmonious coexistence of diverse religious elements in Chinese myths.

MYTHS IN ANCIENT CHU CULTURE

Significant mythological content is found in ancient Chu culture, which spanned the regions now known as Hubei, Hunan and Henan. This culture is characterized by its shamanistic inclinations, blurring the boundaries between human and divine realms. The *Chuci* or *Elegies of Chu*, a compilation of verses from the Chu region, exemplifies this through narratives of soul summoning and divine communication. Several poems depict the journey of the soul beyond the physical body to engage with heavenly beings – a motif that would influence Chinese popular religion, notably religious Daoism, believed to have originated in the Chu area. In contrast, Confucius famously refrained from discussing the supernatural. Despite this, many mythical stories, even those outside the Confucian canon, often promoted Confucian values such as filial piety. In so doing they demonstrated the intricate relationship between religion and mythology in the formation of Chinese cultural and moral principles.

CHINESE COSMOLOGY AND MYTHS

Qi: The Base of the Universe

Ancient Chinese myths are deeply intertwined with discussions on the cosmos's structure and dynamics, positing *qi* as the universe's fundamental element. This concept of *qi* lacks a direct English equivalent. Attempts to define it have included 'stuff', 'fluid', 'pneuma', 'ether', 'material energy' and 'vital force'. However, these translations fall short of capturing the full meaning of qi, generally considered to be an all-encompassing energy vital for the growth of all beings.

Yin-Yang Dichotomy

In this cosmology, *qi* is divided into two opposing yet complementary aspects: *yin* and *yang*. *Yin* symbolizes Earth, passivity, the state of being governed, childhood and the colder seasons, embodying the concept of 'below'. In contrast, *yang* represents Heaven, activity, governance, adulthood and the warmer seasons, associated with 'above'. This dichotomy suggests that a harmonious balance between *yin* and *yang* is crucial for *qi*'s uninterrupted flow. Any imbalance that arises – often attributed to human moral failings – is a potential cause of natural and societal disasters. The concept of duality is so essential to Chinese thought that it permeates the language, with terms such as *da-xiao* (big-small) and *chang-duan* (long-short) reflecting this binary structure.

Five Elements

Beyond *qi*, ancient Chinese philosophy identified Five Elements or agents – Fire, Water, Wood, Metal and Earth – as the building blocks of the universe. Each element was believed to be linked to specific colours and to exert an extensive influence on various cultural domains, including meteorology, human relationships, phenology, geography, anatomy, astrology and politics. The interaction among these elements was understood in two principal ways. The first suggested a generating interaction between each element. Wood generates Fire, Fire generates Earth, Earth generates Metal, Metal generates Water and Water generates Wood. The second theory, in contrast, proposed an interaction of subjugation between each element, in which Wood overcomes Earth, Earth overcomes Water, Water overcomes Fire, Fire overcomes Metal and Metal overcomes Wood. Despite this difference, both theories emphasized an eternal, cyclical balance essential for cosmic and earthly harmony.

DID CREATION MYTHS EXIST IN CHINA?

The question of whether Chinese culture contains creation myths has sparked considerable debate among scholars. Some, such as Frederick W. Mote, David L. Hall and Roger T. Ames, assert that China lacks myths of cosmogony, specifically the concept of *creatio ex nihilo* (creation out of nothing). Conversely, starting with Eduard Erkes, other scholars such as Wolfram Eberhard and, more recently, Paul Goldin have challenged this view, identifying creation myths within a variety of early Chinese texts. Goldin argues against evaluating Chinese narratives through a Western-centric lens, advocating for an understanding of 'creation' within its unique ancient Chinese context.

Beyond the Daoist ontological perspective that positions the Dao as the origin of all things, as depicted in Laozi and other early Daoist writings, several intriguing origin stories are found in Chinese literature. For instance, texts of the third century CE introduce Pangu – a 'creator' who separates Heaven and Earth and, upon his death, transforms his body into various geographical features. It is important to note, however, that the universe, described as a cosmic egg in a state of chaos, pre-existed Pangu. This suggests that ancient Chinese views of creation differ significantly from the Western notion of *creatio ex nihilo*.

THE REPAIR OF HEAVEN AND THE BIRTH OF HUMAN BEINGS

Before the Pangu creation myth, ancient Chinese texts recounted other origin stories, including the myth of Nüwa repairing the sky. This narrative, detailed in the *Huainanzi* from the second century BCE, describes a world in chaos; the pillars of the four compass points are shattered and the nine provinces divided, causing Heaven and Earth to misalign. To rectify this disarray, Nüwa melted stones of five colours to mend the sky and utilized the legs of a turtle to reinforce the corners of the Earth. She also vanquished the Black Dragon, dispelling threats to humanity. The story of Nüwa repairing the heavens with multicoloured stones symbolizes the restoration of cosmic harmony following a turbulent period of imbalance.

Nüwa is also celebrated for creating humans. According to the story, she sculpted the rich and noble from yellow earth and crafted ordinary people from mud streaks. This creation myth not only underscores Nüwa's crucial role in cosmic restoration, but also illustrates the intertwined relationship between divine acts, the natural order and societal hierarchy.

CATASTROPHES IN ANCIENT CHINESE MYTHS

Similar to other ancient civilizations, the fear of natural disasters among ancient Chinese people was well manifested in the catastrophe myths found in early texts. It was said that, prior to the beginning of human civilization in ancient times, the world was fraught with natural threats, and human beings were vulnerable. Among these, the myths of floods reflected the primeval chaos of the universe. As Mark Edward Lewis (2006) suggested, underlying these flood myths was a sophisticated cosmology in which the world was initially described as a chaotic and disordered universe, awaiting a sage who could restore order.

Triggered by the rebellions instigated by sinners such as Gonggong, the fierce floods endangered the lives of all human beings. Consequently, Yu was appointed to control the floods with every effort. According to available evidence, Yu divided the land into nine major areas, allowing the water to flow into different regions. In doing so, Yu successfully mitigated the threats posed by the flood and distinguished the centre of the world from the peripheral areas. Due to his achievements, Yu was chosen as the successor to Shun as the forthcoming ruler. The cosmological significance of Yu's control over the flood was that the universe was no longer in its primeval chaotic state but was in a peaceful order in which human beings were no longer threatened by natural disasters. Moreover, Yu's success in managing the flood set a precedent in ancient Chinese political discourse that a virtuous and competent ruler should have the capability to prevent natural disasters, which, as seen in many official histories of Imperial China, were considered sent by Heaven to warn against the unethical behaviours of the ruling class.

FUXI AND THE *BOOK OF CHANGES*

Nüwa is accompanied in Chinese mythology by her spouse and brother Fuxi, attributed with devising the eight trigrams of the *Book of Changes*. These trigrams, foundational to one of China's most significant divinatory systems, are combinations of broken and unbroken lines that form 64 unique hexagrams. Legend holds that Fuxi was inspired to create the trigrams upon discovering a mystical tablet carried by a snake-horse on a river bank. By delineating Heaven and Earth and observing the dynamics of *yin* and *yang*, Fuxi laid the basis of the divinatory system, reflecting the cosmic principle of change.

CELEBRATING MORAL BEHAVIOURS WHILE PUNISHING EVIL DEEDS

In Chinese mythological narratives, the supernatural domain frequently serves as a lens through which to examine human circumstances and values. Gods were believed to possess the authority to reward virtuous actions and penalize wickedness. Within *Mozi*, a foundational text of ancient Chinese Mohism, we encounter a tale in which Duke Mu of Qin meets Gou Mang, an auxiliary deity with the body of a bird and the face of a human. Gou Mang pledges that Duke Mu's state will flourish. Similarly, another narrative describes Ru Shou's encounter with Duke Guo, who had provided sanctuary to Zhong'er, later known as Duke Wen of Jin, during his period of exile. Echoing Gou Mang's promise, Ru Shou assures Duke Guo of his state's prosperity and tranquillity as a result of his previous aid.

Scholars interpret these stories of divine visitations to the mortal realm as illustrating the belief that celestial beings observe human conduct meticulously. A person's ethical character and actions are seen as pivotal in determining their destiny, as these traits influence whether divine forces respond with kindness or hostility.

CELEBRATING FAITHFUL LOVE

As one of China's four major folktales, the story of the Cowherd and the Weaver Girl enjoys widespread popularity – especially for its link to the Qixi Festival, celebrated on the seventh day of the seventh lunar month. Stemming from ancient narratives such as the *Huainanzi*, this tale narrates a romantic story between the Weaver Girl, represented by the star Vega, and the Cowherd, represented by Altair, who were separated by the celestial river or the Milky Way. Legend has it that on the Qixi Festival magpies form a bridge across the Milky Way, enabling the lovers to reunite. Further embellishments depict the Weaver Girl as divine and the Cowherd as mortal. Following the guidance of a cow, the Cowherd finds the celestial women's bathing site and takes a garment, leading to the Weaver Girl's marriage to him. However, their marriage displeases the Heavenly Emperor, who limits their meetings to just once a year.

This legend is often interpreted as a critique of pre-modern China's patriarchal norms, with the Heavenly Emperor symbolizing supreme authority. Similar themes of societal defiance are echoed in the *Butterfly Lovers*, another celebrated Chinese folk tale.

CHALLENGING THE PATRIARCHAL SOCIETY

Despite traditional China's patriarchal society, in which polygamy was permitted, numerous tales upheld the ideal of faithful love between couples. The *Butterfly Lovers* is a prominent example of these. Often compared to William Shakespeare's tragedy *Romeo and Juliet*, it narrates the story of Zhu Yingtai, a woman from an affluent family who disguises herself as a man to pursue her education. At the academy she befriends Liang Shanbo, who is unaware of her true identity. When Liang eventually learns that Zhu is a woman, the couple fall deeply in love. However, Zhu's family has already arranged her marriage to another man. The story ends tragically with Liang's death. On her way to her arranged marriage, Zhu passes by Liang's grave; it opens up, allowing her to join him in death. Zhu Yingtai's demonstration of loyalty and steadfast love has made her an emblem of righteous wifehood through the ages. The story's persistent popularity in pre-modern China probably mirrors a widespread longing for the freedom of love. Such a desire contrasts sharply with a societal structure in which family patriarchs wielded absolute control over their members' lives, including marriage decisions.

THE MYTHICIZATION OF HISTORY

The *Investiture of the Gods* and the Transition between the Shang and Zhou Dynasties

In pre-modern Chinese literature, certain mythical narratives drew inspiration from historical events. A notable example is the *Investiture of the Gods*, a vernacular novel of the Ming dynasty (1368–1644) that blends mythology, popular religion and Daoism. It recounts the Zhou dynasty's conquest over the Shang dynasty, weaving rich mythological elements into these historical events. The story focuses on Jiang Ziya, a disciple of the Primeval Lord of Heaven, Daoism's supreme deity. Tasked with aiding the future Zhou leaders, King Wen and King Wu,

Jiang Ziya's mission is to dethrone the tyrannical last king of the Shang dynasty. The novel culminates in the deification of nearly 365 virtuous individuals, including Zhou heroes, who are subsequently venerated within the Daoist pantheon.

The Mixture of Various Traditions in *Journey to the West*

Another narrative, *Journey to the West*, is inspired by the pilgrimage of the monk Xuanzang (602–664) to India, which occurred between 627 (or 629) and 645. Motivated by his dissatisfaction with the poor quality of Buddhist scripture translations in China, Xuanzang embarked on a quest to discover the original Buddhist teachings in India. The novel starts with Sun Wukong, the Monkey King, emerging from a magical stone that absorbed the energies of Heaven (*yang*) and Earth (*yin*). The Monkey King gains supernatural abilities through Daoist practices and, after causing turmoil in Heaven, is imprisoned under a mountain by the Buddha. He is later freed by Xuanzang and they proceed on their journey, accompanied by three other spiritual beings. Scholars interpret this quintet as representing the Five Elements of traditional Chinese theory (*see* page 22). The depiction of a Daoist bureaucratic system in Heaven also reflects how people in pre-modern China envisioned the spiritual realm, based on their real-world experiences.

DAOIST TRANSCENDENCE IN CHINESE MYTHS

In pre-modern China, people believed that a human being could achieve transcendence in various ways. One way to do so was to study Daoist practice. A famous example of this is the Great Immortal Sage Wong (Wong Tai Sin), a Daoist deity widely worshipped by people living in the Guangdong area, especially Hong Kong. Wong Tai Sin was said to have been born in Zhejiang Province, China, in the late third century CE. Under the tutelage of a mountain-dwelling Daoist deity, he mastered the alchemical process of refining cinnabar into a drug which, when ingested, conferred immortality. In some accounts he was originally a shepherd. When Wong Tai Sin reached the age of 15, he met an immortal and started to study Daoist practices. His older brother, Wong Co-hei, spent years searching for him after this. Eventually he witnessed his younger brother transforming a rocky outcrop on the side of a hill into a flock of sheep. Wong Co-hei then became Wong Tai Sin's pupil and eventually also attained immortality.

DREAM IN CHINESE MYTH

Dreams hold a pivotal role in Chinese culture and literature, serving as a bridge between the tangible and the intangible. Zhuang Zhou, or Zhuangzi, a prominent figure in early Daoist philosophy, famously dreamed he was a butterfly; he revelled in its joy and freedom, oblivious to his true identity as Zhuang Zhou. Upon awakening, he found himself ensnared in a philosophical conundrum: was he Zhuang Zhou who had dreamed of being a butterfly or a butterfly now dreaming it was Zhuang Zhou? This anecdote underscores the recurring theme in Chinese literature of the fine line between fantasy and reality.

A quintessential example of this theme is *The Dream of the Red Chamber*, an eighteenth-century masterpiece. The narrative begins with a mythological account of Nüwa mending the heavens, leaving behind a single luminous jade stone from the original 36,500; this single stone becomes a birthmark of the protagonist, Jia Baoyu. Symbolically born with this piece of jade in his mouth, Baoyu's life story unfolds among two families, one named 'Zhen' (meaning real) and the other 'Jia' (meaning unreal). Through their names, the story plays cleverly on the duality of reality and illusion. At its core, the novel explores the Buddhist belief that this world is nothing more than a fleeting illusion, a mere dream within a dream.

A LIFETIME IN A DREAM

The concept of a dream encompassing an entire lifetime, one central to *The Dream of the Red Chamber*, found its roots in earlier tales of wonder from the Tang dynasty, exemplified by two notable dream narratives. In 'The World in a Pillow' by Shen Jiji (c. 741– c. 805), a Daoist named Lu Weng offers Lu Sheng a pillow after engaging in a delightful conversation with him at an inn. While the innkeeper steams millet, Lu Sheng rests his head on the pillow and falls into a deep sleep. He dreams of a life in which he marries into the Cui family of Qinghe, rises to officialdom, suffers false accusations from his peers, is re-appointed as Imperial Council and eventually dies peacefully of old age. His awakening from death in the dream jolts him back to reality.

Another story, 'A Dream of Nanke' by Li Gongzuo (d. 850) has a similar theme. It tells the tale of Yu-fen who, after becoming inebriated at a dinner party, rests under a large tree in his front yard. He dreams of being appointed the governor of Nanke by two clerks dressed in purple. Despite years of recognized competence, his career ends when trust in him fades with age. Escorted back to his hometown by the same clerks, he awakens to find himself still lying under the tree.

Both stories weave together key Daoist and Buddhist philosophies, suggesting that life, encompassing the full cycle of birth and death, is no more than an illusion, a fleeting dream.

HUMAN-ANIMAL RELATIONSHIPS

Do not be Enslaved to Beauty

The *Story of the White Maiden* traces its origins back to the Tang dynasty. In 1624 it notably featured in Feng Menglong's (1574–1646) collection, *Stories to Caution the World*. The tale describes how Xu Xian, a young pharmacy assistant, encounters Lady Bai (Lady White), a strikingly beautiful widow, and her attendant, Little Blue. Throughout the narrative Lady White ensnares Xu Xian in a series of predicaments, leading to his repeated banishments. Despite these ordeals, Xu Xian's trust in Lady White persists until he is alerted by the Buddhist monk Fahai to the peril she represents. Ultimately Xu Xian employs a begging bowl, a gift from Fahai, to imprison Lady White; she then transforms herself into a harmless snake, still trapped beneath the bowl. Fahai manages to secure Lady White and Little Blue in a jug, subsequently entombed at Thunder Peak Monastery. Embedded within the story is a poem attributing Xu Xian's legal and personal turmoil to his infatuation with Lady White's allure. The theme of the tale echoes Buddhist teachings that life's sufferings (*dukkha*) arise from our desires for sensual and cognitive gratifications.

The Boundary Between Human and Spiritual Beings

The strange tales or mythical stories in pre-modern China emphasized the belief that even though the supernatural realm is not portrayed as drastically different from the human realm, the clear line between the two must be maintained to avoid unfortunate consequences. The boundary between human beings and spiritual beings must not be overstepped, due to the vulnerability of the human world.

Such vulnerability is best exemplified in the story of Li Chi killing a big serpent, recorded in *In Search of the Spirits* by Gan Bao (286–336?). The tale recounts how a big serpent living in Mount Yunling kept terrifying inhabitants of the nearby village; they had to present nubile girls as human sacrifices to pacify the monster. The big serpent killed nine girls before meeting its end at the hands of Li Chi – a young girl who first recommended herself to be the sacrifice, but was prevented by her parents.

POLITICS AND MYTHS IN ANCIENT CHINA

The Myths of Miraculous Births

In pre-modern China, the principal method of transferring sovereign authority was through hereditary succession. One significant challenge that rulers faced was justifying their dynasty's governance across multiple generations. To address this, particularly during the foundational phase of dynasties, rulers often claimed descent from deities, employing the concept of miraculous birth. Ancient texts abound with stories of the extraordinary births of dynastic founders, attributing their conception not to conventional means but to supernatural phenomena. These accounts served to legitimize the political authority of a ruling house by demonstrating a divine association not shared with ordinary people.

For example, the 'Dark Bird' of the *Book of Songs* recounts a legend in which a woman consumes the egg of a dark bird, leading to the birth of the Shang dynasty's progenitor. Similarly, two poems within the same collection describe how the Zhou dynasty's matriarch conceives her son after stepping on the footprints of a giant. These narratives, alongside the concepts of the heavenly mandate and the theory of the Five Elements, bolster a dynasty's legitimacy by highlighting a sacred lineage, suggesting that the current rulers are distinctively favoured by the gods. This strategy was not exclusive to the Han Chinese; the Manchu dynasty also invoked miraculous birth tales to substantiate their claim to political legitimacy.

The Legends of Abdication

In pre-Imperial China, amid the turmoil of political conflicts, some thinkers advocated abdication as a means of ensuring that the throne was passed to a worthy individual, rather than through hereditary succession. This concept of abdication involved a reigning monarch voluntarily relinquishing power to a virtuous individual rather than to their biological offspring, embodying a meritocratic approach to governance. Philosophers such as Mencius and Mozi cited historical instances of abdication to support the idea under specific conditions. Notably, sage-kings such as Yao and Shun were said to have abdicated in favour of virtuous successors; however, after Yu, the practice shifted back to hereditary rule, with Yu's son ascending the throne.

Scholar Sarah Allan points out that in these abdication tales the incumbent rulers often had unworthy heirs, compelling them to seek virtuous successors from outside their lineage. However, as Yuri Pines observes, the reliance on legendary narratives for discussions of abdication allowed for the creation of counter-narratives that undermined its feasibility. Such narratives ultimately prevented abdication from displacing hereditary succession as the predominant method of transferring power.

Hin Ming Frankie Chik

FURTHER READING

Allan, Sarah, *The Heir and the Sage: Dynastic Legend in Early China*, San Francisco: Chinese Materials Center, 1981.

Allan, Sarah, *The Shape of the Turtle: Myth, Art, and Cosmos in Early China*, Albany: State University of New York Press, 1991.

Bodde, Derk, 'Myths of Ancient China', in *Mythologies of the Ancient World*, edited by Samuel Noah Kramer, pp. 367–408, Garden City: Anchor Books, 1961.

Campany, Robert, *Strange Writing: Anomaly Accounts in Early Medieval China*, Albany: State University of New York Press, 1996.

Campany, Robert, *Signs from the Unseen Realm: Buddhist Miracle Tales from Early Medieval China*, University of Hawaii Press, 2012.

Chang, K.C, *Art, Myth, and Ritual: The Path to Political Authority in Ancient China*, London: Harvard University Press, 1988.

Cho, Sookja, *Transforming Gender and Emotion: The Butterfly Lovers Story in China and Korea*, Ann Arbor: University of Michigan Press, 2018.

Eno, Robert, *The Confucian Creation of Heaven: Philosophy and the Defense of Ritual Mastery*, New York: State University of New York, 1990.

Goldin Paul R, 'The Myth That China Has No Creation Myth', *Monumenta Serica* 56 (2008): 1–22.

Lewis Mark Edward, *The Flood Myths of Early China*, Albany: State University of New York Press, 2006.

Lincoln, Bruce, *Myth, Cosmos, and Society: Indo-European Themes of Creation and Destruction*, Cambridge: Harvard University Press, 1986.

Loewe, Michael, *Divination, Mythology and Monarchy in Han China*, Cambridge: Cambridge University Press, 1994.

Lu, Zongli, *Power of the Words: Chen Prophecy in Chinese Politics, AD 265–618*, Oxford: Lang, 2003.

Major, John S. et al., eds. *The Huainanzi: A Guide to the Theory and Practice of Government in Early Han China*, New York: Columbia University Press, 2010.

Marsili, Filippo, *Heaven is Empty: A Cross-cultural Approach to "Religion" and Empire in Ancient China*, Albany: State University of New York Press, 2018.

Schipper, Mineke, Ye Shuxian and Yin Hubin, eds. *China's Creation and Origin Myths: Cross-cultural Explorations in Oral and Written Traditions*, Leiden: Brill, 2011.

Sterckx, Roel, *The Animal and the Daemon in early China*, Albany: State University of New York Press, 2002.

Tseng, Lillian Lanyin, *Picturing Heaven in Early China*, Cambridge: Harvard University Press, 2011.

Wang, Aihe, *Cosmology and Political Culture in Early China*, Cambridge: Cambridge University Press, 2000.

Wang, Yue Cathy, *Snake Sisters and Ghost Daughters: Feminist Adaptations of Traditional Tales in Chinese Fantasy*, Onix: Wayne State University Press, 2023.

Williams, Nicholas M, *Chinese Poetry as Soul Summoning: Shamanistic Religious Influences on Chinese Literary Tradition*, Amherst: Cambria Press, 2022.

Hin Ming Frankie Chik is currently Visiting Lecturer of Premodern Chinese Literature at the University of Pittsburgh. He studies primarily Chinese thought and history, and also works in related areas such as the religious history of China and the reception history of pre-modern Chinese literature. He is now working on his monograph, in which he examines an understudied dictionary-like collection *Erya* and the idea of Confucian cultural assimilation.

CHINESE MYTHS & LEGENDS

THE CREATION MYTHS

The earliest Chinese myths, believed to have evolved in the primitive society of what is now northern China, are very old indeed, some of them dating back to the eighth century BCE. They were passed on by word of mouth, by a simple people attempting to explain the origins of the cosmos and other astronomical phenomena beyond their comprehension.

The story of Pangu, although generally considered one of China's earliest legends, is actually from a much later period. Some scholars of Chinese mythology suggest that this myth was imported from Indo-China shortly before the advent of Buddhism in the first century BCE. Other scholars attribute the tale specifically to the fourth century Taoist philosopher Ko Hung, author of the *Shen Hsien Chuan* (*Biographies of the Gods*).

But whatever his precise origins, the tale of how Pangu fashioned the universe is now very firmly established in Chinese folklore and a great number of Chinese people still trace their ancestry back to this particular god and his successor, the goddess Nüwa. Ancient Chinese tales which centre on these two characters are commonly known as 'Creation Myths'.

Nüwa and her consort, Fuxi, were created to embellish the mythological notion of the origin of things. Again, the concept of Nüwa is a very ancient one, first mentioned by Lieh Tzu in the fifth century BCE. Nüwa and Fuxi are the great gentle protectors of humanity, while the God of Water, Gonggong, is depicted as the destroyer of the earth. In these stories an interesting tension is introduced between the opposing forces of creativity and destruction.

PANGU AND THE CREATION OF THE UNIVERSE

At the very beginning of time, when only darkness and chaos existed and the heavens and the earth had not yet been properly divided up, the universe resembled the shape of a large egg. And at the centre of this egg, the first living creature one day came into being. After many thousands of years, when he had gathered sufficient strength and energy and had grown to the size of a giant, the creature, who gave himself the name of Pangu, awoke fully refreshed from his long rest and stood upright within his shell. He began to yawn very loudly and to stretch his enormous limbs, and as he did so, the walls of the egg were cracked open and separated into two even portions. The lighter, more fragile, part of the egg floated delicately upwards to form the white silken sheet of the sky, while the heavier, more substantial part, dropped downwards to form the earth's crusty surface.

Now when Pangu observed this, he was happy and proud to have created some light in place of the darkness and chaos out of which he had emerged. But at the same time, he began to fear that the skies and the earth might fuse once more, and he stood and scratched his huge head, pondering a solution to the problem. And after he had thought things through for quite a while, he decided that the only way to keep the two elements at a safe distance from each other was to place his own great bulk between them. So he took up his position, heaving and pushing upwards against the sky with his hands and pressing downwards into the earth with all the weight of his massive feet until a reasonable gap had been formed.

For the next eighteen thousand years, Pangu continued to push the earth and the sky apart, growing taller and taller every day until the gap measured some thirty thousand miles. And when this distance between them had been established, the sky grew firm and solid and the earth became securely fixed far beneath it. Pangu then looked around him and seeing that there was no longer any danger of darkness returning to the universe, he felt at last that he could lay down and rest, for his bones ached and he had grown old and frail over the years. Breathing a heavy sigh, he fell into an exhausted sleep from which he never awoke. But as he lay dying, the various parts of his vast body were miraculously transformed to create the world as we mortals know it today.

Pangu's head became the mountain ranges; his blood became the rivers and streams; the hairs on his head were changed into colourful and fragrant blossoms and his flesh was restored to become the trees and soil. His left eye was transformed into the sun and his right eye became the moon; his breath was revived in the winds and the clouds and his voice resounded anew as thunder and lightning. Even his sweat and tears were put to good use and were transformed into delicate droplets of rain and sweet-smelling morning dew.

And when people later came to inhabit the earth, they worshipped Pangu as a great creator and displayed the utmost respect for all the natural elements, believing them to be his sacred body spread out like a carpet before them beneath the blue arch of the heavens.

NÜWA PEOPLES THE EARTH

When the universe first emerged from chaos, mankind had not yet been created and the firmament and all the territories beneath it were inhabited by Gods or giants who had sprung forth from the body of Pangu. At that time, one particularly powerful Goddess appeared on earth in the company of her chosen heavenly companion. The Goddess's name was Nüwa and her companion's name was Fuxi. Together these deities set out to bring an even greater sense of order and regulation to the world.

And of all the other Gods residing in the heavens, Nüwa was the strangest and most unusual in appearance, for the upper half of her body was shaped like a human being, while the lower part took the form of a snake. Nüwa also possessed the unique ability to change her shape up to seventy times a day and she frequently appeared on earth in several different guises.

Although Nüwa took great pleasure in the wondrous beauty of the new-born world she occupied, deep within she felt it to be a little too silent and she yearned to create something that would fill the empty stillness. One day shortly afterwards, as she walked along the banks of the great Yellow

43

River, she began to imagine spending time in the company of other beings not unlike herself, animated creatures who might talk and laugh with her and with whom she could share her thoughts and feelings. Sitting herself down on the earth, she allowed her fingers to explore its sandy texture and without quite realizing it, began to mould the surrounding clay into tiny figures. But instead of giving them the lower bodies of reptiles, the Goddess furnished her creatures with little legs so they would stand upright. Pleased with the result, she placed the first of them beside her on the earth and was most surprised and overjoyed to see it suddenly come to life, dancing around her and laughing excitedly. She placed another beside it and again the same thing happened. Nüwa was delighted with herself and with her own bare hands she continued to make more and more of her little people as she rested by the river bank.

But as the day wore on, the Goddess grew tired and it was then that she decided to make use of her supernatural powers to complete the task she had begun. So breaking off a length of wood from a nearby mulberry tree, she dredged it through the water until it was coated in mud. Then she shook the branch furiously until several hundred drops of mud landed on the ground and as each drop landed it was instantly transformed into a human being. Then Nüwa pronounced that the beings she had shaped with her own hands should live to become the rich and fortunate people of the world, while those created out of the drops of mud should lead ordinary and humble lives. And realizing that her little creatures should themselves be masters of their own survival, Nüwa separated them into sons and daughters and declared that they should marry and multiply until the whole wide world had become their home and they were free once and for all from the threat of extinction.

THE WAR BETWEEN THE GODS OF FIRE AND WATER

For a great many years after Nüwa had created human beings, the earth remained a peaceful and joyous place and it was not until the final years of the Goddess's reign that mankind first encountered pain and suffering. For Nüwa was extremely protective of the race she had created and considered it her supreme duty to shelter it from all harm and evil. People depended on Nüwa for her guardianship and she, in turn, enabled them to live in comfort and security.

One day, however, two of the Gods who dwelt in the heavens, known as Gonggong and Zhurong, became entangled in a fierce and bitter dispute. No one knew precisely why the two Gods began to shout and threaten one another, but before long they were resolved to do battle against each other and to remain fighting to the bitter end. Gonggong, who was the God of Water, was well known as a violent and ambitious character and his bright red wavy hair perfectly mirrored his fiery and riotous spirit. Zhurong, the God of Fire, was equally belligerent when provoked and his great height and bulk rendered him no less terrifying in appearance.

Several days of fierce fighting ensued between the two of them during which the skies buckled and shifted under the

strain of the combat. An end to this savage battle seemed
to be nowhere in sight, as each God thrust and lunged with
increasing fury and rage, determined to prove himself more
powerful than the other. But on the fourth day, Gonggong
began to weary and Zhurong gained the upper hand, felling
his opponent to the ground and causing him to tumble right
out of the heavens.

Crashing to the earth with a loud bang, Gonggong soon
became acutely aware of the shame and disgrace of his defeat
and decided that he would never again have the courage to
face any of his fellow Gods. He was now resolved to end his
own life and looked around him for some means by which
he might perform this task honourably and successfully. And
seeing a large mountain range in the distance rising in the
shape of a giant pillar to the skies, Gonggong ran towards
it with all the speed he could muster and rammed his head
violently against its base.

As soon as he had done this, a terrifying noise erupted
from within the mountain, and gazing upwards, Gonggong
saw that a great wedge of rock had broken away from the
peak, leaving behind a large gaping hole in the sky. Without
the support of the mountain, the sky began to collapse and
plummet towards the earth's surface, causing great crevasses to
appear on impact. Many of these crevasses released intensely
hot flames which instantly engulfed the earth's vegetation,
while others spouted streams of filthy water which merged to
form a great ocean. And as the flood and destruction spread
throughout the entire world, Nüwa's people no longer knew
where to turn to for help. Thousands of them drowned, while
others wandered the earth in terror and fear, their homes

consumed by the raging flames and their crops destroyed by the swift-flowing water.

Nüwa witnessed all of this in great distress and could not bear to see the race she had created suffer such appalling misery and deprivation. Though she was now old and looking forward to her time of rest, she decided that she must quickly take action to save her people, and it seemed that the only way for her to do this was to repair the heavens as soon as she possibly could with her very own hands.

NÜWA REPAIRS THE SKY

Nüwa rapidly set about gathering the materials she needed to mend the great hole in the sky. One of the first places she visited in her search was the river Yangzi where she stooped down and gathered up as many pebbles as she could hold in both arms. These were carefully chosen in a variety of colours and carried to a forge in the heavens where they were melted down into a thick, gravel-like paste. Once she had returned to earth, Nüwa began to repair the damage, anxiously filling the gaping hole with the paste and smoothing whatever remained of it into the surrounding cracks in the firmament. Then she hurried once more to the river bank and, collecting together the tallest reeds, she built a large, smouldering fire and burnt the reeds until they formed a huge mound of ashes. With these ashes Nüwa sealed the crevasses of the earth, so that water no longer gushed out from beneath its surface and the swollen rivers gradually began to subside.

After she had done this, Nüwa surveyed her work, yet she was still not convinced that she had done enough to prevent the heavens collapsing again in the future. So she went out and captured one of the giant immortal tortoises which were known to swim among the jagged rocks at the deepest point of the ocean and brought it ashore to slaughter it. And when she had killed the creature, she chopped off its four sturdy legs and stood them upright at the four points of the compass as extra support for the heavens. Only now was the Goddess satisfied and she began to gather round her some of her frightened people in an attempt to reassure them that order had finally been restored.

To help them forget the terrible experiences they had been put through, Nüwa made a flute for them out of thirteen sticks of bamboo and with it she began to play the sweetest, most soothing music. All who heard it grew calmer almost at once and the earth slowly began to emerge from the chaos and destruction to which it had been subjected. From that day forth, Nüwa's people honoured her by calling her 'Goddess of music' and many among them took great pride in learning the instrument she had introduced them to.

But even though the heavens had been repaired, the earth was never quite the same again. Gonggong's damage to the mountain had caused the skies to tilt permanently towards the north-west so that the Pole Star, around which the heavens revolved, was dislodged from its position directly overhead. The sun and the moon were also tilted, this time in the direction of the west, leaving a great depression in the south-east. And not only that, but the peak of the mountain which had crashed to the earth had left a huge hollow where it landed in the east into which the rivers and streams of the world flowed incessantly.

Nüwa had done all she could to salvage the earth and shortly afterwards, she died. Her body was transformed into a thousand fairies who watched over the human race on her behalf. Her people believe that the reason China's rivers flow eastwards was because of Gonggong's foolish collision with the mountain, a belief that is still shared by their ancestors today.

TALES OF THE FIVE EMPERORS

After Nüwa had peopled the earth, several of the heavenly gods began to take a greater interest in the world below them. The five most powerful of these gods descended to earth in due course and each was assigned various territories of the new world.

The Yellow Emperor (Huangdi), the most important of the five sovereigns, is a part-mythical, part-historical figure who is reputed to have founded the Chinese nation around 4000 BCE. During his 'historical' reign he is said to have developed a number of important astronomical instruments and mathematical theories, as well as introducing the first calendar to his people and a system for telling the time. He is always depicted as a figure who takes particular pride in humanity and one who consistently reveals a great love of nature and of peaceful existence.

Yet in order to achieve peace, the Yellow Emperor is forced, at one time or another, to battle against the other four gods. These include the Fiery or Red Emperor (Chidi), who is the Yellow Emperor's half-brother by the same mother, the White Emperor (Shaohao), the Black Emperor (Zhuanxu), and the Green Emperor (Tai Hou). The Yellow Emperor is victorious over all of these gods and he divides up the earth into four equal regions. The Red Emperor is placed in charge of the south, the White Emperor is in charge of the west, the Black Emperor rules the north, while the Green Emperor rules the east.

THE YELLOW EMPEROR'S EARTHLY KINGDOM

After he had grown for twenty-five months in his mother's womb, the infant God Huangdi was safely delivered at last, bringing great joy to his celestial father, the God of Thunder. As soon as he appeared, Huangdi had the gift of speech, and in each of his four faces the determination and energy of a born leader shone brightly for all to see. By the time the young God had grown to manhood, he alone among other deities had befriended every known spirit-bird, and a great many phoenixes travelled from afar simply to nest in his garden, or to perch themselves on the palace roof and terraces to serenade him with the sweetest of melodies.

When the five most powerful Gods decided to explore the earth, it was already in the minds of each that one among them should be assigned absolute and supreme control over the others. But the God of Fire, who was later known as the Red Emperor, was reluctant to share power with anyone, especially with his half-brother Huangdi who seemed to be everyone else's natural choice. So when the time of the election came, the Red Emperor launched a vicious attack on the Yellow Emperor, instigating one of the fiercest battles the earth had ever witnessed. It was fought on the field of Banquan where the allies of Huangdi, including wolves, leopards, bears and huge birds of prey, gathered together and rushed at the Red Emperor's troops until every last one of them lay slain.

Once this great battle was over and the Yellow Emperor had been acknowledged by all as supreme ruler, he set about building for himself a divine palace at the top of Kunlun Shan, which reached almost to the clouds. The magnificent royal residence, consisting of no less than five cities and twelve towers surrounded by solid walls of priceless jade, was flanked by nine fire-mountains which burnt day and night casting their warm red glow on the palace walls.

The front entrance faced eastwards and was guarded by the Kaiming, the loyal protector of the Gods, who had nine heads with human faces and the body of a giant panther. The exquisite gardens of the royal palace, where the Emperor's precious pearl trees and jade trees blossomed all year round, were protected by the three-headed Li Zhu Shen who sat underneath the branches never once allowing his three heads to sleep at the same time. This God was also guardian of the dan trees which bore five different exotic fruits once every five years, to be eaten exclusively by the Emperor himself.

From the largest garden, which was known as the Xuan Guan, a smooth path wound its way upwards to the heavens so that many of the most prestigious Gods and the rarest divine beasts chose to make the Emperor's wondrous kingdom their home, content that they had discovered earthly pleasures equal to their heavenly experience. And it was here, in this garden, that the supreme ruler particularly loved to sit each evening, taking time to admire his newly discovered world just as the setting sun bathed it in a gentle golden light. As he looked below him, he saw the reviving spring of Yaoshui flowing jubilantly into the crystal-clear waters of the Yaochi Hu. To the west he saw the great Emerald trees swaying delicately in the breeze, shedding a carpet of jewels on the earth beneath them. When he looked northwards his eyes were fixed upon the towering outline of Zhupi Shan where eagles and hawks soared merrily before their rest. The Yellow Emperor saw that all of this was good and knew that he would spend many happy years taking care of the earth.

THE FIERY EMPEROR AND THE FIRST GRAIN

The Fiery Emperor, who ruled as God of the south, had the head of an ox and the body of a human being. He was also known as the God of the Sun and although in the past he had led his people in a disastrous rebellion against the Yellow Emperor, he was still much loved by his subjects and they held him in the highest esteem. The Fiery Emperor taught mankind how to control and make constructive use of fire through the art of forging, purifying and welding metals so that eventually his subjects were able to use it for cooking, lighting and for making domestic tools and hunting weapons. In those early times, the forests were filled with venomous reptiles and savage wild animals and the Fiery Emperor ordered his people to set fire to the undergrowth to drive away these dangerous and harmful creatures. He was also the first to teach them how to plant grain, together with a whole variety of medicinal herbs that could cure any ailment which might trouble them.

It was said that when the Fiery Emperor first appeared on earth he very wisely observed that there was not enough fruit on the trees, or vegetables in the ground to satisfy the appetite of his people. Knowing that mankind was forced to eat the flesh of other living creatures, the Emperor became unhappy and quickly set about instructing his subjects in the use of the plough and other tools of the land until they learned how to cultivate the soil around them. And when he saw that the soil was ready, the Emperor called for his people to pray aloud for a new and abundant food to rise up before them out of the ground.

As the people raised their faces to the heavens, a red bird carrying nine seedlings in its beak suddenly appeared through the clouds. As it swooped to the ground it began to scatter grains on to the upturned soil. After it had done this, the Fiery Emperor commanded the sun to warm the earth and from the seeds emerged five young cereal plants which began to multiply rapidly until a vast area of land was covered with luscious vegetation.

The fruits of these plants were harvested at the close of day to fill eight hundred wicker baskets. Then the Fiery Emperor showed his people how to set up market stalls and explained to them how to keep time according to the sun in order that they might barter among themselves in the future for whatever food they lacked. But even after having provided all of this, the Fiery Emperor was still not satisfied with his work. And so, taking his divine whip, he began to lash a number of the plants, which caused them to be endowed with healing properties, and he set them aside to be used by mankind whenever disease struck. The people, overjoyed that they were so well cared for, decided that the Fiery Emperor should henceforth go by the name of the Divine Peasant and they built in his honour a giant cauldron for boiling herbs and carried it to the summit of the Shenfu Shan where it stands to this day.

THE BIRD AND THE SEA

The Fiery Emperor had three daughters whom he loved and cared for very much, but it was his youngest daughter who had always occupied a special place in his heart. She was named Nüwa, after the great Goddess who created mankind, and like her sisters she possessed a cheerful disposition and a powerful spirit of adventure.

One day Nüwa went out in search of some amusement and seeing a little boat moored in the tiny harbour at a short distance from the palace gates, she went towards it, untied it and jumped aboard, allowing it to carry her out over the waves of the Eastern Sea. The young girl smiled happily to see the sun sparkle on the water and the graceful gulls circling overhead, but became so preoccupied in her joy that she failed to notice she had drifted out of sight, further and further towards the centre of the ocean. Suddenly, the wind picked up speed and the waves began to crash violently against the side of the boat. There was nothing Nüwa could do to prevent herself being tossed overboard into the foaming spray and even though she struggled with every ounce of strength to save herself, she eventually lost the fight and was sadly drowned.

Just at that time, a small jingwei bird happened to approach the place where Nüwa had fallen. And at that moment, her spirit, resentful of the fact that life had been cut short so unfairly, rose up in anger and entered the creature. Nüwa now lived on in the form of a bird with a speckled head, white beak and red claws, and all day long she circled the skies angrily, vowing to take revenge on the sea which had deprived her of her life and left her father grieving for his beloved child.

It was not long before she conceived of a plan to fill up the sea with anything she could find, hoping that in time there would no longer be any room left for people to drown in it. So every day the little bird flew back and forth from the land out over the Eastern ocean until she grew weary with exhaustion. In her beak she carried pebbles, twigs, feathers and leaves which she dropped into the water below. But this was no easy task, and the sea laughed and jeered at the sight of the tiny bird labouring so strenuously:

"How do you imagine you will ever complete your work," hissed the waves mockingly. "Never in a million years will you be able to fill up the sea with twigs and stones, so why not amuse yourself somewhere else."

But the xiao jingwei would not be deterred: "If it takes me a hundred times a million years, I will not stop what I am doing. I will carry on filling you up until the end of the world, if necessary."

And although the sea continued to laugh even more loudly over the years, the jingwei never ceased to drop into the ocean whatever she managed to collect. Later, after she had found herself a mate and they had produced children together, a

CHINESE MYTHS & LEGENDS

flock of jingwei birds circled above the water, helping to fill up the sea. And they continue to do so to this day in China, where their persistent courage and strength have won the admiration and applause of each and every Chinese citizen.

TAI HOU, THE GREEN EMPEROR

Even in the world of deities, the birth of the Green Emperor, God of the East, was judged quite an extraordinary affair. The story handed down among the other Gods was that the Emperor's mother, a beautiful young mortal named Hua Xu, lived originally in the ancient kingdom of Huaxushi, a place so remote and inaccessible, that many people had begun to question its very existence. Those who believed in this land, however, knew that its inhabitants possessed unique powers and gifts and often they were referred to as partial-Gods. They could move underwater as freely as they did above the earth, for example, and it was said that they could pass through fire without suffering any injury to the flesh. They walked through the air as easily as they walked on the ground and could see through the clouds as clearly as they could through glass.

One day the young girl Hua Xu was out walking across the northern plain of Leize, a name which means 'marshes of thunder', when she happened upon a gigantic footprint in the earth. She had never before encountered an imprint of its size and stooped to the ground to inspect it more closely. Imagining that a strange and wonderful being must have passed through the marshes, she grew very excited and found that she could not suppress the urge to compare the size of the footprint with her own. Slowly and carefully, Hua Xu placed her tiny foot in the enormous hollow and as she did so a strange vibration travelled up from the ground through the entire length of her body.

Shortly afterwards, the young girl found that she was pregnant and she was more than happy to be carrying a child, for there was no doubt in her mind that the Gods had intervened on that strange day to bring about her condition. After nine months Hua Xu gave birth to a son who bore the face of a man and the body of a snake. The elders of the people of Huanxushi advised that he should be named Tai Hou, a name fit for a supreme being they were convinced had been fathered by the God of Thunder.

SHAOHAO, SON OF THE MORNING STAR

The Emperor of the West, Shaohao, was also said to have come into being as the result of a strange and wonderful union. His mother, who was considered to be one of the most beautiful females in the firmament, worked as a weaver-girl in the Palace of Heaven. And it was always the case that after she had sat weaving the whole day, she preferred nothing better than to cruise through the Milky Way in a raft of silver that had been specially built for her use. On these occasions, she would pause for rest underneath the old mulberry tree which reached more than ten thousand feet into the skies. The branches of this tree were covered in huge clusters of shining berries, hidden from the naked eye by delicately spiced, scarlet-coloured leaves. It was a well-known fact that whoever ate the fruit of this tree would immediately receive the gift of immortality and many had journeyed to the centre of the Milky Way with this purpose in mind.

At that time, a very handsome young star-God named Morning Star, who was also known as Prince of the White Emperor, regularly took it upon himself to watch over these berries. Often he came and sat under the Mulberry Tree where he played his stringed instrument and sang the most enchanting songs. One evening, however, Morning Star was surprised to find his usual place occupied by a strange and beautiful maiden. Timidly, he approached her, but there was hardly any need for such caution, for as the maiden raised her head, their eyes met and the two fell in love almost instantly.

The maiden invited the young God aboard her raft and together they floated off into the night sky, along the silver river of the Milky Way down towards the earth and the waves of the sea. And as Morning Star played his magical music, the maiden carved a turtledove from a precious piece of white jade and set it on the top of the mast where it stood as a joint symbol of their mutual love and their deep desire to be guided by each other through the various storms of life. The lovers drifted together over the earth's ocean as their immortal music echoed through the air. And from this joyful union a son was born whom the happy couple named Shaohao, and it was the child's great destiny to become White Emperor of the western realms and to rule wisely over his people.

ZHUANXU, EMPEROR OF THE NORTH

The Yellow Emperor and his wife once had a son called Chang Yi who turned out to be a very disappointing and disobedient child. One day, Chang Yi committed a crime so terrible, even his own father could not bring himself to discuss it, and immediately banished his son to a remote corner of the world where he hoped he would never again set eyes on him. After a time, Chang Yi had a son of his own, a very foolish-looking creature it was said, with a long, thin neck, round, beady eyes, and a pig's snout where his mouth should have been. By some form of miracle, Chang Yi's son also managed to find a mate and eventually married a strong and wholesome woman named A Nu. From this marriage, the Yellow Emperor's great grandson, Zhuanxu, was produced, a God who managed to redeem the family name and who, after a careful trial period, was appointed ruler of the earth's northern territories.

Following the Yellow Emperor's great battle against Chiyou, he began to look around for a successor, for he had grown extremely weary of the rebellion and discontent he had experienced during his long reign. His great-grandson had proven himself a faithful servant and everyone now agreed that Zhuanxu should be the next God to ascend the divine throne.

Chiyou had brought widespread destruction and suffering to the earth which led Zhuanxu to believe that the alliance between mortals and immortals must be dissolved to prevent an even greater disaster in the future. And so he set about the task of separating the people from the Gods and turned his attention first of all to the giant ladder which ran between heaven and earth. For in those days, it was not unusual for people to ascend the ladder to consult with the Gods when they were in trouble, and the Gods, in turn, often made regular visits to the earth's surface. Chiyou had made such a visit when he secretly plotted with the Maio tribe in the south to put an end to the Yellow Emperor's sovereignty. The bloodshed which followed would never again be tolerated by Zhaun Xu and he enlisted the aid of two Gods in his destruction of the ladder.

With their help, the world became an orderly place once more. The Chong Shen was assigned control of the heavens and his task was to ensure that immortals no longer descended to earth. The Li Shen, together with his son Yi, were put in charge of the earth. Yi had the face of a human but his feet grew out of his head to form a fan-shaped bridge to the heavens behind which the sun and the stars set each evening. Zhaun Xu supervised the work of the other Gods and took it upon himself to re-introduce discipline to a race which had become untamed. It was said that he banished all cruel instruments of war and taught mankind respect for his own kind once again. He forbade women to stand in the path of men and severely punished a sister and brother who lived together as husband and wife.

By the time Zhuanxu died, the world was a much more peaceful place and on the day he passed away it was said that the elements rose up in a great lament. Jagged lightning lit up the skies and thunder clouds collided furiously with each other. The north wind howled fiercely and the underground streams burst to the surface in torrents of grief. Legend has it that Zhuanxu was swept away by the water and his upper-half transformed into a fish so that he might remain on the earth in another form, ever watchful of mankind's progress.

CHIYOU CHALLENGES THE YELLOW EMPEROR

Chiyou was a ferocious and ambitious God who had begun life as an aide and companion to the young deity, Huangdi, in the days before he had risen to become Yellow Emperor on earth. During this time, the two had become firm friends and close confidants, but as soon as Huangdi ascended the throne, this favourable relationship came to an abrupt end. For Chiyou could not bear to see his friend achieve the success he secretly longed for, and it became his obsession to find a way to reverse this situation and take the throne for himself.

Chiyou was the eldest of seventy-two brothers, all of them huge and powerful in stature. They each spoke the language of humans, but their bodies below the neckline were those of animals with cloven feet. Their heads were made of iron and their hideous copper faces contained four repulsive eyeballs protruding from mottled foreheads. These brothers ate all kinds of food, but they particularly liked to eat stones and chunks of metal, and their special skill was the manufacture of battle weapons, including sharp lances, spears, axes, shields and strong bows.

Now Chiyou had become convinced that he could easily overthrow the Yellow Emperor and so, gathering together his brothers and other minor Gods who were discontented with the Emperor's reign, he made an arrogant and boisterous descent to earth. First of all, however, he decided to establish a reputation for himself as a great warrior and immediately led a surprise attack on the ageing Fiery Emperor, knowing that he would seize power without a great deal of effort. The Fiery Emperor, who had witnessed his fair share of war, had no desire to lead his people into a climate of further suffering and torment, and soon fled from his home, leaving the way open for Chiyou to take control of the south. Shortly after this event, one of the largest barbarian tribes known as the Miao, who had been severely punished for their misdemeanours under the Fiery Emperor's authority, decided to take their revenge against the ruling monarchy and enthusiastically joined ranks of Chiyou and his brothers.

It was not long before the Yellow Emperor received word of the disturbances in the south, and hearing that it was his old friend who led the armies to rebellion, he at first tried to reason with him. But Chiyou refused to listen and insisted on war as the only path forward. The Yellow Emperor found that he had little choice but to lead his great army of Gods, ghosts, bears, leopards and tigers to the chosen Zhuolu Zhanchang and here the terrible war began in earnest.

It was in Chiyou's nature to stop at nothing to secure victory against his opponent. Every subtle trick and sudden manoeuvre, no matter how underhanded, met with his approval and he had no hesitation in using his magic powers against the enemy. When he observed that his army had not made the progress he desired, he grew impatient and conjured up a thick fog which surrounded the Yellow Emperor and his men. The dense blanket of cloud swirled around them, completely obscuring their vision and they began to stab blindly with their weapons at the thin air. Then suddenly, the wild animals who made up a large part of the Emperor's forces started to panic and to flee in every direction straight into the arms of the enemy. The Yellow Emperor looked on desperately and, realizing that he was helpless to dispel the fog himself, he turned to his ministers and pleaded for help.

Fortunately, a little God named Feng Hou was among the Emperor's men, a deity renowned for his intelligence and inventiveness. And true to his reputation, Feng Hou began to puzzle a solution to the problem and within minutes he was able to offer a suggestion.

"I cannot banish from my mind an image of the Plough which appears in our skies at night-time and always points in the same direction," he informed the Emperor. "Now if only I could design something similar, we would be able to pinpoint our direction no matter which way we were forced to move through the mist."

And so Feng Hou set to work at once, using his magic powers to assist him, and within a very short time he had constructed a device, rather like a compass, which continued to point southwards, regardless of its position. And with this incredible new instrument, the Yellow Emperor finally managed to make his way out of the fog, through to the clear skies once more.

But the battle was far from over, and the Emperor began to plan his revenge for the humiliation Chiyou had brought upon his men. At once, he summoned another of his Gods before him, a dragon-shaped deity named Ying Long, who possessed the ability to make rain at will, and commanded him to produce a great flood that would overwhelm the enemy. But Chiyou had already anticipated that the Yellow Emperor would not gladly suffer his defeat, and before the dragon had even begun to prepare himself for the task ahead, Chiyou had called upon the Master of Wind and the Master of Rain who together brought heavy rains and howling winds upon the Yellow Emperor's army, leaving them close to defeat once more.

As a last desperate measure, the Emperor introduced one of his own daughters into the battlefield. Ba was not a beautiful Goddess, but she had the power to generate tremendous heat in her body, enough heat to dry up the rain which now threatened to overcome her father's legions. So Ba stood among them and before long, the rains had evaporated from the earth and the sun began to shine brilliantly through the clouds. Its bright rays dazzled Chiyou's men which enabled Ying Long to charge forward unnoticed, and as he did so, hundreds of enemy bodies were crushed beneath his giant feet, lying scattered behind him on the plains.

And seeing this result, the Yellow Emperor managed to recover some of his dignity and pride, but his army lay exhausted and the morale of his men was very low. He was worried also that they would not be able to withstand another onslaught, for although Chiyou had retreated, the Emperor was certain he would soon return with reinforcements. He knew that he must quickly find something to lift the spirit of his men, and after much thought it suddenly came to him What he needed most was to fill their ears with the sound o a victory drum, a drum which would resound with more powe and volume than anyone had ever before imagined possible.

"With such a drum, I would bring fear to the enemy and hope to my own men," the Emperor thought to himself. "Two of my finest warriors must go out on my behalf and fetch a very special skin needed to produce this instrument."

And having decided that the great beast from the Liubo Shan possessed the only skin which would suffice, the Yellow Emperor dispatched two of his messengers to kill the strange creature. It resembled an ox without horns, he told them, and they would find it floating on the waves of the Eastern Sea. Sometimes the beast was known to open its mouth to spit out great tongues of lightning, and its roar, it was said, was worse than that of any wild cat of the forests.

But in spite of the creature's terrifying description, the Emperor's men found the courage to capture and skin it without coming to any great harm. After they had done so, they carried the hide back to the battlefield where it was stretched over an enormous bamboo frame to create an impressively large drum. At first, the Yellow Emperor was satisfied with the result, but when his men began to beat upon it with their hands, he decided that the sound was not loud enough to please him. So again, he sent two of his finest warriors on an expedition, and this time they went in search of the God of Thunder, Lei Shen. They found the God sleeping peacefully and crept up on him to remove both his thigh bones as the Emperor had commanded them to do. With these thigh bones a suitable pair of drumsticks was made and handed over to the principal drummer who stood awaiting his signal to beat on the giant instrument.

At last, the drum was struck nine times, releasing a noise louder than the fiercest thunder into the air. Chiyou's men stood paralysed with terror and fear as all around them the earth began to quake and the mountains to tremble. But this was the opportunity the Yellow Emperor's men had waited for and they rushed forward with furious energy, killing as many of Chiyou's brothers and the Miao warriors as they could lay their hands on. And when the battlefield was stained with blood and the casualties were too heavy for Chiyou to bear much longer, he called for his remaining men to withdraw from the fighting.

Refusing to surrender to the Yellow Emperor, the defeated leader fled to the north of the country to seek the help of a group of giants who took particular delight in warfare. These giants were from a tribe known as the Kua Fu and with their help Chiyou revived the strength of his army and prepared himself for the next attack.

THE YELLOW EMPEROR RETURNS TO THE HEAVENS

Chiyou had spent three days and three nights after his defeat at the battle of Zhuolu in the kingdom of the Kua Fu giants gathering rebel forces for his ongoing war against the Yellow Emperor. Both sides, it seemed, were now evenly matched once more and Chiyou relished the thought of a return to battle. But the Yellow Emperor saw that a renewal of conflict would only result in more loss of life and he was deeply disturbed and saddened by the prospect.

On the day before the second great battle was due to commence, the Emperor was sitting deep in thought in his favourite garden at the palace of Kunlun Shan when a strange

Goddess suddenly appeared before him. She told him she was the Goddess of the Ninth Heaven and that she had been sent to help him in his plight.

"I fear for the lives of my men," the Yellow Emperor told her, "and I long for some new battle plan that will put an end to all this bloodshed."

So the Goddess sat down on the soft grass and began to reveal to him a number of new strategies conceived by the highest, most powerful Gods of the heavens. And having reassured the Emperor that his trouble would soon be at an end, she presented him with a shining new sword furnished of red copper that had been mined in the sacred Kunwu Shan.

"Treat this weapon with respect," she told him as she disappeared back into the clouds, "and its magic powers will never fail you."

The next morning, the Emperor returned to the battlefield armed with his new strategies and the sacred weapon the Goddess had given him. And in battle after battle, he managed to overcome Chiyou's forces until at last they were all defeated and Chiyou himself was captured alive. The evil God was dragged in manacles and chains before the Yellow Emperor, but he showed no sign of remorse for the anguish he had caused and the destruction he had brought to the earth. The Yellow Emperor shook his head sadly, knowing that he now had little option but to order his prisoner's execution. The death sentence was duly announced, but Chiyou struggled so fiercely that the shackles around his ankles and wrists were stained crimson with blood.

When it was certain that he lay dead, Chiyou's manacles were cast into the wilderness where it is said they were transformed into a forest of maple trees whose leaves never failed to turn bright red each year, stained with the blood and anger of the fallen God.

And now that relative peace had been restored to the world once more, the Yellow Emperor spent his remaining time on earth re-building the environment around him. He taught the people how to construct houses for themselves where they could shelter from the rains; he brought them the gift of music and he also introduced them to the skill of writing. Mankind wanted to believe that the Yellow Emperor would always be with them on earth, but soon a divine dragon appeared in the skies, beckoning him back to the heavens. The time had arrived for the Yellow Emperor to answer this call and to acknowledge an end to the long reign of the Gods on earth. And so in the company of his fifty officials and all the other willing immortals whose stay had also run its course, he climbed on to the dragon's back and was carried up into the sky back to the heavens to take up his position again as crowned head of the celestial realms.

GIANTS IN EARLY
CHINESE LEGEND

In Chinese mythology, the earthly home, or 'Place of the Giant People', was said to have been in the region of the east sea, close to the Dayan Shan. On top of Bo gu Shan lived the descendants of the dragons, giants who grew in the womb for thirty-six years before emerging fully matured and usually covered in long black hair. They could be up to fifty feet in height, with footprints six feet in length. Like their winged ancestors, they could fly before walking, and some lived as long as eighteen thousand years.

XING TIAN, THE HEADLESS GIANT

Once there was a giant named Xing Tian who was full of ambition and great plans for his future. At one time, he had been an official of the Fiery Emperor, but when Chiyou had conquered the region, he had quickly switched loyalties and offered his services to the new, corrupt usurper of the south. It greatly disturbed the giant to hear reports of the bloody deaths of Chiyou's men at the hands of the Yellow Emperor and he wanted nothing less than to meet the Emperor face to face and challenge him to single combat until one of them lay dead.

So Xing Tian took up his axe and his shield and set off for the divine palace at the top of Kunlun Shan, seething with anger and rage as he thundered along. But the Yellow Emperor had received word of the giant's approach and seized his most precious sword ready to meet him head on. For days the two battled furiously, lashing out savagely with their weapons as they fought into the clouds and down the side of the mountain. They fought along all the great mountain ranges of northern China until eventually they reached the place known as the Long Sheep range in the north-east.

And it was here that the Yellow Emperor caught the giant off-guard and, raising his sword high into the air just at the level of the giant's shoulder, he slashed sideways with his blade until he had sliced off Xing Tian's head. A terrifying scream escaped the gaping, bloody mouth of the giant as his head began to topple forward, crashing with a loud thud to the ground and rolling down the hill like a massive boulder.

The giant stood frozen in absolute horror, and then he began feeling desperately with his hands around the hole above his shoulders where his head ought to have been. Soon panic had taken control of him and he thrashed about wildly with his weapon, carving up trees and tossing huge rocks into the air until the valleys began to shake and the sky began to cloud over with dust from the debris.

Seeing the giant's great fury, the Yellow Emperor grew fearful that Xing Tian might actually find his head and put it back on his shoulders again. So he swiftly drew his sword and sliced open the mountain underneath which the head had finally come to rest. Then he kicked the head into the chasm and sealed up the gap once more.

For ten thousand years afterwards the giant roamed the mountainside searching for his head. But in all that time he never found what he was looking for although he remained defiant that he would one day face the Yellow Emperor again. Some people say that the giant grew to be very resourceful, and to help him in his long search he used his two breasts for eyes and his navel for a mouth.

KUA FU CHASES THE SUN

The underworld of the north where the most ferocious giants had lived since the dawn of time was centred around a wild range of black mountains. And underneath the tallest of these mountains the giant Kua Fu, gatekeeper of the dark city, had built for himself a home. Kua Fu was an enormous creature with three eyeballs and a snake hanging from each ear, yet in spite of his intimidating appearance he was said to be a fairly good-natured giant, though not the most intelligent of his race.

Kua Fu took great pleasure in everything to do with the sun. He loved to feel its warm rays on his great body, and nothing delighted him more than to watch the golden orb rise from its bed in the east each morning. He was never too keen, however, to witness it disappear below the horizon in the evenings and longed for the day when the sun would not have to sleep at night.

And as he sat watching the sun descend in the sky one particular evening, Kua Fu began thinking to himself:

"Surely I can do something to rid the world of this depressing darkness. Perhaps I could follow the sun and find out where it hides itself at night. Or better still, I could use my great height to catch it just as it begins to slide towards the west and fix it firmly in the centre of the sky so that it never disappears again."

So the following morning, Kua Fu set off in pursuit of the sun, stepping over mountains and rivers with his very long legs, all the time reaching upwards, attempting to grab hold of the shining sphere above him. Before long, however, evening had approached, and the sun began to glow a warm red, bathing the giant in a soothing, relaxing heat. Puffing and panting with exhaustion, Kua Fu stretched his huge frame to its full length in a last great effort to seize his prize. But as he did so, he was overcome by an unbearable thirst, the like of which he had never experienced before. He raced at once to a nearby stream and drank its entire contents down in one mouthful. Still his thirst had not been quenched, so he proceeded to the Weishui He and again gulped down the water until the river ran dry. But now he was even more thirsty and he felt as if he had only swallowed a single drop.

He began to chase all over the earth, pausing at every stream and lake, seeking to drown the fiery heat that raged within his body. Nothing seemed to have any effect on him, though he had by now covered a distance of eight thousand miles, draining the waters from every possible source he encountered. There was, however, one place that he had not yet visited where surely he would find enough water to satisfy him. That place was the great lake in the province of Henan where it was said the clearest, purest water flowed from the mountain streams into the lake's great cavern.

The giant summoned all his remaining strength and plodded along heavily in the direction of this last water hole. But he had only travelled a short distance before he collapsed to the ground, weak with thirst and exhaustion. The last golden rays of the sun curved towards his outstretched body, softening the creases on his weary forehead, and melting away his suffering. Kua Fu's eyelids began to droop freely and a smile spread its way across his face as he fell into a deep, deep, eternal sleep.

At dawn on the following morning, the sun rose as usual in the east, but the sleeping figure of the giant was no longer anywhere to be seen. In its place a great mountain had risen up towards the sky. And on the western side of the mountain a thick grove of trees had sprung up overnight. These trees were laden with the ripest, most succulent peaches whose sweet juices had the power to quench the most raging thirst of any passer-by. Many believe that the giant's body formed this beautiful site and that is why it is still named Kua Fu Mountain in his honour.

MYTHS OF THE
YIN GUO

The stories of this chapter centre on the adventures of some of the most popular heroes of the ancient Yin Guo, from Dijun and Xihe, to Yi, the indomitable archer; from Yao, the wise and benevolent Emperor, to Yu, the saviour of the human race. The welfare of the people is the dominant concern of Yao's reign, and the struggle to maintain order on earth when it is threatened by the hasty intervention of angry gods, or the foolish behaviour of lesser deities, is a recurring theme in these tales.

As with the earlier stories, many of the figures presented here are reputed to be genuinely historical. More often than not, however, characters are endowed with superhuman strength and magical skills, typical of the Chinese mythological tradition of blending fact and fiction, myth and history. Yu, for example, who succeeds Yao to the throne after the brief reign of Emperor Shun (2205–2197 BCE) is an outstanding legendary hero, who first appears in the shape of a giant dragon and controls the great floodwaters on earth. He is at the same time, however, the historical founder of the Xia Chao, a powerful leader of the Chinese nation, ultimately responsible for the division of China into nine provinces.

THE TEN SUNS OF DIJUN AND XIHE

The God of the East, Dijun, had married the Goddess of the Sun, Xihe, and they lived together on the far eastern side of the world just at the edge of the great Eastern Ocean. Shortly after their marriage, the Goddess gave birth to ten suns, each of them a fiery, energetic, golden globe, and she placed the children lovingly in the giant Fusang shu close to the sea where they could frolic and bathe whenever they became overheated.

Each morning before breakfast, the suns took it in turns to spring from the enormous tree into the ocean below in preparation for their mother's visit when one of them would be lifted into her chariot and driven across the sky to bring light and warmth to the world. Usually the two remained together all day until they had travelled as far as the western abyss known as the Yu Yuan. Then, when her sun had grown weary and the light had begun to fade from his body, Xihe returned him to the Fusang shu where he slept the night peacefully with his nine brothers. On the following morning, the Goddess would collect another of her suns, sit him beside her in her chariot, and follow exactly the same route across the sky. In this way, the earth was evenly and regularly heated, crops grew tall and healthy, and the people rarely suffered from the cold.

But one night, the ten suns began to complain among themselves that they had not yet been allowed to spend an entire day playing together without at least one of them being absent. And realizing how unhappy this situation made them feel, they decided to rebel against their mother and to break free of the tedious routine she insisted they follow. So the next morning, before the Goddess had arrived, all ten of them leapt into the skies at once, dancing joyfully above the earth, intent on making the most of their forbidden freedom. They were more than pleased to see the great dazzling light they were able to generate as they shone together, and made a solemn vow that they would never again allow themselves to become separated during the daytime.

The ten suns had not once paused to consider the disastrous consequences of their rebellion on the world below. For with ten powerful beams directed at the earth, crops began to wilt, rivers began to dry up, food became scarce and people began to suffer burns and wretched hunger pangs. They prayed for rains to drive away the suns, but none appeared. They called upon the great sorceress Nu Chou to perform her acts of magic, but her spells had no effect. They hid beneath the great trees of the forests for shade, but these were stripped of leaves and offered little or no protection. And now great hungry beasts of prey and dreaded monsters emerged from the wilderness and began to devour the human beings they encountered, unable to satisfy their huge appetites any longer. The destruction spread to every corner of the earth and the people were utterly miserable and filled with despair. They turned to their Emperor for help, knowing he was at a loss to know what to do, but he was their only hope, and they prayed that he would soon be visited by the God of Wisdom.

YI, THE ARCHER, IS SUMMONED

Tijun and Xihe were horrified to see the effect their unruly children were having upon the earth and pleaded with them to return to their home in the Fusang shu. But in spite of their entreaties, the ten suns continued on as before, adamant that they would not return to their former lifestyle. Emperor Yao now grew very impatient, and summoning Dijun to appear before him, he demanded that the God teach his suns to behave. Dijun heard the Emperor's plea but still he could not bring himself to raise a hand against the suns he loved so dearly. It was eventually settled between them, however, that one of Yao's officials in the heavens, known as Yi, should quickly descend to earth and do whatever he must to prevent any further catastrophe.

Yi was not a God of very impressive stature, but his fame as one of the most gifted archers in the heavens was widespread, for it was well known that he could shoot a sparrow down in full flight from a distance of fifty miles. Now Dijun went to meet with Yi to explain the problem his suns had created, and he handed the archer a new red bow and a quiver of white arrows and advised him what he must do.

"Try not to hurt my suns any more than you need to," he told Yi, "but take this bow and ensure that you bring them under control. See to it that the wicked beasts devouring mankind are also slain and that order and calm are restored once more to the earth."

Yi readily accepted this challenge and, taking with him his wife Chang'e, he departed the Heavenly Palace and made his descent to the world below. Emperor Yao was overjoyed to see the couple approach and immediately organized a tour of the land for them, where Yi witnessed for himself the devastation brought about by Dijun's children, as he came face to face with half-burnt, starving people roaming aimlessly over the scorched, cracked earth.

And witnessing all of this terrible suffering, Yi grew more and more furious with the suns of Dijun and it slipped his mind entirely that he had promised to treat them leniently. "The time is now past for reasoning or persuasion," Yi thought to himself, and he strode to the highest mountain, tightened the string of his powerful bow and took aim with the first of his arrows. The weapon shot up into the sky and travelled straight through the centre of one of the suns, causing it to erupt into a thousand sparks as it split open and spun out of control to the ground, transforming itself on impact into a strange three-legged raven.

Now there were only nine suns left in the sky and Yi fitted the next arrow to his bow. One after another the arrows flew through the air, expertly hitting their targets, until the earth slowly began to cool down. But when the Emperor saw that there were only two suns left in the sky and that Yi had already taken aim, he wisely remembered that at least one sun should survive to brighten the earth and so he crept up behind the archer and stole the last of the white arrows from his quiver.

Having fulfilled his undertaking to rid Emperor Yao of the nine suns, Yi turned his attention to the task of hunting down the various hideous monsters threatening the earth. Gathering a fresh supply of arrows, he made his way southwards to fight the man-eating monster of the marsh with six feet and a human head, known as Zao Chi. And with the help of his divine bow, he quickly overcame the creature, piercing his huge heart with an arrow of steel. Travelling northwards, he tackled a great many other ferocious beasts, including the nine-headed monster, Jiu Ying, wading into a deep, black pool and throttling the fiend with his own bare hands. After that, he moved onwards to the Qingqiu marshes of the east where he came upon the terrible vulture Dafeng, a gigantic bird of unnatural strength with a wing span so enormous that whenever the bird took to the air, a great typhoon blew up around it. And on this occasion, Yi knew that his single remaining arrow would only wound the bird, so he tied a long black cord to the shaft of the arrow before taking aim. Then as the creature flew past, Yi shot him in the chest and even though the vulture pulled strongly on the cord as it attempted to make towards a place of safety, Yi dragged it to the ground, plunging his knife repeatedly into its breast until all life had gone from it.

All over the earth, people looked upon Yi as a great hero, the God who had single-handedly rescued them from destruction. Numerous banquets and ceremonial feasts were held in his honour, all of them attended by the Emperor himself, who could not do enough to thank Yi for his assistance. Emperor Yao invited Yi to make his home on earth, promising to build him the a very fine palace overlooking Jade Mountain, but Yi was anxious to return to the heavens in triumph where he felt he rightly belonged and where, in any event, Dijun eagerly awaited an account of his exploits.

CHANG'E'S BETRAYAL

After Yi, the great archer, had returned to the heavens with his wife, he immediately went in search of the God Dijun to report on the success of his mission on earth. He had managed to save mankind from the evil destruction of the ten suns, as Dijun had requested him, and was still basking in the glory of this mammoth achievement. Yi fully expected a reception similar to the one he had been given on earth, but instead he found an angry and unforgiving God waiting to receive him. Dijun did not welcome the archer with open arms, but walked forward and spoke only a few harsh words.

"I feel no warmth or gratitude in my heart towards you," he said to Yi in the bitterest of voices, "you have murdered all but one of my suns, and now I cannot bear to have you in my sight. So I have decided that from this day forth, you and your wife will be banished to the earth to live among the mortals you appear to have enjoyed serving so well. Because of the foul deed you have committed, it is my judgment that you no longer merit the status of Gods and neither of you will ever be permitted to enter the Heavens again."

And although Yi argued against his sentence, Dijun would not listen to a single word of his plea. Slowly, the archer made his way homewards, shocked and saddened by the breach of friendship and weighted down by the certain knowledge that his wife would not react well to the news.

And as expected, when Chang'e had been told that she and her husband had been exiled to the earth, she was absolutely furious. Much more so than Yi, she revelled in the pleasures and privileges the Gods alone enjoyed, and throughout their married life together, she had never attempted to hide the fact that she had little or no tolerance for the inferior company of mortals. Now she began to regret ever tying herself in matrimony to the archer, for she felt strongly that she was being unduly punished for his hot-headed behaviour. Surely her banishment was totally unjust! And why was it that she was being punished for her husband's foolish actions? These thoughts circled around her head as she reluctantly gathered up her things, and she promised herself that she would never cease to reproach Yi, or allow him a day's rest, until he had made amends for what he had done to her.

The couple's earthly home was as comfortable as Yi could make it and all day long he trudged through the forests in search of the luxuries his wife demanded – the most tender deer-flesh, or the most exotic, sun-ripened berries. But often when he would return exhausted with these items, Chang'e would fling them away, declaring that she had no appetite for unsophisticated mortal food. And then she would begin to bemoan their dreadful misfortune, over and over again, while Yi sat there gloomily, his head in his hands, wishing that he had never set eyes on the suns of Dijun.

One evening, when Chang'e had been thinking particularly long and hard about her miserable existence on earth, she went and stood before her husband and announced that she had made firm plans for their future.

"'I have had more than enough of this wretched place," she told Yi, "and I have no intention of dying here like a mortal and descending to the Underworld afterwards. If you want to keep me, Yi, you must do what I ask of you and go to the west, to the Mountain of Kunlun. For I have heard that the Queen Mother of the West, who lives there, keeps a very special substance. People call it the elixir of immortality and it is said that whoever takes this potion will be granted eternal life."

Now Yi had also heard a report of this strange queen and her magic medicine, and noticing that some of the old sparkle danced in his wife's eyes as she spoke about it, he could not find it in his heart to refuse her this request even though he knew that the journey ahead would be a treacherous one. For the Queen Mother of the West lived close to the earthly palace of the Yellow Emperor, a region encircled by fire mountains and a deep moat filled with boiling, hissing water which no mortal had ever yet penetrated. The Queen herself may have had the human face of a woman, but her teeth, it was said, were those of a tiger and her hair was long and matted, covering her ugly, scaly body which ended in a leopard's tail.

It was fortunate for Yi that he still possessed some of his God-like powers, since these enabled him to pass through the scorching flames and to swim through the intense heat of the water without coming to any harm. And having reached the opening of the cave where the queen rested, he decided that the best way to approach her was to greet her openly and honestly and tell her his story from start to finish in the hope that she might help him.

To the archer's immense relief, the Queen Mother of the West listened to all he had to say with an open mind, and certainly the image he painted of his innocent wife forced to suffer equal hardship because of what he had done, invited a genuine heartfelt sympathy. The queen suddenly reached into a copper box close by and withdrew a small leather pouch which she handed to Yi.

"The magic medicine inside of this pouch is very precious indeed," she told him. "It has been collected from the immortal trees on Kunlun Shan which flower only every three thousand years and bear fruit only every six thousand years. If two people eat this amount, which is all I have to give you, they will both have eternal life in the world of men. But if only one person swallows it all, that person will have the complete immortality of the Gods. Now take the medicine away with you and guard it well, for its value is beyond all measure."

And so Yi returned to his home and to his anxious wife, feeling as if a great burden had been lifted from his shoulders. For the first time in many years, his wife appeared happy to see him and she kissed his cheek as he presented her with the pouch and began to relate the entire story of his adventure, including everything the queen had told him about the magic potion. Chang'e agreed with her husband that they should prepare a great feast to celebrate the end to their mortal lives and she took it upon herself to guard the medicine while her husband went in search of something very special for them to eat.

But as soon as Yi had disappeared into the trees, Chang'e began to stare at the little pouch and her thoughts travelled to the days when she lived among the Gods in Heaven, breathing in the scent of beautiful flowers or reclining in the warm sunshine listening to the soothing tones of immortal music drifting gently on the breeze. A deep resentment against her husband rose up within her as she indulged this daydream of a divine kingdom she considered her rightful home and she knew that she would never be content simply with eternal life on earth. She could not let go of what Yi had trustingly told her, that there was only enough elixir to make one of them fully immortal again, and now she allowed her selfish desire to overcome her. Without hesitating a moment longer, Chang'e quickly opened up the pouch and swallowed the entire contents all at once.

The effect of the medicine was almost immediate and Chang'e felt her body become lighter and lighter until her feet began to lift themselves off the ground as they had done in the past so many times before.

"How glorious it is to be a Goddess again," she thought to herself as she floated happily towards the flickering stars in the direction of the heavens. She rose higher and higher through the air until the earth below resembled a tiny egg and the skies around her were completely silent and still. But now a sudden fear told hold of the Goddess, for it began to dawn on her that she was entirely alone, cut off from her husband Yi and other earthly mortals, yet not safely arrived in the world of deities. And as she thought more about her return to the Heavens it occurred to her for the first time that she may not necessarily receive a warm welcome there.

"How can I confront these other Gods," she said to herself, "when they will certainly scorn me for taking all of the elixir myself and for abandoning my poor husband. Perhaps it is not such a good idea to return straight to Heaven."

Chang'e gazed around her and saw that she had must make an unhappy choice, either to return to the unwelcoming, grey earth, or move onwards towards the cold, silvery moon. "It is probably quite lonely on the moon," she thought, "still, it seems the best place to go to for a short length of time until the Gods have forgotten my crime." And so, she floated off towards the moon, determined that she would move on from here before too long.

But the moon was far more desolate and dispiriting than she had imagined possible, a cold, hostile place, totally uninhabited, apart from one rabbit who sat forlornly under a cassia tree. Chang'e could not bear it a moment longer, and having decided that even a host of angry Gods presented a more desirable alternative, she attempted to rise again into the air. But she soon discovered that her powers had deserted her and that a strange metamorphosis was taking place in her body. Her back stiffened suddenly and then curved forwards. Her breasts separated and flattened, causing her stomach to bulge outwards. Small swellings began to appear all over her skin which lost its translucence and changed to a dull, murky green. Her mouth stretched wider and wider to the edge of her face where her ears once rested and her eyes grew larger and larger until they formed two ugly black rounds.

Once a beautiful and faithful wife, the greedy and disloyal Chang'e had finally met with her punishment and was transformed into a giant toad. And in this form she remained until the end of time, doomed to keep a lonely watch over the earth below while yearning, every passing moment, to be with the husband she had so falsely deceived.

HOU JI, THE ICE-CHILD

Jiang Yuan was one of four wives of Di Ku, God of the East. For many years the couple had tried to have a child together but they had not been successful and their marriage was not a very happy one as a result. One day, however, Jiang Yaun was walking along by the riverbank when she spotted a trail of large footprints in the earth. She was intrigued by them and began to follow where they led, placing her own tiny feet in the hollows of the ground. She was unaware that by doing this, she would conceive a child, and not long afterwards she gave birth to a son, an event which under normal circumstances would have brought her great joy.

But Jiang Yuan was filled with shame to see the tiny bundle wriggling in her arms, knowing that she had absolutely no knowledge of its father. And realizing that she would have great difficulty explaining the infant's birth to her husband, Jiang Yaun made up her mind to dispose of the child before she became a victim of scandalous gossip and derision. So she took the baby to a deserted country lane and left him to perish in the cold among the sheep and cattle. But then a strange thing happened. For instead of rejecting the baby and trampling him to death, the sheep and cattle treated him as one of their own, carrying him to a nearby barn where they nestled up close to him to keep him warm and suckled him with their own milk until he grew fit and strong.

Now Jiang Yuan had sent her scouts into the countryside to make sure that her unwanted child no longer lived. The news that he had survived and that he was being cared for by the animals of the pastures threw her into a fit of rage and she ordered her men to take the infant deep into the forests, to the most deserted spot they could find, where he was to be abandoned without any food or water. Jiang Yuan's messengers performed their duty exactly as they had been commanded, but again, fate intervened to save the child.

For one morning, a group of woodcutters who had travelled into the heart of the forest to find sturdier trees, spotted the child crawling through the undergrowth. Alarmed by his nakedness and grimy appearance, they immediately swept him up off the ground and carried him back to their village. Here, the woman Jingti, who was herself without child, took charge of the infant. She wrapped him in warm clothing and filled him with nourishing food until gradually he grew plump and healthy. His foster-mother doted on her son and it brought her great pleasure to see him thrive in her care.

But again, Jiang Yuan managed to track down the child and this time she was resolved to stop at nothing until she was certain of his destruction. And so, as a last resort, she carried him herself to a vast frozen river in the north where she stripped him naked and threw him on to the ice. For two years, the infant remained on the frozen waters, but from the very first day, he was protected from the piercing cold by a flock of birds who took it in turn to fly down with morsels of food and to shelter him under their feathered wings.

The people grew curious to know why the birds swooped on to the icy surface of the river every day when clearly there were no fish to be had. Eventually a group of them set off across the ice to investigate further and soon they came upon the young child, curled up against the warm breast of a motherly seagull. They were amazed at the sight and took it as a sign that the child they had discovered was no ordinary mortal, but a very precious gift from the Gods. They rescued the young boy and named him Hou Ji and as they watched him grow among them, his outstanding talents began to manifest themselves one by one.

Hou Ji became an excellent farmer in time, but he did not follow any conventional model. He was a born leader and from a very early age he had learned to distinguish between every type of cereal and edible grain. He made agricultural tools for the people, such as hoes and spades, and soon the land delivered up every variety of crop, including wheat, beans, rice and large, succulent wild melons. The people had a bountiful supply of food and when the Emperor himself heard of Hou Ji's great work he appointed him a minister of the state so that his knowledge of agriculture would spread throughout the nation.

When Hou Ji died he left behind a 'Five-Crop-Stone' which guaranteed the Chinese people a constant supply of food even in times of famine. He was buried on the Duguang Pingyuan, a magnificent region of rolling hills and clear-flowing rivers where the land has always remained exceptionally fertile.

GUN BATTLES THE GREAT FLOOD

King Yao, the first mortal emperor of China, was judged an outstanding monarch by his subjects, one of the wisest, most devoted rulers that had ever risen to power. Humble and charitable almost to a fault, Yao never allowed himself luxuries of any kind. He wore sackcloth in summer and only a deerskin during the winter months and spent his entire life making sure that his people had everything they could possibly need to keep them satisfied. If the Emperor spotted a man without clothes, he would remove the shirt from his own back and hand it over to the unfortunate person. If his people were short of food, he blamed himself for their suffering. If they committed a crime, he was immediately understanding and took personal responsibility for the breach of law and order.

Yet in spite of Yao's remarkably warm and tolerant nature, he was destined to suffer repeated misfortunes during his lifetime and his reign was plagued by disasters of every kind, including drought, starvation, disease and floods. But perhaps the worst period of the Emperor's rule came immediately after he had rid the earth of the suns of Dijun, when he had just breathed a sigh of relief and had set to work restoring the shattered morale of his nation.

During these days immediately following the destruction of the suns, when chaos still ruled the earth and the world of mortals failed to communicate a peaceful and harmonious atmosphere, the High God, Tiandi, happened to peer down from the Heavens and began to shake his head disappointedly. Everywhere the God looked, he saw people living miserable and wretched lives. Flames had devoured the homes of many and now they squabbled bitterly among themselves, desperate to secure basic food and provisions even by the most dishonest means.

Now Tiandi was not a God renowned for his patience and he saw only that mankind had begun to tread a path of wickedness and corruption. And taking swift action, he sent the God of Water to the earth's surface, commanding him to create a flood that would punish mankind for its debauched behaviour. This flood, he announced, would last for a period of no less than twenty-two years, after which time, it was hoped that the world would be properly cleansed of all evil.

So day after day the rains beat down upon the soil, pulverizing the crops which remained, flooding the houses, swelling the rivers to bursting point, until eventually the whole of the earth resembled one vast ocean. Those who were fortunate enough to avoid drowning, floated on the treacherous waters in search of tall trees or high mountains where they might come to rest. But even if they managed to reach dry land, they were then forced to compete with the fiercest beasts of the earth for food, so that many were mercilessly devoured even as they celebrated the fact that they had been saved.

Only one God among the deities of the heavens appeared to feel any sympathy for the innocent people suffering such appalling misery on earth. The God's name was Gun and he was the grandson of the Yellow Emperor. Now Gun took it upon himself to plead with Tiandi to put an end to the heavy rains, but the High God would not listen to a word of what he had to say and so Gun was forced to continue roaming the heavens, powerless to help the drowning people.

One day, however, as the young God sat alone dejectedly, pondering the destruction caused by the ongoing flood, he was approached by two of his friends, an eagle and a tortoise. And seeing their companion so downcast, the two enquired what they might do to lift his spirits.

"The only thing that would make me happy right now," Gun answered them, "would be to stop this water pouring out of the skies. But I have no idea how I can bring this about."

"It is not such a difficult task," replied the eagle, "if you feel you have courage enough to pay a visit to Tiandi's palace. For he is the keeper of the Shirang, a very precious substance which has exactly the same appearance of soil or clay. But if you can manage to drop some of this magical clay into the ocean, it will swell up to form a great dam that will hold back the flood waters."

It remains a great mystery to this day precisely how Gun overcame every obstacle to retrieve a handful of the magic soil, but he managed this task successfully and immediately departed for the earth where he flung the clay into the ocean. Almost at once, mountains began to spring up from the water and soon great stretches of land appeared everywhere as the huge waves began to subside. Filled with gratitude, the gaunt-faced people crawled down from the trees and out of their remote hiding places and began to hail Gun as the saviour of mankind.

But the High God, Tiandi, was not at all pleased with Gun's theft of the Shirang and its subsequent healing effect on the world below. Enraged by this challenge to his authority, he ordered the God of Fire, Zhurong, to go down to earth to murder the God who had betrayed him. The two met in combat on Yushan Shan, but Gun was no match for Zhurong and the God of Fire quickly overcame his opponent, striking him down without difficulty after they had exchanged only a few blows. And now the flood waters burst through the dam Gun had created, crashing on to the dried-out earth which became completely submerged once again.

Gun had sacrificed his life on Yushan Shan for the good of mankind, but he had died without completing his work and so his spirit refused to rest within the shell of his dead body. For three years, his remains lay in a special vault in the mountains, watched over by the people who greatly mourned his loss. But in all this time, Gun's body showed no sign of decomposing, for a new life had begun to grow inside of him, waiting for the day when it would be mature enough to emerge.

After these three years had passed and Gun's body had still not wasted away, Tiandi grew very concerned, fearing that the dead God was being transformed into an evil spirit destined to plague him for the rest of his days. So Tiandi sent one of his most trusted officials down to earth to carve up Gun's remains, presenting him with a divine sword called the Wudao. But a fantastic thing occurred as soon as the official's blade had slashed open Gun's belly. For instead of the blood he had anticipated would emerge from the opening, a large and mighty golden dragon sprung forth in its place. This dragon was Yu, the son of Gun, who had inherited all the strength and courage of his father and who had entered the world in all his magnificent glory to complete Gun's unfinished work.

YU CONTROLS THE FLOOD

The appearance of a great golden dragon in the skies, whose sole purpose it was to save mankind from destruction, encouraged the High God, Tiandi, to question whether or not the punishment he had meted out to the people below had been a little too severe. The mysterious creature was fiercely determined and persistent, he noticed, and to allow any further grievances between them was not the most prudent way forward. So Tiandi decided to yield to the dragon's wishes and put an end to the suffering on earth at long last.

Yu's mission so far had been an easy one. Tiandi not only ordered the God of Water to call a halt to the downpour, he also gave Yu enough Shirang to construct another great dam to hold back the flood waters. He sent the dragon Ying Long down to earth to assist him in repairing the widespread damage. Yu received this help gratefully and day and night channelled all his available energy into the task at hand.

Now all would have gone on smoothly, and the earth been restored to its original condition in little or no time, but for the God of Water, Gonggong, who decided to cause as much trouble as possible for Yu. For it was Gonggong who had originally created the flood and to see his great work undone by a mere boy-dragon was more than he could tolerate. No one had yet dared to disobey Yu's commands, but Gonggong ignored every last one of them, entirely underestimating the dragon's strength and the powerful influence he exerted over his followers. And seeing that Gonggong would not be reasoned with, Yu called together all the fairies, spirits and giants of the earth, so that not one remained to fight alongside Gonggong. Then Yu challenged the God of Water to single combat, an encounter Gonggong now wished he could avoid, for in no time, Yu had defeated him and skewered his ugly head upon his sword.

And after he had vanquished the God of Water, Yu went among the people handing them pieces of the magic clay so that they could decide for themselves where mountain ranges should appear and where stretches of land would flourish most. But it was not enough simply to rebuild the earth again, nor was the giant dam a permanent safeguard against flooding in the future. Yu realized that something more had to be done and so, dragging his great tail in the earth, he began to hollow out the soil, digging a long, tunnel-like structure through which the water could easily and swiftly flow, away from the land in the direction of the sea. Throughout the country, people followed his example and soon an entire network of shallow gullies began to appear, draining the surplus water from the plains. In this way, Yu brought the flood under control and created the great rivers of China that still flow eastwards towards the ocean to this very day.

THE MARRIAGE OF YU

Yu had spent thirty years on earth regulating the waters before it even occurred to him that he had earned a well-deserved rest and that perhaps the time had now arrived to make plans for his own future. Never in the past had he paused to consider the possibility that he might one day marry, but suddenly he felt lonely and in need of a wife who could love him and attend to him in old age. He had no idea how he might go about choosing a wife, however, and decided to put his trust in the Gods, waiting patiently for a sign from the divine powers above.

One morning, he observed a strange white fox with nine tails making its way towards him and he felt at once that the animal must be a heavenly messenger sent to help him in his quest. The fox approached and began to sing a strange little song which Yu listened to attentively, confident that its words would somehow enlighten him. The fox's song cheered him immensely and left him in little doubt that his search for a suitable wife was drawing to a close:

> He who meets with the fox of nine tails
> Will soon become king of the land.
> He who weds the chief's daughter on Tu Shan
> Will become a prosperous man.

Nu Jiao was reputed to be one of the most beautiful maiden in China and she dwelt in the distant valley of Tu on the summit of the great mountain. Ever since childhood, she had heard nothing but favourable reports of Yu and by now she wa familiar with everything he had accomplished on earth. She had come to admire him from a distance as a God of legendary stature, and in her heart she had always entertained the hope that one day they would meet. And so when Yu appeared unexpectedly and asked for her hand in marriage, Nu Jiao could scarcely believe her good fortune and agreed at once to become his bride.

The two departed her father's kingdom and travelled southwards where they set up home and began a very happy married life together. It was not long before Nu Jiao became pregnant and the couple were overjoyed at the prospect of a son who would carry on his father's good work. For although the majority of the floods had been checked, the task of clearing the debris and ensuring that no similar disasters occurred in the future was still very much incomplete. And as the days passed by, the responsibility of overseeing more and more of this kind of work fell on Yu's experienced shoulders. Often he was forced to spend days away from home and occasionally he was away for several weeks at a time.

Now when the time was close at hand for Nu Jiao to deliver her child, Yu was unfortunately summoned to help restore the Huanyan Shan which had begun to collapse and slide treacherously into the sea. And knowing that his wife would be anxious during his absence, Yu offered her the following words of comfort:

"If the task ahead were not so dangerous I would allow you to accompany me," he told her. "But I won't be very far away and I will take this drum with me and beat on it loudly when it safe for you to join me."

Nu Jiao was relieved to hear this and she bade her husband farewell and watched him disappear into the forest.

As soon as he was within range of the great mountain, Yu transformed himself into a giant black bear with mighty claws and powerful shoulders in preparation for the gruelling work ahead. Then, after he had tied the drum to a tree behind him, he stooped to the ground and tossed a boulder high into a crevice of the mountain where he could see it had originally broken loose. One after another he tossed the huge boulders in the same direction until almost all the gaps in the mountain had been filled in and the towering structure took on a more solid appearance again. But just as his work was coming to an end, Yu allowed one of the boulders to slip from his upraised arms and it slid over his shoulder, striking the drum that remained tied to the tree.

At once, Nu Jiao prepared a small parcel of food for her husband and set off in the direction of Huanyan Shan. Arriving at the place where the drum dangled in the breeze, she looked around for Yu, but was confronted instead by a terrifying black bear. Screaming in fright, Nu Jiao ran as fast as her legs would carry her towards her home, pursued by Yu who failed to realize that he had not changed back into his human shape. The young woman ran onwards in panic and dread, faster and faster until all colour had drained from her face and her muscles grew stiff from the chase. At last, she dropped down to the earth exhausted and beaten, and within seconds she was transformed into a stone.

Stunned and horrified by what had happened, Yu called out to his wife: "Give me my son, my only precious son." Immediately, the stone burst open and a small baby tumbled o to the earth. Yu named the child Qi, meaning 'cracked stone', and the story of his unusual birth earned him great fame even before he had grown to manhood.

MYTHS OF THE STARS

According to Chinese ideas, the sun, moon and planets influence sublunary events, especially the life and death of human beings, and changes in their colour tell of approaching calamities. Alterations in the appearance of the sun announce misfortunes to the State or its head, as revolts, famines, or the death of the emperor; when the moon waxes red, or turns pale, men should be in awe of the unlucky times foretold.

The sun and the moon are both included by the Chinese among the stars, the spirit of the sun king being 'Qijiang of the Solar Palace', that of the moon queen 'Chang'e of the Lunar Palace.' The sun is symbolized by the figure of a raven in a circle, and the moon by a hare on its hind legs pounding rice in a mortar, or by a three-legged toad. The moon is a special object of worship in autumn, and moon cakes dedicated to it are sold at this season.

All the stars are ranged into constellations, and an emperor is installed over them, who resides at the North Pole; five monarchs also live in the five stars in Leo, where there is a palace called Wu Di Zuo, or 'Throne of the Five Emperors.' In this celestial government there are also an heir-apparent, empresses, sons and daughters, and tribunals, and the constellations receive the names of men, animals and other terrestrial objects. The Great Bear, or Dipper, is worshipped as the residence of the Fates, where the duration of life and other events relating to mankind are measured and meted out. Fears are excited by unusual phenomena among the heavenly bodies.

It is here that we also encounter Taisui, the celestial spirit who presides over the year. He is the President of the Ministry of Time, a stellar god who corresponds to the planet Jupiter. This god is much to be feared. Whoever offends against him is sure to be destroyed. He strikes when least expected to.

THE HERDSMAN AND THE WEAVER GIRL

Many, many hundreds of years ago there lived in the palace of the High God in heaven a little weaver girl who spun and wove the most beautiful garments for the Gods, using colours and patterns more gorgeous than anything anyone had ever seen before. The High God was delighted with her efforts, but worried that she worked too hard, and for such long hours every day, and he decided to reward her diligence by giving her a rest from her labours. He determined to send her down to earth to live among mortals for a short time, to allow her to experience new and different pleasures. To ensure that the girl was well cared for, the High God chose for her a husband for her time on earth, a herdsman called Chen-Li, who lived with his two elder brothers on a farm by a great river.

The brothers had divided up the farm on their parents' death, and Chen-Li, being the youngest, had received nothing but an old ox, and the least fertile, most unproductive, piece of land. Here he built himself a rough home, and toiled day and night to make a living from the barren soil; although his life was hard he never complained, nor harboured a grudge against his brothers, for he was an honest youth of stout heart, which is indeed why the High God chose him for the weaver girl.

One evening Chen-Li was sitting watching the sun set over the distant mountains as his old ox munched the grass nearby. A feeling of great loneliness came over him, and he said to himself, "If only I had someone to share my life with, all my hard work would seem worthwhile." To his complete astonishment, the ox looked up and answered him, saying, "Do not be so sad, master. I can help you to find a wife who will bring you great joy." The ox then explained that it was really the Ox Star, sent to earth by the High God as a punishment, to work out its penance in labouring for mankind. It did not mention that it had also been given specific instructions regarding Chen-Li and the weaver girl, but went on to say: "If you go upstream you will find a beautiful, clear pool, shaded by willows and rushes. There the Heavenly Maidens bathe each afternoon; if you were to steal the clothes of one of them she would be unable to fly back to Heaven, and would have to, according to custom, become your wife."

Chen-Li did as the ox suggested, and the next afternoon he followed the river upstream, where he found the clear pool, shaded by willows. As he peered through the rushes, he saw the most beautiful girls he had ever set eyes on, laughing and splashing in the crystal waters. Spying their clothes piled on the banks of the pool, he leapt forward and snatched one of the piles; the noise disturbed the girls, who flew from the pool, took up their clothes, and soared away, up into the sky. Only one girl was left, naked in the pool, the little weaver girl, who looked shyly at Chen-Li and said, "Good Sir, if you would be generous enough to return my clothes, I will gladly come with you and become your wife." Chen-Li handed her clothes to her without hesitation, so strongly did he believe her promise. Then the girl dressed and, true to her word, followed him home and became his wife.

The couple were extremely happy in their simple existence, so much so that the weaver girl forgot all about the palace of the High God, and her place among the immortals. And in the fullness of time she bore the herdsman a fine son and a beautiful daughter, whom they loved dearly. However, the High God did not forget her, and grew impatient for her return. Eventually, when it became clear that she had no intention of leaving Chenh-Li, he sent down to earth his soldiers to bring her back. The weaver girl was distressed beyond all measure at leaving Chen-Li and her two children, but the soldiers were adamant, and carried her away, up into the sky. Chen-Li looked on in horror, unable to prevent this catastrophe, and he cried out in anguish, "What can I do? What can I do?"

The old ox saw his grief, and taking pity on Chen-Li said, "Master, my earthly form will die soon so that I can return to my celestial home; when I am dead, take off my hide and wrap it around you, and you will be able to follow your beloved." Saying this, the creature lay down and died at Chen-Li's feet, and, quickly, he did as the ox had instructed him. He picked up his son in one arm and his daughter in the other, and threw the leather hide around him. Instantly, all three soared up into the sky, and began to chase after the weaver girl, who was fast disappearing into the distance.

The High God watched this pursuit with much displeasure, and when he saw that Chen-Li would soon catch up with the weaver girl, he threw down his white silk scarf, which flowed and shimmered like fire between the lovers, forming a great river. Chen-Li called across the fiery torrent to his beloved, but to no avail, since neither could cross it. Defeated, he returned to his desolate home.

When the High God saw how much the weaver girl missed Chen-Li and her children, and how terribly they missed her, his anger abated, and he decreed that once a year, on the seventh day of the seventh month, all the magpies in the world would fly up into Heaven and form a bridge across the fiery river, so that the lovers could cross to each other and meet face to face. Whenever they met, the weaver girl would weep, and her tears fall to earth as drizzling rain; then all the women on earth would sorrow, and say, "Our sister is weeping again."

Chen-Li and the little weaver girl spent so much time in the sky, they eventually turned into stars; that is why, when we look up into the night sky, we can still see them both shining there. The fiery river is the Milky Way, on one side is Vega, the bright star that is the weaver girl, and on the other side shines Aquila, with two small stars beside it; which are Chen-Li and his two children. And if you look closely at the Milky Way on the night of the seventh day of the seventh month you will see these two stars meet as the two lovers are reunited for a few, precious hours, giving courage and hope to parted lovers throughout the world.

THE STEED SUMMIT

Qijiang **lived** in the reign of Xianyuan Huangdi, who appointed him Director of Construction and Furnishing. When Hsien-yüan went on his visit to Emei Shan, a mountain in Sichuan, Qijiang obtained permission to accompany him. Their object was to be initiated into the doctrine of immortality.

The Emperor was instructed in the secrets of the doctrine by Taiyi Huangren, the spirit of this famous mountain, who, when he was about to take his departure, begged him to allow Qijiang to remain with him. The new hermit went out every day to gather the flowering plants which formed the only food of his master, Taiyi Huangren, and he also took to eating these flowers, so that his body gradually became spiritualized.

One day Taiyi Huangren sent him to cut some bamboos on the summit of Emei Shan, far away from the place where they lived. When he reached the base of the summit, all of a sudden three giddy peaks confronted him, so dangerous that even the monkeys and other animals dared not attempt to scale them. But he took his courage in his hands, climbed the steep slope and by sheer energy reached the summit. Having cut the bamboos, he tried to descend, but the rocks rose like a wall in sharp points all round him and he could not find a foothold anywhere. Then, though laden with the bamboos, he threw himself into the air and was borne on the wings of the wind. He came to earth safe and sound at the foot of the mountain and ran with the bamboos to his master. On account of this feat he was considered advanced enough to be admitted to instruction in the doctrine.

SHEN YI, THE DIVINE ARCHER

The Emperor Yao, one day, while walking in the streets of Huai-yang, met a man carrying a bow and arrows, the bow being bound round with a piece of red stuff. This was Qijiang Ziyu. He told the Emperor he was a skilful archer and could fly in the air on the wings of the wind. Yao, to test his skill, ordered him to shoot one of his arrows at a pine-tree on the top of a neighbouring mountain. Ch'ih shot an arrow which transfixed the tree, and then jumped on to a current of air to go and fetch the arrow back. Because of this the Emperor named him Shen Yi, 'the Divine Archer,' attached him to his suite, and appointed him Chief Mechanician of all Works in Wood. He continued to live only on flowers.

At this time terrible calamities began to lay waste the land. Ten suns appeared in the sky, the heat of which burnt up all the crops; dreadful storms uprooted trees and overturned houses; floods overspread the country. Near the Dongting Hu a serpent, a thousand feet long, devoured human beings, and wild boars of enormous size did great damage in the eastern part of the kingdom. Yao ordered Shen Yi to go and slay the devils and monsters who were causing all this mischief, placing three hundred men at his service for that purpose.

Shen Yi took up his post on Qingqiu Shan to study the cause of the devastating storms, and found that these tempests were released by Fei Lian, the Spirit of the Wind, who blew them out of a sack. The ensuing conflict ended in Fei Lian suing for mercy and swearing friendship to his victor, whereupon the storms ceased.

After this first victory Shen Yi led his troops to the banks of the Xi He, West River, at Lin Shan. Here he discovered that on three neighbouring peaks nine extraordinary birds were blowing out fire and thus forming nine new suns in the sky. Shen Yi shot nine arrows in succession, pierced the birds, and immediately the nine false suns resolved themselves into red clouds and melted away. Shen Yi and his soldiers found the nine arrows stuck in nine red stones at the top of the mountain.

Shen Yi then led his soldiers to Gaoliang, where the river had risen and formed an immense torrent. He shot an arrow into the water, which thereupon withdrew to its source. In the flood he saw a man clothed in white, riding a white horse and accompanied by a dozen attendants. He quickly discharged an arrow, striking him in the left eye, and the horseman at once took to flight. He was accompanied by a young woman named Heng'e, the younger sister of He Bo, the Spirit of the Waters. Shen Yi shot an arrow into her hair. She turned and thanked him for sparing her life, adding: "I will agree to be your wife." After these events had been duly reported to the Emperor Yao, the wedding took place.

Three months later Yao ordered Shen Yi to go and kill the great Tung-t'ing serpent. An arrow in the left eye laid him out stark and dead. The wild boars also were all caught in traps and slain. As a reward for these achievements Yao canonized Shen Yi with the title of Marquis Pacifier of the Country.

SHEN YI BECOMES IMMORTAL

About this time Taiwu Furen, the third daughter of Xi Wang Mu, had entered a nunnery on Nanmin Shan, to the north of Luofu Shan, where her mother's palace was situated. She mounted a dragon to visit her mother, and all along the course left a streak of light in her wake. One day the Emperor Yao, from the top of Qingyun Shan, saw this track of light, and asked Shen Yi the cause of this unusual phenomenon. The latter mounted the current of luminous air, and letting it carry him whither it listed, found himself on Luofu Shan, in front of the door of the mountain, which was guarded by a great spiritual monster. On seeing Shen Yi this creature called together a large number of phoenixes and other birds of gigantic size and set them at Shen Yi. One arrow, however, settled the matter. They all fled, the door opened, and a lady followed by ten attendants presented herself. She was no other than Jin Mu herself. Shen Yi, having saluted her and explained the object of his visit, was admitted to the goddess's palace, and royally entertained.

"I have heard," said Shen Yi to her, "that you possess the pills of immortality; I beg you to give me one or two." "You are a well-known architect," replied Jin Mu; "please build me a palace near this mountain." Together they went to inspect a celebrated site known as Baiyugui Shan, 'White Jade-tortoise Mountain,' and fixed upon it as the location of the new abode of the goddess. Shen Yi had all the spirits of the mountain to work for him. The walls were built of jade, sweet-smelling woods were used for the framework and wainscoting, the roof was of glass, the steps of agate. In a fortnight's time sixteen palace buildings stretched magnificently along the side of the mountain. Jin Mu gave to the architect a wonderful pill which would bestow upon him immortality as well as the faculty of being able at will to fly through the air. "But," she said, "it must not be eaten now: you must first go through a twelve-month preparatory course of exercise and diet, without which the pill will not have all the desired results." Shen Yi thanked the goddess, took leave of her, and, returning to the Emperor, related to him all that had happened.

On reaching home, the archer hid his precious pill under a rafter, lest anyone should steal it, and then began the preparatory course in immortality.

At this time there appeared in the south a strange man named Zuo Qi, 'Chisel-tooth.' He had round eyes and a long projecting tooth. He was a well-known criminal. Yao ordered Shen Yi and his small band of brave followers to deal with this new enemy. This extraordinary man lived in a cave, and when Shen Yi and his men arrived he emerged brandishing a padlock. Shen Yi broke his long tooth by shooting an arrow at it, and Zuo Qi fled, but was struck in the back and laid low by another arrow from Shen Yi. The victor took the broken tooth with him as a trophy.

Heng'e, during her husband's absence, saw a white light which seemed to issue from a beam in the roof, while a most delicious odour filled every room. By the aid of a ladder she reached up to the spot whence the light came, found the pill of immortality, and ate it. She suddenly felt that she was freed from the operation of the laws of gravity and as if she had wings, and was just essaying her first flight when Shen Yi returned. He went to look for his pill, and, not finding it, asked Heng'e what had happened.

The young wife, seized with fear, opened the window and flew out. Shen Yi took his bow and pursued her. The moon was full, the night clear, and he saw his wife flying rapidly in front of him, only about the size of a toad. Just when he was redoubling his pace to catch her up a blast of wind struck him to the ground like a dead leaf.

Heng'e continued her flight until she reached a luminous sphere, shining like glass, of enormous size, and very cold. The only vegetation consisted of cinnamon-trees. No living being was to be seen. All of a sudden, she began to cough, and vomited the covering of the pill of immortality, which was changed into a rabbit as white as the purest jade. This was the ancestor of the spirituality of the yin, or female, principle. Heng'e noticed a bitter taste in her mouth, drank some dew, and, feeling hungry, ate some cinnamon. She took up her abode in this sphere.

As to Shen Yi, he was carried by the hurricane up into a high mountain. Finding himself before the door of a palace, he was invited to enter, and found that it was the palace of Donghua Dijun, otherwise Dong Wanggong, the husband of Xi Wang Mu.

The God of the Immortals said to Shen Yi: "You must not be annoyed with Heng'e. Everybody's fate is settled beforehand. Your labours are nearing an end, and you will become an Immortal. It was I who let loose the whirlwind that brought you here. Heng'e, through having borrowed the forces which by right belong to you, is now an Immortal in the Palace of the Moon. As for you, you deserve much for having so bravely fought the nine false suns. As a reward, you shall have the Palace of the Sun. Thus, the yin and the yang will be united in marriage." This said, Donghua Dijun ordered his servants to bring a red Chinese sarsaparilla cake, with a lunar talisman.

"Eat this cake," he said; "it will protect you from the heat of the solar hearth. And by wearing this talisman you will be able at will to visit the lunar palace of Heng'e; but the converse does not hold good, for your wife will not have access to the solar palace." This is why the light of the moon has its birth in the sun, and decreases in proportion to its distance from the sun, the moon being light or dark according as the sun comes and goes. Shen Yi ate the sarsaparilla cake, attached the talisman to his body, thanked the god, and prepared to leave. Dong Wanggong said to him: "The sun rises and sets at fixed times; you do not yet know the laws of day and night; it is absolutely necessary for you to take with you the bird with the golden plumage, which will sing to advise you of the exact times of the rising, culmination, and setting of the sun." "Where is this bird to be found?" asked Shen Yi. "It is the one you hear calling Ia! Ia! It is the ancestor of the spirituality of the yang, or male, principle. Through having eaten the active principle of the sun, it has assumed the form of a three-footed bird, which perches on the fu-sang tree in the middle of the Eastern Sea. This tree is several thousands of feet in height and of gigantic girth. The bird keeps near the source of the dawn, and when it sees the sun taking his morning bath gives vent to a cry that shakes the heavens and wakes up all humanity. That is why I ordered Ling Zhenzi to put it in a cage on Taohua Shan, Peach-blossom Hill; since then its cries have been less harsh. Go and fetch it and take it to the Palace of the Sun. Then you will understand all the laws of the daily movements." He then wrote a charm which Shen Yi was to present to Ling Zhenzi to make him open the cage and hand the golden bird over to him.

The charm worked, and Ling Zhenzi opened the cage. The bird of golden plumage had a sonorous voice and majestic bearing. "This bird," he said, "lays eggs which hatch out nestlings with red combs, who answer him every morning when he starts crowing. He is usually called the cock of heaven, and the cocks down here which crow morning and evening are descendants of the celestial cock."

Shen Yi, riding on the celestial bird, traversed the air and reached the disk of the sun just at mid-day. He found himself carried into the centre of an immense horizon, as large as the earth, and did not perceive the rotatory movement of the sun. He then enjoyed complete happiness without care or trouble. The thought of the happy hours passed with his wife Heng'e, however, came back to memory, and, borne on a ray of sunlight, he flew to the moon. He saw the cinnamon-trees and the frozen-looking horizon. Going to a secluded spot, he found Heng'e there all alone. On seeing him she was about to run away, but Shen Yi took her hand and reassured her. "I am now living in the solar palace," he said; "do not let the past annoy you." Shen Yi cut down some cinnamon-trees, used them for pillars, shaped some precious stones, and so built a palace, which he named Guanghan Gong, 'Palace of Great Cold.' From that time forth, on the fifteenth day of every moon, he went to visit her in her palace. That is the conjunction of the yang and yin, male and female principles, which causes the great brilliancy of the moon at that epoch.

Shen Yi, on returning to his solar kingdom, built a wonderful palace, which he called the Palace of the Lonely Park. From that time, the sun and moon each had their ruling sovereign.

When the old Emperor was informed that Shen Yi and his wife had both gone up to Heaven he was much grieved to lose the man who had rendered him such valuable service, and bestowed upon him the posthumous title of Zong Pu, 'Governor of Countries.' In the representations of this god and goddess the former is shown holding the sun, the latter the moon.

A VICTIM OF DA JI

Bo Yi Kao was the eldest son of Wen Wang, and governed the kingdom during the seven years that the old King was detained as a prisoner of the tyrant Zhou. He did everything possible to procure his father's release. Knowing the tastes of the cruel King, he sent him for his harem ten of the prettiest women who could be found, accompanied by seven chariots made of perfumed wood, and a white-faced monkey of marvellous intelligence. Besides these he included in his presents a magic carpet, on which it was necessary only to sit in order to recover immediately from the effects of drunkenness.

Unfortunately for Bo Yi Kao, Zhou's favourite concubine, Da Ji, conceived a passion for him and had recourse to all sorts of ruses to catch him in her net; but his conduct was throughout irreproachable. Angered by his indifference, she tried slander in order to bring about his ruin. But at first this did not have the result she expected. Zhou, after inquiry, was convinced of the innocence of Po. But an accident spoiled everything. In the middle of an amusing séance the monkey which had been given to the King by Po perceived some sweets in the hand of Da Ji, and, jumping on to her body, snatched them from Her. The King and his concubine were furious, Zhou had the monkey killed forthwith, and Da Ji accused Bo Yi Kao of having brought the animal into the palace with the object of making an attempt on the lives of the King and herself. But the Prince explained that the monkey, being only an animal, could not grasp even the first idea of entering into a conspiracy.

Shortly after this Po committed an unpardonable fault which changed the goodwill of the King into mortal enmity. He allowed himself to go so far as to suggest to the King that he should break off his relations with this infamous woman, the source of all the woes which were desolating the kingdom, and when Da Ji on this account grossly insulted him he struck her with his lute.

For this offence, Da Ji caused him to be crucified in the palace. Large nails were driven through his hands and feet, and his flesh was cut off in pieces. Not content with ruining Bo Yi Kao, this wretched woman wished also to ruin Wen Wang. She therefore advised the King to have the flesh of the murdered man made up into rissoles and sent as a present to his father. If he refused to eat the flesh of his own son he was to be accused of contempt for the King, and there would thus be a pretext for having him executed. Wen Wang, being versed in divination and the science of the ba gua, Eight Trigrams, knew that these rissoles contained the flesh of his son, and to avoid the snare spread for him he ate three of the rissoles in the presence of the royal envoys. On their return the latter reported this to the King, who found himself helpless on learning of Wen Wang's conduct.

Bo Yi Kao was canonized and appointed ruler of the constellation Ziwei of the North Polar heavens.

LEGEND OF TAISUI

Taisui was the son of the Emperor Zhou, the last of the Yin Chao. His mother was Jiang Hou. When he was born he looked like a lump of formless flesh. The infamous Da Ji, the favourite concubine of this wicked Emperor, at once informed him that a monster had been born in the palace, and the over-credulous sovereign ordered that it should immediately be cast outside the city. Shen Zhenren, who was passing, saw the small abandoned one, and said: "This is an Immortal who has just been born." With his knife, he cut open the caul which enveloped it, and the child was exposed.

His protector carried him to the cave Shui Lian, where he led the life of a hermit, and entrusted the infant to He Xiangu, who acted as his nurse and brought him up.

The child's hermit-name was Yin Jiao meaning 'Yin the Deserted of the Suburb'. When he had reached an age when he was sufficiently intelligent, his nurse informed him that he was not her son, but really the son of the Emperor Zhou, who, deceived by the calumnies of his favourite Da Ji, had taken him for an evil monster and had him cast out of the palace. His mother had been thrown down from an upper storey and killed. Yin Jiao went to his rescuer and begged him to allow him to avenge his mother's death. The Goddess Tian Fei, the Heavenly Concubine, picked out two magic weapons from the armoury in the cave, a battle-axe and club, both of gold, and gave them to Yin Jiao. When the Shang army was defeated at Mu Ye, Yin Jiao broke into a tower where Da Ji was, seized her, and brought her before the victor, King Wu, who gave him permission to split her head open with his battle-axe. But Da Ji was a spiritual hen-pheasant. She transformed herself into smoke and disappeared. To reward Yin Jiao for his filial piety and bravery in fighting the demons, Yu Di canonized him with the title Taisui Yin.

Taisui is the celestial spirit who presides over the year. He is the President of the Ministry of Time.

MYTHS OF THUNDER, LIGHTNING, WIND & RAIN

The number of spirits and guardians associated with the elements in Chinese legend is vast. Each of these elements is managed by a Ministry in the Heavens, composed of a large number of celestial officials. Members of these ministries are the most powerful of the guardian spirits, since they control the unpredictable forces on earth, such as fire, thunder, lightning, wind and rain.

Natural disasters caused by these forces occur again and again in Chinese mythology. It is always crucial in these stories to maintain a favourable relationship with the God in charge. The Ministry of Thunder and Storms, to take but one example, has a complicated infrastructure. It is presided over by the Ancestor of Thunder, Lei Zu, followed by other officials in order of seniority: Lei Gong, the Duke of Thunder, Tian Mu, the Mother of Lightning, Feng Po, the Count of Wind, Yu Shi, the Master of Rain and a string of other lesser Gods.

In temples Lei Zu is placed in the centre with the other four to right and left. He is a divinity with three eyes, one in the middle of his forehead, from which, when open, a ray of white light streams to a distance of more than two feet. Mounted on a black unicorn, he can travel millions of miles in the twinkling of an eye.

The Spirit of Thunder is represented as an ugly, black, bat-winged demon with clawed feet, a monkey's head, and an eagle's beak, who holds a steel chisel in one hand and a spiritual hammer in the other, with which he beats numerous drums strung about him. This produces the terrific noise of thunder. According to the Chinese, it is the sound of these drums and not the lightning which causes death.

WEN CHONG, MINISTER OF THUNDER

This story tells of Wen Chong, a minister of the tyrant king Zhou who fought against the armies of the Zhou dynasty. Being defeated, he fled to the mountains of Yen, Yan Shan, where he met Qi Jingzi, one of the alleged discoverers of fire, and joined battle with him; the latter, however, flashed his yin-yang mirror at a unicorn and put it out of action. Lei Chên-tzu, one of Wu Wang's marshals, then struck the animal with his staff, severing it in two.

Wen Chong escaped in the direction of the mountains of Jue long Ling, where another marshal, Yun Zhongzi, barred his way. Yün's hands had the power of producing lightning, and eight columns of mysterious fire suddenly came out of the earth, completely enveloping Wen Chong. They were thirty feet high and ten feet in circumference. Ninety fiery dragons came out of each and flew away up into the air. The sky was like a furnace, and the earth shook with the awful claps of thunder. In this fiery prison Wen Chong died.

When the new dynasty finally proved victorious, Jiang Ziya, by order of Yuanshi Tianzun, conferred on Wen Chong the supreme direction of the Ministry of Thunder, appointing him celestial prince and defender of the laws governing the distribution of clouds and rain. His full title was Celestial and Highly Honoured Head of the Nine Orbits of the Heavens, Voice of the Thunder, and Regulator of the Universe. His birthday is celebrated on the twenty-fourth day of the sixth moon.

LEI GONG, DUKE OF THUNDER

The Duke of Thunder, Lei Gong, is represented in Chinese legend as an ugly black creature with clawed feet and a monkey's head. In his hand he holds a chisel which he uses to beat on a drum, producing the ferocious noise of thunder. A popular story about him recalls how one day, a youth who had been chopping firewood high in the mountains noticed a thunderstorm approaching and took shelter under a large tree. Suddenly a great fork of lightning struck the tree, trapping the Duke of Thunder underneath its great weight as it fell to the ground. Lei Gong begged the youth to release him, promising to reward him handsomely, until finally the terrified youth agreed to his request. In return for his help, the Duke of Thunder presented him with a book which would teach him to conjure up storms and tempests.

"When you need rain," the God told him, "call on one of my four brothers and they will come to your aid. But don't call on me unless it is really necessary because my mood is often unpredictable."

After he had said this, Lei Gong disappeared and the youth headed back to his village.

Within no time he had become a popular figure among the people who regularly took the opportunity to celebrate his great powers in the local inn. One night, however, the youth became so drunk and disorderly he was arrested and carried off by the police. The following morning, as he was led to court, he called upon the God of Thunder to save him from imprisonment. The God responded immediately and thundered through the air so loudly that the windows of the courthouse were shattered by the noise. Cowering to the floor in terror, the magistrate ordered the youth to be released and dismissed him from the court without imposing any sentence.

From this day onwards, the youth used his power to save many people. For whenever he saw that there was danger of the land becoming dried out, he ordered a great storm to appear overhead and the rains to saturate the soil below.

LEI ZHENZI, SON OF THUNDER

Lei Zhenzi a Son of Thunder, was hatched from an egg after a clap of thunder and found by the soldiers of Wen Wang in some brushwood near an old tomb. The infant's chief characteristic was its brilliant eyes. Wen Wang, who already had ninety-nine children, adopted it as his hundredth, but gave it to a hermit named Yün Chung-tzŭ to rear as his disciple. The hermit showed him the way to rescue his adopted father from the tyrant who held him prisoner. In searching for a powerful weapon, the child found two apricots on the hillside and ate them both. He then noticed that wings had grown on his shoulders and was too ashamed to return home.

But the hermit, who knew intuitively what had happened, sent a servant to look for him. When they met the servant said: "Do you know that your face is completely altered?" The mysterious fruit had not only caused Lei Zhenzi to grow wings, known as Wings of the Wind and Thunder, but his face had become green, his nose long and pointed, and two tusks protruded horizontally from each side of his mouth, while his eyes shone like mirrors.

Lei Zhenzi now went and rescued Wen Wang, dispersing his enemies by means of his mystical power and bringing the old man back on his shoulders. Having brought him to safety, he returned to the hermit.

THE SPIRIT OF LIGHTNING

Dong Wanggong, the King of the Immortals, was playing at pitch-pot with Yunü. He lost; whereupon Heaven smiled and from its half-open mouth a ray of light came out. This was lightning; it is regarded as feminine because it is supposed to come from the earth, which is of the yin (or female) principle.

The Mother of Lightning is represented as a female figure, gorgeously dressed in blue, green, red, and white, holding in either hand a mirror from which streams two flashes of light.

Lightning, say the Chinese, is caused by the rubbing together of the yin and the yang – just as sparks of fire may be produced by the friction of two substances.

FÊNG PO, GOD OF THE WIND

Fêng Po, the God of the Wind, is represented as an old man with a white beard, yellow cloak, and blue and red cap. He holds a large sack, and directs the wind which comes from its mouth in any direction he pleases.

He is regarded as a stellar divinity under the control of the star Ch'i, because the wind blows at the time when the moon leaves that celestial mansion. He is also said to be a dragon called Fei Lian, at first one of the supporters of the rebel Qiyu, who was defeated by Huangdi. Having been transformed into a spiritual monster, he stirred up tremendous winds in the southern regions. The Emperor Yao sent Shen Yi with three hundred soldiers to quiet the storms and appease Qiyu's relatives, who were wreaking their vengeance on the people. Shen Yi ordered the people to spread a long cloth in front of their houses, fixing it with stones. The wind, blowing against this, had to change its direction. Shen Yi then flew on the wind to the top of a high mountain, where he saw a monster at the base. It had the shape of a huge yellow and white sack and kept inhaling and exhaling in great gusts. Shen Yi, concluding that this was the cause of all these storms, shot an arrow and hit the monster, whereupon it took refuge in a deep cave. Here it turned on Shen Yi and, drawing a sword, dared him to attack the Mother of the Winds. Shen Yi, however, bravely faced the monster and discharged another arrow, this time hitting it in the knee. The monster immediately threw down its sword and begged that its life might be spared.

YU SHI, MASTER OF RAIN

Yu Shi, the Master of Rain, clad in yellow scale-armour, with a blue hat and yellow busby, stands on a cloud and from a watering can pours rain upon the earth. Like many other gods, however, he is represented in various forms. Sometimes he holds a plate, on which is a small dragon, in his left hand, while with his right he pours down the rain.

Legend tells that the God of Rain is Qi Songzi, who appeared during a terrible drought in the reign of Shennong, and owing to his reputed magical power was requested by the latter to bring rain from the sky. "Nothing is easier," he replied; "pour a bottleful of water into an earthen bowl and give it to me." This being done, he plucked from a neighbouring mountain a branch of a tree, soaked it in the water, and with it sprinkled the earth. Immediately clouds gathered and rain fell in torrents, filling the rivers to overflowing. Qi Songzi was then honoured as the God of Rain, and his images show him holding the mystic bowl. He resides in the K'un-lun Mountains, and has many extraordinary peculiarities, such as the power to go through water without getting wet, to pass through fire without being burned and to float in space.

THE ONE-LEGGED BIRD

At the time when Xuanming Daren instructed Fei Lian in the secrets of magic, the latter saw a wonderful bird which drew in water with its beak and blew it out again in the shape of rain. Fei Lian tamed it, and would take it about in his sleeve.

Later on a one-legged bird was seen in the palace of the Qi Wangzi walking up and down and hopping in front of the throne. Being much puzzled, the Prince sent a messenger to Lu to inquire of Confucius concerning this strange behaviour. "This bird is a shang yang" said Confucius; "its appearance is a sign of rain. In former times the children used to amuse themselves by hopping on one foot, knitting their eyebrows, and saying: 'It will rain, because the shang yang is disporting himself.' Since this bird has gone to Ch'i, heavy rain will fall. The people should be told to dig channels and repair the dykes, for the whole country will be inundated." Not only Ch'i, but all the adjacent kingdoms were flooded; all sustained grievous damage except Ch'i, where the necessary precautions had been taken. This caused Duke Jing to exclaim: "Alas! How few listen to the words of the sages!"

MA YUANSHUAI, GENERALISSIMO OF THE WEST

Ma Yuanshuai is a three-eyed monster condemned by Ju Lai to reincarnation for excessive cruelty in the extermination of evil spirits.

In order to obey this command he entered the womb of Ma Jinmu in the form of five globes of fire. Being a precocious youth, he could fight when only three days old and killed the Dragon king of the Eastern Sea. From his instructor he received a spiritual work dealing with wind and thunder, and a triangular piece of stone which he could change at will into anything he liked. By order of Yu Di he subdued the Spirits of the Wind and Fire, the Blue Dragon, the King of the Five Dragons, and the Spirit of the Five Hundred Fire Ducks, all without injury to himself. For these and many other enterprises he was rewarded by Yu Di with various magic articles and with the title of Generalissimo of the West, and is regarded as so successful an interceder with Yu Di that he is prayed to for all sorts of benefits.

MYTHS OF THE WATERS

In the spirit world there is a Ministry that controls all things connected with the waters on earth, salt or fresh. Its main divisions are the Department of Salt Waters, presided over by four Dragon-kings – those of the East, South, West and North – and the Department of Sweet Waters, presided over by Si Wang (Si Tu) of the four great rivers – the Blue (Jiang), Yellow (He), Huai, and Qi – and the Dragon spirits who control the Secondary Waters, the rivers, springs, lakes, pools, rapids.

The dragons are spirits of the waters. In a sense the dragon is the type of a man, self-controlled, and with powers that verge on the supernatural. In China the dragon is not a power for evil, instead he controls the rain, and so holds in his power prosperity and peace. He is the essence of the yang, or male, principle.

The dragon is also represented as the father of the great emperors of ancient times. His bones, teeth and saliva are employed as a medicine. He has the power of transformation and of rendering himself visible or invisible at will. In the spring he ascends to the skies and in the autumn buries himself in the watery depths. Some are wingless and rise into the air by their own inherent power. There is the celestial dragon, who guards the mansions of the gods and supports them so that they do not fall; the divine dragon, who causes the winds to blow and produces rain for the benefit of mankind; the earth dragon, who marks out the courses of rivers and streams; the dragon of the hidden treasures, who watches over the wealth concealed from mortals; and the five Sea Dragon Kings who live in gorgeous palaces in the depths of the sea.

THE FOOLISH DRAGON

This is the part of the great Buddha legend referring to the dragon. In years gone by, a dragon living in the great sea saw that his wife's health was not good. He, seeing her colour fade away, said: "My dear, what shall I get you to eat?" Mrs Dragon was silent. Just tell me and I will get it," pleaded the affectionate husband. "You cannot do it; why trouble?" she replied. "Trust me, and you shall have your heart's desire," said the dragon. "Well, I want a monkey's heart to eat." "Why, Mrs Dragon, the monkeys live in the mountain forests! How can I get one of their hearts?" "Well, I am going to die; I know I am."

So the dragon went on shore, and, spying a monkey on the top of a tree, said: "Hail, shining one, are you not afraid you will fall?" "No, I have no such fear." "Why eat of one tree? Cross the sea, and you will find forests of fruit and flowers." "How can I cross?" "Get on my back." The dragon with his tiny load went seaward and then suddenly dived down. "Where are you going?" said the monkey with the salt water in his eyes and mouth. "Oh! My dear sir! my wife is very sad and ill and has taken a fancy to your heart." "What shall I do?" thought the monkey. He then spoke, "Illustrious friend, why did not you tell me? I left my heart on the top of the tree; take me back, and I will get it for Mrs Dragon." The dragon returned to the shore. As the monkey was slow in coming down from the tree, the dragon said: "Hurry up, little friend, I am waiting." Then the monkey thought within himself, "What a fool this dragon is!"

Then Buddha said to his followers: "At this time I was the monkey."

AN UNAUTHORIZED PORTRAIT

Po Shi, a Taoist priest, told Qin Shi Huangdi, the First Emperor, that an enormous oyster vomited from the sea a mysterious substance which accumulated in the form of a tower and was known as 'the market of the sea'. Every year, at a certain period, the breath from his mouth was like the rays of the sun. The Emperor expressed a wish to see it, so Po Shi said he would write a letter to the God of the Sea and he next day the Emperor could witness the wonderful sight.

The Emperor then remembered a dream he had had the year before in which he saw two men fighting for the sun. The one killed the other and carried it off. He therefore wished to visit the country where the sun rose. Po Shi said that all that was necessary was to throw rocks into the sea and build a bridge across them. Immediately he rang his magic bell, the earth shook and rocks began to rise up; but as they moved too slowly e struck them with his whip and blood came from them, which eft red marks in many places. The row of rocks extended as far s the shore of the sun country, but to build the bridge across em was found to be beyond the reach of human skill.

So Po Shi sent another messenger to the God of the Sea, requesting him to raise a pillar and place a beam across it which could be used as a bridge. The submarine spirits came and placed themselves at the service of the Emperor, who asked for an interview with the god. To this the god agreed on condition that no one should make a portrait of him, he being very ugly. Instantly a stone gangway one hundred thousand feet long rose out of the sea, and the Emperor, mounting his horse, went with his courtiers to the palace of the god. Among his followers was Lu Dongshi, who tried to draw a portrait of the god by using his foot under the surface of the water. Detecting this manoeuvre the god was incensed and said to the Emperor: "You have broken your word; did you bring Lu here to insult me? Retire at once, or evil will befall you." The Emperor, seeing that the situation was precarious, mounted his horse and galloped off. As soon as he reached the beach, the stone causeway sank and all his suite perished in the waves. One of the Court magicians said to the Emperor: "This god ought to be feared as much as the God of Thunder; then he could be made to help us. Today a grave mistake has been made." For several days after the incident the waves beat upon the beach with increasing fury. The Emperor then built a temple and a pagoda to the god of Zhifu Shan and Wenteng Shan respectively; by which he was apparently appeased.

THE SHIPWRECKED SERVANT

Once the Eight Immortals were on their way to Chang Shan to celebrate the birthday anniversary of Xian Wen the God of Longevity. They had with them a servant who bore the presents they intended to offer to the god. When they reached the seashore the Immortals walked on the waves without any difficulty, but Lan Caihe remarked that the servant was unable to follow them and said that a means of transport must be found for him. So Cao Guojiu took a plank of cypress-wood and made a raft. But when they were in mid-ocean a typhoon arose and upset the raft and servant and presents sank to the bottom of the sea.

Regarding this as the hostile act of a water devil, the Immortals said they must demand an explanation from the Dragon King, Ao Qin. Li Tieguai took his gourd and, directing the mouth toward the bottom of the sea, created so brilliant a light that it illuminated the whole palace of the Sea King. Ao Qin, surprised, asked where this powerful light came from. He sent a messenger to ascertain its cause.

To this messenger the Immortals made their complaint. "All we want," they added, "is that the Dragon King shall restore to us our servant and the presents." On this being reported to Ao Qin he suspected his son of being the cause and, having established his guilt, severely reprimanded him. The young Prince took his sword and, followed by an escort, went to find those who had made the complaint to his father. As soon as he caught sight of the Immortals he began to inveigh against them.

Han Xiangzi, not liking this undeserved abuse, changed his flute into a fishing line and as soon as the Dragon prince was within reach caught him on the hook, intending to keep him as a hostage. The Prince's escort returned at once and informed Ao Qin of what had happened. The latter declared that his son was in the wrong and proposed to restore the shipwrecked servant and the presents. The Court officers, however, held a different opinion. "These Immortals," they said, "dare to hold captive your Majesty's son merely on account of a few lost presents and a shipwrecked servant. This is a great insult, which we ask permission to avenge." Eventually they won over Ao Qin, and the armies of the deep gathered for the fray. The Immortals called to their aid the other Taoist Immortals and Heroes and thus two formidable armies found themselves face to face.

Several attempts were made by other divinities to avert the conflict, but without success. The battle was a strenuous one. Ao Qin received a ball of fire full on his head and his army was threatened with disaster when Cizhang Dashi appeared with his bottle of lustral water. Using a willow-branch, he sprinkled the combatants with this magic fluid, causing all their magic powers to disappear.

Shui Guan, the Ruler of the Watery Elements, then arrived and reproached Ao Qin; he assured him that if the matter were to come to the knowledge of Shang Di, the Supreme Ruler, he would not only be severely punished but would risk losing his post. Ao Qin expressed penitence restored the servant and the presents and made full apology to the Eight Immortals.

THE SPIRITS OF THE WELL

One day Zhang Daoling, the 'father of modern Taoism,' wa on Homing Shan with his disciple Wang Chang. "See, he said, "that shaft of white light on Yang Shan. There ar undoubtedly some bad spirits there. Let us go and bring them to reason." When they reached the foot of the mountain they met twelve women who had the appearance of evil spirits. Zhang Daoling asked them where the shaft of white light came from. They answered that it was the yin (female) principle of the earth. "Where is the source of the salt water?" he asked again. "That pond in front of you," they replied, "in which lives a very wicked dragon." Zhang Daoling tried to force the dragon to come out, but without success. Then he drew a phoenix with golden wings on a charm and hurled it into the air over the pond. The dragon took fright and fled, the pond immediately drying up. After that Zhang Daoling took his sword and stuck it in the ground. A well full of salt water appeared on the spot.

The twelve women each offered Zhang Daoling a jade ring and asked that they might become his wives. He took the rings and, pressing them together in his hands, made one large single ring. "I will throw this ring into the well," he said, "and the one of you who recovers it shall be my wife." All the twelve women jumped into the well to get the ring. Then Zhang Daoling put a cover over it and fastened it down, telling them that from now on they were the spirits of the well and would never be allowed to come out.

Shortly after this Zhang Daoling met a hunter. He urged him not to kill living beings, but to change his occupation to that of a salt burner, instructing him how to draw out the salt from salt-water wells. The people of that district were helped both by being able to obtain the salt and by being no longer molested by the twelve female spirits. A temple, called Temple of the Prince Qi, was built by them, and the territory of Ling

Zhou was given to Zhang Daoling in recognition of the benefits he had granted the people.

THE DRAGON KING'S DAUGHTER

There was once a student named Liu Yi, who lived in the central region of China, near the great lakes. One day, as he was returning from the capital having successfully taken his examinations, he saw on the road ahead of him a young woman herding a flock of sheep. She was the most beautiful woman Liu had ever seen, but she was deeply distressed, tears coursing down her fair cheeks, her whole body shaking with sobs. Liu's heart went out to the girl, and he got down from his donkey and asked her if there was any way in which he could be of assistance. The girl thanked him through her tears, and explained the cause of her grief.

"My father is the Dragon King of Dongting Hu," she explained, "and many months ago he married me to the son of the God of the Jing river, whom I do not love. My husband is cruel to me, and his family torment me, but I cannot complain to my father as Dongting Hu is too far away for me to travel, and the family intercept my messages to him. I know my father would help if he but knew of my grief, but I am so utterly alone and friendless."

Liu was so touched by the girl's plight that he offered to take the message to her father himself, but he could not see how it could be done.

"Although the shores of Dongting Hu are my home," he said, "I am a mere human. How could I ever reach your father's palace in the terrifying depths of the lake?"

The girl replied, "If you are strong in heart, go to the sacred tangerine tree on the northern shore of the lake. Tie your sash around its trunk, and knock on it three times. From there you will be led to the palace."

Liu willingly agreed to undertake the journey, and the girl handed him a letter from the folds of her gown. As he remounted his donkey, he called out, "When you return to Dongting, I sincerely hope that we shall meet again." Then, spurring the animal on, he set off. After a few minutes he looked back, but the girl had disappeared together with her sheep.

Liu went straight to the northern shore of Dongting Hu, and finding the sacred tangerine tree, he tied his sash around its trunk and knocked on it three times as the girl had said. At once the waves of the lake parted, and a man rose up from the depths, and asked Liu what he wanted.

"I must talk to your king," Liu said. "It is a matter of the utmost importance."

The man nodded, and placed a blindfold over Liu's eyes. Liu became aware of a silence engulfing him, and his body became colder and colder, but he did not flinch. After a time, the blindfold was removed, and Liu found he was in a great palace, beautifully decorated with pearl and other precious stones, and all the warmth flooded back into his body. His guide showed him into a vast chamber, and there, on a mighty throne, sat the Dragon King.

Liu bowed low, and humbly proffered the girl's letter, explaining where and how he had met her on the road from the capital. The Dragon King read the letter, and as he did so great tears rolled down his face, and his huge hands shook. Then he instructed a servant to take the letter to the queen, and said to

Liu, "I thank you for all your trouble. You have taken pity on my daughter, while I did nothing to save her from her suffering. I shall never forget your kindness to her, and your bravery in making this journey."

At that moment he was interrupted by a loud wailing from the queen's chamber, and the sound of weeping. "Quickly," ordered the king with a worried frown, "tell them to be quiet, or they will arouse Qiantang."

"Who is Qiantang?" asked Liu, surprised that anything should disturb such a mighty ruler.

The Dragon King explained that Qiantang was his younger brother, once ruler of Lake Qiantang. His quick temper had caused such floods and devastation, even threatening the Five Holy Peaks, that the High God had banished him from the lake, and forgiven him on the understanding that his brother guarantee his good behaviour. "This news would infuriate him, as he is extremely fond of his niece, and would instantly demand revenge."

As he spoke, there was a tremendous crash, and the chamber filled with smoke. In a tumult of lightning, thunder and rain, a huge red dragon tore through the hall, clouds streaming from his nostrils, and a mighty roar issuing from his throat. Liu fell to the ground in terror, but the dragon left as quickly as it had appeared.

"That was Qiantang," the Dragon King explained, helping the terrified Liu to his feet. "I must apologize for his frightening you like that." He called for wine and food, and graciously set them before Liu, who soon forgot his fear, as they talked about Liu's career, and life in the capital. A short while later they were cut short by the arrival of the queen and her train.

smiling and laughing amongst themselves. And Liu saw to his amazement that the Dragon King's daughter, whom he had met on the road, was in the group. The king embraced her, and he begged her forgiveness for allowing her to marry such a wretch, and she warmly thanked Liu for his help in rescuing her.

At that moment an elegant, dignified young man walked into the chamber and was introduced to Liu as Qiantang. Once he overcame his initial fear, Liu was delighted to find him a charming individual, courteously thanking Liu for his help, and toasting his health. Qiantang explained to his brother that he had fought the Jing River God and his men, and then visited the High God to explain his actions and apologize if he had done wrong. "He has generously forgiven me," he said, "and I now apologize to you, my brother for my fury in your palace, and to you, honoured guest, for scaring you."

"I am glad the High God has forgiven you," said the king. "And I willingly do so too, but you must be less hasty in future. And now tell me of the battle with the God of the Jing river."

"It was nothing," said Qiantang. "I slew six hundred thousand of his men, and destroyed two hundred square miles of his land, and the battle was as good as won."

"And what of my daughter's erstwhile husband?"

"I ate him," replied Qiantang casually, and the conversation was over.

The next day a great feast was held in Liu's honour; the Dragon King lavished gifts on him, and Qiantang drank to his health innumerable times. After much delicious food, and even more wine, Qiantang took Liu aside and said to him, "The king's daughter has been saved thanks to you. She is a fine woman, aware of how much she owes to you, and as it is clear that you are in love with her, I suggest that you marry her straight away."

Liu did not know what to say; although he was, as Qiantang had guessed, very much in love with the girl, marriage to the daughter of a God was not to be taken lightly. Nor was the suggestion of a rather drunken dragon to be taken too seriously, especially when Liu considered the possibility of Qiantang's anger at his presumption, if the dragon changed his mind when sober. So, regretfully, Liu talked the tipsy Qiantang out of his idea, and the next day left the palace for his home, laden with gifts, and accompanied by many servants. In his heart, though, he still longed for the Dragon Princess.

Months passed, and the now-wealthy Liu, knowing he could not pine for ever, married a local girl, but she was stricken with fever and soon died. To stave off his loneliness, Liu married again, but his second wife too caught the fever, and soon died. Despairing more and more, Liu married a girl from outside the region, who soon bore him a son. As time went by, Liu began to notice that his wife looked more and more like the Dragon Princess, the lost love of his youth, and after his second son had been born, the woman finally admitted that she was indeed the Dragon King's daughter. She had been bitterly disappointed when Liu turned down her uncle's suggestion, and kept remembering his last words to her on the road from the capital: 'When you return to Dongting, I sincerely hope that we shall meet again.' When Liu's second wife had died, she had seized her opportunity to become the third.

The couple lived together in great happiness, and raised a large family. They frequently visited the Dragon King's palace beneath the deep waters of Dongting Hu, and as

Liu became older, they stayed there for longer and longer periods. Eventually they left the land of mortal men entirely, and took up residence with the immortal Dragon King and Queen, and Qiantang, in their immortal home beneath the waves.

THE OLD MOTHER OF THE WATERS

The Old Mother of the Waters, Shuimu Niangniang, inundated the ancient city of Sizhou in Anhui almost every year. A report was presented to Yu Huang, Lord of the Skies, begging him to put an end to the menace who devastated the country and cost so many lives. The Lord of the Skies commanded the Great Kings of the Skies and their generals to raise troops and take the field in order to capture this goddess of the waters and deprive her of the power of doing further mischief. But her tricks triumphed over force and the city continued to be periodically devastated by inundations.

One day Shuimu Niangniang was seen near the city gate carrying two buckets of water. Li Laojun suspected some plot, but, an open attack being too risky, he preferred to adopt a ruse. He went and bought a donkey, led it to the buckets of water and let it drink their contents. Unfortunately the animal could not drink all the water, so that a little remained at the bottom of the buckets. Now these magical buckets contained the sources of the five great lakes, which held enough water to inundate the whole of China. Shuimu Niangniang overturned one of the buckets and the water that had remained in it was enough to cause a formidable flood, which submerged the unfortunate town, and buried it forever under the immense sheet of water called the Hungze Hu.

So great a crime deserved an exemplary punishment and accordingly Yu Huang sent reinforcements to his armies and a pursuit of the goddess was planned.

Sun Houzi, the Monkey Sun, the rapid courier – who in a single skip could travel thirty-six thousand miles – started in pursuit and caught her up, but the astute goddess was clever enough to slip through his fingers. Sun Houzi, furious at this setback, went to ask Guanyin Pusa to come to his aid. She promised to do so. As one may imagine, the furious race she had had to escape from her enemy had given Shuimu Niangniang a good appetite. Exhausted with fatigue and with an empty stomach, she caught sight of a woman selling vermicelli, who had just prepared two bowls of it and was awaiting customers. Shuimu Niangniang went up to her and began to eat the strength-giving food with enthusiasm. No sooner had she eaten half of the vermicelli than it changed in her stomach into iron chains, which wound round her intestines. The end of the chain protruded from her mouth and the contents of the bowl became another long chain which welded itself to the end and stuck out beyond her lips. The vermicelli-seller was none other than Guanyin Pusa herself, who had conceived this idea as a means of ridding herself of this evil goddess. She ordered Sun Houzi to take her down a deep well at the foot of a mountain in Xuyi Xian and to fasten her securely there. It is there that Shuimu Niangniang remains in her liquid prison. The end of the chain is to be seen when the water is low.

XU SUN, THE DRAGON SLAYER

At forty-one years of age, when Xu Sun was Magistrate of Ching-yang, near the modern Zhijiang Xian, in Hubei, during times of drought he had only to touch a piece of tile to turn it into gold in order to relieve the people of their distress. He also saved many lives by curing sickness through the use of talismans and magic formulae.

During the period of the dynastic troubles, he resigned and joined the famous magician Kuo Po. Together they went to the minister Wang Tun, who had risen against the Eastern Chin dynasty. Kuo Po's remonstrance only irritated the minister, who cut off his head.

Xu Sun then threw his chalice on the ridgepole of the room, causing it to be whirled into the air. As Wang Tun watched this unfold, Hsü disappeared and escaped. When he reached Luchiang Kou, in Anhui, he boarded a boat, which two dragons towed into the offing and then raised into the air. In an instant they had borne it to the Lushan Mountains, to the south of Jiujiang, in Jiangxi. The perplexed boatman opened the window of his boat and looked out. The dragons, finding themselves discovered by an infidel, set the boat down on the top of the mountain and fled.

In this country was a dragon, or spiritual alligator, which transformed itself into a young man named Shen Lang. He married Jia Yu, daughter of the Chief Judge of T'an Zhou. The young people lived in rooms below the official apartments. During spring and summer Shen Lang roamed in the rivers and lakes. One day Hsü met him, recognized him as a dragon and knew that he was the cause of the numerous floods that were devastating Jiangxi Province. He determined to find a means of getting rid of him.

Shen Lang, aware of the steps being taken against him, changed himself into a yellow ox and fled. Hsü at once transformed himself into a black ox and started in pursuit. The yellow ox jumped down a well to hide, but the black ox followed suit. The yellow ox then jumped out again and escaped to Changsha, where he reassumed a human form.

Xu Sun, returning to the town, hastened to the yamên and called to Shen Lang to come out and show himself, addressing him in a severe tone of voice: "Dragon, how dare you hide yourself there under a borrowed form?" Shen Lang then reassumed the form of a spiritual alligator and Xu Sun ordered the spiritual soldiers to kill him. He then commanded his two sons to come out of their abode. By merely spurting a mouthful of water on them he transformed them into young dragons. Jia Yu was told to vacate the rooms at once and in the twinkling of an eye the whole yamên sank beneath the earth. Nothing but a lake remained where it had been.

After his victory over the dragon, Xu Sun assembled the members of his family on Xi Shan, outside the city of Nanchang Fu and all ascended to Heaven in full daylight, taking with them even the dogs and chickens. He was then 133 years old. Subsequently a temple was erected to him and he was canonized as Just Prince, Admirable and Beneficent.

THE MARRIAGE OF THE RIVER GOD

In Yeh Xian there was a witch and some official attendant who every year collected money from the people for the marriage of the River god. The witch would select a pretty girl of low birth and say that she should be the Queen of the River god. The girl was bathed and clothed in a beautiful dress made of expensive silk. She was then taken to the bank of the river to a monastery which was beautifully decorated with scrolls and banners. A feast was held and the girl was placed on a bed that was floated out on the tide till it disappeared under the waters.

Many families with beautiful daughters moved to distant places and gradually the city became deserted. The common belief in Yeh was that if no queen was offered to the River god a flood would come and drown the people.

One day Ximen Bao, Magistrate of Yeh Xian, said to his attendants: "When the marriage of the River god takes place I wish to say farewell to the chosen girl."

Accordingly Ximen Bao was present to witness the ceremony. About three thousand people had come together. Standing beside the old witch were ten of her female disciples, "Call the girl out," said Ximen Bao. After seeing her, Ximen Bao said to the witch: "She is not fair. Go you to the River god and tell him that we will find a fairer maid and present her to him later on." His attendants then seized the witch and threw her into the river.

After a little while Ximen Bao said: "Why does she stay so long? Send a disciple to call her back." One of the disciples was thrown into the river. Another and yet another followed. The magistrate then said: "The witches are females and therefore cannot bring me a reply." So one of the official attendants of the witch was thrown into the river.

Ximen Bao stood on the bank for a long time, apparently awaiting a reply. The spectators were alarmed. Ximen Bao then ordered his attendants to send the remaining disciples of the witch and the other official attendants to recall their mistress. The wretches threw themselves on their knees and knocked their heads on the ground, which was stained with the blood from their foreheads, and with tears confessed their sin. "The River god detains his guest too long," said Ximen Bao at length. "Let us adjourn."

After this no one dared to celebrate the marriage of the River god.

THE BUILDING OF BEIJING

When the Mongol Yuan dynasty had been destroyed and the Emperor Hongwu had succeeded in firmly establishing that of the Great Ming, Da Ming, he made Jinling (the present Nanjing) his capital and held his Court there with great splendour. Envoys from every province within the 'Four Seas' would assemble there to witness his greatness.

The Emperor had many sons and daughters by his different consorts and concubines, each mother in her inmost heart fondly hoping that her own son would be selected by his father to succeed him.

Although the Empress had a son, who was the heir-apparent, she felt envious of those ladies who had likewise been blessed with children for fear one of the princes should supplant her son in the affection of the Emperor and in the succession. This envy displayed itself on every occasion; she was greatly beloved by the Emperor and exerted all her influence with him to get the other young princes removed from Court. Through her means most of them were sent to the different provinces as governors.

One of the consorts of Hongwu, the Lady Weng, had a son named Zhudi. This young prince was very handsome and graceful; he was, moreover, of an amiable disposition. He was the fourth son of the Emperor and his pleasing manner had made him a great favourite, not only with his father, but with every one about the Court. The Empress noticed the evident affection the Emperor had for this prince, so she plotted to get him removed from the Court as soon as possible. By a judicious use of flattery and cajolery, she ultimately persuaded the Emperor to appoint the prince governor of the Yen country. He was to be known as Yan Wang, Prince of Yen.

Soon afterwards the young Prince left Jinling to proceed to his post. As he left, however, a Taoist priest called Liu Bowen, who had a great affection for the Prince, put a sealed packet into his hand and told him to open it when he found himself in difficulty, distress or danger; a glance at the first portion that came to his hand would invariably suggest some remedy for the evil, whatever it was. After doing so he was again to seal the packet, without further looking into its contents, till some other emergency arose necessitating advice or assistance, when he would again find it. The Prince departed on his journey and in time arrived safely at his destination.

When Zhudi arrived in Yen it was a mere barren wilderness with very few inhabitants; those there lived in huts and scattered hamlets and there was no city to afford protection to the people and to defend then from robbers or would-be attackers.

When the Prince saw what a desolate looking place he had been appointed to – and thought of the long years he was probably destined to spend there – he grew very melancholy and nothing his attendants said or did could alleviate his sorrow.

All at once the Prince thought of the packet that the old Taoist priest had given him; he began to search for it – for in the bustle and excitement of travelling he had forgotten all about it – in hope that it might suggest something to better his prospects. Having found the packet, he quickly broke it open to see what instructions it contained; taking out the first paper which came to hand, he read the following:

"When you reach Beijing Fu (now Beijing) you must build a city there and name it Nocha Cheng, the City of Nocha. But, as the work will be costly, you must issue a proclamation inviting the wealthy to subscribe the necessary funds for building it. At the back of this paper is a plan of the city; you must be careful to act according to the instructions accompanying it."

The Prince inspected the plan, carefully read the instructions and found even the minutest details fully explained. He was struck with the grandeur of the design of the proposed city and immediately acted on the instructions contained in the packet; proclamations were posted up and large sums were soon subscribed, ten of the wealthiest families who had accompanied him from Jinling being the largest contributors, supporting the plan not only with their purses, by giving immense sums, but by their influence among their less wealthy neighbours.

When enough money had been subscribed, a day was chosen on which to start building. Trenches where the foundations of the walls were to be were first dug out, according to the plan found in the packet. The foundations themselves consisted of layers of stone quarried from the western hills; bricks of an immense size were made and burnt in the neighbourhood; the moat was dug out and the earth from it used to fill in the centre of the walls; the whole circuit of the walls having battlements and embrasures. Above each of the nine gates of the city immense three-storied towers were built.

Near the front entrance of the city, facing each other, were built the Temples of Heaven and of Earth. Behind it the beautiful 'Coal Hill' (better known as 'Prospect Hill') was raised; while in the square in front of the Great Gate of the palace was buried an immense quantity of charcoal (that and the coal being stored as a precaution in case of siege).

The palace, containing many superb buildings, was built in a style of exceeding splendour; in the various enclosures were beautiful gardens and lakes; in the different courtyards, too, seventy-two wells were dug and thirty-six golden tanks placed. The whole of the buildings and grounds was surrounded by a lofty wall and a stone paved moat, in which the lotus and other beautiful flowers bloomed, and in the clear waters of which numerous gold and silver fish could be found.

The city was similar to that of Jinling. When everything was completed the Prince compared it with the plan and found that the city tallied with it in every respect. He was delighted and called for the ten wealthy persons who had been the chief contributors and gave each of them a pair of 'couchant dragon' silk- or satin-embroidered cuffs and allowed them great privileges. Up to the present time there is the common saying: "Since then the 'dragon-cuffed' gentlefolks have flourished."

All the people were loud in praise of the beauty and strength of the newly built city. Merchants from every province hastened to Beijing, attracted by the news they heard of its magnificence and of the prospect of selling their wares. The people were prosperous and happy, food was plentiful, the troops brave, the monarch just, his ministers virtuous and all enjoyed the blessings of peace. All was tranquil.

However, one day one of the Prince's ministers reported that "the wells are thirsty and the rivers dried up" – there was no water and the people were all alarmed. At once the Prince called his counsellors together to devise some means of remedying this disaster and causing the water to return to the wells and springs, but no one could suggest a suitable plan.

The reason for the scarcity of water was that there was a dragon's cave outside the east gate of the city at a place called Leichen Kou, 'Thunder-clap Mouth' or 'Pass'. The dragon had not been seen for many years, but it was well known that he lived there. In digging out the earth to build the wall, the workmen had broken into this dragon's cave, without knowing the consequences that would result. The dragon was angry and determined to move away from the new city, but the she-dragon said: "We have lived here thousands of years, and shall we suffer the Prince of Yen to drive us forth thus? If we do go we will collect all the water, place it in our baskets and at midnight we will appear in a dream to the Prince requesting permission to retire. If he gives us permission to do so and allows us also to take our baskets of water with us, he will fall into our trap – for we shall take the water with his own consent."

The two dragons then transformed themselves into an old man and an old woman, went to the chamber of the Prince, who was asleep, and appeared to him in a dream. Kneeling before him, they cried: "O Lord of a Thousand Years, we have come before you to beg leave to retire from this place and to beseech you out of your great bounty to give us permission to take these two baskets of water with us."

The Prince readily agreed, little dreaming of the danger he was facing. The dragons were delighted, and quickly left; they filled the baskets with all the water there was in Beijing and carried them off with them.

When the Prince woke he paid no attention to his dream till he heard the report of the scarcity of water. Deciding there might be some hidden meaning in it, he opened the packet again and discovered that his dream visitors had been dragons who had taken the waters of Beijing away with them in their magic baskets. He returned to the packet once more, which contained directions for the recovery of the water.

The Prince quickly donned his armour, mounted his black horse and, with spear in hand, dashed out of the west gate of the city. He soon caught up with the water-stealing dragons, who still retained the forms they had appeared to him in his dream. On a cart were the two identical baskets he had seen; in front of the cart, dragging it, was the old woman, while behind, pushing it, was the old man.

When the Prince saw them he galloped up to the cart and, without pausing, thrust his spear into one of the baskets, making a great hole, out of which the water rushed so rapidly that the Prince became frightened. He dashed off at full speed to save himself from being swallowed up by the waters, which in a very short time had risen more than thirty feet and had flooded the surrounding country. On galloped the Prince, followed by the roaring water, till he reached a hill, up which he urged his startled horse. When he reached the top he found that it stood out of the water like an island, completely surrounded; the water was seething and swirling round the hill in a frightful manner, but he could see neither of the dragons.

The Prince was alarmed at his perilous position, when suddenly a Buddhist priest appeared before him, with clasped hands and bent head, who told him not be alarmed, as with Heaven's assistance he would soon disperse the water. Then the priest recited a short prayer or spell and the waters receded as rapidly as they had risen, finally returning to their proper channels.

The broken basket became a large deep hole, in the centre of which was a fountain which threw up a vast body of clear water. From the midst of this arose a pagoda, which rose and fell with the water, floating on the top like a vessel; the spire thrusting itself far up into the sky, and swaying about like the mast of a ship in a storm.

The Prince returned to the city filled with wonder at what he had seen, and with joy at having so successfully carried out the directions contained in the packet. On all sides he was greeted by his delighted people, hailing him as the saviour of Beijing. Since that time Beijing has never had the misfortune to be without water.

The pagoda is called the Pagoda on the Hill of the Imperial Spring. The spring is still there and day and night its clear waters bubble up and flow eastward to Beijing, which would now be a barren wilderness but for the Prince's pursuit of the water.

THE SPIRITS OF THE YELLOW RIVER

The spirits of the Yellow River are called Dai Wang – Great King. For many hundreds of years past the river inspectors had continued to report that all sorts of monsters show themselves in the waves of the stream, at times in the shape of dragons, at others in that of cattle and horses, and whenever such a creature makes an appearance a great flood follows. Hence temples are built along the river banks. The higher spirits of the river are honored as kings, the lower ones as captains, and hardly a day goes by without their being honored with sacrifices or theatrical performances. Whenever, after a dam has been broken, the leak is closed again, the emperor sends officials with sacrifices and ten great bars of Tibetan incense. This incense is burned in a great sacrificial censer in the temple court, and the river inspectors and their subordinates all go to the temple to thank the gods for their aid. These river gods, it is said, are good and faithful servants of former rulers, who died in consequence of their toil in keeping the dams unbroken. After they died their spirits became river-kings; in their physical bodies, however, they appear as lizards, snakes and frogs.

The mightiest of all the river-kings is the Golden Dragon-King. He frequently appears in the shape of a small golden snake with a square head, low forehead and four red dots over his eyes. He can make himself large or small at will, and cause the waters to rise and fall. He appears and vanishes unexpectedly, and lives in the mouths of the Yellow River and the Imperial Canal. But in addition to the Golden Dragon-King there are dozens of river-kings and captains, each of whom has his own place. The sailors of the Yellow River all have exact lists in which the lives and deeds of the river-spirits are described in detail.

The river-spirits love to see theatrical performances. Opposite every temple is a stage. In the hall stands the little spirit-tablet of the river-king, and on the altar in front of it a small bowl of golden lacquer filled with clean sand. When a little snake appears in it, the river-king has arrived. Then the priests strike the gong and beat the drum and read from the holy books. The official is at once informed and he sends for a company of actors. Before they begin to perform the actors go up to the temple, kneel, and beg the king to let them know which play they are to give. And the river-god picks one out and points to it with his head; or else he writes signs in the sand with his tail. The actors then at once begin to perform the desired play.

The river-god cares naught for the fortunes or misfortunes of human beings. He appears suddenly and disappears in the same way, as best suits him.

Between the outer and the inner dam of the Yellow River are a number of settlements. Now it often happens that the yellow water moves to the very edge of the inner walls. Rising perpendicularly, like a wall, it gradually advances. When people see it coming they hastily burn incense, bow in prayer before the waters, and promise the river-god a theatrical performance. Then the water retires and the word goes round: "The river-god has asked for a play again!"

In a village in that section there once dwelt a wealthy man. He built a stone wall, twenty feet high, around the village, to keep away the water. He did not believe in the spirits of the river, but trusted in his strong wall and was quite unconcerned.

One evening the yellow water suddenly rose and towered in a straight line before the village. The rich man had them shoot cannon at it. Then the water grew stormy, and surrounded the wall to such a height that it reached the openings in the battlements. The water foamed and hissed, and seemed about to pour over the wall. Then everyone in the village was very much frightened. They dragged up the rich man and he had to kneel and beg for pardon. They promised the river-god a theatrical performance, but in vain; but when they promised to build him a temple in the middle of the village and give regular performances, the water sank more and more and gradually returned to its bed. And the village fields suffered no damage, for the earth, fertilized by the yellow slime, yielded a double crop.

Once a scholar was crossing the fields with a friend in order to visit a relative. On their way they passed a temple of the river-god where a new play was just being performed. The friend asked the scholar to go in with him and look on. When they entered the temple court they saw two great snakes upon the front pillars, who had wound themselves about the columns, and were thrusting out their heads as though watching the performance. In the hall of the temple stood the altar with the bowl of sand. In it lay a small snake with a golden body, a green head and red dots above his eyes. His neck was thrust up and his glittering little eyes never left the stage. The friend bowed and the scholar followed his example.

Softly he said to his friend: "What are the three river-gods called?"

"The one in the temple," was the reply, "is the Golden Dragon-King. The two on the columns are two captains. They do not dare to sit in the temple together with the king."

This surprised the scholar, and in his heart he thought: "Such a tiny snake! How can it possess a god's power? It would have to show me its might before I would worship it."

He had not yet expressed these secret thoughts before the little snake suddenly stretched forth his head from the bowl, above the altar. Before the altar burned two enormous candles. They weighed more than ten pounds and were as thick as small trees. Their flame burned like the flare of a torch. The snake now thrust his head into the middle of the candle-flame. The flame must have been at least an inch broad, and was burning red. Suddenly its radiance turned blue, and was split into two tongues. The candle was so enormous and its fire so hot that even copper and iron would have melted in it; but it did not harm the snake.

Then the snake crawled into the censer. The censer was made of iron, and was so large one could not clasp it with both arms. Its cover showed a dragon design in open-work. The snake crawled in and out of the holes in this cover, and wound his way through all of them, so that he looked like an embroidery in threads of gold. Finally all the openings of the cover, large and small, were filled by the snake. In order to do so, he must have made himself several dozen feet long. Then he stretched out his head at the top of the censer and once more watched the play.

Thereupon the scholar was frightened, he bowed twice and prayed: "Great King, you have taken this trouble on my account! I honor you from my heart!"

No sooner had he spoken these words than, in a moment the little snake was back in his bowl, and just as small as he had been before.

In Dsiningdschou they were celebrating the river god' birthday in his temple. They were giving him a theatrica performance for a birthday present. The spectators crowde around as thick as a wall, when who should pass but a simpl peasant from the country, who said in a loud voice: "Why, that is nothing but a tiny worm! It is a great piece of folly to honor it like a king!"

Before ever he had finished speaking the snake flew out of the temple. He grew and grew, and wound himself three times around the stage. He became as thick around as a small pail, and his head seemed like that of a dragon. His eyes sparkled like golden lamps, and he spat out red flame with his tongue. When he coiled and uncoiled the whole stage trembled and it seemed as though it would break down. The actors stopped their music and fell down on the stage in prayer. The whole multitude was seized with terror and bowed to the ground. Then some of the old men came along, cast the peasant on the ground, and gave him a good thrashing. So he had to cast himself on his knees before the snake and worship him. Then all heard a noise as though a great many firecrackers were being shot off. This lasted for some time, and then the snake disappeared.

East of Shandong lies the city of Dongzhou. There rises an observation-tower with a great temple. At its feet lies the water-city, with a sea-gate at the North, through which the flood-tide rises up to the city. A camp of the boundary guard is established at this gate.

Once upon a time there was an officer who had been transferred to this camp as captain. He had formerly belonged to the land forces, and had not yet been long at his new post. He gave some friends of his a banquet, and before the pavilion in which they feasted lay a great stone shaped somewhat like a table. Suddenly a little snake was seen crawling on this stone. It was spotted with green, and had red dots on its square head. The soldiers were about to kill the little creature, when the captain went out to look into the matter. When he had looked he laughed and said: "You must not harm him! He is the river-king of Dsiningdschou. When I was stationed in Dsiningdschou he sometimes visited me, and then I always gave sacrifices and performances in his honor. Now he has come here expressly in order to wish his old friend luck, and to see him once more."

There was a band in camp; the bandsmen could dance and play like a real theatrical troupe. The captain quickly had them begin a performance, had another banquet with wine and delicate foods prepared, and invited the river-god to sit down to the table.

Gradually evening came and yet the river-god made no move to go.

So the captain stepped up to him with a bow and said: "Here we are far removed from the Yellow River, and these people have never yet heard your name spoken. Your visit has been a great honor for me. But the women and fools who have crowded together chattering outside, are afraid of hearing about you. Now you have visited your old friend, and I am sure you wish to get back home again."

With these words he had a litter brought up; cymbals were beaten and fire-works set off, and finally a salute of nine guns was fired to escort him on his way. Then the little snake crawled into the litter, and the captain followed after. In this order they reached the port, and just when it was about time to say farewell, the snake was already swimming in the water. He had grown much larger, nodded to the captain with his head, and disappeared.

Then there were doubts and questionings: "But the river-god lives a thousand miles away from here, how does he get to this place?"

Said the captain: "He is so powerful that he can get to any place, and besides, from where he dwells a waterway leads to the sea. To come down that way and swim to sea is something he can do in a moment's time!"

MYTHS OF FIRE

The celestial organization of Fire is the fifth Ministry, which is presided over by a President, Luo Xuan, 'Stellar Sovereign of the Fire-virtue,' with five subordinate ministers, four of whom are star-gods, and the fifth a 'celestial prince who receives fire': Jiehuo Tianjun. Like so many other Chinese deities, the five were all ministers of the tyrant emperor Zhou.

LUO XUAN AND THE MINISTRY OF FIRE

It is believed that Luo Xuan was originally a Taoist priest known as Yenchong Xian, of the island Huolong, meaning 'Fire-dragon.' His face was the colour of ripe fruit of the jujube-tree, his hair and beard red, the former done up in the shape of a fish-tail. He is also said to have had three eyes. He wore a red cloak ornamented with the ba gua; his horse snorted flames from its nostrils and fire darted from its hoofs.

While fighting in the service of the son of the tyrant emperor, Luo Xuan suddenly changed himself into a giant with three heads and six arms. In each of his hands he held a magic weapon. These were a seal which reflected the heavens and the earth, a wheel of the five fire-dragons, a gourd containing ten thousand fire-crows, and, in the other hands, two swords which floated like smoke and a tall column of smoke enclosing swords of fire.

Having arrived at the city of Xiqi, Luo Xuan sent forth his smoke-column and the air was filled with swords of fire. The ten thousand fire-crows, emerging from the gourd, spread themselves over the town and a terrible fire broke out, the whole place being ablaze in just a few minutes.

It was then that Princess Longzhi, daughter of Wangmu Niangniang appeared in the sky. She spread her shroud of mist and dew over the city and the fire was extinguished by a heavy downpour of rain. All the mysterious mechanisms of Luo Xuan lost their power and the magician took to his heels down the side of the mountain. There he was met by Li, the Pagoda-bearer, who threw his golden pagoda into the air. The pagoda fell on Luo Xuan's head and broke his skull.

THE LEGEND OF QIJINGZI

Of the various fire-gods, Ch'ih Ching-tzǔ, the principle of spiritual fire, is one of the five spirits representing the Five Elements. He is Fire personified, which has its birth in the south on Shitang Shan. He himself and everything connected with him – his skin, hair, beard, trousers and cloak of leaves – are all of the colour of fire, though he is sometimes represented with a blue cap resembling the blue tip of a flame.

He appeared in the presence of Huang Lao in a fire cloud. It was he who obtained fire from the wood of the mulberry tree. The heat of this fire, joined with the moisture of water, developed the germs of terrestrial beings.

THE RED EMPEROR

Zhu Rong was a legendary emperor who made his first appearance in the time of Xianyuan. In his youth he asked Kuangshou Lao ren, 'Old Longevity,' to grant him immortality. "The time has not yet come," replied Old Longevity; "before it does you have to become an emperor. I will give you the means of reaching the end you desire. Give orders that after you are dead you are to be buried on the southern slope of the sacred mountain Hêng Shan; there you will learn the doctrine of Ch'ih Ching-tzŭ and will become immortal."

The Xianyuan Huangdi, having abdicated the throne, sent for Zhu Rong and bestowed upon him the crown. Zhu Rong, having become emperor, taught the people the use of fire and the advantages to be derived from it.

In those early times the forests were filled with venomous reptiles and savage animals; he ordered the peasants to set fire to the brushwood to drive away these dangerous neighbours and keep them at a distance. He also taught his subjects the art of purifying, forging and welding metals by the action of fire. He was nicknamed Qidi, 'the Red Emperor.' He reigned for more than two hundred years, and became an immortal. His capital was the ancient Kuei cheng, north-east of Xinzheng Xian. His tomb is on the southern slope of Heng Shan. The peak is known as Zhu Rong Feng. His descendants, who went to live in the south, were the ancestors of the Directors of Fire.

HUILU, GOD OF FIRE

The most popular God of Fire is Huilu, a celebrated magician who lived some time before the reign of Tiku, the father of Yao the Great, and had a mysterious bird named Pifang and a hundred other fire birds shut up in a gourd. He had only to let them out to set up an extensive fire that would extend over the whole country.

Huangdi ordered Zhu Rong to fight Huilu and also to subdue the rebel Zhiyu. Zhu Rong had a large bracelet of pure gold – a most wonderful and effective weapon. He hurled it into the air and it fell on Huilu's neck, throwing him to the ground and rendering him incapable of moving. Finding resistance impossible, he asked for mercy from his victor and promised to be his follower in the spiritual contests. Subsequently he always called himself Huoshi Zhitu, 'the Disciple of the Master of Fire.'

SHENNONG, THE FIRE EMPEROR

When Shennong, the God of Agriculture, succeeded the Fuxi Huangdi on the throne he adopted fire a the emblem of his government, just as Huangdi adopte the symbol of Earth. He came to be called Huodi, th 'Fire emperor.'

Shennong taught his subjects the use of fire for smelting metals and making implements and weapons, and the use of oil in lamps. All the divisions of his official hierarchy were connected in some way with this element – there were the Ministers of Fire generally, the officers of Fire of the North, South, etc. He subsequently become doubly the patron of fire and a second fire symbol was added to his name, changing it from Huo Ti, 'Fire Emperor,' to Yandi, 'Blazing Emperor'.

MYTHS OF EPIDEMICS
& EXORCISM

Here we encounter some of the more interesting tales of the gods of Epidemics and of Exorcism, who belong to a number of celestial Ministries.

The composition of the Ministry of Epidemics is arranged differently in different historical works as Epidemics (regarded as epidemics on earth, but as demons in Heaven) of the Centre, Spring, Summer, Autumn and Winter, or as the marshals clothed in yellow, green, red, white and blue respectively, or as the Officers of the East, West, South and North, with two additional members: a Taoist who quells the plague and the Grand Master who urges people to do right.

The Ministry of Exorcism, on the other hand, is a Taoist invention and is composed of seven chief ministers, whose duty is to expel evil spirits from dwellings and generally to counteract the annoyances of infernal demons. The two gods usually referred to in the popular legends are Panguan and Zhongkui. The first is the Guardian of the Living and the Dead in the Otherworld. He was originally a scholar named Cuizhao, who became the Minister of Ceremonies. After his death he was appointed to the spiritual post mentioned above. His best-known achievement is his prolongation of the life of the Tang Taizong Huangdi by twenty years by changing i, 'one,' into san, 'three,' in the life register kept by the gods. However, the original Panguan, 'the Decider of Life in Hades', has been gradually supplanted in popular favour by Zhongkui, 'the Protector against Evil Spirits'.

THE FIVE SPIRITS OF THE PLAGUE

With regard to the Ministry of Seasonal Epidemics, it is told that in the sixth moon of the eleventh year of the reign of Sui Gaozu Huangdi, five men appeared in the air, clothed in robes of five colours, each carrying different objects in his hands: the first a spoon and earthenware vase, the second a leather bag and sword, the third a fan, the fourth a club, the fifth a jug of fire.

The Emperor asked his Grand Historiographer who these were and if they were benevolent or evil spirits. The official answered: "These are the five powers of the five directions. Their appearance indicates the imminence of epidemics, which will last throughout the four seasons of the year." "What remedy is there, and how am I to protect the people?" inquired the Emperor. "There is no remedy," replied the official, "for epidemics are sent by Heaven." During that year the mortality was very great. The Emperor built a temple to the five men and granted them the title of Marshals to the Five Spirits of the Plague. During that and the following dynasty sacrifices were offered to them on the fifth day of the fifth moon.

THE LEGEND OF LÜ YUE

Lü Yue, the President of the Ministry of Epidemics was an old Taoist hermit living at Jiulong Dao ('Nine-dragon Island') who became an Immortal. The four members of the Ministry were his disciples. He wore a red garment had a blue face, red hair, long teeth and three eyes. His war horse was named the Myopic Camel. He carried a magic sword and was in the service of Zhou Wang, whose armies were concentrated at Xiqi. In a duel with Mucha, brother of Nezha, he had his arm severed by a sword. In another battle with Huang Tianhua, son of Huang Feihu, he appeared with three heads and six arms. In his many hands he held the celestial seal, plague microbes, the flag of plague, the plague sword and two mysterious swords. His faces were green and large teeth protruded from his mouths. Huang Tianhua threw his magic weapon and hit him on the leg. Just at that moment Jiang Ziya arrived with his whip and felled him with a blow. However, he was able to rise again and took to flight.

Resolved to avenge his defeat, he joined General Xufang who was commanding an army corps at Chuanyun Guan. Round the mountain he organized a system of entrenchments and of infection against their enemies. Yang Jian released his celestial hound which bit Lü Yue on the crown of his head. Then Yang Ren, armed with his magic fan, pursued Lü Yue and compelled him to retreat to his fortress. Lü Yue mounted the central raised part of the embattled wall and opened all his plague-disseminating umbrellas, with the intent of infecting Yang Ren, but the latter, simply by waving his fan, reduced all the umbrellas to dust and also burned the fort, and with it Lü Yue.

THE FIVE GRADUATES

There is an interesting legend concerning five other gods of epidemics. These gods are called the Wuyue, 'Five Mountains,' and are worshipped in the temple Sanyi Guo at Jukao, especially in outbreaks of contagious diseases and fevers. A sufferer goes to the temple and promises offerings to the gods in the event of recovery. The customary offering is five small wheaten loaves (called shao ping) and a pound of meat.

The Wuyue are stellar devils whom Yu Huang sent to be reincarnated on earth. Their names were Tian Boxue, Dong Hongwen, Cai Wenzhu, Zhao Wuzhen, and Huang Yingtu. They were all noted for their brilliant intellects and were clever scholars who successfully passed their graduate's examination.

The story goes that when Li Shimin ascended the throne he called together all the literati of the Empire to take the Doctor's Examination in the capital. Our five graduates started for the metropolis, but, losing their way, were robbed and had to beg help in order to reach the end of their journey. By good luck they all met in the Sanyi Guo temple and told each other the various hardships they had endured. But when they eventually reached the capital the examination was over and they were out in the streets without resources. So they took an oath of brotherhood for life and death. They pawned some of the few clothes they possessed and bought some musical instruments, turning themselves into a band of strolling musicians. The first bought a drum, the second a seven-stringed guitar, the third a mandolin, the fourth a clarinet and the fifth and youngest composed songs.

They went through the streets of the capital giving their concerts, and Fate decreed that Li Shimin should hear their melodies. Charmed with the sweet sounds, he asked Xu Maogong where this band of exceptional musicians came from. Having made inquiries, the minister related their experiences to the Emperor. Li Shimin ordered them to be brought to him and after hearing them play and sing he appointed them to his private suite. They were to accompany him wherever he went.

Meanwhile, the Emperor bore malice toward Zhang Tianshi, the Master of the Taoists, because he refused to pay the taxes on his property and conceived a plan to bring about his destruction. He caused a spacious subterranean chamber to be dug under the reception hall of his palace. A wire passed through the ceiling to where the Emperor sat. This was so that the signal for the music to begin or stop could be given at will. Having stationed the five musicians in this subterranean chamber, he summoned the Master of the Taoists and invited him to a banquet. During the course of this he pulled the wire and a subterranean babel began.

The Emperor pretended to be terrified and allowed himself to fall to the ground. Then, addressing himself to the Tianshi, he said: "I know that you can at will catch the devilish hobgoblins which molest human beings. You can hear for yourself the infernal row they make in my palace. I order you under penalty of death to put a stop to their pranks and to exterminate them."

Having said this, the Emperor left. The Master of the Taoists brought his projecting mirror and began to seek for the evil spirits. In vain he inspected the palace and its precincts; he could discover nothing. In despair threw his mirror on the floor of the reception hall.

A minute later, sad and pensive, he stooped to pick it up; when he saw reflected in it the subterranean room and the musicians! At once he drew five talismans on yellow paper, burned them and ordered his celestial general, Zhao Gongming, to take his sword and kill the five musicians. The order was promptly executed, but when the Tianshi informed the Emperor, he could not believe it was true. He went to his seat and pulled the wire, but all remained silent. A second and third time he gave the signal, but without response. He then ordered his Grand Officer to ascertain what had happened. The officer found the five graduates bathed in their blood and lifeless.

The Emperor, furious, reproached the Master of the Taoists. "But," replied the Tianshi, "was it not your Majesty who ordered me under pain of death to exterminate the authors of this pandemonium?" Li Shimin could not reply. He dismissed the Master of the Taoists and ordered the five victims to be buried.

After the funeral ceremonies, apparitions appeared at night in the place where they had been killed, and the palace became a babel. The spirits threw bricks and broke the tiles on the roofs.

The Emperor ordered his uncomfortable visitors to go to the Tianshi who had murdered them. They obeyed and, seizing the garments of the Master of the Taoists, swore not to allow him any rest if he would not restore them to life.

To appease them the Taoist said: "I am going to give each of you a wonderful object. You are then to return and spread epidemics among wicked people, beginning in the imperial palace and with the Emperor himself, with the object of forcing him to canonize you."

One received a fan, another a gourd filled with fire, the third a metallic ring to encircle people's heads, the fourth a stick made of wolves' teeth and the fifth a cup of lustral water.

The spirit graduates left full of joy and made their first experiment on Li Shimin. The first gave him feverish chills by waving his fan, the second burned him with the fire from his gourd, the third encircled his head with the ring, causing him violent headache, the fourth struck him with his stick and the fifth poured out his cup of lustral water on his head.

The same night a similar tragedy took place in the palace of the Empress and the two chief imperial concubines.

Taipo Jinxing, however, informed Yu Huang what had happened and, touched with compassion, he sent three Immortals with pills and talismans which cured the Empress and the ladies of the palace.

Li Shimin, having also recovered his health, summoned the five deceased graduates and expressed his regret for the unfortunate series of events. He said to them: "To the south of the capital is the Sanyi Guo miao. I will change its name to Xiangshan Wuyue Shen, 'Fragrant Hill of the Five Mountain Spirits.' On the twenty-eighth day of the ninth moon betake yourselves to that temple to receive the seals of your canonization." He granted them the title of Ti, 'Emperor.'

THE EXORCISM OF EMPTINESS AND DEVASTATION

This legend tells of the Emperor Tang Minghuang who, after an expedition to Li Shan in Shaanxi, was attacked by fever. During a nightmare he saw a small demon fantastically dressed in red trousers, with a shoe on one foot but not on the other and a shoe hanging from his girdle.

Having broken through a bamboo gate, the demon took possession of an embroidered box and a jade flute and then began to make a tour of the palace. The Emperor grew angry and questioned him. "Your humble servant," replied the little demon, "is named Xu Hao, 'Emptiness and Devastation,'" "I have never heard of such a person," said the Emperor. The demon replied, "Hsü means to desire Emptiness, because in Emptiness one can fly just as one wishes; Hao, 'Devastation,' changes people's joy to sadness."

The Emperor, irritated by this flippancy, was about to call his guard, when suddenly a great devil appeared wearing a tattered head-covering and a blue robe. He had a horn clasp on his belt and official boots on his feet. The devil went up to the sprite, tore out one of his eyes, crushed it up and ate it. The Emperor asked the newcomer who he was. "Your humble servant," he replied, "is Zhong Kui, Physician of Tungnan Shan in Shaanxi. In the reign-period Tang Gaozu Wu Di I was rejected and unjustly defrauded of a first class in the public examinations. Overwhelmed with shame, I committed suicide on the steps of the imperial palace. The Emperor ordered me to be buried in a green robe [reserved for members of the imperial clan], and out of gratitude for that favour I swore to protect the sovereign in any part of the Empire against the evil plots of the demon Xu Hao." At these words the Emperor awoke and found that the fever had left him.

His Majesty called for Wu Daozi (one of the most celebrated Chinese artists) to paint the portrait of the person he had seen in his dream. The work was so well done that the Emperor recognized it as the actual demon he had seen in his sleep and rewarded the artist handsomely. The portrait is said to have been still in the imperial palace during the Song dynasty.

TALES OF THE GODDESS OF MERCY

The most popular Goddess of the Buddhist faith is the beautiful Guanyin, a deity originally represented as a man. This transition from a male deity into a female one seems to have emerged sometime during the Northern Song dynasty (960–1126 CE) and is reflected in Guanyin's miraculous appearance in human form in the saga of Miaoshan that follows.

According to the ancient myth, Guanyin was about to enter Heaven when she heard a cry of anguish from the earth beneath her and could not prevent herself from investigating its source. Hence her name translates as 'one who hears the cries of the world'.

Guanyin is the patron saint of Tibetan Buddhism, the patron Goddess of mothers, the guardian of the storm-tossed fisherman and the overall protector of mankind. If, in the midst of a fire she is called upon, the fire ceases to burn. If during a battle her name is called, the sword and spear of the enemy prove harmless. If prone to evil thoughts, the heart is immediately purified when she is summoned. Her image is that of a Madonna figure with a child in her arms. All over China this Goddess is revered and it is this image that appears not only in temples of worship but also in households and other public places.

THE BIRTH OF MIAOSHAN

In the twenty-first year of the reign of Ta Hao (the Great Great One) of the Golden Heavenly Dynasty, a man named Po Jia, whose first name was Luo Yu – an enterprising kinglet of Xi Yi – seized the throne for twenty years after fighting a war for three years. His kingdom was known as Xing Lin and the title of his reign as Miao Chuang.

The kingdom of Xing Lin was situated between India on the west, the kingdom of Tian Cheng on the south and the kingdom of Siam on the north. Of this kingdom the two pillars of State were the Grand Minister Zhao Chen and the General Qu Jie. The Bao De Huanghou, whose maiden name was Boya, and the King Miao Chuang had lived nearly half a century without having a son to succeed to the throne. This was a source of great grief to them. Boya suggested to the King that the God of Hua Shan, the sacred mountain in the west, had the reputation of being always willing to help; and that if he prayed to him and asked his pardon for having shed so much blood during the wars which preceded his accession to the throne he might obtain an heir.

Welcoming this suggestion, the King sent for Zhao Chen and ordered him to dispatch the two Chief Ministers of Ceremonies, Xi Hengnan and Zhi Tu, to the temple of Hua Shan with instructions to request fifty Buddhist and Taoist priests to pray for seven days and seven nights in order that the

King might obtain a son. When that period was over, the King and Queen would go in person to offer sacrifices in the temple.

The envoys took with them many rare and valuable presents and for seven days and seven nights the temple resounded with the sound of drums, bells and all kinds of instruments, intermingled with the voices of the praying priests. On their arrival the King and Queen offered sacrifices to the god of the sacred mountain.

But the God of Hua Shan knew that the King had been deprived of a male heir as a punishment for the extensive loss of life during his three years' war. The priests, however, interceded for him, urging that the King had come in person to offer the sacrifices, so the God could not altogether reject his prayer. So he ordered Qianli Yan, 'Thousand-li Eye,' and Shunfeng Er, 'Favourable-wind Ear,' to go quickly and find out if there were not some worthy person who was on the point of being reincarnated into this world.

The two messengers shortly returned and stated that in India, in the village of Zhishu Yuan in the Jiuling Shan, there lived a good man named Shi Qinchang whose ancestors had observed all the ascetic rules of the Buddhists for three generations. This man was the father of three children – the eldest Shih Wen, the second Shi Jin and the third Shi Shan – all worthy followers of the great Buddha.

Meanwhile, Wang Che, a bandit chief and thirty of his band of men, finding themselves pursued and harassed by the Indian soldiers, without provisions or shelter and dying of hunger, went to Shih Wen and begged for something to eat. Knowing that they were evildoers, Shih Wen and his two brothers refused to give them anything; if they starved, they said, the peasants would no longer suffer from their attacks. So the robbers decided that it was a case of life for life and broke into the house of a rich family of the name of Tai, burning their home, killing a hundred men, women and children, and carrying off everything they possessed.

The local tuti (or Local God) made a report to Yu Huang at once.

"This Shi jia," replied the god, "for three generations has given itself up to good works, and certainly the robbers were not deserving of any pity. However, it is impossible to deny that the three brothers Shih, in refusing them food, morally compelled them to loot the Tai family's house, putting all to the sword or flames. Is this not the same as if they had committed the crime themselves? Let them be arrested and put in chains in the celestial prison and let them never see the light of the sun again."

"Since," said the messenger to the God of Hua Shan, "your gratitude toward Miao Chuang compels you to grant him an heir, why not ask Yu Huang to pardon their crime and reincarnate them in the womb of the Queen Boya, so that they may begin a new terrestrial existence and give themselves up to good works?" As a result, the God of Hua Shan called the Spirit of the Wind and gave him a message for Yu Huang.

The message was as follows: "King Miao Chuang has offered sacrifice to me and begged me to grant him an heir. But since by his wars he has caused the deaths of a large number of human beings, he does not deserve to have his request granted. Now these three brothers Shih have offended your Majesty by forcing Wang Che to be guilty of murder and robbery. I pray you to take into account their past good works and pardon their crime, giving them an opportunity of expiating it by causing them all three to be reborn, but of the female sex, in the womb of Boya the Queen. In this way they will be able to atone for their crime and save many souls." Yu Huang was pleased to comply and he ordered the Spirit of the North Pole to release the three captives and take their souls to the palace of King Miao Chuang, where in three years' time they would be changed into females in the womb of Queen Boya.

The King, who was anxiously expecting the birth of an heir, was informed one morning that a daughter had been born to him. She was named Miao Qing. A year went by and another daughter was born. This one was named Miao Yin. When, at the end of the third year, another daughter was born, the King, beside himself with rage, called his Zhao Zhen Dazai and said to him, "I am past fifty, and have no male child to succeed me on the throne. My dynasty will therefore become extinct. Of what use have been all my labours and all my victories?" Zhao Chen tried to console him, saying, "Heaven has granted you three daughters: no human power can change this divine decree. When these princesses have grown up, we will choose three sons-in-law for your Majesty, and you can elect your successor from among them. Who will dare to dispute his right to the throne?"

The King named the third daughter Miaoshan. She became noted for her modesty and many other good qualities and scrupulously observed all the tenets of the Buddhist doctrines. Virtuous living seemed, indeed, to be like second nature.

MIAOSHAN'S AMBITION

One day, when the three daughters of King Miao Chuang were playing in the palace garden of Perpetual Spring,

Miaoshan said to her sisters, "Riches and glory are like the rain in spring or the morning dew; a little while, and all is gone. Kings and emperors think to enjoy to the end the good fortune which places them in a rank apart from other human beings; but sickness lays them low in their coffins, and all is over. Where are now all those powerful dynasties which have laid down the law to the world? As for me, I desire nothing more than a peaceful retreat on a lone mountain, there to attempt the attainment of perfection. If someday I can reach a high degree of goodness, then, borne on the clouds of Heaven, I will travel throughout the universe, passing in the twinkling of an eye from east to west. I will rescue my father and mother, and bring them to Heaven; I will save the miserable and afflicted on earth; I will convert the spirits which do evil, and cause them to do good. That is my only ambition."

No sooner had she finished speaking than a lady of the Court came to announce that the King had found sons-in-law for his two elder daughters. The wedding feast was to be the very next day. "Be quick," she added, "and prepare your presents, your dresses and so forth, for the King's order is imperative." The husband chosen for Miao Qing was a First Academician named Zhao Kui. His personal name was Deta, and he was the son of a celebrated minister of the reigning dynasty. Miao Yin's husband-to-be was a military officer named He Feng, whose personal name was Chaoyang. He had passed first in the examination for the Military Doctorate. The marriage ceremonies were magnificent. Festivity followed festivity; the newlyweds were duly installed in their palaces and general happiness prevailed.

There now remained only Miaoshan. The King and Queen wished to find for her a man famous for knowledge and virtue, capable of ruling the kingdom and worthy of being the successor to the throne. So the King called her and explained to her all his plans regarding her and how all his hopes rested on her.

"It is a crime," she replied, "for me not to comply with my father's wishes; but you must pardon me if my ideas differ from yours."

"Tell me what your ideas are," said the King. "I do not wish to marry," she said. "I wish to attain to perfection and to Buddhahood. Then I promise that I will not be ungrateful to you."

"Wretch of a daughter," cried the King in anger, "you think you can teach me, the head of the State and ruler of so great a people! Has anyone ever known a daughter of a king become a nun? Can a good woman be found in that class? Put aside all these mad ideas of a nunnery and tell me at once if you will marry a First Academician or a Military First Graduate."

"Who is there," answered the girl, "who does not love the royal dignity? What person who does not aspire to the happiness of marriage? However, I wish to become a nun. With respect to the riches and glory of this world, my heart is as cold as a dead cinder and I feel a keen desire to make it ever purer and purer."

The King was furious and wished to cast her out from his presence. Miaoshan, knowing she could not openly disobey his orders, took another course. "If you absolutely insist upon my marrying," she said, "I will consent; only I must marry a physician."

"A physician!" growled the King. "Are men of good family and talents wanting in my kingdom? What an absurd idea, to want to marry a physician!"

CHINESE MYTHS & LEGENDS

"My wish is," said Miaoshan, "to heal humanity of all its ills; of cold, heat, lust, old age and all infirmities. I wish to equalize all classes, putting rich and poor on the same footing, to have community of goods, without distinction of persons. If you will grant me my wish, I can still in this way become a Buddha, a Saviour of Mankind. There is no necessity to call in the diviners to choose an auspicious day. I am ready to be married now."

At these words the King was mad with rage. "Wicked imbecile!" he cried, "What diabolical suggestions are these that you dare to make in my presence?" Without further ado he called He Tao, who on that day was officer of the palace guard. When he had arrived and kneeled to receive the King's commands, the latter said: "This wicked nun dishonours me. Take from her her Court robes and drive her from my presence. Take her to the Queen's garden and let her perish there of cold: that will be one care less for my troubled heart."

Miaoshan fell on her face and thanked the King. She went with the officer to the Queen's garden, where she began to lead her retired hermit life with the moon for companion and the wind for friend, content to see all obstacles overthrown on her way to Nirvana – the highest state of spiritual bliss – and glad to exchange the pleasures of the palace for the sweetness of solitude.

THE NUNNERY OF THE WHITE BIRD

After many futile attempts to dissuade Miaoshan from her purpose, one day the King and Queen sent Miao Hong and Cui Hong to make a last attempt to bring their misguided daughter to her senses. Miaoshan, annoyed at this renewed attempt, ordered them never again to come and torment her with their silly prattle. "I have found out," she added, "that there is a well-known temple at Ju Zhou in Longshu Xian. This Buddhist temple is known as the Nunnery of the White Bird. In it five hundred nuns give themselves up to the study of the true doctrine and the way of perfection. Go then and ask the Queen to obtain the King's permission for me to retire there. If you can do me this favour, I will not fail to reward you later."

Miao Chuang summoned the messengers and inquired the result of their efforts. "She is more unapproachable than ever," they replied; "she has even ordered us to ask the Queen to obtain your Majesty's permission to retire to the Nunnery of the White Bird in Longshu Xian."

The King gave his permission, but sent strict orders to the nunnery instructing the nuns to do all in their power to dissuade the Princess from remaining.

This Nunnery of the White Bird had been built by Huangdi and the five hundred nuns who lived in it had as Superior a lady named Yi Yu, who was remarkable for her virtue. On receipt of the royal mandate, she had summoned Zheng Chengchang, the choir mistress, and informed her that Princess Miaoshan would shortly arrive at the temple. She requested her to receive the visitor courteously, but at the same time to do all she could to dissuade her from adopting the life of a nun. Having given these instructions, the Superior, accompanied by two novices went to meet Miaoshan at the gate of the temple. On her arrival they saluted her. The Princess returned the salute, but said: "I have just left the world in order to place myself under your orders: why do you come and salute me on my arrival? I beg you to be so good as to take me into the temple, in order that I may pay my respects to the Buddha." Yi Yu led her into the principal hall and instructed the nuns to light incense sticks, ring the bells and beat the drums. The visit to the temple finished, she went into the preaching hall, where she greeted her instructresses. The latter obeyed the King's command and tried to persuade the Princess to return to her home but, as none of their arguments had any effect, they decided to give her a trial. She was to be put in charge of the kitchen, where she could prepare the food for the nunnery and generally be at the service of all. If she did not do a good job, they could dismiss her.

Miaoshan joyfully agreed, and went to make her humble submission to the Buddha. She knelt before Ju Lai and made offering to him, praying: "Great Buddha, full of goodness and mercy, your humble servant wishes to leave the world. Grant that I may never yield to the temptations which will be sent to try my faith." Miaoshan further promised to observe all the regulations of the nunnery and to obey the superiors.

This generous self-sacrifice touched the heart of Yu Huang, the Master of Heaven, who summoned the Spirit of the North Star and instructed him as follows:

"Miaoshan, the third daughter of King Miao Chuang, has renounced the world in order to devote herself to the attainment of perfection. Her father has consigned her to the Nunnery of the White Bird. She has happily undertaken the burden of all the work in the nunnery. If she is left without help, who is there who will be willing to adopt the virtuous life? Go quickly and order the Three Agents, the Gods of the Five Sacred Peaks, the Eight Ministers of the Heavenly Dragon, Jie Lan and the tuti to send her help at once. Tell the Sea Dragon to dig her a well near the kitchen, a tiger to bring her firewood, birds to collect vegetables for the nuns and all the spirits of Heaven to help her in her duties, so that she may give herself up without disturbance to the pursuit of perfection. See that my commands are promptly obeyed." The Spirit of the North Star complied without delay.

Seeing all these gods arrive to help the novice, the Superior, Yi Yu, spoke with the choir mistress, saying: "We assigned to the Princess the burdensome work of the kitchen because she refused to return to the world; but since she began her duties the gods of the eight caves of Heaven have come to offer her fruit, Jie Lan sweeps the kitchen, the dragon has dug a well, the God of the Hearth and the tiger bring her fuel, birds collect vegetables for her, the nunnery bell every evening at dusk booms of itself, as if struck by some mysterious hand. Obviously miracles are being performed. Hasten and fetch the King and beg his Majesty to recall his daughter."

Zheng Chengchang travelled to the palace and informed the King of all that had happened. The King called Hu Pili, the chief of the guard, and ordered him to go the Nunnery of the White Bird and burn it to the ground, together with the nuns. When he reached the place the commander surrounded the nunnery with his soldiers and set fire to it. The five hundred doomed nuns invoked the aid of Heaven and earth, and then, addressing Miaoshan, said: "It is you who have brought upon us this terrible disaster."

"It is true," said Miaoshan. "I alone am the cause of your destruction." She then knelt down and prayed to Heaven: "Great Sovereign of the Universe, your servant is the daughter of King Miao Chuang; you are the grandson of Lun

Wang. Will you not rescue your younger sister? You have left your palace; I also have left mine. You in former times took yourself to the snowy mountains to attain perfection; I came here with the same object. Will you not save us from this fiery destruction?"

Her prayer ended, Miaoshan took a bamboo hairpin from her hair. She pricked the roof of her mouth with it and spat the flowing blood toward Heaven. Immediately great clouds gathered in all parts of the sky and sent down heavy rain, which put out the fire that threatened the nunnery. The nuns threw themselves on their knees and thanked her for having saved their lives.

THE EXECUTION OF MIAOSHAN

After witnessing the extraordinary event at the Nunnery of the White Bird, Hu Pili rushed back to inform the King. The King was enraged. He ordered Hu Pili to go back at once and bring his daughter in chains. He was to behead her on the spot.

But the Queen, who had heard of this new plot, begged the King to grant her daughter one last chance. "If you will give permission," she said, "I will have a magnificent pavilion built at the side of the road where Miaoshan will pass in chains on the way to her execution. We will go there with our two other daughters and our sons-in-law. As she passes we will have music, songs and feasting – everything likely to impress her and make her contrast our luxurious life with her miserable plight. This will surely make her repent."

"I agree," said the King, "to counter-order her execution until your preparations are complete." Nevertheless, when the time came, Miaoshan showed nothing but disdain for all this worldly show, and to all advances replied only: "I love not these pompous vanities; I swear that I prefer death to the so-called joys of this world." She was then led to the place of execution. All the Court was present. Sacrifices were made to her as to one already dead. In the midst of all this the Queen appeared. She ordered the officials to return to their posts, so that she might once more urge her daughter to repent. But Miaoshan only listened in silence with downcast eyes.

The King felt great disgust at the thought of shedding his daughter's blood. He ordered her to be imprisoned in the palace so that he might make a last effort to save her. "I am the King," he said; "my orders cannot be lightly set aside. Disobedience to them involves punishment and in spite of my paternal love for you, if you persist in your present attitude, you will be executed tomorrow in front of the palace gate."

The tuti, hearing the King's verdict, immediately went to Yu Huang and reported to him the sentence that had been pronounced against Miaoshan. Yu Huang exclaimed: "Save Buddha, there is none in the west so noble as this Princess. Tomorrow, at the appointed hour, go to the scene of execution, break the swords and splinter the lances they will use to kill her. See that she suffers no pain. At the moment of her death transform yourself into a tiger and bring her body to the pine wood. Having deposited it in a safe place, put a magic pill in her mouth to arrest decay. Her triumphant soul on its return from the lower regions must find it in a perfect state of preservation in order to be able to re-enter it and animate it afresh. After that she must go to Xiang Shan on Putuo Dao, where she will reach the highest state of perfection."

On the appointed day, Commander Hu Pili led the condemned Princess to the place of execution. Troops had been stationed there to maintain order. The tuti was in attendance at the palace gates. Miaoshan was radiant with joy. "Today," she said, "I leave the world for a better life. Hasten to take my life, but beware of mutilating my body."

The King's warrant arrived, and suddenly the sky became overcast and darkness fell upon the earth. A bright light surrounded Miaoshan, and when the sword of the executioner fell upon the neck of the victim it was broken in two. Then they thrust at her with a spear, but the weapon fell to pieces. After that the King ordered that she be strangled with a silken cord. A few moments later a tiger leapt into the execution ground, dispersed the executioners, put the body of Miaoshan on his back and disappeared into the pine forest. Hu Pili rushed to the palace. He told the King full all that had happened and received a reward of two ingots of gold.

Meanwhile, Miaoshan's soul, which remained unhurt, was carried on a cloud. She awoke, as from a dream, lifted her head and looked round but she could not see her body. "My father has just had me strangled," she sighed. "How is it that I find myself in this place? Here are neither mountains, nor trees, nor vegetation; no sun, moon, nor stars; no habitation, no sound, no cackling of a fowl nor barking of a dog. How can I live in this desolate region?"

Suddenly a young man appeared carrying a large banner. He was dressed in blue, shining with a brilliant light. He said to her: "By order of Yan Wang, the King of the Hells, I come to take you to the eighteen infernal regions."

"What is this cursed place where I am now?" asked Miaoshan.

"This is the lower world, Hell," he replied. "Your refusal to marry, and the magnanimity with which you chose death rather than break your resolutions, deserve the recognition of Yu Huang. The ten gods of the lower regions, impressed by your eminent virtue, have sent me to you. Fear nothing and follow me."

So Miaoshan began her visit to all the infernal regions. The Gods of the Ten Hells came to congratulate her. "Who am I," asked Miaoshan, "that you should take the trouble to show me such respect?"

"We have heard," they replied, "that when you recite your prayers all evil disappears as if by magic. We should like to hear you pray."

"I consent," replied Miaoshan, "on condition that all the condemned ones in the ten infernal regions be released from their chains in order to listen to me."

At the appointed time the condemned were led in by Niutou ('Ox-head') and Mamian ('Horse-face'), the two chief constables of Hell, and Miaoshan began her prayers. No sooner had she finished than Hell was suddenly transformed into a paradise of joy, and the instruments of torture into lotus-flowers.

Panguan, the keeper of the Register of the Living and the Dead, presented a memorial to Yan Wang stating that since Miaoshan's arrival there was no more pain in Hell; and all the condemned were beside themselves with happiness. "Since it has always been decreed," he added, "that, in justice, there must be both a Heaven and a Hell, if you do not send this saint back to earth, there will no longer be any Hell, but only a Heaven."

"Since that is so," said Yan Wang, "let forty-eight flag bearers escort her across the Styx Bridge so that she may be taken to the pine forest to re-enter her body and resume her life in the upper world."

The King of the Hells, having paid his respects to her, asked the youth in blue to take her soul back to her body, which she found lying under a pine tree. Having re-entered it, Miaoshan found herself alive again. A bitter sigh escaped from her lips. "I remember," she said, "all that I saw and heard in Hell. I sigh for the moment which will find me free of all impediments, and yet my soul has re-entered my body. Here, without any lonely mountain on which to give myself up to the pursuit of perfection, what will become of me?" Great tears welled from her eyes.

Just then Ju Lai Buddha appeared. "Why have you come to this place?" he asked. Miaoshan explained why the King had put her to death and how after her descent into Hell her soul had re-entered her body. "I greatly pity your misfortune," Ju Lai said, "but there is no one to help you. I also am alone. Why should we not marry? We could build ourselves a hut and pass our days in peace. What say you?" "Sir," she replied, "you must not make impossible suggestions. I died and came to life again. How can you speak so lightly? Do me the pleasure of withdrawing from my presence."

"Well," said the visitor, "he to whom you are speaking is no other than the Buddha of the West. I came to test your virtue. This place is not suitable for your devotional exercises; I invite you to come to Xiang Shan."

Miaoshan threw herself on her knees and said: "My bodily eyes deceived me. I never thought that your Majesty would come to a place like this. Pardon my seeming want of respect. Where is this Xiang Shan?"

"Xiang Shan is a very old monastery," Ju Lai replied, "built in the earliest historical times. It is inhabited by Immortals. It is situated in the sea, on Putuo Dao. There you will be able to reach the highest perfection."

"How far off is this island?" Miaoshan asked. "More than a thousand miles," Ju Lai replied. "I fear," she said, "I could not bear the fatigue of so long a journey." "Calm yourself," he replied. "I have brought with me a magic peach, of a kind not to be found in any earthly orchard. Once you have eaten it, you will experience neither hunger nor thirst; old age and death will have no power over you: you will live for ever."

Miaoshan ate the magic peach, left Ju Lai and started on the way to Xiang Shan. From the clouds the Spirit of the North Star saw her making her way toward P'u T'o. He called the Guardian of the Soil of Xiang Shan and said to him: "Miaoshan is on her way to your country; the way is long and difficult. I ask you take the form of a tiger and carry her to her journey's end."

The tuti transformed himself into a tiger and stationed himself in the middle of the road along which Miaoshan must pass. As Miaoshan approached the tiger she said, "I am a poor girl devoid of filial piety. I have disobeyed my father's commands; devour me, and make an end of me."

The tiger then spoke, saying: "I am not a real tiger, but the Guardian of the Soil of Xiang Shan. I have received instructions to carry you there. Get on my back."

"Since you have received these instructions," said the girl, "I will obey, and when I have attained to perfection I will not forget your kindness."

The tiger went off like a flash of lightning, and in the twinkling of an eye Miaoshan found herself at the foot of the rocky slopes of Putuo Dao.

MIAOSHAN ATTAINS PERFECTION

After nine years in the retreat of Putuo Dao Miaoshan had reached the pinnacle of perfection. Dizang Wang then came to Xiang Shan, and was so astonished at her virtue that he inquired of the local tuti as to what had brought about this wonderful result. "With the exception of Ju Lai, in all the west no one equals her in dignity and perfection. She is the Queen of the three Qian Pusa's and of all the beings on earth who have skin and blood. We regard her as our sovereign in all things. Therefore, on the nineteenth day of the eleventh moon we will enthrone her."

The tuti sent out his invitations for the ceremony. The Dragon king of the Western Sea, the Gods of the Five Sacred Mountains, the one hundred and twenty Emperor saints, the thirty-six officials of the Ministry of Time, the celestial functionaries in charge of wind, rain, thunder and lightning, the Three Causes, the Five Saints, the Eight Immortals, the Ten Kings of the Hells – all were present on the appointed day. Miaoshan took her seat on the lotus throne and the assembled gods proclaimed her sovereign of Heaven and earth and a Buddha. Furthermore, they decided that it was not right that she should remain alone at Xiang Shan; so they begged her to choose a worthy young man and a virtuous young woman to serve her in the temple.

The tuti was entrusted with the task of finding them. In his search he met a young priest named Shan Cai. After the death of his parents he had become a hermit on Dahua Shan and was still a novice in the science of perfection. Miaoshan ordered him to be brought to her. "Who are you?" she asked.

"I am a poor orphan priest of no merit," he replied. "From my earliest youth I have led the life of a hermit. I have been told that your power is equalled only by your goodness, so I have ventured to come to pray you to show me how to attain to perfection."

"My only fear," replied Miaoshan, "is that your desire for perfection may not be sincere."

"I have now no parents," the priest continued, "and I have come a very long way to find you. How can I be wanting in sincerity?"

"What special degree of ability have you attained during your course of perfection?" asked Miaoshan.

"I have no skill," replied Shan Cai, "but I rely for everything on your great pity, and under your guidance I hope to reach the required ability."

"Very well," said Miaoshan, "take up your station on the top of yonder peak, and wait till I find a means of transporting you."

Miaoshan called the tuti and asked him to go and beg all the Immortals to disguise themselves as pirates and to besiege the mountain, waving torches and threatening with swords and spears to kill her. "Then I will seek refuge on the summit, and will leap over the precipice to prove Shan Cai's fidelity and affection."

A minute later a ferocious gang of robbers rushed up to the temple of Xiang Shan. Miaoshan cried for help, rushed up the steep incline, missed her footing and rolled down into the ravine. Shan Cai, seeing her fall into the abyss, without hesitation flung himself after her in order to rescue her. When he reached her, he asked: "What have you to fear from the robbers? You have nothing for them to steal; why throw yourself over the precipice, exposing yourself to certain death?"

Miaoshan saw that he was weeping, and wept too. "I must comply with the wish of Heaven," she said.

Shan Cai, inconsolable, prayed Heaven and earth to save his protectress. Miaoshan said to him: "You should not have risked your life by throwing yourself over the precipice, I have not yet transformed you. But you did a brave thing and I know that you have a good heart. Now, look down there." "Oh," said he, "if I am not mistaken, that is a corpse." "Yes," she replied, "that is your former body. Now you are transformed you can rise at will and fly in the air." Shan Cai bowed low to thank her. She said to him: "From now on you must say your prayers by my side and not leave me for a single day."

'BROTHER AND SISTER'

With her spiritual sight Miaoshan perceived at the bottom of the Southern Sea the third son of Long Wang, who, in carrying out his father's orders, was making his way through the waves in the form of a carp. While doing so, he was caught in a fisherman's net and taken to the market at Yue Zhou where he was offered for sale. Miaoshan at once sen her faithful Shan Cai, disguised as a servant, to buy him. She gave him the money to purchase the fish, which he was to take to the foot of the rocks at P'u T'o and set free in the sea. The son of Long Wang heartily thanked his deliverer, and on his return to the palace he told his father what had occurred. The King said: "As a reward, make her a present of a luminous pearl, so that she may recite her prayers by its light at night time."

Long Nü, the daughter of Long Wang's third son, asked her grandfather's permission to take the gift to Miaoshan and beg that she might be allowed to study the doctrine of the sages under her guidance. After having proved her sincerity, she was accepted as a pupil. Shan Cai called her his sister, and Long Nü reciprocated by calling him her dear brother. Both lived as brother and sister by Miaoshan's side.

THE KING'S PUNISHMENT

After King Miao Chuang had burned the Nunnery of the White Bird and killed his daughter, Jie Lan Fo presented a petition to Yu Huang praying that the crime be not allowed to go unpunished. Yu Huang, justly irritated, ordered Panguan to consult the Register of the Living and the Dead to see how long this homicidal King had yet to live. Panguan turned over the pages of his register and saw that according to the divine ordinances the King's reign on the throne of King Lin should last for twenty years, but that this period had not yet expired. "That which has been decreed is unable to be changed," said Yu Huang, "but I will punish him by sending him illness." He called the God of Epidemics, and ordered him to afflict the King's body with ulcers, of a kind which could not be healed except by remedies to be given him by his daughter Miaoshan.

The order was promptly executed and the King could get no rest by day or by night. His two daughters and their husbands spent their time feasting while he tossed about in agony on his sickbed. The most famous physicians were called in but the pain only grew worse. Despair took hold of the patient. He then proclaimed that he would grant the succession to the throne to any person who would provide him with an effectual remedy to restore him to health.

Miaoshan had learnt all that was taking place at the palace. She assumed the form of a priest doctor, clothed herself in a priest's gown and attached to her girdle a gourd containing pills and other medicines. Then she went straight to the palace gate, read the royal edict posted there, and tore it down. Some members of the palace guard seized her, and inquired angrily: "Who are you that you should dare to tear down the royal proclamation?"

"I, a poor priest, am also a doctor," she replied. "I read the edict posted on the palace gates. The King is looking for a doctor who can heal him. I am a doctor of an old cultured family and propose to restore him to health."

"If you are of a cultured family, why did you become a priest?" they asked. "Would it not have been better to gain your living honestly in practising your art than to shave your head and go loafing about the world? Besides, all the highest physicians have tried in vain to cure the King; do you imagine that you will be more skilful than all the aged practitioners?"

"Set your minds at ease," she replied. "I have received from my ancestors the most effective remedies and I guarantee that I shall restore the King to health," The palace guard informed the King and in the end the priest was admitted. Having reached the royal bed chamber, he sat still awhile in order to calm himself before feeling the pulse, and to have complete control of all his faculties while examining the King. When he felt quite sure of himself, he approached the King's bed, took the King's hand, felt his pulse, carefully diagnosed the nature of the illness and assured himself that it was easily curable.

One serious difficulty, however, presented itself, and that was that the right medicine was almost impossible to obtain. The King showed his displeasure by saying: "For every illness there is a medical prescription and for every prescription a specific medicine; how can you say that the diagnosis is easy, but that there is no remedy?"

"Your Majesty," replied the priest, "the remedy for your illness is not to be found in any pharmacy, and no one would agree to sell it."

The King became angry and ordered those about him to drive away the priest, who left smiling.

The following night the King dreamt of an old man who said to him: "This priest alone can cure your illness and, if you ask him, he himself will give you the right remedy." The King awoke as soon as these words had been uttered and begged the Queen to recall the priest. When the priest returned the King related his dream and begged him to give him the remedy required. "What, after all, is this remedy that I must have in order to be cured?" he asked.

"There must be the hand and eye of a living person, from which to compound the ointment which alone can save you," answered the priest.

The King called out: "This priest is fooling me! Who would ever give his hand or his eye? Even if anyone would, I could never have the heart to make use of them."

"Nevertheless," said the priest, "there is no other effective remedy."

"Then where can I obtain this remedy?" asked the King.

"Your Majesty must send your ministers, who must observe the Buddhist rules of abstinence, to Xiang Shan, where they will be given what is required."

"Where is Xiang Shan, and how far from here?"

"About a thousand or more miles, but I myself will indicate the route to be followed. In a very short time they will return."

The King, who was suffering terribly, was more contented when he heard that the journey could be made quickly. He called his two ministers, Zhao Chen and Liu Qin, and instructed them to lose no time in starting for Xiang Shan. They were warned to scrupulously observe the Buddhist rules of abstinence. Meanwhile, the king ordered the Minister of Ceremonies to detain the priest in the palace until their return.

The two sons-in-law of the King, He Feng and Zhao Kui, had already made secret preparations to succeed to the throne as soon as the King should breathe his last. They were surprised to learn that the priest had hopes of curing the King's illness and that he was waiting in the palace until the remedy was brought to him. Fearing that they might be disappointed in their ambition, and that after his recovery the King would give the crown to the priest, they entered into a conspiracy with an unscrupulous courtier named He Li. They needed to act quickly because the ministers would soon be back. That same night He Li was to give to the King a poisoned drink made, he would say, by the priest to numb the King's pain until the return of his two ministers. Shortly after, an assassin, Su Ta, was to murder the priest. Both the King and the priest would meet their death and the kingdom would pass to the King's two sons-in-law.

Miaoshan had returned to Xiang Shan, leaving the bodily form of the priest in the palace. She saw the two traitors preparing the poison and was aware of their wicked intentions. Calling the spirit Yu Yi, she told him to fly to the palace and change the poison about to be administered to the King into a harmless soup and to bind the assassin hand and foot.

At midnight He Li carried the poisoned drink and knocked at the door of the royal apartment. He said to the Queen that the priest had prepared a soothing potion while waiting for the return of the ministers. "I come," he said, "to offer it to his Majesty." The Queen took the bowl in her hands and was about to give it to the King, when Yu Yi arrived unannounced. Quickly he snatched the bowl from the Queen and poured the contents on the ground; at the same moment he knocked over those present in the room, so that they all rolled on the floor.

At the same time, the assassin Su Ta entered the priest's room and struck him with his sword. Instantly the assassin, without knowing how, found himself wrapped up in the priest's robe and thrown to the ground. He struggled and tried to free himself but found that his hands had been rendered useless by some mysterious power and that there was no escape. The spirit Yu Yi then returned to Xiang Shan and reported to Miaoshan.

The next morning, the two sons-in-law of the King heard of the turn things had taken during the night. The whole palace was in a state of great confusion.

When he was informed that the priest had been killed, the King called Qu Tinglie and ordered him to have the murderer arrested. Su Ta was tortured and confessed all that he knew. Together with He Li he was condemned to be cut into a thousand pieces.

The two sons-in-law were seized and executed. It was only through the Queen's intervention that their wives were spared. The infuriated King, however, ordered that his two daughters should be imprisoned in the palace.

In the meantime, Zhao Chen and Liu Qin had reached Xiang Shan. When they were brought to Miaoshan the ministers took out the King's letter and read it to her.

"I, Miao Chuang, Xing Lin Wang, have learned that there dwells at Xiang Shan an Immortal whose power and compassion have no equal in the whole world. I have passed my fiftieth year, and am afflicted with ulcers that all remedies have failed to cure. Today a priest has assured me that at Xiang Shan I can obtain the hand and eye of a living person, with which he will prepare an ointment able to restore me to health. Relying on his word and on the goodness of the Immortal to whom he has directed me, I venture to beg that those two parts of a living body necessary to heal my ulcers be sent to me. I assure you of my everlasting gratitude, fully confident that my request will not be refused."

The next morning Miaoshan urged the ministers to take a knife and cut off her left hand and gouge out her left eye. Liu Qin took the knife but did not dare to obey the order. "Be quick," urged the Immortal; "you have been commanded to return as soon as possible; why do you hesitate as if you were a young girl?" Liu Qin was forced to do it. He plunged in the knife, and the red blood flooded the ground, spreading an odour like sweet incense. The hand and eye were placed on a golden plate, and, having paid their grateful respects to the Immortal, the envoys left.

After they had gone, Miaoshan – who had transformed herself in order to allow the envoys to remove her hand and eye – told Shan Cai that she was now going to prepare the ointment that would cure the King. "Should the Queen," she added, "send for another eye and hand, I will transform myself again and you can give them to her." No sooner had she finished speaking than she mounted a cloud and disappeared in space. The two ministers reached the palace and presented the Queen with the gruesome remedy. She wept, overcome with gratitude and emotion. "What Immortal," she asked, "can have been so charitable as to sacrifice a hand and eye for the King's benefit?" Then suddenly she uttered a great cry, as she recognized the hand of her daughter.

"Who else, in fact, but his child," she continued amid her sobs, "could have had the courage to give her hand to save her father's life?" "What are you saying?" said the King. "In the world there are many hands like this." Just then the priest entered the King's apartment. "This great Immortal has long devoted herself to the attainment of perfection," he said. "She has healed a great many people. Give me the hand and eye." He took them and quickly produced an ointment which, he told the King, was to be applied to his left side. No sooner had it touched his skin than the pain on his left side disappeared as if by magic; no sign of ulcers was to be seen on that side, but his right side remained as swollen and painful as before.

"Why is it," asked the King, "that this remedy, which is so effective for the left side, should not be applied to the right?" "Because," replied the priest, "the left hand and eye of the saint cures only the left side. If you wish to be completely cured, you must send your officers to obtain the right eye and right hand also." The King accordingly dispatched his envoys again with a letter of thanks, and begging as a further favour that the cure should be completed by the healing of his right side.

On the arrival of the envoys Shan Cai met them in the mutilated form of Miaoshan. He told them to cut off his right hand, pluck out his right eye and put them on a plate. At the sight of the four bleeding wounds, Liu Qin could not stop himself from calling out indignantly: "This priest is a wicked man to make a martyr of a woman in order to obtain the succession!"

Having said this, he left with his companion for the kingdom of Xing Lin. On their return the King was overwhelmed with joy. The priest quickly prepared the ointment, and the King applied it to his right side. At once the ulcers disappeared like the darkness of night before the rising sun. The whole Court congratulated the King and praised the priest. The King gave the latter the title Priest of the Brilliant Eye. He fell on his face to return thanks and added: "I, a poor priest, have left the world, and have only one wish, namely, that your Majesty should govern your subjects with justice and sympathy and that all the officials of the realm should prove themselves men of integrity. As for me, I am used to roaming about. I have no desire for any royal estate. My happiness exceeds all earthly joys."

The priest then waved the sleeve of his cloak and a cloud descended from Heaven. Seating himself on it, the priest disappeared in the sky. From the cloud a note containing the following words was seen to fall: "I am one of the Teachers of the West. I came to cure the King's illness, and so to glorify the True Doctrine."

All who witnessed this miracle exclaimed with one voice: "This priest is the Living Buddha, who is going back to Heaven!" The note was taken to King Miao Chuang, who exclaimed: "Who am I that I should deserve that one of the rulers of Heaven should deign to descend and cure me by the sacrifice of hands and eyes?"

"What was the face of the saintly person like who gave you the remedy?" he then asked Zhao Chen.

"It was like that of your deceased daughter, Miaoshan," he replied.

"When you removed her hands and eyes did she seem to suffer?"

"I saw a great flow of blood, and my heart failed, but the face of the victim seemed radiant with happiness."

"This certainly must be my daughter Miaoshan, who has attained to perfection," said the King. "Who but she would have given hands and eyes? Purify yourselves and observe the rules of abstinence. Go quickly to Xiang Shan to return thanks to the saint for this favour. I myself will soon make a pilgrimage there to return thanks in person."

THE KING'S REPENTANCE

Three years later the King and Queen, with the noblemen of their Court, set out to visit Xiang Shan. On the way the monarchs were captured by the Green Lion, or God of Fire, and the White Elephant, or Spirit of the Water – the two guardians of the Temple of Buddha – who transported them to a dark cavern in the mountains. A terrific battle then took place between the evil spirits on the one side and some hosts of heavenly genii, who had been summoned to the rescue, on the other. While its issue was still uncertain, reinforcements under the Red Child Devil, who could resist fire, and the Dragon king of the Eastern Sea, who could subdue water, finally defeated the enemy and the prisoners were released.

The King and Queen now resumed their pilgrimage, and Miaoshan instructed Shan Cai to receive the monarchs when they arrived to offer incense. She herself took up her place on the altar, her eyes torn out, her hands cut off and her wrists all dripping with blood. The King recognized his daughter and bitterly reproached himself; the Queen fell swooning at her feet. Miaoshan then spoke and tried to comfort them. She told them of all that she had experienced since the day when she had been executed and how she had attained to immortal perfection. She then went on: "In order to punish you for having caused the deaths of all those who perished in the wars preceding your accession to the throne and also to avenge the burning of the Nunnery of the White Bird, Yu Huang afflicted you with those terrible ulcers. It was then that I changed myself into a priest in order to heal you and gave my eyes and hands, with which I prepared the ointment that cured you. It was I, moreover, who secured your liberty from Buddha when you were imprisoned in the cave by the Green Lion and the White Elephant."

At these words the King threw himself with his face on the ground, offered incense, worshipped Heaven, earth, the sun and the moon, saying with a voice broken by sobs: "I committed a great crime in killing my daughter, who has sacrificed her eyes and hands in order to cure my sickness."

No sooner were these words uttered than Miaoshan reassumed her normal form and, descending from the altar, approached her parents and sisters. Her body had again its original completeness; and in the presence of its perfect beauty and finding themselves reunited as one family, all wept for joy.

"Well," said Miaoshan to her father, "will you now force me to marry and prevent my devoting myself to the attainment of perfection?"

"Speak no more of that," replied the King. "I was in the wrong. If you had not reached perfection, I should not now be alive. I have made up my mind to exchange my sceptre for the pursuit of the perfect life, which I wish to lead together with you."

Then he addressed his Zhao Zhen Dazai, saying: "Your devotion to the service of the State has rendered you worthy to wear the crown: I surrender it to you." The Court proclaimed Zhao Chen Xing Lin Wang, said farewell to Miao Chuang and set out for their kingdom accompanied by their new sovereign.

Buddha had summoned the White Elephant and the Green Lion, and was on the point of sentencing them to eternal damnation when the compassionate Miaoshan interceded for them. "Certainly you deserve no forgiveness," he said, "but I cannot refuse a request made by Miaoshan, whose clemency is without limit. I give you over to her, to serve and obey her in everything. Follow her."

MIAOSHAN BECOMES A BUDDHA

The guardian spirit on duty that day then announced the arrival of a messenger from Yu Huang. It was Taipo Jinxing, who was the bearer of a divine decree, which he handed to Miaoshan. It read as follows: "I, the august Emperor, make known to you this decree: Miao Chuang, Xing Lin Wang, forgetful alike of Heaven and Hell, the six virtues, and metempsychosis, has led a blameworthy life; but your nine years of penitence, the filial piety which caused you to sacrifice your own body to effect his cure, in short, all your virtues, have redeemed his faults. Your eyes can see and your ears can hear all the good and bad deeds and words of men. You are the object of my especial regard. Therefore I make proclamation of this decree of canonization.

"Miaoshan will have the title of Very Merciful and Very Compassionate P'u-sa, Saviour of the Afflicted, Miraculous and Always Helpful Protectress of Mortals. On your lofty precious lotus-flower throne, you will be the Sovereign of the Southern Seas and of P'u T'o Isle. Your two sisters, until now tainted with earthly pleasures, will gradually progress till they reach true perfection. Miao Qing will have the title of Very Virtuous P'u-sa, the Completely Beautiful, Rider of the Green Lion. Miao Yin will be honoured with the title of Very Virtuous and Completely Resplendent P'u-sa, Rider of the White Elephant. King Miao Chuang is raised to the dignity of Virtuous Conquering P'u-sa, Surveyor of Mortals. Queen Boya receives the title of P'u-sa of Ten Thousand Virtues, Surveyor of Famous Women. Shan Cai has the title of Golden Youth.

Long Nü has the title of Jade Maiden." Finally he said, "During all time incense is to be burned before all the members of this canonized group."

THE GODS OF CHINA

The ordinary Chinese people seemed to have had little difficulty amalgamating and absorbing a number of different religious beliefs, resulting in popular superstitions that convey the diverse influences of Confucianism, Taoism and Buddhism.

Confucius was a pragmatic man, whose main concern was for the smooth running of the state where individuals took personal responsibility for the creation of a harmonious atmosphere on earth, reflecting that of the Heavens. Taoism argued that there was a natural order in the world determining the behaviour of all things and that even inanimate objects had an existence of their own. Buddhism contributed to society the concept of the transmigration of souls and introduced the notion of an Underworld, presided over by the gatekeeper, Yan Wang. Overall, Chinese people believed that there was a great deal of communication between heaven and earth. It was widely believed that the Gods lived on earth in the capacity of divine officials, and returned to the heavens regularly to report on the progress of humanity.

The dualistic idea of the Otherworld being a replica of this one is nowhere more clearly illustrated than in the nine celestial Ministries or official Boards, with their chiefs and staffs presiding over the spiritual hierarchies. Generally, the functions of the officers of the celestial Boards are to protect mankind from the evils represented in the title of the Board. In all cases the duties seem to be remedial. As the God of War is the God who protects people from the evils of war, so the vast hierarchy of these various divinities is conceived as functioning for the good of mankind.

But besides the Gods who hold definite official posts in these various Ministries, there are also a very large number who are protecting patrons of the people.

MR REDCOAT, THE GOD OF GOOD LUCK

During the Tang dynasty, in the reign-period Jianzhong (780–84 CE) shidai de Tang Dezong, the Taiyin Gongzhu noticed that Lu Qi, a native of Hua Zhou, had the bones of an Immortal and wanted to marry him.

Her neighbour, Ma Po, introduced him one day into the Crystal Palace for an interview with his future wife. The Princess gave him the choice of three careers: to live in the Dragon Prince's Palace with the guarantee of immortal life, to enjoy immortality among the people on the earth, or to have the honour of becoming a minister of the Empire. Lu Qi first answered that he would like to live in the Crystal Palace. The young lady was overjoyed and said to him: "I am Taiyin Gongzhu. I will inform Shang Di, the Supreme Ruler, at once." A moment later the arrival of a celestial messenger was announced. Two officers bearing flags preceded him and took him to the foot of the flight of steps. The messenger presented himself as Zhu Yi, the envoy of Shang Di.

Addressing himself to Lu Qi, he asked: "Do you wish to live in the Crystal Palace?" The latter did not reply. T'ai Yin urged him to give his answer, but he remained silent. In despair the Princess went to her apartment and brought out five pieces of precious cloth, which she presented to the divine envoy, begging him to have patience and wait a little longer for the answer. After some time, Zhu Yi repeated his question. Then Lu Qi in answered a firm voice: "I have devoted my life to the hard labour of study and wish to attain to the dignity of minister on this earth."

T'ai Yin ordered Ma Po to lead Lu Qi from the palace. From that day his face became transformed: he developed the lips of a dragon, the head of a panther and the green face of an Immortal. He took his degree and was promoted to be Director of the Censorate. The Emperor, appreciating the good sense shown in his advice, appointed him a minister of the Empire.

From this legend it would seem that Zhu Yi is the purveyor of official posts. However, in practice, he is more generally seen as the protector of weak candidates, as the God of Good Luck for those who present themselves at examinations with a somewhat light understanding of literary knowledge. The special legend relating to this role is known everywhere in China. It is as follows:

An examiner, busily correcting the essays of the candidates, after a superficial look of one of the essays, put it on one side as obviously inferior. He is quite determined not to pass the candidate who has written it. Then the essay, moved by some mysterious power, was replaced in front of his eyes, as if to invite him to examine it more closely. At the same time an old man, clothed in a red garment, suddenly appeared before him and by a nod of his head made him understand that he should pass the essay. The examiner, surprised at the novelty of the incident and fortified by the approval of his supernatural visitor, admitted the author of the essay to the literary degree.

Zhu Yi is invoked by the literati as a powerful protector and aid to success. When anyone with a poor chance of passing presents himself at an exam, his friends encourage him by the popular saying: "Who knows but that Mr Redcoat will nod his head?"

GUAN DI, THE GOD OF WAR

A young man whose name was Yunchang was born near Jie Liang in He Dong (now the town of Jiezhou in Shanxi). The boy had a difficult nature and, having exasperated his parents, he was shut up in a room from which he escaped by breaking through the window. In one of the neighbouring houses he heard a young lady and an old man weeping. Running to the foot of the wall of the compound, he asked the reason for their grief. The old man replied that though his daughter was already engaged, the uncle of the local official, smitten by her beauty, wished to make her his concubine. His petitions to the official had only been rejected with curses.

Beside himself with rage, the youth seized a sword and went and killed both the official and his uncle. He escaped through the Tong Guan, the pass to Shaanxi. Having successfully avoided capture by the barrier officials, he knelt down at the side of a brook to wash his face. As he did so he discovered his appearance was completely transformed. His complexion had become reddish-grey and he was absolutely unrecognizable. He then presented himself with assurance before the officers, who asked him his name. "My name is Kuan," he replied. It was by that name that he was then known.

One day Kuan arrived at the town of Zhuzhou, in Zhili. There he met Zhang Fei, a butcher who had been selling his meat all morning. At noon the butcher lowered what remained of his meat into a well. He placed a stone weighing twenty-five pounds over the mouth of the well and said with a sneer: "If anyone can lift that stone and take my meat, I will make him a present of it!" Guan Yu, going up to the edge of the well, lifted the stone with the same ease as he would a tile, took the meat and made off. Zhang Fei pursued him and eventually the two came to blows, but no one dared to separate them. Just then Liu Bei, a hawker of straw shoes arrived, and put a stop to the fight. The community of ideas which they found they possessed soon gave rise to a firm friendship between the three men.

Another account represents Liu Bei and Zhang Fei as having entered a village inn to drink wine, when a man of gigantic stature pushing a wheelbarrow stopped at the door to rest. As he sat himself down he hailed the waiter, saying: "Bring me some wine quickly, because I have to rush to the town to enlist in the army."

Liu Bei looked at this man, nine feet in height, with a beard two feet long. His face was the colour of the fruit of the jujube tree and his lips were carmine. Eyebrows like sleeping silkworms shaded his phoenix eyes, which were a scarlet red. Terrible was his appearance.

"What is your name?" asked Liu Bei. "My family name is Kuan, my own name is Yu, my surname Yun Chang," he replied. "I am from the He Dong country. For the last five or six years I have been wandering around the world as a fugitive to escape from my pursuers, because I killed a powerful man of my country who was oppressing the poor people. I hear that they are collecting a body of troops to crush the brigands, and I should like to join the expedition."

Zhang Fei (also named Zhang Yi De), is described as eight feet in height, with round shining eyes in a panther's head and a pointed chin bristling with a tiger's beard. His voice resembled the rumbling of thunder. His enthusiasm was like that of a fiery steed. He was a native of Zhu Jun, where he owned some fertile farms. He was a butcher and wine merchant.

Liu Bei, surnamed Xuan De, (otherwise Xiang Zhu), was the third member of the group.

The three men went to Zhang Fei's farm. The following day they met in his peach orchard and sealed their friendship with an oath. Having bought a black ox and a white horse, with the various accessories to perform a sacrifice, they killed the victims, burnt the incense of friendship, and after twice prostrating themselves took this oath:

"We three, Liu Bei, Guan Yu, and Zhang Fei, already united by mutual friendship, although belonging to different clans, now bind ourselves by the union of our hearts and join our forces in order to help each other in times of danger. We wish to pay to the State our debt of loyal citizens and give peace to our black-haired compatriots. We do not inquire if we were born in the same year, the same month or on the same day, but we desire only that the same year, the same month and the same day may find us united in death. May Heaven our King and Earth our Queen see clearly our hearts! If any one of us violate justice or forget benefits, may Heaven and Man unite to punish him!"

The oath having been formally taken, Liu Bei was saluted as elder brother, Guan Yu as the second and Zhang Fei as the youngest. Their sacrifice to Heaven and earth over, they killed an ox and served a feast, to which they invited over three hundred of the soldiers from the district. They all drank copiously until they were intoxicated. Liu Bei enrolled the peasants; Zhang Fei bought them horses and arms; and then they set out to make war on the Yellow Turbans (Huang Qinzai).

Guan Yu proved himself worthy of the affection which Liu Bei showed him; brave and generous, he never turned aside from danger. His fidelity was shown especially on one occasion when, having been taken prisoner by Cao Cao, together with two of Liu Bei's wives and having been allotted a common sleeping apartment with his fellow captives, he preserved the ladies' reputation and his own trustworthiness by standing at the door of the room all night with a lighted lantern in his hand.

Guan Yu remained faithful to his oath, even though tempted with a marquisate by the great Cao Cao, but he was eventually captured by Sun Quan and put to death in 219 CE. Long celebrated as the most renowned of China's military heroes, he was ennobled in 1120 CE as Faithful and Loyal Duke. Eight years later he was given the still more glorious title of Magnificent Prince and Pacificator. The Yuan Wendi added the appellation Warrior Prince and Civilizer and, finally, the Ming Wanli Huangdi in 1594, gave him the title of Faithful and Loyal Great Ti, Supporter of Heaven and Protector of the Kingdom. He therefore became a god, a ti, and has ever since received worship as Guan Di or Wu Di, the God of War.

Temples erected in his honour are to be seen in all parts of the country. He is one of the most popular gods of China. During the last half-century of the Manchu Period his fame greatly increased. In 1856 he is said to have appeared in the heavens and successfully turned the tide of battle in favour of the Imperialists. His portrait hangs in every tent but his worship is not confined to the officials and the army. Many trades and professions have elected him as a patron saint. The sword of the public executioner used to be kept within the precincts of his temple and after an execution the presiding magistrate would stop there to worship for fear the ghost of the criminal might follow him home. He knew that the spirit would not dare to enter Guan Di's presence.

THE DIAMOND KINGS OF HEAVEN

On the right and left sides of the entrance hall of Buddhist temples, two on each side, are the gigantic figures of the four great Si Da Jingang or Tianwang, the Diamond Kings of Heaven. They are the protectors or governors of the continents lying in the direction of the four cardinal points from Mount Sumêru, the centre of the world. They are four brothers named respectively Moli Qing (Pure), or Zeng Zhang, Moli Hong (Vast), or Kuang Mu, Moli Hai (Sea), or Tao Wen, and Moli Shou (Age), or Qiguo. They are said to bestow all kinds of happiness on those who honour the Three Treasures, Buddha, the Law and the Priesthood.

Kings and nations who neglect the Law lose their protection. They are described as follows:

Moli Qing, the eldest, is twenty-four feet tall. He has a beard, the hairs of which are like copper wire. He carries a magnificent jade ring and a spear and always fights on foot. He also has a magic sword, 'Blue Cloud,' on the blade of which are engraved the characters Di, Shui, Huo, Feng (Earth, Water, Fire, Wind). When brandished, the magic sword causes a black wind which produces tens of thousands of spears. These spears pierce the bodies of men and turn them to dust. The wind is followed by a fire which fills the air with tens of thousands of golden fiery serpents. A thick smoke also rises out of the ground which blinds and burns men, none being able to escape.

Moli Hong carries in his hand an umbrella called the Umbrella of Chaos, formed of pearls with spiritual properties. Opening this marvellous implement causes the heavens and earth to be covered with thick darkness. Turning it upside down produces violent storms of wind and thunder and universal earthquakes.

Moli Hai holds a four-stringed guitar, the twanging of which supernaturally affects the earth, water, fire or wind. When it is played all the world listens and the camps of the enemy take fire.

Moli Shou has two whips and a panther-skin bag, the home of a creature resembling a white rat, known as Huahu Tiao. When at large this creature assumes the form of a white winged elephant, which devours men. He sometimes also has a snake or other man-eating creature, always ready to obey his commands.

The legend of the Four Diamond Kings goes that at the time of the consolidation of the Zhou dynasty in the twelfth and eleventh centuries BCE, Jiang Ziya (chief counsellor to

Wen Wang) and General Huang Feihu were defending the town and mountain of Xiqi. The supporters of the house of Shang appealed to the four genii Mo, who lived at Jiameng Guan, praying for them to come to their aid. They agreed and raised an army of one hundred thousand celestial soldiers. They travelled through towns, fields and mountains and arrived at the north gate of Xiqi in less than a day, where Moli Qing pitched his camp and entrenched his soldiers.

Hearing of this, Huang Feihu hurried to warn Jiang Ziya of the danger that threatened him. "The four great generals who have just arrived at the north gate," he said, "are marvellously powerful genii, experts in all the mysteries of magic and use of wonderful charms. It is feared that we will not be able to resist them."

Many fierce battles ensued. At first these went in favour of the Jingang, thanks to their magical weapons and especially to Moli Shou's Huahu Tiao, who terrorized the enemy by devouring their bravest warriors.

Unfortunately for the Jingang, the brute attacked and swallowed Yang Jian, the nephew of Yu Huang. This genie, on entering the body of the monster, split his heart apart and cut him in two. Then, as he could transform himself at will, he assumed the shape of Huahu Tiao and went off to Moli Shou, who unsuspectingly put him back into his bag.

The Four Kings held a festival to celebrate their triumph and having drunk copiously soon fell asleep. During the night Yang Jian came out of the bag with the intention stealing the three magical weapons of the Jingang. But he succeeded only in carrying off the umbrella of Moli Hong. In a subsequent battle Nezha, the son of Vadjrâ-pani (the God of Thunder), broke the jade ring of Moli Qing. Misfortune followed misfortune. Deprived of their magical weapons, the Jingang began to lose heart. To complete their embarrassment, Huang T'ien Hua brought a matchless magical weapon to the attack called the 'Heart-piercer'. This was a spike seven-and-a-half inches long, enclosed in a silk sheath. It projected a ray of light so strong that eyes were blinded by it.

Huang Tianhua, hard pressed by Moli Qing, drew the mysterious spike from its sheath and hurled it at his adversary. It entered his neck and with a deep groan the giant fell dead.

Moli Hong and Moli Hai hastened to avenge their brother, but before they could come within striking distance of Huang Ti'en Hua his formidable spike reached their hearts and they lay prone at his feet.

The one remaining hope for the sole survivor was in Huahu Tiao. Moli Shou, not knowing that the creature had been slain, put his hand into the bag to pull him out. Immediately after which Yang Jian, who had re-entered the bag, bit his hand off at the wrist. There remained nothing but a stump of bone. In this moment of intense agony Moli Shou fell an easy prey to Huang Tianhua. The magical spike pierced his heart and he fell bathed in his own blood. So perished the last of the Jingang.

THE THREE PURE ONES

Turning to the gods of Taoism, we find that the triad or trinity consists of three Supreme Gods, each in his own Heaven. These three Heavens, the Sanqing ('Three Pure Ones'), were formed from the three airs, which are subdivisions of the one primordial air.

The first Heaven is Yuqing. In it reigns the first member of the Taoist triad. He inhabits the Jade Mountain. The entrance to his palace is named the Golden Door. He is the source of all truth, as the sun is the source of all light.

Various authorities give his name differently – Yuanshi Tianzun, or Luo Qingxin, and call him Tian Bao (meaning 'the Treasure of Heaven'). Some state that the name of the ruler of this first Heaven is Yu Huang and it is he who occupies this supreme position. The Three Pure Ones are above him in rank, but he (the Pearly Emperor) is entrusted to oversee the world. He has all the power of Heaven and earth in his hands. He is the correlative of Heaven, or rather Heaven itself.

The second Heaven, Shangqing, is ruled by the second person of the triad, named Lingbao Tianzun, or Tao Jun. He is the custodian of the sacred books. He has existed from the beginning of the world. He calculates time, dividing it into different periods. He occupies the upper pole of the world. He determines the movements and interaction, or regulates the relations of the yin and the yang – the two great principles of nature.

In the third Heaven, Taiqing, the Taoists place Laozi, the promulgator of the true doctrine drawn up by Lingbao Tianzun. He is alternatively called Shen Bao ('the Treasure of the Spirits') and Taishang Laojun ('the Most Eminent Aged Ruler'). Under various assumed names he appears as the teacher of kings and emperors, the reformer of successive generations.

This three-storied Taoist Heaven, or three Heavens, is the result of Taoists' desire not to be out-rivalled by the Buddhists. For Buddha, the Law and the Priesthood they substitute the Tao (or Reason), the Classics and the Priesthood.

With regards to the organization of the Taoist Heavens, Y

Huang has the names of eight hundred Taoist divinities and a multitude of Immortals on his register. These are all divided into three categories: Saints (Shengren), Heroes (Zhenren), and Immortals (Xianren), occupying the three Heavens respectively in that order.

THE THREE CAUSES

Connected with Taoism (but not exclusively associated with that religion) is the worship of the Three Causes, the deities presiding over three departments of physical nature – Heaven, earth and water. They are known by various names: San Guan ('the Three Agents'), San Yuan ('the Three Origins'), San Guan Da Di ('the Three Great Emperor Agents') and Taishang San Guan ('the Three Supreme Agents'). This worship has passed through four main phases, as follows.

The first comprises Heaven, earth and water, or Tian, Ti, Shui – the sources of happiness, forgiveness of sins and deliverance from evil, respectively. Their names, written on labels and offered to Heaven (on a mountain), earth (by burial) and water (by immersion), are supposed to cure sickness. This idea dates from the Han dynasty, being first noted about 172 CE.

The second, San Yuan dating from 407 CE under the Wei dynasty, identified the Three Agents with three dates of which they were respectively made the patrons. The year was divided into three unequal parts: the first to the seventh moon, the seventh to the tenth and the tenth to the twelfth. Of these, the fifteenth day of the first, seventh and tenth moons, respectively became the three principal dates of these periods. The Agent of Heaven became the principal patron of the first division, honoured on the fifteenth day of the first moon, and so on.

The third phase, San Guan, resulted from the first two being found too complicated for popular favour. The San Guan were the three sons of a man, Chen Zizhun, who was so handsome and intelligent that the three daughters of Long Wang, the Dragon King, fell in love with him and went to live with him. The eldest girl was the mother of the Superior Cause, the second of the Medium Cause and the third of the Inferior Cause. All these were gifted with supernatural powers. Yuanshi Tianzun canonized them as the Three Great Emperor Agents of Heaven, earth and water, governors of all beings, devils or gods in the three regions of the universe. As in the first phase, the Tian Guan confers happiness, the Di Guan grants remission of sins and the Shui Guan delivers from evil or misfortune.

The fourth phase consisted simply in the substitution by the priests for the abstract or time-principles of the three great sovereigns of ancient times, Yao, Shun, and Yu. The literati, proud of the achievements of their ancient rulers, were quick to offer incense to them. Temples, or San Yuan Gong, sprang up in many parts of the Empire.

THE FIRST CAUSE

Yuanshi Tianzun (or the First Cause), the Highest in Heaven, is generally placed at the head of the Taoist triad. He i said never to have existed but in the fertile imagination o the Laozijia sectarians. According to them Yuanshi Tianzun had neither origin nor master, but is himself the cause of al beings, which is why he is called the First Cause. The name assigned to him is Luo Qingxin.

As first member of the triad and sovereign ruler of the First Heaven, he is raised in rank above all the other gods. He was born before all beginnings. His substance is imperishable. It is formed essentially of uncreated air, invisible and without perceptible limits. No one has been able to penetrate to the beginnings of his existence. The source of all truth, he at each renovation of the worlds gives out the mysterious doctrine that confers immortality. All who reach this knowledge achieve eternal life, become refined like the spirits, or instantly become Immortals, even while on earth.

Originally, Yuanshi Tianzun was not a member of the Taoist triad. He resided above the Three Heavens, above the Three Pure Ones, surviving the destructions and renovations of the universe, as an immovable rock in the midst of a stormy sea. He set the stars in motion and caused the planets to revolve. The chief of his secret police was Cao Jun, the Kitchen-god, who rendered to him an account of the good and evil deeds of each family. His executive agent was Lei Zu, the God of Thunder, and his subordinates. The seven stars of the North Pole were the palace of his ministers, whose offices were on the various sacred mountains. Nowadays, however, Yuanshi Tianzun is generally neglected for Yu Huang.

YU HUANG, THE JADE EMPEROR

Yu Huang means 'the Jade Emperor,' or 'the Pure August One,' jade symbolizing purity. He is also known by the name Yu Huang Shangdi, 'the Pure August Emperor on High.'

The history of this deity, who later received many titles and became the most popular god, a very Chinese Jupiter, seems to be somewhat as follows: In 1005 CE the Emperor Cheng Zong of the Song dynasty was forced to sign a disgraceful peace with the Tunguses or Kitans and the dynasty was in danger of losing the support of the nation. In order to hoodwink the people the Emperor announced with great pomp and ceremony that he was in direct communication with the gods of Heaven. In doing this he was following the advice of his crafty and unreliable minister Wang Qinjiao, who had often tried to persuade him that the pretended revelations attributed to Fuxi, Yu Wang and others were only pure inventions to induce obedience.

The Emperor, having studied his part well, assembled his ministers in the tenth moon of the year 1012, and made the following declaration to them: "In a dream I had a visit from an Immortal, who brought me a letter from Yu Huang, the purpose of which was as follows: 'I have already sent you by your ancestor Zhao (Tai Zu) two celestial letters. Now I am going to send him in person to visit you.'" A little while later his ancestor Taizu, the founder of the dynasty, came according to Yu Huang's promise and Cheng Zong quickly informed his ministers of it. This is the origin of Yu Huang. He was born of a fraud and came ready made from the brain of an emperor.

Fearing of being admonished for the fraud by another of his ministers, the scholar Wang Tan, the Emperor decided to put a golden gag in his mouth. So one day, having invited him to a banquet, he overwhelmed him with flattery and made him drunk with good wine. "I would like the members of your family also to taste this wine," he added, "so I am making you a present of a cask of it." When Wang Tan returned home, he found the cask filled with precious pearls. Out of gratitude to the Emperor he kept silent as to the fraud and made no further opposition to his plans. However on his death bed he asked that his head be shaved like a priest's and that he be dressed in priestly robes so that he might make amends for his crime of feebleness before the Emperor.

Kangxi, the great Emperor of the Qing chao, who had already declared that if it is wrong to impute deceit to a man it is still more reprehensible to impute a fraud to Heaven, stigmatized him as follows: "Wang Tan committed two faults: the first was in showing himself a vile flatterer of his Prince during his life; the second was in becoming a worshipper of Buddha at his death."

History side, the legend of Yu Huang relates that in ancient times there was a kingdom named Guangyan Miao Luoguo, whose king was Jingde and whose queen was Bao Yue. Though getting on in years, the Queen had no son. The Taoist priests were summoned to the palace to perform their rites. They recited prayers in the hope of obtaining an heir to the throne.

During the ensuing night the Queen had a vision. Laojun appeared to her, riding a dragon and carrying a male child in his arms. He floated down through the air in her direction. The Queen begged him to give her the child as an heir to the throne. 'I am quite willing," he said. "Here it is." She fell on her knees and thanked him. When she awoke, she found herself pregnant. At the end of a year the Prince was born. From an early age he was compassionate and generous to the poor. On the death of his father he ascended the throne, but after reigning only a few days he abdicated in favour of his chief minister and became a hermit at Puming, in Shaanxi, and also on Xiu Yan Shan, in Yunnan. Having attained to perfection, he passed the rest of his days during sickness and saving life; and it was in the exercise of these charitable deeds that he died. The emperors Cheng Zong and Hui Zong, of the Song dynasty, loaded him with all the various titles associated with his name today.

Both Buddhists and Taoists claim him as their own, the former identifying him with Indra, in which case Yu Huang is a Buddhist deity incorporated into the Taoist pantheon. He has also been taken to be the subject of a 'nature myth.' The Emperor Jingde, his father, is the sun, the Queen Bao Yue the moon, and the marriage symbolizes the rebirth of the vivifying power which clothes nature with green plants and beautiful flowers.

THE LEGEND OF TONGTIAN JIAOZHU

In modern Taoism Tongtian Jiaozhu is regarded as the first of the Patriarchs and one of the most powerful genii of the sect. His master was Hongjun Laozu. He wore a red robe embroidered with white cranes and rode a guiniu – a monster resembling a buffalo, with one long horn like a unicorn. His palace, the Biyu Gong, was situated on Zizhi Yai Shan.

This genie took the part of Zhou Wang and helped him to resist Wu Wang's armies. First, he sent his disciple Topao Dao ren to Jiepai Guan. He gave him four precious swords and the plan of a fort which he was to construct and to name Zhuxian Zhen, 'the Citadel of all the Immortals.'

Topao Dao ren carried out his orders, but he had to fight a battle with Kuang Chengzi, and the latter, armed with a celestial seal, struck his adversary so hard that he fell to the ground and had to take refuge in flight.

Tongtian Jiaozhu came to the defence of his disciple and to restore the morale of his forces. Unfortunately, a posse of gods arrived to aid Wu Wang's powerful general, Jiang Ziya. The first who attacked Tongtian Jiaozhu was Laozi, who struck him several times with his stick. Then came Chunti, armed with his cane. The buffalo of Tongtian Jiaozhu stamped him under foot, and Chunti was thrown to the earth. He only just had time to rise quickly and mount into the air amid a great cloud of dust.

There could be no doubt that the fight was going against Tongtian Jiaozhu; to complete his feeling of unease Jianteng Dao ren split the air and fell on him unexpectedly. With a violent blow of his staff he cast him down and compelled him to give up the struggle.

Tongtian Jiaozhu then prepared plans for a new fortified camp beyond Tong Guan. He tried to take the offensive once more, but again Laozi stopped him with a blow of his stick. Yuanshi Tianzun wounded his shoulder with his precious stone Juyi, and Chunti Dao ren waved his 'Branch of the Seven Virtues.' Immediately the magic sword of Tongtian Jiaozhu was reduced to splinters and he saved himself only by flight.

Hongjun Laozu, the master of these three genii, seeing his three beloved disciples in the melee, resolved to make peace between them. He assembled all three in a tent in Jiang Ziya's camp, made them kneel before him, then reproached Tongtian Jiaozhu for having taken the part of the tyrant Zhou, and recommended them to live in harmony in future. After finishing his speech, he produced three pills and ordered each of the genii to swallow one. When they had done so, Hongjun Laozu said to them: "I have given you these pills to ensure an absolute truce among you. Know that the first who entertains a thought of discord in his heart will find that the pill will explode in his stomach and cause his instant death."

Hongjun Laozu then took Tongtian Jiaozhu away with him on his cloud to Heaven.

THE IMMORTALS

An Immortal, according to the Taoist, is a solitary man of the mountains. He appears to die, but does not. After 'death' his body retains all the qualities of the living. The body or corpse is for him only a means of transition, a phase of metamorphosis – a cocoon or chrysalis, the temporary home of the butterfly. To reach this state a hygienic regimen both of the body and mind must be observed. All luxury, greed and ambition must be avoided. But negation is not enough. In the system of nourishment all the elements which strengthen the essence of the constituent yin and yang principles must be found by means of medicine, chemistry and exercise. When the maximum vital force has been acquired the means of preserving it and keeping it from the attacks of death and disease must be discovered; in a word, he must spiritualize himself – render himself completely independent of matter.

Mugong or Dong Wanggong, the God of the Immortals, was also called Yijun Ming and Yu Huang Jun, the Prince Yu Huang. Legend has it that the primitive vapour congealed, remained inactive for a time and then produced living beings, beginning with the formation of Mugong, the purest substance of the Eastern Air and sovereign of the active male principle yang and of all the countries of the East. His palace is in the misty heavens violet clouds form its dome, blue clouds its walls. Hsien T'ung, 'the Immortal Youth,' and Yunü, 'the Jade Maiden,' are his servants. He keeps the register of all the Immortals, male and female.

Similarly, Xi Wang Mu was formed of the pure quintessence of the Western Air, in the legendary continent of Shên Chou. She is often called the Golden Mother of the Tortoise. Her family name is variously given as Hou, Yang and Ho. Her own name was Hui, and first name Wingjing. She had nine sons and twenty-four daughters.

As Mugong, formed of the Eastern Air, is the active principle of the male air and sovereign of the Eastern Air, so Xi Wang Mu, born of the Western Air, is the passive or female principle (yin) and sovereign of the Western Air. These two principles, co-operating, give rise to Heaven and earth and all the beings of the universe, and therefore become the two principles of life and of the subsistence of all that exists. She is the head of the troop of genii dwelling on the K'un-lun Mountains (the Taoist equivalent of the Buddhist Sumêru).

Xi Wang Mu's palace is situated in the high mountains of the snowy K'un-lun. It is about 333 miles in circuit; a rampart of massive gold surrounds its battlements of precious stones. Its right wing rises on the edge of the Kingfishers' River. It is the usual abode of the Immortals, who are divided into seven special categories according to the colour of their garments – red, blue, black, violet, yellow, green and 'nature colour.' There is a marvellous fountain built of precious stones, where the periodical banquet of the Immortals is held. This feast is called Pantao Hui, 'the Feast of Peaches.' It takes place on the borders of the Yaochi (Lake of Gems) and is attended by both male and female Immortals. Besides several superfine meats, they are served with bears' paws, monkeys' lips, dragons' liver, phoenix marrow and peaches gathered in the orchard, endowed with the mystic virtue of granting longevity on all who have the good luck to taste them. It was by these peaches that the date of the banquet was fixed. The tree put forth leaves once every three thousand years, and it required three thousand years after that for the fruit to ripen. These were Xi Wang Mu's birthdays, when all the Immortals assembled for the great feast.

THE EIGHT IMMORTALS

During the Mongol or Yuan dynasty in the thirteenth century, a group of Taoist deities who were known as the 'Eight Immortals', or Pa Hsien, became the new focus of a whole catalogue of Chinese legends, achieving a rapid and widespread popularity. Partly historical and partly mythical figures, the Eight Immortals were said to share a home together in the Eastern Paradise on the isles of Penglai. Characters similar to these Gods were celebrated in earlier Taoist tales, but now for the first time they appeared as a group, whose different personalities were intended to represent the whole spectrum of society ranging from young to old, rich to poor, whether male or female in gender. The Chinese were very fond of these characters and their numerous eccentricities, and increasingly they became a favourite subject for artists. They appeared together frequently in paintings, or on pottery and elaborate tapestries, or as statuettes and larger sculptures.

The most famous of the Eight Immortals was known as Li Tieguai, a name which means 'Li of the Iron Crutch'. Among the group, he was perhaps the most gifted disciple of Taoism, an immortal reputed to have acquired his great wisdom from the spirit of Lao Tzu himself. After the course of instruction had been completed, it was said that the Great Master summoned Li to the Heavens to assess his ability more closely. Li willingly answered the call and his soul left his body and journeyed upwards towards the firmament.

But before Li departed the earth, he placed one of his own pupils, known as Lang Ling, in charge of his body, ordering him to guard it well for a period of seven days until he returned to reclaim it. After only six days had elapsed, however, the student was called to his mother's deathbed, and because he was reluctant to leave the body exposed to scavengers, he decided to cremate it before he departed.

When Li returned to earth he found only a mound of ashes where his body once lay and his spirit was forced to wander about in search of another host. Fortunately, however, a beggar had just died of starvation in the nearby woods, and Li entered the body without any further delay. But as soon as he had done so, he began to regret his decision, for the deceased beggar had only had one leg, his head was ugly and pointed, and the hair around his face was long and dishevelled. Li wished to leave the vile body he had entered, but Lao Tzu advised him that this would not be wise. So instead, the Great Master of the Heavens sent him a gold band to keep his matted hair in place and an iron crutch to help him move about more easily.

And one of the first benevolent acts Li performed in this human body was to visit the home of his negligent pupil, where he poured the contents of his gourd into the mouth of Lang Ling's dead mother, bringing her back to life instantly. For two hundred years Li roamed the earth in this way, converting people to Taoism and healing them with his medicine. He represents the sick and his emblems are an iron stick and a gourd.

The second of the Eight Immortals was called Han Zhongli, a powerful military figure, who in his younger days rose to become Marshal of the Empire. After Han became converted to Taoism, however, he chose to live the life of a hermit in Yangqiao Shan. Here, he studied the ways of immortality and stored whatever secrets he discovered in a large jade casket within his cave. Some say that Han Zhongli was highly skilled in the ways of alchemy and that during the great famine he changed base metals, such as copper and pewter, into silver which he then distributed to the poor, saving thousands of lives. A fan of feathers, or the peach of immortality are his emblems, and he is associated with military affairs.

During a visit to Yangqiao Shan, Lu Dongbin, the son of a high-ranking government official and a clever young scholar, met with Han Zhongli, who invited him into his cave to share some rice wine with him. Tired from his journey, Lu Dongbin readily accepted the invitation, but as soon as he tasted the wine he fell into a deep sleep. And while he slept, he had an unpleasant dream which altered the course of his life.

He dreamt that he had married well, fathered several healthy children, and that he had risen to a position of great prominence in his work before his fiftieth year. After this time, he looked forward to a peaceful retirement, but for some reason, he was exiled in disgrace and his family put to death for his misdemeanours. For the rest of his days, he was condemned to a futile and lonely existence from which he could find no escape. Lü awoke from his dream with a start and began to interpret its meaning. At length, he became convinced of the vanity of worldly dignities and begged Han Zhongli to accept him as a disciple in order that he might train to be one of the Eight Immortals. He is commonly associated with scholars and is always portrayed carrying a sword.

The fourth Immortal, Changguo Lao, was also a famous hermit who lived in the Hengzhou Shan. He usually appeared seated on a white donkey which he was able to fold up like a piece of paper and which would resume its former shape once he had sprinkled water on it. Changguo Lao claimed that he was a descendant of Emperor Yao and his special magical powers enabled him to bring fertility to young couples. His emblem is a white mule, or a phoenix feather, and he represents the old.

Cao Guojiu, who is associated with the nobility and whose emblem is a scribe's tablet, became an Immortal after he renounced the wickedness of his worldly life. Tsao was the eldest of two brothers whose sister was married to the Di, Renzong. One day the Empress invited a young graduate and his wife to dine with her at the palace, but disaster struck when the younger brother, Ching-chih, who was notorious for his bad behaviour, allowed himself to become besotted by the lady and decided to murder her husband. After he had committed this crime, the soul of the husband demanded justice from the God Pao and Jingzhi was immediately thrown in prison. Knowing his brother would inevitably face the death penalty, Cao Guojiu encouraged him to kill the graduate's wife so that no evidence of his crime would remain. But the wife escaped to inform Pao of this second attack and Cao Guojiu was also thrown in prison to face execution.

Eventually, the Empress intervened on her brothers' behalf and begged the Emperor to grant them both an amnesty. As soon as this happened, Tsao was so grateful he decided to abandon his life of luxury and to live by the doctrines of Taoism. For the remainder of his days Cao Guojiu lived as a hermit devoting himself to the practice of perfection.

The sixth and seventh Immortals were very young men. Han Xiangzi was the grand-nephew of one of the greatest poets of the Tang dynasty, and from an early age he was schooled by his uncle in the ways of poetry until eventually his ability far surpassed that of the older man. Shortly afterwards, the youth became a disciple of Lu Dongbin and at the end of his instruction he was required to climb to the top of the Immortalizing Peach Tree. As he did so, he lost his balance and fell dead to the ground. Miraculously, however, he came to life once more, for he had attained the gift of immortality during the descent. Han Xiangzi is always depicted carrying either a flower-basket or a peach and he represents cultured society.

Lan Caihe, a strolling actor and singer of about sixteen years of age, dressed himself in a tattered blue gown and a black wooden belt, and always wore only one shoe. His life was spent urging people to convert to Taoism and he denounced the material comforts of mortals. When given money, he either strung it on a cord and used it as an instrument to beat time as he sang, or scattered it to the ground for the poor to pick up. His emblem is a lute and he represents the poor.

Only one of the Eight Immortals, He Xiangu was a woman and she was always depicted holding a lotus flower or the peach of immortality, presented to her by Lu Dongbin after she had lost her way through the mountains. While still very young, she chose to live a simple life of celibacy and prayer on Yunmu Ling Shan. Here, she found a stone known as the Yunmu Shi, 'mother-of-pearl', and was told in a dream to powder the stone and to swallow its dust should she wish to become an Immortal. He Xiangu followed this instruction and spent the rest of her days floating around the mountains, picking wild berries which she carried to her mother. Her emblem is a lotus and she represents young, unmarried girls.

ZHANG DAOLING, THE HEAVENLY TEACHER

Zhang Daoling, the first Taoist pope, was born in 35 CE, in the reign of the Emperor Kuang Wudi of the Han dynasty. His birthplace is variously given as the Tianmu Shan, 'Eye of Heaven Mountain,' in Lin'an Xian, in Zhejiang, and Fengyang Fu, in Anhui. He devoted himself wholly to study and meditation, declining all offers to enter the service of the State. He preferred to live in the mountains of Western China, where he persevered in the study of alchemy and in cultivating the virtues of purity and mental abstraction. From the hands of Laozi he received a mystic treatise. Any by following the instructions in it he was successful in his search for the elixir of life.

One day when he was engaged in experimenting with the 'Dragon-tiger elixir' a spiritual being appeared to him and said: "On Posong Shan is a stone house in which are concealed the writings of the Three Emperors of antiquity and a canonical work. By obtaining these you may ascend to Heaven, if you undergo the course of discipline they prescribe."

Zhang Daoling found these works and by means of them he obtained the power of flying, of hearing distant sounds and of leaving his body. After going through a thousand days of discipline and after receiving instruction from a goddess, who taught him to walk about among the stars, he began to fight with the king of the demons, to divide mountains and seas and to command the wind and thunder. All the demons fled before him. On account of the immense slaughter of demons by this hero, the wind and thunder were reduced to subjection, and various divinities hurried to acknowledge their faults. In nine years he gained the power to ascend to Heaven.

Zhang Daoling may rightly be considered as the true founder of modern Taoism. The recipes for the pills of immortality contained in the mysterious books, and the invention of talismans for the cure of all sorts of diseases, not only elevated him to the high position he has since occupied in the minds of his numerous disciples, but enabled them in turn to successfully exploit this new source of power and wealth. From that time the Taoist sect began to specialize in the art of healing. Protecting or curing talismans bearing the Master's seal were purchased for enormous sums. It is therefore seen that he was after all a deceiver of the people, and unbelievers or rival partisans of other sects have dubbed him a 'rice thief'.

He is generally represented as dressed in richly decorated garments, brandishing his magic sword with his right hand, holding a cup containing the draught of immortality in his left, and riding a tiger which in one paw grasps his magic seal and with the others tramples down the five venomous creatures: lizard, snake, spider, toad and centipede. Pictures of him with these accessories are pasted up in houses on the fifth day of the fifth moon to protect from calamity and sickness.

Another legend relating to Zhang Daoling is that, not wishing to ascend to Heaven too soon, he took of only half of the pill of immortality, dividing the other half among several of his admirers. Also that he had at least two selves or personalities, one of which used to amuse itself in a boat on a small lake in front of his house. The other self would receive his visitors, entertaining them with food, drink and conversation.

On one occasion this self said to them: "You are unable to quit the world altogether as I can, but by imitating my example in the matter of family relations you could obtain a medicine which would prolong your lives by several centuries. I have given the crucible in which Huangdi prepared the draught of immortality to my disciple Wang Chang. Later on, a man will come from the East, who will also make use of it. He will arrive on the seventh day of the first moon."

Exactly on that day a man named Zhao Sheng arrived from the East. Chang then led all three hundred of his disciples to the highest peak of the Yuntai. Below them they saw a peach tree growing near a pointed rock, stretching out its branches like arms above a fathomless abyss. It was a large tree, covered with ripe fruit.

Chang said to his disciples: "I will communicate a spiritual formula to the one among you who will dare to gather the fruit of that tree." They all leaned over to look, but each declared the feat to be impossible. Zhao Sheng alone had the courage to rush out to the point of the rock and up the tree stretching out into space. He stood and gathered the peaches, placing them in the folds of his cloak, as many as it would hold, but when he wished to climb back up the precipitous slope, his hands slipped on the smooth rock and all his attempts were in vain. So he threw the peaches, three hundred and two in all, one by one up to Zhang Daoling, who distributed them. Each disciple ate one, as did Chang, who reserved the remaining one for Zhao Sheng, whom he helped to climb up again. To do this Chang extended his arm to a length of thirty feet, everyone present marvelling at the miracle.

After Chao had eaten his peach Chang stood on the edge of the precipice and said with a laugh, "Zhao Sheng was brave enough to climb out to that tree and his foot never tripped. I too will make the attempt. If I succeed I will have a big peach as a reward."

Having said this, he leapt into space and jumped into the branches of the peach tree. Wang Chang and Zhao Sheng also jumped into the tree and stood one on each side of him. There Chang communicated to them the mysterious formula. Three days later they returned to their homes; then, having made final arrangements, they returned once more to the mountain peak. From here, in the presence of the other disciples, who followed them with their eyes until they had completely disappeared from view, all three ascended to Heaven in broad daylight.

The name of Zhang Daoling, the Heavenly Teacher, is a household name in China. He is the earthly representative of the Pearly Emperor in Heaven and the Commander-in-Chief of the hosts of Taoism. He, the chief of the wizards, the 'true man,' as he is known, wields an immense spiritual power throughout the land. The present pope boasts of an unbroken line for many generations. His family obtained possession of the Dragon-tiger Mountain in Jiangxi around 1000 CE.

TAI YI, THE GREAT ONE

Temples are found in various parts of China dedicated to Tai Yi, the Great One, or Great Unity.

When Emperor Wu Di (140–86 BCE) of the Han dynasty was in search of the secret of immortality, and various suggestions had proved unsatisfactory, he turned to a Taoist priest named Miao Chi. The priest told the Emperor that his lack of success was due to his omission to sacrifice to Tai Yi, the first of the celestial spirits. The Emperor, believing his word, ordered the Grand Master of Sacrifices to re-establish this worship at the capital.

He carefully followed the prescriptions of Miao Chi. This enraged the literati, who resolved to ruin him. One day, when the Emperor was about to drink one of his potions, one of the chief courtiers seized the cup and drank the contents himself. The Emperor was about to have him slain, when he said: "Your Majesty's order is unnecessary; if the potion confers immortality, I cannot be killed; if, on the other hand, it does not, your Majesty should reward me for disproving the pretensions of the Taoist priest." The Emperor, however, was not convinced.

One account represents Tai Yi as having lived in the time of Shennong, the Divine Husbandman, who visited him to consult with him on the subjects of diseases and fortune. He was Xian Yuan's medical teacher. His medical knowledge was handed down to future generations. He was one of those who, with the Immortals, was invited to the great Peach Assembly of the Western Royal Mother.

As the spirit of the star Tai Yi he resides in the Eastern Palace, listening for the cries of sufferers in order to save them. With a boat of lotus flowers of nine colours he ferries men over to the shore of salvation. Holding in his hand a willow branch, he scatters from it the dew of the doctrine.

Tai Yi is variously represented as the Ruler of the Five Celestial Sovereigns, Cosmic Matter before it congealed into concrete shapes, the Triune Spirit of Heaven, earth, and Tai Yi as three separate entities, an unknown Spirit, and the Spirit of the Pole Star.

TOU MU, GODDESS OF THE NORTH STAR

Tou Mu, the Bushel Mother, or Goddess of the North Star, worshipped by both Buddhists and Taoists, is the Indian Maritchi, and was made a stellar divinity by the Taoists.

She is said to have been the mother of the nine Ren Huang or Human Sovereigns of fabulous antiquity, who succeeded the lines of Celestial and Terrestrial Sovereigns. In the Taoist religion she occupies the same relative position as Guanyin, who may be said to be the heart of Buddhism. Having attained to a profound knowledge of celestial mysteries, she shone with heavenly light, could cross the seas, and pass from the sun to the moon. She also had a kind heart for the sufferings of humanity. The Zhou Yu Wang, in the north, married her on hearing of her many virtues. They had nine sons. Yuanshi Tianzun came to earth to invite her, her husband and nine sons to enjoy the delights of Heaven. He placed her in the palace Tou Shu, the Pivot of the Pole, because all the other stars revolve round it, and gave her the title of Queen of the Doctrine of Primitive Heaven. Her nine sons have their palaces in the neighbouring stars.

Tou Mu wears the Buddhist crown, is seated on a lotus throne, has three eyes, eighteen arms, and holds various precious objects in her numerous hands, such as a bow, spear, sword, flag, dragon's head, pagoda, five chariots, sun's disk, moon's disk, etc. She has control of the books of life and death, and all who wish to prolong their days worship at her shrine. Her devotees abstain from animal food on the third and twenty-seventh day of every month.

Of her sons, two are the Northern and Southern Bushels; the latter, dressed in red, rules birth; the former, in white, rules death. "A young Esau once found them on the South Mountain, under a tree, playing chess, and by an offer of venison his lease of life was extended from nineteen to ninety-nine years."

SNORTER AND BLOWER

At the time of the overthrow of the Shang and establishment of the Zhou dynasty in 1122 BCE there lived two marshals, Cheng Long and Chen Qi. These were Heng and Ha, the Snorter and Blower respectively. The former was the chief superintendent of supplies for the armies of the tyrant emperor Zhou, the Nero of China. The latter was in charge of obtaining food for the same army.

Legend has it that from his master, Tu O, the celebrated Taoist magician of the K'un-lun Mountains, Heng acquired a marvellous power. When he snorted, his nostrils emitted two white columns of light, which destroyed his enemies, body and soul. It was through him the Zhou gained numerous victories. One day he was captured, bound and taken to the general of

Zhou. His life was spared and he was made general superintendent of army stores as well as generalissimo of five army corps.

Later on he found himself face to face with the Blower. The latter had learned from the magician how to store a supply of yellow gas in his chest which, when he blew it out, annihilated anyone it struck. By this means he caused large gaps to be made in the ranks of the enemy.

Being opposed to each other, one snorting out great streaks of white light, the other blowing streams of yellow gas, the battle continued until the Blower was wounded in the shoulder by Nezha, of the Zhou army, and pierced in the stomach with a spear by Huang Feihu, Yellow Flying Tiger.

The Snorter in turn was slain in this fight by Marshal Jin Dasheng, 'Golden Big Pint,' an ox spirit who was blessed with the mysterious power of producing the celebrated niu huang, ox-yellow, or bezoar. Facing the Snorter, with a noise like thunder he spat a piece of bezoar as large as a rice bowl in his face. It struck him on the nose and split his nostrils. He fell to the earth and was cut in two by a blow from his victor's sword.

After the Zhou dynasty had been fully established Jiang Ziya canonized the two marshals Heng and Ha, and granted them the offices of guardians of the Buddhist temple gates, where their gigantic images may be seen.

BLUE DRAGON AND WHITE TIGER

The functions carried out by Heng and Ha at the gates of Buddhist temples are in Taoist temples done by Blue Dragon and White Tiger. The former, the Spirit of the Blue

Dragon Star, was Deng Jiugong, one of the chief generals of the last emperor of the Yin Chao. He had a son named Deng Xiu and a daughter named Chanyu.

The story goes that the army of Deng Jiugong was camped at Sanshan Guan, when he received orders to go to the battle then taking place at Xiqi. There, in standing up to Nezha and Huang Feihu, he had his left arm broken by the former's magic bracelet. Fortunately for him, his subordinate, Tu Xingsun, a renowned magician, gave him a remedy which quickly healed the fracture.

His daughter then came on the scene to avenge her father. She had a magic weapon, the Five-fire Stone, which she hurled full in the face of Yang Jian. But the Immortal was not wounded. His celestial dog jumped at Chanyu and bit her neck, so that she was forced to flee. Tu Xingsun, however, healed the wound.

After a banquet, Deng Jiugong promised his daughter in marriage to Tu Xingsun if he would gain him the victory at Xiqi. Jiang Ziya then persuaded T'u's magic master, Ju Liusun, to call his disciple over to his camp, where he asked him why he was fighting against the new dynasty. "Because," he replied, "Jiugong has promised me his daughter in marriage as a reward of success."

So Jiang Ziya promised to obtain the bride and sent a force to seize her. As a result of the fighting that ensued, Jiugong was beaten and retreated in confusion, leaving Chanyu in the hands of the victors. During the next few days the marriage was celebrated with great ceremony in the victor's camp. According to custom, the bride returned for some days to her father's house, and while there she strongly urged Jiugong to submit. Following her advice, he went over to Jiang Ziya's party.

In the ensuing battles he fought valiantly on the side of his former enemy and killed many famous warriors, but he was eventually attacked by the Blower, from whose mouth a column of yellow gas struck him, throwing him from his horse. He was held prisoner and executed by order of General Qiu Yin. Jiang Ziya granted him the kingdom of the Blue Dragon Star.

The Spirit of the White Tiger Star is Yin Chengxiu. His father, Yin Pobai, a high courtier of the tyrant Zhou Wang, was sent to negotiate peace with Jiang Ziya, but was seized and put to death by Marquis Jiang Wenhuan. His son, attempting to avenge his father's murder, was pierced by a spear. His head was cut off and carried in triumph to Jiang Ziya.

As compensation he was canonized as the Spirit of the White Tiger Star.

THE CITY GOD

Chenghuang is the Celestial Mandarin or City god. Every fortified city or town in China is surrounded by a wall, or ch'êng, composed usually of two battlemented walls, the space between which is filled with earth. This earth is dug from the ground outside, making a ditch, or huang, running parallel with the ch'êng. The Chenghuang is the spiritual official of the city or town. All the numerous Chenghuang constitute a celestial Ministry of Justice, presided over by a Chenghuang-in-chief.

The origin of the worship of the Chenghuang dates back to the time of the great Emperor Yao (2357 BCE), who instituted a sacrifice called Ba Cha in honour of eight spirits, of whom the seventh, Shui Yong corresponded to the dyke and rampart known later as Chenghuang. Since the Song dynasty sacrifices have been offered to the Chenghuang all over the country, though now and then some towns have adopted another or special god as their Chenghuang, such as Zhou Xin, adopted as the Chenghuang of Hangzhou, the capital of Zhejiang Province.

Concerning Zhou Xin, who had a 'face of ice and iron,' and was so much dreaded for his severity that old and young fled at his approach, it is told that once when he was trying a case a storm blew some leaves on to his table. In spite of diligent search the tree to which this kind of leaf belonged could not be found anywhere in the neighbourhood, but was eventually discovered in a Buddhist temple a long way off. The judge declared that the priests of this temple must be guilty of murder. By his order the tree was felled, and in its trunk was found the body of a woman who had been assassinated. The priests were convicted of the murder.

THE CITY GOD OF YAN CHENG

The Chenghuang Pusa is the patron god of a city, his position in the unseen world similar to that of a zhi xian (district magistrate) among men, if the city under his care is a hsien; but if the city hold the rank of a fu, it has (or used to have) two Chenghuang Pusas, one a prefect, and the other a district magistrate.

One part of his duty consists of sending small demons to carry off the spirits of the dying, of which spirits he then acts as ruler and judge. He is supposed to exercise special care over the kugui, or spirits which have no descendants to worship and offer sacrifices to them. During the Seventh Month Festival he is carried around the city in his chair to maintain order among them, while the people offer food to them and burn paper money for their benefit. He is also carried in procession at the Qingming Festival and on the first day of the tenth month.

This is the legend of the Chenghuang Pusa of the city of Yan Cheng (Salt City), who is in the extremely unfortunate predicament of having no skin to his face.

Once upon a time in Yan Cheng lived an orphan boy who was brought up by his uncle and aunt. He was just entering his teens when his aunt lost a gold hairpin and accused him of having stolen it. The boy, whose conscience was clear in this matter, thought of a plan that might prove his innocence.

"Let's go tomorrow to Chenghuang Pusa's temple," he said, "and I will swear an oath before the god, so that he may show my innocence." So they went to the temple, and the boy, solemnly addressing the idol, said "If I have taken my aunt's gold pin, may my foot twist, and may I fall as I go out of your temple door!"

However, as he stepped over the threshold his foot did twist and he fell to the ground. Of course, everybody was firmly convinced of his guilt and what could the poor boy say when his own appeal to the god had turned against him?

After such a proof of his wickedness his aunt had no room in her house for her orphan nephew. And he himself no longer wanted to stay with people who suspected him of theft. So he left the home that had sheltered him for years and wandered out alone into the cold hard world. The boy encountered many hardships, but with rare bravery he persevered in his studies and at the age of twenty odd years became a mandarin.

In course of time our hero returned to Yan Cheng to visit his uncle and aunt. While he was there he took himself to the temple of the deity who had dealt so harshly with him and prayed for a revelation as to the whereabouts of the lost hairpin.

He slept that night in the temple and was rewarded by a vision in which the Chenghuang Pusa told him that the pin would be found under the floor of his aunt's house.

He rushed back and informed his relatives, who took up the boards in the place indicated, and lo and behold there lay the long-lost pin! The women of the house then remembered that the pin had been used in pasting together the various layers of the soles of shoes and, when night came, had been carelessly left on the table. No doubt rats, attracted by the smell of the paste which clung to it, had carried it off to their domains under the floor.

The young mandarin joyfully returned to the temple and offered sacrifices by way of thanksgiving to the Chenghuang Pusa for bringing his innocence to light, but he could not stop himself from giving the god a gentle reproach: "You made me fall down and so led people to think I was guilty, and now you accept my gifts. Aren't you ashamed to do such a thing? You have no face!" As he uttered the words all the plaster fell from the face of the idol and was smashed into fragments.

From that day forward the Chenghuang Pusa of Yan Cheng has had no skin on his face. People have tried to patch up the disfigured features, but in vain: the plaster always falls off and the face remains skinless.

Some try to defend the Chenghuang Pusa by saying that he was not at home on the day when his temple was visited by the accused boy and his relatives, and that one of the little demons employed by him to carry off dead people's spirits perpetrated a practical joke on the poor boy out of sheer mischief.

In that case it is certainly hard that his skin should so persistently testify against him by refusing to remain on his face!

THE KITCHEN GOD

Cao Jun, the kitchen god, is said to be a Taoist invention, but is universally worshipped by all families in China. Traditionally about sixty million pictures of him were regularly worshipped twice a month, at the new and full moon.

His temple was a small niche above the kitchen stove where an incense stick burned continuously. From this position, the Kitchen God kept an account of how well the family behaved, compiling his annual report for the attention of the Supreme Being of the Heavens. At New Year, he was destined to return to the firmament to present his report and he was sent on his way with a great deal of ceremony. Firecrackers were lit and a lavish meal prepared to improve his mood. His mouth was smeared with honey, so that only 'sweet' words would escape his lips when he stood before the Supreme Being. He was entrusted with the power to punish and reward members of the family under his supervision. He is also called 'the God of the Stove.'

The origin of his worship, according to the legend, is that a Taoist priest named Li Shaojun obtained from the Kitchen god the double favour of exemption from growing old and of being able to live without eating. He then went to the Han Xiaowudi of the Han dynasty, and promised him that he would benefit by the powers of the god provided that he would consent to patronize and encourage his religion. It was by this means, he added, that the Emperor Huangdi obtained his knowledge of alchemy, which enabled him to make gold.

The Emperor asked the priest to bring him his divine patron, and one night the image of Cao Jun appeared to him. Deceived by this trick, dazzled by the ingots of gold which he too should obtain, and determined to risk everything for the pill of immortality which was among the benefits promised, the Emperor made a solemn sacrifice to the God of the Kitchen. This was the first time that a sacrifice had been officially offered to this new deity.

Li Shaojun gradually lost the confidence of the Emperor and, at his wits' end, conceived the plan of writing some phrases on a piece of silk and then forcing them to be swallowed by an ox. This done, he announced that a wonderful script would be found in the animal's stomach. The ox was killed and the script was found there as predicted, but Li's unlucky star decreed that the Emperor should recognize his handwriting, and he was put to death. Nevertheless, the worship of the Kitchen god continued and increased.

THE GOD OF HAPPINESS

The God of Happiness, Fushen, owes his origin to the fondness of the Liang Wudi of the Liang dynasty for dwarfs as servants and comedians in his palace. The number levied from the Taozhou district in Hunan became greater and greater until one day a Criminal Judge of Tao Chou named Yang Xiji represented to the Emperor that, according to law, the dwarfs were his subjects but not his slaves. Being touched by this remark, the Emperor ordered the levy to be stopped.

Overjoyed at their liberation from this hardship, the people of that district set up images of Yang and offered sacrifices to him. He was revered as the Spirit of Happiness. It was in this simple way that there became a god is worshipped almost as universally as the God of Riches.

THE GOD OF RICHES

As with many other Chinese gods, the God of Wealth, Cai Shen, has been ascribed to several different people. The original and best known until later times was Zhao Gongming. The accounts of him also differ but the following is the most popular.

When Jiang Ziya was fighting for the Zhou dynasty against the last of the Shang emperors, Zhao Gongming, then a hermit on Emei Shan, took the part of the latter.

He performed many wonderful feats. He could ride a black tiger and hurl pearls which burst like bombshells. But he was eventually overcome by the form of witchcraft known in Wales as Ciurp Creadh. Jiang Ziya made a straw image of him, wrote his name on it, burned incense and worshipped before it for twenty days. On the twenty-first day he shot arrows made of peach wood into its eyes and heart. At that same moment Kung-ming, then in the enemy's camp, felt ill and fainted, and uttering a cry gave up the ghost.

Later on Jiang Ziya persuaded Yuanshi Tianzun to release the spirits of the heroes who had died in battle from the Otherworld, and when Zhao Gongming was led into his presence he praised his bravery and canonized him as President of the Ministry of Riches and Prosperity.

The God of Riches is universally worshipped in China. Talismans, trees of which the branches are strings of cash, and the fruits ingots of gold, to be obtained merely by shaking them down, a magic inexhaustible casket full of gold and silver – these and other spiritual sources of wealth are associated with this much-adored deity. He is represented in the guise of a visitor accompanied by a crowd of attendants laden down with all the treasures that the hearts of men, women and children could desire.

THE GOD OF LONGEVITY

The God of Longevity, Shouxing, was first a stellar deity and only later represented in human form. It was a constellation formed of the two star-groups Qiao and Kang, the first two on the list of twenty-eight constellations. Hence it was called the Star of Longevity. When it appears the nation enjoys peace. When it disappears there will be war. Qin Shi Huangdi, the First Emperor, was the first to offer sacrifices to this star, the Old Man of the South Pole, at She Po, in 246 BCE. Since then the worship has been continued regularly until modern times.

But desire for something personal than a star led to this god being represented as an old man. Connected with this is a long legend which turns on the point that after the father of Zhao Yan had been told that his son would not live beyond the age of nineteen, the transposition from shijiu (nineteen) to jiushi (ninety) was made by one of two gamblers, who turned out to be the Spirit of the North Pole. He is the one who fixes the time of death, as the Spirit of the South Pole does of birth.

The deity is a domestic god, usually spoken of as Shouxing Lao Touzi, 'Longevity Star Old-pate'. He is represented as riding a stag, with a flying bat above his head. He holds a large peach in his hand, and attached to his long staff are a gourd and a scroll. The stag and the bat both indicate fu, happiness. The peach, gourd and scroll are symbols of longevity.

THE DOOR GODS

It was the important task of these Gods to ward off undesirable visitors and evil spirits from Chinese households and often pictures of ferocious warriors were pinned on either side of the door for this purpose. In the more modern version of this legend, these pictures represented two war ministers of the Emperor Taizong of Tang. These two ministers of outstanding ability were deified after death to become the Door Gods.

The story unfolds that one day the Emperor fell gravely ill with a high fever and during the night he imagined he heard demons in the passageway attempting to gain entry to his chamber. The Emperor grew increasingly delirious and everyone became concerned for his health. Eventually it was decided that two of his finest warriors, Jin Shubao and Hu Jingde, should stand guard overnight outside his door.

For the first time in many weeks, the Emperor slept soundly and peacefully. Next morning, he thanked his men heartily and from that time onwards his health continued to improve. Soon he felt well enough to release his men from their nocturnal duty, but he ordered them to have their portraits painted, looking as fierce as they possibly could, so that he could paste these on his bedroom door to keep evil spirits away in the future.

FOX LEGENDS

Among the many animals worshipped by the Chinese, those at times seen emerging from coffins or graves naturally hold a prominent place. They are supposed to be the transmigrated souls of deceased human beings. We should therefore expect animals such as the fox, stoat and weasel to be closely associated with the worship of ghosts and spirits and that they should be the subjects of, or included in, a large number of Chinese legends. This we find. Of these animals, the fox is mentioned in Chinese legends perhaps more often than any other.

Generally, the fox is a creature of ill omen, long-lived (living to eight hundred or even a thousand years), with a peculiar virtue in every part of his body, able to produce fire by striking the ground with his tail, cunning, cautious, sceptical, able to see into the future, to transform himself (usually into old men, scholars or pretty young maidens) and fond of playing pranks and tormenting mankind.

FRIENDSHIP WITH FOXES

A certain man had an enormous stack of straw, as big as a hill, in which his servants, taking what they needed, ha made quite a large hole. In this hole a fox made his home and would often show himself to the master of the house under the form of an old man. One day the old man invited the master to come into his home. At first he declined, but after being pressed, he accepted. When he got inside he saw a long suite of handsome apartments.

The pair sat down and exquisitely perfumed tea and wine were brought. But the place was so gloomy that there was no difference between night and day. Once the entertainment was over, the guest took his leave. But as he left he looked back and found that the beautiful rooms and their contents had all disappeared. The old man himself was in the habit of going away in the evening and returning with the first streaks of morning light; and as no one was able to follow him, one day the master of the house asked him where he went. The old man replied that a friend invited him to drink wine. The master begged to be allowed to accompany him, a proposal to which the old man very reluctantly consented. However, he seized the master by the arm and away they went as though riding on the wings of the wind.

They soon reached a city and walked into a restaurant, where there were a number of people drinking together and making a great noise. The old man led his companion to a gallery above, from which they could look down on the feasters below. He himself went down and brought back all kinds of nice food and wine from the tables, without appearing to be seen or noticed by any of the company.

After a while a man dressed in red garments came forward and laid some exquisite dishes on the table. At once the master asked the old man to go down and get him some of these. "Ah," replied the old man, "that is an upright man: I cannot approach him." Considering this, the master said to himself, "By seeking the companionship of a fox, I am deflected from the true course. From now on I too will be an upright man."

No sooner had he formed this resolution than he suddenly lost all control of his body. He fell from the gallery down among the revellers below. These gentlemen were astonished. Looking up, he himself saw there was no gallery to the house – only a large beam on which he had been sitting. He told the revellers the story of how he had come to be in the restaurant. Those present made up a purse for him to pay his travelling expenses; for he was at Yutai – a thousand li from home.

THE MARRIAGE LOTTERY

A certain labourer, named Ma Tianjun, lost his wife when he was just twenty years of age, and was too poor to take another. One day, when out hoeing in the fields, he watched a nice looking young lady leave the path and come tripping across the furrows toward him. She had such a refined look that Ma concluded she must have lost her way and began to make some playful remarks. "You go along home," cried the young lady, "and I'll be with you before long."

Ma doubted this rather extraordinary promise, but she vowed and declared she would not break her word; and then Ma went off, telling her that his front door faced the north. At midnight the young lady arrived. Ma saw that her hands and face were covered with fine hair, which quickly made him suspect that she was a fox. She did not deny the accusation;

and accordingly Ma said to her, "If you really are one of those wonderful creatures you will be able to get me anything I want; and I should be much obliged if you would start by giving me some money to relieve my poverty." The young lady said she would.

The following evening when she came again, Ma asked her where the money was. "Dear me!" replied she, "I forgot it." As she was going away Ma reminded her of what he wanted, but on the following evening she made precisely the same excuse, promising to bring it another day. A few nights afterwards, Ma asked her once more for the money. This time she drew two pieces of silver from her sleeve, each weighing about five or six ounces. They were both of fine quality. Ma was very pleased. He stored them away in a cupboard.

Some months later Ma happened to need some money, so he took out these pieces. However the person he showed them to said they were only pewter, and easily bit off a portion of one of them with his teeth. Ma was alarmed and put the pieces away. When evening came he confronted the young lady. "It's all your bad luck," she retorted.

"Real gold would be too much for your inferior destiny." There was an end of that; but Ma went on to say, "I always heard that fox girls were of surpassing beauty; how is it you are not?" "Oh," replied the young lady, "we always adapt ourselves to our company. Now you haven't the luck of an ounce of silver to call your own; and what would you do, for instance, with a beautiful princess? My beauty may not be good enough for the aristocracy; but among your big-footed, bent-backed rustics, why, it may safely be called 'surpassing'!"

A few months went by, and then one day the young lady came and gave Ma three ounces of silver, saying, "You have often asked me for money, but in consequence of your bad luck I have always refrained from giving you any. Now, however, your marriage is at hand, and I here give you the cost of a wife, which you may also regard as a parting gift from me." Ma replied that he was not engaged, to which the young lady answered that in a few days a go-between would visit him to arrange the affair. "And what will she be like?" asked Ma. "Why, as your aspirations are for 'surpassing' beauty," replied the young lady, "of course she will be possessed of surpassing beauty." "I hardly expect that," said Ma; "at any rate, three ounces of silver will not be enough to get a wife." "Marriages," explained the young lady, "are made in the moon; mortals have nothing to do with them." "And why must you be going away like this?" inquired Ma. "Because," answered she, "for us to meet only by night is not the proper thing. I had better get you another wife and have done with you." Then when morning came she departed, giving Ma a pinch of yellow powder, saying, "In case you are ill after we are separated, this will cure you."

Sure enough, the next day a go-between did come. Ma immediately asked what the proposed bride was like; to which the go-between replied that she was very passable looking. Four or five ounces of silver was fixed as the marriage present. Ma had no difficulty on that score, but declared he must have a peep at the young lady. The go-between said she was a respectable girl and would never allow herself to be seen. However, it was arranged that they should go to the house together, and wait for a good opportunity.

So off they went, Ma remaining outside while the go-between went in, returning in a little while to tell him it was alright. "A relative of mine lives in the same court. Just now I saw the young lady sitting in the hall. We have only got to pretend we are going to see my relative and you will be able to catch a glimpse of her." Ma agreed and so they went through the hall, where he saw the young lady sitting down with her head bent forward while someone was scratching her back. She seemed to be all that the go-between had said; but when they came to discuss the money it appeared that the young lady only wanted one or two ounces of silver, just to buy herself a few clothes. Ma thought this was a very small amount, so he gave the go-between a present for her trouble, which just finished up the three ounces his fox friend had given him. An auspicious day was chosen and the young lady came over to his house. Ma was shocked to discover the girl was humpbacked and pigeon-breasted, with a short neck like a tortoise and feet which were ten inches long! The meaning of his fox friend's remarks then flashed upon him.

THE MAGNANIMOUS GIRL

At Jinling there lived a talented young man named Ku, who was very poor. Having an elderly mother he was reluctant to leave home, so he employed himself in writing or painting for people. Ku always gave his mother the proceeds – going on this way until he was twenty-five years of age without taking a wife. Opposite to their house was another building, which had long been unoccupied. One day an old woman and a

CHINESE MYTHS & LEGENDS

young girl moved in, but there being no gentleman with them young Ku did not make any inquiries as to who they were or where they had come from.

Then one day, just as Ku was entering his house he observed a young lady come out of his mother's door. She was about eighteen or nineteen years old, very clever and refined looking and when she noticed Mr Ku she did not run away, but seemed quite self-possessed.

"It was the young lady over the way; she came to borrow my scissors and measure," said his mother, "and she told me that there is only her mother and herself. They don't seem to belong to the lower classes. I asked her why she didn't get married, to which she replied that her mother was old. I must go and call on her tomorrow and find out how the land lies. If she doesn't expect too much, you could take care of her mother for her."

So the next day Ku's mother went over to the girl's house. She discovered that the girl's mother was deaf and that they were evidently poor, apparently not having a day's food in the house. Ku's mother asked how they were able to survive and the old lady said they trusted for food to her daughter's ten fingers. She then threw out some hints about uniting the two families, to which the old lady seemed to agree. The daughter, however, would not consent. Mrs Ku returned home and told her son, saying, "Perhaps she thinks we are too poor. She doesn't speak or laugh, is very nice looking, and as pure as snow; truly no ordinary girl." That was the end of that.

Until one day, Ku was sitting in his study when a young man arrived at his door. The stranger said he was from a neighbouring village and employed Ku to draw a picture for him. The two youths soon struck up a firm friendship and met regularly. Later it happened that the stranger happened to see the young lady of over the way. "Who is that?" he said, following her with his eyes. Ku told him and then he said, "She is certainly pretty, but rather stern in her appearance."

One day Ku's mother told him the girl had come to beg a little rice, as they had had nothing to eat all day. "She's a good daughter," said his mother, "and I'm very sorry for her. We must try and help them a little." So Ku picked up a sack of rice and, knocking at their door, presented it with his mother's compliments. The young lady took the rice, but said nothing. After that she got into the habit of coming over and helping Ku's mother with her work and household affairs, almost as if she had been her daughter-in-law, for which Ku was very grateful to her. Whenever he had anything nice he always sent some of it in to her mother, though the young lady herself never once took the trouble to thank him.

So things went on until Ku's mother got an abscess on her leg. She lay writhing in agony day and night. Then the young lady devoted herself to the invalid, waiting on her and giving her medicine with such care and attention that at last the sick woman cried out, "Oh that I could secure such a daughter-in-law as you to see this old body into its grave!" The young lady soothed her and replied, "Your son is a hundred times more filial than I, a poor widow's only daughter." "But even a filial son makes a bad nurse," answered the patient; "besides, I am now drawing toward the evening of my life, when my body will be exposed to the mists and the dews, and I am deeply saddened about our ancestral worship and the continuance of our line." As she was speaking Ku walked in. His mother, weeping, said, "I am deeply indebted to this young lady; do not forget to repay her goodness." Ku made a low bow, but the young lady said, "Sir, when you were kind to my mother, I did not thank you; why then thank me?" Ku was becoming more attached to her than ever, but could never get her to show him the slightest warmth from her cold demeanour toward him. One day, however, he managed to squeeze her hand, after which she told him never to do so again. Then for some time he neither saw nor heard anything of her.

She had taken a violent dislike to the young stranger who had befriended Ku. One evening, when he was sitting talking with Ku, the young lady appeared. After a while she got angry at something he said. She drew from her robe a glittering knife about a foot long. The young man, seeing her do this, ran out in terror. She ran after him, only to find that he had vanished. She then threw her dagger up into the air, and with a streak of light like a rainbow, something came tumbling down with a flop. Ku grabbed a light and ran to see what it was. There lay a white fox, head in one place and body in another. "There is your friend," cried the girl, "I knew he would cause me to destroy him sooner or later." Ku dragged it into the house and said, "Let's wait until tomorrow to talk it over; we will be calmer then."

When the young lady arrived the following day Ku inquired about her knowledge of the black art. She told Ku not to trouble himself about such things and to keep it secret or it might be prejudicial to his happiness. Ku then pleaded with her to consent to their union, to which she replied that she had already been as it were a daughter-in-law to his mother, and there was no need to push the thing further. "Is it because I am poor?" asked Ku. "Well, I am not rich," she answered, "but the fact is I had rather not." Then she left. The next evening when

Ku went across to their house to try once more to persuade her the young lady had disappeared, and was never seen again.

THE BOON-COMPANION

Once upon a time there was a young man named Che, who was not particularly well off, but at the same time very fond of his wine; so much so that without his three cups of liquor every night he was quite unable to sleep. Bottles were seldom absent from the head of his bed.

One night he had woken up and was turning over and over, when he imagined someone was in the bed with him. But then, thinking it was only the clothes that had slipped off, he put out his hand to feel and in doing so touched something silky like a cat. Striking a light, he found it was a fox, lying in a drunken sleep like a dog. Then looking at his wine bottle he saw that it had been emptied. "A boon-companion," he said laughing. To avoid startling the animal, he covered it up and lay down to sleep with his arm across it, leaving the candle alight so as to see what transformation it might undergo. About midnight the fox stretched itself and Che cried, "Well, to be sure, you've had a nice sleep!" He then drew off the clothes and saw an elegant young man in a scholar's dress; but the young man jumped up, and, bowing low, returned his host many thanks for not cutting off his head. "Oh," replied Che, "I am not averse to liquor myself; in fact they say I'm too much given to it. If you have no objection, we'll be a pair of drinking chums." So they lay down and went to sleep again, Che urging the young man to visit him often, saying that they must have faith in each other.

The fox agreed to this, but when Che awoke in the morning his bedfellow had already disappeared.

That evening he prepared a goblet of first-rate wine in expectation of his friend's arrival. At nightfall sure enough he came. They then sat together drinking and the fox cracked so many jokes that Che said he regretted he had not known him before. "And truly I don't know how to repay your kindness," replied the fox, "in preparing all this nice wine for me." "Oh," said Che, "what's a pint or so of wine? Nothing worth speaking of." "Well," replied the fox, "you are only a poor scholar and money isn't so easy to get. I must see if I can't secure a little wine capital for you." The next evening when he arrived he said to Che, "Two miles down toward the south-east you will find some silver lying by the wayside. Go early in the morning and get it." So in the morning Che set off and actually obtained two lumps of silver, with which he bought some choice morsels to help them out with their wine that evening. The fox now told him that there was a vault in his backyard which he ought to open; and when he did so he found more than a hundred strings of cash. "Now then," cried Che, delighted, "I shall have no more anxiety about funds for buying wine with all this in my purse!" "Ah," replied the fox, "the water in a puddle is not inexhaustible. I must do something further for you." Some days afterward the fox said to Che, "Buckwheat is very cheap in the market just now. Something is to be done in that line." Accordingly Che bought over forty tons, much to the ridicule of others; but before long there was a bad drought and all kinds of grain and beans were spoilt. Only buckwheat would grow, and Che sold off his stock at a profit of one thousand per cent. With his wealth beginning to increase, he bought two hundred acres of rich land and always planted his crops – corn, millet, or what not – on the advice of the fox secretly given to him beforehand. The fox looked on Che's wife as a sister and on Che's children as his own, but when Che later died it never came to the house again.

JIA ZILONG FINDS THE STONE

At Chang'an there lived a scholar named Jia Zilong, who one day noticed a very refined looking stranger. After making inquiries about him, Chia learned that he was a Mr Chen who had taken lodgings nearby. Accordingly, Chia called on him the next day and sent in his card, but did not see Chen, who happened to be out at the time. The same thing happened three times and eventually Chia employed someone to watch and let him know when Mr Chen was at home. However, even then the latter would not come out to receive his guest and Chia had to go in and find him. The two then entered into conversation and soon became mutually charmed with each other.

Before long Chia sent off a servant to bring wine from a neighbouring wine shop. Mr Chen proved himself a pleasant companion, and when the wine was nearly finished he went to a box and took some wine cups from it and a large and beautiful jade tankard. Into the tankard he poured a single cup of wine and immediately it was filled to the brim. They then began to help themselves from the tankard; but however much they took out, the contents never seemed to diminish. Chia was astonished at this and begged Mr Chen to tell him how it was done. "Ah," replied Mr Chen, "I tried to avoid making your acquaintance solely because of your one bad quality – avarice. The art I practise is a secret known only to the Immortals: how can I divulge it to you?" "You do me wrong," rejoined Chia, "in attributing avarice to me. The avaricious, indeed, are always poor." Mr Chen laughed, and they separated for that day; but from that time they were constantly together, and all ceremony between them was laid aside.

Whenever Chia wanted money Mr Chen would bring out a black stone and, muttering a charm, would rub it on a tile or a brick, which was instantly changed into a lump of silver. This silver he would give to Chia. It was always just as much as he actually needed, no more no less; and if ever Chia asked for more Mr Chen would rally him on the subject of avarice.

Finally Chia determined to try to get possession of this stone; and one day, when Mr Chen was sleeping off the fumes of a drinking bout, he tried to extract it from his clothes. However, Chen detected him at once and declared that they could no longer be friends. The next day he left the place altogether.

About a year later Chia was wandering by the riverbank, when he saw a handsome looking stone, similar to that in the possession of Mr Chen. He picked it up and carried it home with him at once. After a few days had passed, suddenly Mr Chen himself arrived at Chia's house. He explained that the stone in question possessed the property of changing anything into gold, and that it had been given to him long before by a certain Taoist priest whom he had followed as a disciple. "Alas!" he added, "I got tipsy and lost it; but divination told me where it was, and if you will now restore it to me I will take care to repay your kindness." "You have divined rightly," Chia replied; "the stone is with me; but remember, if you please, that the poor Guan Zhong shared the wealth of his friend Bao Shu." At this hint Mr Chen said he would give Chia one hundred ounces of silver. Chia replied that one hundred ounces was a fair offer, but that he would far sooner have Mr Chen teach him the formula to utter when rubbing the stone on anything, so that he might try the thing once himself. But Mr Chen was afraid to do this.

Chia cried out, "You are an Immortal yourself; you must know well enough that I would never deceive a friend." So Mr Chen was persuaded to teach him the formula. Chia would have tried the art on the immense stone washing block which was lying close at hand had Mr Chen not seized his arm and begged him not to do anything so outrageous. Chia then picked up half a brick and laid it on the washing block, saying to Mr Chen, "This little piece is not too much, surely?" Accordingly Mr Chen relaxed his hold and let Chia proceed, which he did by promptly ignoring the half brick and quickly rubbing the stone on the washing block. Mr Chen turned pale when he saw him do this. He made a dash forward to get hold of the stone, but it was too late; the washing- block was already a solid mass of silver. Chia quietly handed him back the stone. "Alas! Alas!" cried Mr Chen in despair, "What is to be done now? For, having granted such wealth on a mortal, Heaven will surely punish me. Oh, if you would save me, give away one hundred coffins and one hundred suits of wadded clothes." "My friend," replied Chia, "my object in getting money was not to hoard it up like a miser." Mr Chen was delighted at this.

During the next three years Chia engaged in trade, always taking care to fulfil his promise to Mr Chen. Then one day

Mr Chen reappeared and, grasping Chia's hand, said to him, "Trustworthy and noble friend, when we last parted the Spirit of Happiness impeached me before God and my name was erased from the list of angels. But now that you have carried out my request that sentence has been rescinded. Go on as you have begun, without ceasing." Chia asked Mr Chen what office he filled in Heaven; to which the latter replied that he was only a fox who, by a sinless life, had finally attained to that clear perception of the truth which leads to immortality. Wine was then brought, and the two friends enjoyed themselves together as of old; and even when Chia had passed ninety years of age the fox still used to visit him from time to time.

THE CRANE MAIDEN &
OTHER FABLES

The tales that follow demonstrate the mixture of beliefs and religions that were a part of ancient China. In many of the stories the immortal Gods and human beings interact, not exactly as equals, but not within the rigid hierarchy one might expect; it is perfectly feasible, even customary, for the daughter of a God to marry a human, and for such marriages to be successful. Often, we are also transported into a world of spirits and demons, capable of inhabiting animals with malicious intent. Similarly, humans can become transformed into animals or birds, either as a punishment, through grief, or through the will of the Gods.

The image which we perhaps associate most with Chinese myth is that of the dragon. The Chinese dragon breathes cloud, not fire, and is a creature of awesome beauty. Although quick to anger and terrible in its fury, the dragon was mostly a force for good, representing the male principle, the yang, just as the phoenix represents the female, the yin. Similarly, the monkey represents the irrepressibility of the human spirit, as well as its tendency to mischief and evil.

Most of the tales told here do not have such a formal meaning. Some may try to explain how various animals came into being, others might be parables illustrating foolishness, or steadfastness, or wisdom. But above all they are for entertainment and enjoyment, telling of a mythical time when Gods and dragons walked the earth, and when human destiny was determined by magic spirits.

HOW MONKEY BECAME IMMORTAL

Monkey had been born from a stone egg on top of the Mountain of Fruit and Flowers, and had received many special powers from the stone. He had led his tribe of monkeys to a safe home behind a waterfall on top of the mountain of his birth, and become their beloved king, ruling wisely for hundreds of years. Their way of life was extremely pleasant, they had all they needed to eat and drink, and were safe from enemies. Yet Monkey was not content.

"However happy we are here," he told his followers, "we still have Death to fear. One day Lord Yama of the Underworld will send for us, and we will have to obey. I have heard of Lord Buddha and the other Gods who cannot die, and I intend to find them and learn the secret of immortality."

Monkey set off for the world of men, and soon learned the whereabouts of a holy man, Master Subhodi, who knew the way to eternal life. Subhodi knew in advance of Monkey's coming, and realizing this was no ordinary animal, accepted him as a pupil, and gave him a new name: Sun, the Enlightened One. Monkey spent twenty years with Master Subhodi, learning of the road to eternal life, and many other skills. He learned to change his shape as he pleased, and to travel thousands of miles in a single leap. And armed with this knowledge he returned to his home.

There he found that a demon had taken control of his tribe, and although he conquered the demon, Monkey realized he needed a proper weapon for the future. He seized upon the iron pillar of the Dragon King of the Eastern Sea. This could be changed at will, from an eight-foot staff for fighting, to a tiny needle that Monkey could carry behind his ear, and he kept it with him at all times.

One day two men came for him with a warrant of death from Lord Yama, and tried to drag his soul to the Underworld. Monkey cried out in vain that he knew the way to eternal life, for the men only tied him more tightly. With a desperate struggle, Monkey freed himself, and taking the needle from behind his ear, turned it into a staff, and knocked the men to the ground. Then, incensed with rage, Monkey charged into the Underworld itself, beating anyone in his way with his cudgel.

"Bring out the register of the dead," he demanded. The book was brought to him by the terrified judges, whereupon he found the page with his name on, and the names of all his tribe, and ripped it from the register, tearing it into a thousand pieces. "Now I am free from your power," he cried, and charged back out of the Underworld to his own land. The other monkeys assured him he had been asleep, and must have dreamt all this, but Monkey knew in his heart that it had really happened, and that death held no more sway over them.

Appalled by the trouble Monkey was causing, the Jade Emperor, the most powerful God, offered him high office in Heaven, so that the Gods could secretly keep him under their control. Monkey gladly accepted and was made Master of the Heavenly Stables, but he soon realized this was a derisory post, created only to tame him, and he stormed out of Heaven and returned home. The Jade Emperor sent guards to recapture him, but Monkey defeated them, and the Gods sent to seize him. Eventually the Jade Emperor appeased him by offering him a magnificent palace in Heaven, and a proper position as Superintendent of the Heavenly Peach Garden.

Now Monkey knew that the peaches in this garden, which ripened only once every six thousand years, conferred immortality on anyone who ate them, and so he ignored the order not to touch any of them, and devoured a huge number. Unstoppable now, and furious too that he had not been invited to the great Feast of Peaches, given to the Gods by Wangmu, Goddess of the Immortals, Monkey was intent on revenge. So, when the preparations were complete, he put all the servants under a spell, and ate and drank all the food and wine prepared for the guests. Dizzy with drink, Monkey staggered into the deserted palace of Lao Chun, where he stumbled across the five gourds in which were kept the seeds of immortality, and, ever inquisitive, he ate them all. Assured doubly of immortality, Monkey returned home.

The Jade Emperor and all the Gods and Goddesses were furious with monkey, but none could defeat him in battle. Until, that is, the Jade Emperor's nephew, Erlang, aided by Lao Chun and the celestial dog Tiankou, managed to chain him, and bring him, securely bound, back to Heaven. Monkey was sentenced to death, and placed in Lao Chun's furnace, in which the seeds of immortality were made. But Monkey was now so powerful that he burst free from the crucible, stronger than ever, and proclaimed himself ruler of the Universe.

At this, Buddha appeared, and demanded of Monkey what powers he had that entitled him to make such a claim. Monkey replied that he was immortal, invulnerable, that he could change shape at will, and could travel thousands of miles in a single leap. Buddha smiled, and taking Monkey in the palm of his hand, said, "If you can jump from out of my hand, I will make you ruler of the Universe and all it contains."

Monkey laughed at this, and in two mighty leaps found himself opposite the five red pillars that mark the edge of the Universe. Delighted, he wrote his name on one of them as proof that he had been there, and returned to the Buddha.

"I have been to the ends of the Universe in two bounds," he bragged. "And now I seek my reward."

"The ends of the Universe?" asked the Buddha, "You never left the palm of my hand." And Buddha showed Monkey his fingers, on one of which was Monkey's name in his own writing. Monkey realized the five pillars were merely the five fingers of the Buddha, and that the whole Universe was contained in his hand, and that he could never be defeated. Afraid for the first time in his life, Monkey tried to run away, but Buddha closed his hand over him, and changing his fingers into the five elements of earth, air, fire, water and wood, created a great mountain in which he imprisoned Monkey.

"There you must stay until you have fully repented and are free of your sins," Buddha told him. "At that time someone will come and intercede for you, and then you may be free." And crushed under the mountains the dejected Monkey was forced to stay.

THE PAIR OF FOOLS

Once, a poor villager called Lin unexpectedly found ten pieces of silver, riches beyond anything he had ever owned before. After his first flush of exhilaration at finding such wealth, Lin realized that he must hide the money, as he worked in the fields all day, and it could so easily be stolen from him. He looked despairingly around his sparse, mud-walled hut for a hiding place for the silver, but there was no furniture, no secret cupboards, nothing. Then suddenly he thought of the wall itself, and pausing only to check through the door that no one was coming, he hollowed out a cavity in the mud wall, and poured the silver pieces into it. He quickly covered the hole with fresh mud, and guarded his door against all visitors until the mud had dried and there was no sign of the hiding place.

However, the next morning, before he left for the fields, Lin had another attack of nerves. If someone did come into his hut looking for money, there was only one place it could be hidden. There was no furniture, no secret cupboards, only the wall itself. It would be the first place any thief would look. Then Lin had a flash of inspiration, and picking up his brush and ink, he wrote on the wall: "There are no silver pieces hidden in this wall." Reassured, he went off to the fields for his day's work.

A few hours later Lin's neighbour, Wan, came to look for him. Seeing no sign of Lin, his eyes were drawn to the writing on the wall, and he chuckled to himself: "Of course there are no silver pieces hidden in the wall, why should there be?" Then a second thought struck him: Why would Lin say there weren't any, unless there actually were?

Pausing only to check through the door that no one was coming, Wan attacked the wall with vigour and found the ten pieces of silver almost immediately. Delighted, he ran home with them to his own hut, where he was struck by an attack of nerves. What if they searched his hut and found the money, and he was taken before the Judge and tortured until he confessed, and then sentenced to death? He must stop anyone from suspecting his guilt. Suddenly, Wan had a flash of inspiration, and picking up his brush and ink, he wrote on the front of his door: "I, Wan, an honest man, did not steal the ten silver pieces from the hole in the wall of Lin's hut."

THE SILKWORM

Many centuries ago a certain man was called up to fight for his Emperor, in the war that was raging on the Chinese borders far, far from his home. The man was distraught at leaving his wife and family, but, being a loyal subject he promptly went away to fulfil his duty. As he left, he instructed the family to look after their farm as best they could, and not to worry unduly as to his fate in the battles that were to come, as all life is in the hands of the Gods.

Try though they might to obey his parting instructions, the family missed him terribly, none more so than his daughter. In her loneliness, the young girl took solace in tending the family's horse, a creature that had been her father's for many years, and one that he loved dearly. Every day she would tenderly groom its fine coat, brush its silky mane, and make sure it had clean hay and enough oats to eat, talking to it all the while about how much she missed her father, and how she prayed nightly for his return. However, what little news reached them from the borders became more and more alarming, and the family began to doubt in their hearts if they would ever see their husband and father again.

One day, the daughter was in the stable tending the old horse and thinking of her father, barely able to hold back her tears in her fear for his safety. "If only you could gallop from here to the wars and rescue him from his peril," she murmured. "If anyone could do that, I swear that I would gladly marry him at once, and serve him joyfully all my days, whatever his state or situation in life."

Immediately the horse reared up violently, and with a loud whinny, tore at the leash that held him, breaking it in two, although it was made of the strongest leather. With a mighty kick of its powerful front legs, it splintered the stable door and galloped across the courtyard and out of sight before the startled girl could stop it, or even call out to the servants. When it became clear that the horse was not going to return, she made her way sadly to the house to tell of its disappearance, not mentioning the oath she had sworn in front of the animal.

Many days later, the runaway horse reached the Chinese borders, and despite the confusion and destruction caused by the war, managed to find its owner in the camp where he was billeted. The man was astonished to see his old horse, and even more surprised when he could find no message from his family on the animal. Immediately, he feared the worst, and became convinced that some disaster had befallen them, and although he was a brave and true subject, his fears for his family overcame his loyalty.

He secretly saddled up the horse, and under cover of darkness he eluded the guards and galloped as fast as possible back to his homeland, and to his farm.

His family were amazed and delighted to find him home again; tears of joy rolled down their cheeks seeing him alive and unharmed by the horrors of war. Only his daughter seemed less than overwhelmed by his return, and avoided his gaze whenever he looked at her, and answered his questions briefly, without emotion. The man was surprised to find nothing amiss in the household, after all his fears and misgivings, but presumed that the horse had come to fetch him out of devotion, and an understanding that his family missed him so much. In gratitude he lavished attention on the faithful beast, gave it the best oats and hay and the finest stable, and groomed it himself. The horse, however, refused all food and kindness, and just moped in the corner of its stall, making no sound at all. Only when the daughter of the house came near, which she did as rarely as possible, did the animal seem to come alive; then it would rear up, and whinny and froth at the mouth, so that it took several servants to restrain it.

The father became increasingly worried about the horse, which was becoming distressingly thin. Noticing the effect his daughter had on the beast, he asked her one day if she knew why the animal was behaving in so peculiar a fashion. At first the young girl lied, and said she has no idea of the cause of the problem, but eventually, because she was an honest girl, she told her father of the promise she had made in the stable to marry whomsoever would return her father to her, whatever his state or station in life. The father became extremely angry at her lack of sense and modesty, and confined the girl to her room in the house. He forbade her to so much as peep out of the door if the horse was in the courtyard, so as not to disturb it further; for although the man was very grateful to the horse for its years of service, and its intelligence in finding him in the front lines, he still could not imagine allowing a dumb animal to marry his daughter.

The horse continued to pine and mope, and deprived of even a glimpse of the girl, wasted away more and more, day by day. Eventually the father realized there was only one thing he could do, and sadly he took up his bow and arrow and shot the horse to put it out of its misery. The animal gave a piteous whimper, and died, still looking at the house in which it knew the daughter was imprisoned. The man took off the horse's skin, and placed it in the sun to dry, and then went to tell his daughter what he had been compelled to do. She was thrilled to hear that her problem was solved, and that she would not have to marry a horse, and ran into the courtyard to greet the sun for the first time in days. As she passed the dead creature's hide, it suddenly lifted as if on a gust of wind, and wrapped itself tightly around the girl's shoulders, and then her whole body, and started to spin her round like a top. Whirling faster and faster, the girl cried out, but no one could stop her, and she disappeared out of the farm and into the countryside, carried away on the wind, her cries growing ever fainter.

Appalled, her father ran after the whirlwind his daughter had become, and followed it for many days, although it appeared to get smaller and smaller the further it travelled, until it was barely visible to the naked eye. At last, the whirlwind stopped by a mulberry bush, and breathlessly, the exhausted father rushed up to it. There, on a mulberry bough, he found a small worm feeding on the leaf, and seeing that this was all that was left of his daughter, he took it home, grieving in his heart. He and his wife cared for the worm with tenderness, feeding it thick mulberry leaves every day, and after a week the worm produced a fine thread that glistened and shone, and was soft and cool when woven, and more beautiful to look at than any cloth they had ever seen. They called it silk, and bred more and more of the worms, which became famous throughout the land. And in time silk became one of China's most acclaimed and desired products, and many people profited through its sale, so that in years to come silk weavers throughout the country worshipped thankfully the silkworm girl who had given them such a great treasure through her love for her father.

THE CRANE MAIDEN

Tian Kunlun was a bachelor, who lived alone with his elderly mother whose one desire in life was to see her son happily married before she died. It was a desire that Tian keenly shared, but they had little money, and he had little chance of finding a suitable bride.

Not far from their home was a beautiful pool of clear, fresh water, shaded by willows, and fringed with rushes. One day, as Tian was on his way to the fields, he heard the sound of girls' laughter coming from the pool, and creeping as silently as he could through the rushes, Tian edged nearer to the water to see whose voice sounded so sweet. Before him he saw three of the loveliest maidens he had ever set eyes on, playing and splashing in the pool, their clothes piled on the bank near him. Entranced, Tian watched for a while, gazing at their beauty, when suddenly he sneezed loudly.

Instantly the three young women turned into three white cranes, and beating their fine wings, they flew from the water. Two of them swooped and picked up their clothes and soared away, up and up into the clear sky, but the third was not fast enough, and Tian managed to reach her clothes before her. The bird circled him for a moment, and then returned to the water, again taking on the form of the beautiful maiden Tian had seen first. Bashfully, she begged him to return her clothes, but first he insisted on knowing who she was.

"I am a daughter of the High God, and those were two of my sisters," the girl answered. "Our father gave us the clothes to pass between Heaven and earth; without them I cannot return to our home." Again the girl pleaded with Tian to return them, adding, "If you do give them back I shall gladly become your wife."

Tian accepted the offer, thinking what a perfect wife the daughter of the High God would make any man, but he feared that if he returned her clothes, she would simply fly away, and he would never see her again. Instead, he gave her his own coat and leggings, and carried her clothes home with him; the crane maiden unwillingly following behind him.

Tian's mother was thrilled that her son was to marry such a beautiful and high-born girl, and their wedding feast was long and lavish, all their friends and neighbours sharing in their joy. The couple lived together, and learned to love each other, and after a time they had a son, whom they called Tian Zhang, and on whom they both doted.

Some years later, Tian was called away to fight in the wars on the borders of China, many many miles from his home. Before he left, he called his mother to him and showed her his wife's celestial clothes and begged her to keep them well hidden, so that she could never put them on and fly away to Heaven. She promised she would, and found a safe hiding place. Tian then said a tearful farewell to his wife and son, and set off for the wars.

After his departure, the young wife asked her mother-in-law every day for a look at her old clothes, just one quick look.

"If you will let me see them only the once I shall be happy," she told the old lady. Seeing how desperate the girl was to see them, and fearing for her health if she continued as she was, the woman relented. She fetched the clothes from the bottom of a large chest in her own room, and showed them to her. The crane maiden wept with joy to see them and hugged them to her breast. Then, in a flash, she threw off her human clothes, put on the celestial garments, and, instantly was transformed into a beautiful white crane. Then she flew out the window before the old lady could stop her, up, up into the clear sky.

When Tian returned from the wars, his mother told him the news of the crane maiden's flight, but both knew that there was nothing they could do to bring her back. Tian readily forgave his mother, but his little son was inconsolable, always crying out her name, and looking longingly out of the window, hoping she would return. He wandered the fields looking for her, weeping, and would accept no comfort from his father or grandmother. One day his cries were heard by a wise old man who sat beneath a willow, and who knew the cause of the boy's grief.

"Go to the pool near your home," he told the child, "and you will see three ladies all dressed in white; the one that ignores you will be your mother."

Tian Zhang did as he was told, and sure enough, there were three girls all in white silk, as the wise man had said. There was the crane maiden, who had so missed her little son, that she had begged her sisters to accompany her back to earth to see that he was happy and well cared for, and to look once more at his face. Tian Zhang boldly walked up to the women, and two of them cried out, "Sister, here is your child to see you," but the crane maiden looked away, her eyes wet with tears of guilt and joy intermingled. The boy then knew that this was his mother, and ran to her, and seeing this, the girl broke down and took him in her arms, embracing him as if she would never let him go, weeping, and crying, "My son, my son."

After some time, one of the sisters said, "Sister, it is time for us to go. If you cannot bear to be parted from the child, we will take him back to Heaven with us."

Between them they lifted the child and flew up, up into the clear sky, all the way to the palace of the High God. He was delighted his daughter was no longer unhappy, and also greatly taken with his grandson, whom he taught personally, telling him of all the things of Heaven and earth. The child was quick to learn, and after a few days the High God gave him eight books, and sent him back to earth with these words: "Study well, my son, for all knowledge is in these, and you may use them to give great benefit to the earth."

So Tian Zhang returned to earth, where he found that not a few days, but twenty years had passed on earth, and that he was a young man. He tried to find his earthly family, but his grandmother had died, and his father left for the mountains of the West in grief for having lost mother, wife and child. So Tian Zhang devoted his life to studying the eight books, and armed with the knowledge the High God had given him, he became a renowned scholar and judge. He was granted a high place at the Emperor's court, and was famed throughout the land for his wisdom and his desire to help mankind.

And thousands of miles away, in the mountains of the West, the aged Tian heard of his son's fame, and was content.

THE CUCKOO

There was once a God called Wang, who lived in Heaven, but whose love for the earth and its people was so great that he used to visit it regularly, using his powers to help struggling humanity, and to right wrongs. On one such visit he met a woman, like him an immortal, who had been forced from her original home at the bottom of a deep well, and was now living in the kingdom of Shu, which we would now call Sichuan. The two immortals fell instantly in love with each other, and were soon married; Wang left his home in Heaven and came to live in Shu with his new bride, where they reigned together as king and queen.

Wang and his wife were excellent rulers, kind and caring. Wang taught the farmers how to get the most from their land, which crops would grow best, and how to observe the seasons, so that soon the whole kingdom prospered. Amid all this peace and happiness, only one thing still troubled Wang, the one thing over which he had no power to help his people. Every year the mighty Yangzi river would flood, breaking its banks and destroying vast tracts of farming land, sweeping across all before it, crops, livestock, and people alike. Try as he might, with all the powers of an immortal, Wang could do nothing to control this force of nature, and he bitterly grieved over his impotence.

One day a messenger came to Wang's palace to report a miracle: a corpse had been found floating in the great Yangzi, but floating upstream against the current. Moreover, as soon as the body had been pulled out of the river, it had revived and asked to see the king. Amazed at this report, Wang had the stranger brought before him, and asked him his story. The man said that he came from Chu, several thousand miles downstream from where they now stood, and that he had tripped over a log and fallen into the river. He was unable to explain why he had drifted upstream, but he impressed Wang enormously with his knowledge and understanding of the river and its ways, and he talked of the methods they used in Chu to control the floods, and the damage they could cause. Wang immediately asked the stranger if he could help with their problem, and when the man agreed to try, Wang made him Minister of the River, and accorded him much honour at court.

Not many weeks had passed before the river came into flood again, and the new Minister journeyed far along its banks to try and determine the cause. It did not take him long to find his answer: in the higher country the river ran through a series of ravines too narrow to take the flood waters caused by melting snow on the mountain peaks. This made the river break its banks. He instructed engineers to bore drainage channels through the rock from the main channel, allowing the water to disperse safely, and so preventing flooding further downstream in the valuable farmlands.

Wang was so ashamed that he had not thought of this himself, and so impressed by the stranger's abilities as an engineer, that he decided the stranger would make a better king for his people than himself. Accordingly, he gave over the kingship to the Minister and secretly left the court to go and live in isolation in the mountains of the West. He had been there a very short time, however, when rumours reached him of a disturbing nature. It was said that while the man from Chu had been in the mountains, Wang had seduced his wife, who had come to court only recently, and that the stranger, on his return, had found the two of them together. The rumour told that Wang had handed over the throne in shame and guilt, in return for the man's silence, and had been banished to a life in exile.

So stricken was Wang on hearing this vile and ungrateful gossip, and so regretful of his act of generosity in handing over the throne for the good of his people, that he wasted away in his mountain retreat, and died broken-hearted. The Gods turned his spirit into a cuckoo, whose mournful cry in Chinese calls out 'Better return', reminding people for all time, and especially in the Spring at the time of planting, of Wang's grief at leaving his people, and the land of Shu that he loved.

THE WOODEN BRIDGE INN

There was once a travelling merchant called Zhao, whose trade took him all over China, and who prided himself on knowing all the roads, and all the inns on those roads, throughout the country. One day, however, finding himself in a strange district with his donkey tiring by the mile, he had to admit his ignorance of the area, so he stopped to ask a farmer where he could find accommodation for the night, and, if possible, purchase a new donkey as he had much further to travel.

The farmer replied that travellers always stayed at the Wooden Bridge Inn, run by a woman called Third Lady.

"And does this Third Lady sell donkeys?" Zhao asked the man. "Oh, yes. Best donkeys in the district," the man replied. But when Zhao asked where these fine animals came from, the man looked uneasy, and would not look Zhao in the eye. "Better ask her that," he said, "I have absolutely no idea, I'm afraid." And without further comment, he returned quickly to his field, and did not look back.

Zhao walked his weary animal the mile or so to the Wooden Bridge Inn, which was an inviting and comfortable building, presided over by a young woman who greeted Zhao warmly. She introduced herself as Third Lady, and invited him to join the six or seven other guests, who were already drinking cups of wine. Zhao stabled his donkey around the back, and joined the others for a delicious dinner of fish, vegetables and rice. While chatting to the other merchants, he admired their capable hostess's ability to make them all welcome, plying her guests with wine until they were quite drunk. Zhao, however, was not a drinking man, and left the wine alone, preferring to drink only tea.

As midnight approached, the other guests soon fell into a drunken slumber, and Zhao was given a clean and comfortable bed alongside a rush partition, where he lay for a while, musing on his fortune in finding such a pleasant resting place. Just as he was about to drift into sleep, he was startled by a low rumble on the other side of the partition, and fearful that someone might be doing harm to his hostess, he peered through a chink in the rush matting. There was Third Lady, alone, dragging a large trunk across the floor of her room, and Zhao watched as she knelt before it, opened the lid, and took out a little wooden man. Intrigued, Zhao watched as she next brought out a little wooden ox and a little wooden plough, hitched them together and set the man behind the plough. Then, from a small phial, she sprinkled water over the figures, and to Zhao's utter amazement, they began to move, and in no time at all had ploughed up the floor of the room.

Third Lady then gave a tiny seed basket to the little man, who proceeded to sow the field that the floor had become, and immediately green shoots of wheat sprang from the soil, ripened, and were harvested by the tiny farmer, who gave the crop to his mistress. Third Lady quickly ground the corn into flour, and under Zhao's astonished gaze, made cakes from it, which she put into the oven to bake. She returned the now lifeless figures to the trunk, and pushed it back to the corner of the room. She then retired for the night, leaving Zhao to lie alone in the darkness, wondering at what he had witnessed.

When dawn broke, the guests arose, and Third Lady courteously offered them a breakfast of tea and freshly baked wheat cakes. Zhao thanked her profusely, but was determined not to eat his cake, hiding it up his sleeve instead. He then went to fetch his donkey from the stable, ready for the next stage of his journey. As he left the Wooden Bridge Inn, he happened to glance through the door, and he froze in astonishment. The other guests, finishing off their cakes, all suddenly became frenzied, their clothes turning into rough animal hair, their ears growing absurdly long, their voices changing to a grating bray. Within minutes the room was filled with six or seven donkeys, which Third Lady promptly herded with a stick out of the back of the Inn, towards the stables.

Zhao hurried his donkey on its way, grateful to have escaped such a terrible fate; he went on to the capital where his business was, saying not a word to anyone about what he had seen. And when he had concluded his trade, he prepared to return home, stopping off only to buy some wheat cakes identical to the ones Third Lady had made for her guests.

On his return journey, he again stayed at the Wooden Bridge Inn, where the hostess welcomed him warmly. This time Zhao was the only guest, and Third Lady cooked him an excellent dinner, and bade him drink the wine freely, which he again declined. At midnight, he retired to the same comfortable bed, and was roused again some time later by the same low, rumbling noise of the trunk being pulled into position. Zhao did not even bother to look through the partition, he just allowed himself to drift away into a deep sleep.

The next morning, Third Lady again offered him tea and wheat cakes, but Zhao, bringing out those he had bought in the city, said, "Gracious Lady, please try one of these, they are from the capital, and are said to be particularly fine," and he handed her the cake of her own making that he had taken a few days before. Third Lady had little option but to thank him, and eat the cake. She took only one bite and immediately her hair grew rough, her ears grew absurdly long, and she turned into a donkey. Zhao examined the beast, and was delighted to find it was a strong, powerful beast, infinitely superior to his own decrepit animal, which he promptly set free. Staying only long enough to open the trunk, take out the figures and burn them, so they could do no more harm, Zhao then spurred his new mount homewards.

For five years Zhao had excellent service from his strange donkey, until one day he was riding through Chang'an. An old man came up to him, and looking at the donkey, cried 'Third Lady of the Wooden Bridge Inn! I would hardly have recognized you. How you have changed!' Then turning to Zhao, he said 'I congratulate you on preventing her from causing more grief but she has served her penance now. Please let her go free. Zhao dismounted, and unloaded the beast, which brayed loudly in gratitude. The old man took his sword, and split the creature's stomach in two, and out sprang Third Lady. With a cry of shame, and without looking at Zhao or the old man, she ran into the wilderness, and no living person ever saw or heard from her again.

THE THREE PRECIOUS PACKETS

In the freezing depths of a particularly severe winter, a poor student called Niu was travelling to the capital to take his law examinations, so that he could start on the ladder of success that might eventually lead to him becoming magistrate. As the snow fell, and night darkened around him, Niu stopped at a small inn for some food and shelter. His meagre finances allowed him a bowl of noodles, and some he rice-wine, and he sat contentedly warming himself in front of the fire.

Suddenly, the door of the inn was thrown open, and in a flurry of snow, an old man staggered into the room. He was dressed in rags, had no shoes on his feet, and was clearly half-frozen, his teeth chattering too much to allow him to speak. Without waiting to be asked, Niu leapt from his seat and offered the man his place in front of the fire, which the wretch took with a grateful nod. Soon he began to recover, but when the landlord asked him what he wanted, he replied, "I only have money for a bowl of tea, and then I will be off again." The landlord grunted and went off to get the tea, but Niu, poor though he was, could not bear to think of the man having to face the freezing weather again that night without food. He insisted that the man share his noodles, and when they were rapidly eaten, he ordered more, and then more still, until the stranger had eaten five full bowls. He then stood to go, but Niu insisted he share his bedding and get a good night's rest before facing the winter's anger in the morning. Once again, the man gratefully accepted, and fell asleep almost immediately.

In the morning, Niu settled up with the landlord, using up almost all his money in the process, and was about to leave, when the stranger woke and said, "Please wait, I have something to give you." He took Niu outside the inn, and said, "Although I am in beggar's rags, I am actually a messenger from the Underworld; for your kindness to me last night, when you could ill afford it, I would like to give you these in return," and from his pocket he took three small, folded packets. "When you are faced with impossible difficulties, you must burn incense and open one of these; it will help you, but only when your circumstances seem hopeless." Niu took the packets, and all at once the stranger disappeared on the wind.

Niu continued on his way to the capital, not really believing what the man had said. There he continued his studies and waited for the examinations, but the city was terribly expensive, and he was soon forced to cut down on food to the point where he was close to starvation, his studies suffering badly as a consequence. He was about to return to his village in despair, when he remembered the three packets and, lighting a stick of incense, he opened the first of them. Inside was a slip of paper which read, "Go and sit outside the Bodhi Temple at noon." The Bodhi Temple was some miles distant, but Niu went there through the cold, and sat in the freezing snow outside the building, all the while thinking that he must be wasting his time. After a time a monk came out and asked him what he wanted. Niu replied that he just wanted to sit there for a while, and taking pity on this strange man, the monk brought him some tea, and started talking to him. He asked Niu his name, and when Niu told him, the monk reeled backwards in astonishment.

"Are you related to the late Magistrate Niu of Jinyang?" he asked, and Niu replied that he was the man's nephew. After asking a few further questions, to assure himself that Niu really was the dead man's relative, the monk said, "Your uncle was a great benefactor of this temple, but he also left three thousand strings of coins with me for safe keeping. When he died, I was at a loss as to what to do with them, but now that you have miraculously come here, you must take them as his next of kin."

The astonished Niu was now a very wealthy man, able to live in complete comfort, and concentrate entirely on his studies. However, try as he might, he could not pass the examinations necessary to fulfil his ambition of becoming a Magistrate, and he began to despair. After failing for the third time, Niu was about to give up and return to his village, when he again remembered the three packets, and quickly finding the remaining pair, he lit a stick of incense and opened the second. Inside was a slip of paper which read, 'Go and eat in Shu's restaurant.' Rather baffled, Niu did as he was told. He ordered tea, and sat in the restaurant, wondering what he was doing there. Then, from behind a partition on his right, Niu heard two men in a private room talking, and he could not help overhearing their conversation. "I am worried," said one, "that the questions are too easy. After all, this is an important examination, and we do not want to let standards slip."

The other replied, "Tell me the quotations you have set, and I will tell you what I think." The first man then ran through the list of quotations that were to be set as exam topics, and the astonished Niu realized that he was being told exactly what would be required of him at the next round of examinations. Rushing home, he wrote down all he had heard, and when the time came for the exams he passed with flying colours.

So impressive were his results that he was given an important official post, and very soon became a Magistrate, as he had always wished. He became famous for his fairness and wisdom, and also for his kindness, never turning away any person in need. He always carried with him the last of the three packets, but felt that he would never have to open it, so great was his good fortune. However, when still in middle age, Niu fell ill, and nothing that the doctors or the priests could do seemed able to cure him. At last, with his strength failing, Niu decided to open the last packet. He lit a stick of incense and opened the packet; inside there was a slip of paper which read, "Make your will."

Niu knew now that his life was ending. He carefully put all his affairs in order, and said farewell to his family and friends. Then he died, peacefully, and full of contentment at a life well spent, mourned by the whole city, and remembered with love and admiration by the entire population.

THE HAUNTED PAVILION

Many years ago a student was walking along a road south of Anyang, heading towards that city. In those days it was common for students to travel the country, seeking knowledge from ancient sites and men of learning throughout China: 'wandering with sword and lute' as it was known.

On this particular night the student arrived at a village some twelve miles short of Anyang, and as night was closing in fast, he asked an old woman if there was an inn nearby. She replied, saying that the nearest inn was some miles distant, whereupon the student remarked that he had just passed a pavilion on the road and that he would rest there. Such pavilions were common in China at that time, used as resting places for weary travellers, and looked after by neighbouring villagers.

The old woman went white at the student's words, and told him he must on no account stay in the shelter, as it was cursed with demons, and no one who had stayed there had ever lived to tell the tale. But the student laughed off the dire warning, saying that he thought he could take care of himself, and brushing aside the protestations of the villagers, he set off for the pavilion.

Night fell, but the student did not sleep; instead he lit a lamp and read aloud to himself from one of his books. Time passed; for a long while nothing stirred, until, on the stroke of midnight, the student heard footsteps on the road outside. Peering out of the door, he saw a man in black. The man stopped and called the master of the pavilion.

"Here I am," came a voice from just behind him, causing the student to jump in surprise. "What do you want?"

"Who is in the pavilion?" the man in black asked.

"A scholar is in the pavilion, but he is reading his book and not yet asleep," the voice replied.

At this the man in black sighed, and turned towards the village, and the scholar returned to his reading. Some while later he again heard footsteps, and this time, as he peered of the door, he saw a man in a red hat stop on the road outside the pavilion.

"Master of the Pavilion!" the man cried.

"Here I am," came the voice from just behind him.

"Who is in the pavilion?" the man in the red hat asked.

"A scholar is in the pavilion, but he is reading his book and not yet asleep," the voice replied.

At this the man in the red hat sighed too and turned towards the village. Then the student waited for a few minutes, until he was sure there was no one else coming down the road. He crept out of the door, and standing on the road, called out, "Master of the Pavilion!"

"Here I am," came the voice from within.

"Who is in the pavilion?" the student asked.

"A scholar is in the pavilion, but he is reading his book and not yet asleep," the voice replied.

The scholar sighed, and then asked, "Who was the man in black?"

"That was the black swine of the North," the voice answered.

"And who was the man in the red hat?"

"That was the Red Cock of the West."

"And who are you?" the student asked.

"I am the Old Scorpion," came the reply. At this, the student slipped back into the pavilion, and stayed awake all night, reading his book undisturbed.

The next morning the villagers rushed to the pavilion to see if the student had survived the night, and were astonished to see him sitting on the veranda, strumming his lute. As they gathered round him, bombarding him with questions, the student held up his hand for silence.

"Follow me," he said, "and I will remove the curse from this building." Then he went back inside the pavilion, followed by the villagers. He pulled aside a rotting screen in one corner of the room, and there behind it was a huge black scorpion, many feet long, and ready to strike. With one sweep of his sword, the student split the creature from head to tail, and it fell lifeless to the floor.

Next he asked the villagers where they kept a black pig. "In the house north of the pavilion," they answered, and showed him the place. There was a huge black pig, its eyes glinting with demonic fury. Again the student drew his sword, and in moments the pig lay dead at his feet.

"Now, where do you keep a large red rooster?" he asked.

"In a shed to the west of the pavilion," they answered, and showed him the place. There was an enormous red cockerel, with a huge red comb, and long, sharp talons. With another swish of the student's sword, the bird was decapitated, and lay dead at his feet.

The scholar explained to the startled villagers how he had discovered the identities of the demons, and from that day on, no traveller's rest was ever against disturbed in the pavilion south of Anyang.

THE DRAGON'S PEARL

Many hundreds of years ago a mother and her son lived together by the banks of the Min Jiang in the province of Shu, which we now call Sichuan. They were extremely poor, and the young boy had to look after his mother, who was very old and very ill. Although he worked long hours cutting and selling grass for animal food; he barely made enough to support them both, and was always afraid that ruin lay just around the next corner.

One summer, as the earth grew brown through lack of rain, and the supply of good grass became even more sparse than usual, the young boy was forced to journey farther and farther from home to make any living at all; higher and higher into the mountains he went in search of pasture. Then one day, tired and thirsty, the boy was just about to set out empty-handed on the long homeward journey, when he came across a patch of the most verdant, tall grass he had ever seen, waving in the breeze, and giving off a pleasing scent of Spring. The boy was

CHINESE MYTHS & LEGENDS

so delighted that he cut down the whole patch, and joyfully carried it down the mountain to his village. He sold the grass for more than he often earned in a week, and for once he and his sick mother were able to eat a good meal of fish and rice.

The next day the boy returned to the same area, hoping to find a similar patch of grass nearby, but to his complete amazement, the very spot which he had harvested the day before had grown again fully, as green and luscious as before. Once again, he cut down the whole patch and returned home. This happened day after day, and the boy and his mother were delighted by the upturn in their fortunes. The only disadvantage was the distance the boy had to travel every day, a long, hazardous journey into the mountains, and it occurred to him that if this was a magic patch of grass, it should grow equally well in his village as it did in the mountains.

The very next day he made several journeys to the mountains, and dug up the patch, grass, roots, soil and all, and carried it back to a spot just near his house, where he carefully re-laid the plot of earth. As he was doing so, he found to his wonder and delight, hidden in the roots of the grass, the largest, most beautiful pearl he had ever seen. He rushed to show it to his mother, and even with her failing sight, she realized that it must be of enormous value. They decided to keep it safely hidden until the boy could go to the city to sell it in the market there. The old woman hid it at the bottom of their large rice jar, which contained just enough to cover the stone, and the boy went back to re-laying the magic grass patch.

The next day he rushed out of bed to go and harvest his crop, only to find that, far from luxuriant pasture he had expected, the grass on the patch was withered, brown, and obviously dying.

The boy wept for his folly in moving the earth and destroying its magic, and went inside to confess his failure to his mother. As he was going into the house, he heard his mother cry out, and rushing to her, found her standing in amazement over the rice jar. It was full to the brim with rice, and on the top of the jar lay the pearl, glinting in the morning sun. Then they knew that this must be a magic pearl. They placed it in their virtually empty money box, and sure enough, the next morning, they discovered that it too was absolutely full, the pearl sitting on top of the golden pile like a jewel on top of a crown.

Mother and son used their magic pearl wisely, and became quite wealthy; naturally in a small village this fortune did not go unremarked, and the neighbours who had been kind to the mother and son in their times of hardship now found themselves handsomely repaid, and those in need found ready relief for their distress.

However, the villagers were curious as to the source of this new wealth, and it did not take long for the story of the fabulous pearl to become known. One day the boy found himself surrounded by people demanding to see the stone. Foolishly he took it from its hiding place and showed it to the assembled throng. Some of the crowd grew threatening, jostling and pushing, and asking why the boy should be allowed to keep such a lucky find. The son saw that the situation was about to turn ugly, and without thinking, he put the pearl into his mouth to keep it safe. But in the uproar he accidentally swallowed it with a loud gulp.

Immediately, the boy felt as if he was on fire, his throat and then his stomach was consumed with a heat so intense he did not know how to endure it. He ran to his house and threw the contents of the water bucket down his throat, but it had no impact on the searing pain; he dashed to the well, and pulled up bucket after bucket of water, but to no avail. Although he drank gallon after gallon he was still burning up, and in a frenzy of despair he threw himself down on the banks of the Min and began to lap up the river as fast as he could, until eventually he had drunk it absolutely dry. As the last drop of the mighty river disappeared down his throat, there was a huge crack of thunder, and a violent storm erupted. The earth shook, lightning flashed across the sky, rain lashed down from the heavens, and the terrified villagers all fell to the ground in fear. Still the boy was shaking like a leaf, and his frightened mother grabbed hold of his legs, which suddenly started to grow. Horns sprouted on his forehead, scales appeared in place of his skin, and his eyes grew wider, and seemed to spit fire. Racked by convulsions the boy grew bigger and bigger. The horrified mother saw that he was turning into a dragon before her very eyes, and understood that the pearl must have belonged to the dragon guardian of the river. For every water dragon has a magic pearl which is its most treasured possession.

The river was now filling up with all the rain, and the dragon-boy started to slither towards it, his weeping mother still clinging to his scaly legs. With a powerful jerk, he managed to shake her free, but even as he headed for the torrent, he could still hear her despairing cries. Each time she called out, he turned his huge body to look at her, each writhing motion throwing up mud-banks at the side of the river, until, with a last anguished roar, he slid beneath the waves for the last time and disappeared for ever. And to this day the mud banks on the Min Jiang are called the 'Looking Back at Mother' banks, in memory of the dragon-boy and his magic pearl.

THE FOOLISH OLD MAN AND THE MOUNTAINS

There was once a very old man, more than ninety years old, called Yugong. He lived with his family in the mountains of the West and their house stood right in front of two great peaks, Taihang and Wangwu. Every time the old man went anywhere, he had to cross the two peaks, and he hated them with all his soul for always exhausting him.

Eventually he could stand it no longer, and calling his family together, told them that they were going to move the peaks out of the way.

"Where will you put all the earth?" asked his wife, who thought the whole plan insane.

"We'll just carry it all to the shores of the great lake," replied Yugong. And all the men of the family set to work, right down to his youngest nephew.

They carried bucket after bucket, sack after sack of earth and rock away, all the way to the shores of the great lake, but still the mountains seemed no smaller, the climb in the mornings no less strenuous. The wise old man who lived nearby saw all this and laughed at Yugong.

"This is madness," he cried. "You are old, Yugong, your life is like a candle guttering in the wind; stop this nonsense now."

"Stop now?" replied Yugong. "Don't be absurd. When I die my sons will carry on the work, and their sons after them. The work will continue on down the generations until the great task is finished. You really are no wiser than my youngest nephew."

And the wise man kept silent, as he had no answer to this.

Now it so happened that a God overheard this exchange,

305

and he went to the High God to warn him of the old man's ambition, fearing the two peaks might one day actually disappear. But the High God was so impressed by Yugong's fortitude and determination that he sent two giants to help the old man, and they took the mountains away, one to Yongnan in the South, and the other to Shuodong in the East. And the old man was able to live out his remaining years without ever again having to climb over the twin peaks.

THE GUARDIAN OF THE GATE OF HEAVEN

In Buddhist temples you will find a figure of a man holding a model of a pagoda in his hand. He is Li, the Prime Minister of Heaven and father of Nezha. He was a general under the tyrant Zhou and commander of Chentang Guan at the time when the bloody war was being waged that resulted in the extinction of the Yin Chao.

Nezha is one of the most frequently mentioned heroes in Chinese romance; he is represented in one account as being Yu Huang's shield bearer, sixty feet in height, his three heads with nine eyes crowned by a golden wheel, his eight hands each holding a magic weapon and his mouth vomiting blue clouds. At the sound of his voice, we are told, the heavens shook and the foundations of the earth trembled. His duty was to bring into submission all the demons which desolated the world.

Li Ching's wife, Yin Shih, bore him three sons, the eldest Jincha, the second Mucha, and the third Nezha, generally known as 'the Third Prince.'

One night, Yin Shi dreamed that a Taoist priest entered her room. She indignantly exclaimed: "How dare you come into my room in this indiscreet manner?" The priest replied: "Woman, receive the child of the unicorn!" Before she could reply the Taoist pushed an object to her bosom.

Yin Shi awoke in a fright, a cold sweat all over her body. Having woken her husband, she told him of her dream. At that moment she was seized with the pains of childbirth. Li Jing left the room, uneasy at what seemed to be inauspicious omens. A little later two servants ran to him, crying out: "Your wife has given birth to a monstrous freak!"

Li Jing seized his sword and went into his wife's room, which he found filled with a red light and a most extraordinary odour. A ball of flesh was rolling on the floor like a wheel; with a blow of his sword he cut it open and a baby emerged, surrounded by a halo of red light. Its face was very white, a gold bracelet was on its right wrist and it wore a pair of red silk trousers, from which came rays of dazzling golden light. The bracelet was 'the horizon of Heaven and earth,' and the two precious objects belonged to the cave Jinguang Dong of Taiyi Zhenren, the priest who had bestowed them upon him when he appeared to his mother during her sleep. The child itself was an avatar of Ling Chuzi, 'the Intelligent Pearl.'

Then next day Taiyi Zhenren returned and asked Li Ching's permission to see the newborn baby. "He shall be called Nezha," he said, "and will become my disciple."

At seven years of age Nezha was already six feet in height. One day he asked his mother if he might go for a walk outside the town. His mother granted him permission on condition that he was accompanied by a servant. She also told him not to remain too long outside the wall, for his father should become anxious.

It was in the fifth moon: the heat was excessive. Nezha had not gone far before he was sweating profusely. Some way ahead he saw a clump of trees. He decided to go there and, settling himself in the shade, opened his coat and breathed the fresher air with relief. In front of him he saw a stream of limpid green water running between two rows of willows – the water gently flowing round a rock. The child ran to the banks of the stream and said to his guardian: "I am covered with perspiration, and will bathe from the rock." "Be quick," said the servant; "if your father returns home before you he will be anxious." Nezha stripped himself, took his red silk trousers and dipped them in the water, intending to use them as a towel. No sooner were the magic trousers immersed in the stream than the water began to boil and Heaven and earth trembled. The water of the Jiuwan He ('Nine-bends River') turned completely red and Long Wang's palace shook to its foundations. The Dragon king, surprised at seeing the walls of his crystal palace shaking, called his officers and asked: "How is it that the palace threatens to collapse? There should not be an earthquake at this time." He ordered one of his attendants to go at once and find out what evil was causing the commotion. When the officer reached the river he saw that the water was red but noticed nothing else except a boy dipping a band of silk in the stream. He called out angrily: "That child should be thrown into the water for making the river red and causing Long Wang's palace to shake." Nezha replied, "Who is that who speaks so brutally?"

Then he jumped aside, realizing that the man intended to seize him. He took his gold bracelet and hurled it in the air. It fell on the head of the officer and Nezha left him dead on the rock. Then he picked up his bracelet and said smiling: "His blood has stained my precious horizon of Heaven and earth." He then washed it in the water.

"How is it that the officer does not return?" inquired Long Wang. At that moment attendants came to inform him that the messenger had been murdered by a boy.

Ao Ping, the third son of Long Wang, immediately placed himself at the head of a troop of marines, and with his trident in his hand he left the palace precincts. The warriors dashed into the river, raising on every side waves mountains high. Seeing the water rising, Nezha stood up on the rock and was confronted by Ao Ping mounted on a sea monster. "Who slew my messenger?" cried the warrior. "I did," answered Nezha. "Who are you?" demanded Ao Ping.

"I am Nezha, the third son of Li Jing of Chentang Guan. I came here to bathe and refresh myself. Your messenger cursed me, and I killed him."

"Rascal! Do you not know that your victim was a deputy of the King of Heaven? How dare you kill him and then boast of your crime?" Ao Ping then thrust at the boy with his trident, but Nezha evaded the thrust.

"Who are you?" Nezha asked in turn.

"I am Ao Ping, the third son of Long Wang."

"Ah, you are a blusterer," jeered the boy. "If you dare to touch me I will skin you alive, you and your mud eels!"

"You make me choke with rage," shouted Ao Ping, at the same time thrusting again with his trident.

Furious at this renewed attack, Nezha spread his silk trousers in the air. Thousands of balls of fire flew out of them, felling

Long Wang's son. Nezha put his foot on Ao Ping's head and struck it with his magic bracelet, causing Ao Ping to turn into his true form of a dragon.

"I am now going to pull out your sinews," he said, "in order to make a belt for my father."

Nezha was as good as his word, and Ao Ping's escort ran and informed Long Wang of the fate of his son. The Dragon king went to Li Jing and demanded an explanation.

Being entirely ignorant of what had taken place, Li Jing went to Nezha to question him.

Li Jing found Nezha in the garden, busily weaving the belt of dragon sinew. "You have brought the most awful misfortunes upon us," he exclaimed. "Come and give an account of your conduct." "Have no fear," Nezha replied; "his son's sinews are still intact. I will give them back to him if he wishes."

When they entered the house he saluted the Dragon king, made a curt apology, and offered to return his son's sinews. The father, moved with grief at the sight of the proofs of the tragedy, said bitterly to Li Ching: "You have such a son and yet dare to deny his guilt, though you heard him admitting it! Tomorrow I shall report the matter to Yu Huang." Having said this, he departed.

Li Jing was overwhelmed at the enormity of his son's crime. His wife, hearing his cries of grief, went to her husband. "What obnoxious creature is this that you have brought into the world?" he said to her angrily. "He has slain two spirits, the son of Long Wang and a steward sent by the King of Heaven. Tomorrow the Dragon king is to lodge a complaint with Yu Huang, and two or three days from now will see the end of our existence."

The poor mother began to weep. "What!" she sobbed, "you whom I suffered so much for, you are to be the cause of our ruin and death!"

Nezha, seeing his parents so distracted, fell on his knees. "Let me tell you once for all," he said, "that I am no ordinary mortal. I am the disciple of Taiyi Zhenren. The magic weapons I received from him – it is they that brought on me the undying hatred of Long Wang. But he cannot prevail. Today I will go and ask my master's advice. The guilty alone should suffer the penalty; it is unjust that his parents should suffer."

Nezha then left for Qianyuan Shan. He entered the cave of his master Taiyi Zhenren, to whom he told of his adventures. The master considered the grave consequences of the murders. He then ordered Nezha to bare his breast. With his finger he drew on the skin a magic formula, after which he gave him some secret instructions. "Now," he said, "go to the gate of Heaven and await the arrival of Long Wang, who plans to accuse you before Yu Huang. Then you must come again to consult me, so that your parents may not be molested because of your misdeeds."

When Nezha reached the gate of Heaven it was closed. He searched in vain for Long Wang, but after a while he saw him approaching. Long Wang did not see Nezha, as the formula written by Taiyi Zhenren rendered him invisible. As Long Wang approached the gate, Nezha ran up to him and struck him so hard with his golden bracelet that he fell to the ground. Then Nezha stamped on him, cursing him.

The Dragon-king now recognized his assailant and sharply reproached him with his crimes, but the only reparation he got was a renewal of kicks and blows. Then, partially lifting Long

Wang's cloak and raising his shield, Nezha tore off about forty scales from his body. Blood flowed copiously and under stress of the pain the Dragon king begged his foe to spare his life. To this Nezha consented on condition that he relinquished his purpose of accusing him before Yu Huang.

"Now," went on Nezha, "change yourself into a small serpent so that I may take you back without fear of your escaping."

Long Wang took the form of a small blue dragon and followed Nezha to his father's house. After entering the house Long Wang resumed his normal form and accused Nezha of attacking him. "I will go with all the Dragon kings and lay an accusation before Yu Huang," he said. Then he transformed himself into a gust of wind and disappeared.

"Things are going from bad to worse," sighed Li Ching, His son, however, consoled him: "I beg you, my father, not to let the future trouble you. I am the chosen one of the gods. My master is Taiyi Zhenren. He has assured me that he can easily protect us."

Next Nezha went out and climbed a tower that overlooked the entrance of the fort. There he found a wonderful bow and three magic arrows. Nezha did not know that this was the spiritual weapon belonging to the fort. "My master informed me that I am destined to fight to establish the coming Zhou dynasty; I ought therefore to perfect myself in the use of weapons. This is a good opportunity." So he seized the bow and shot an arrow toward the south west. A red trail indicated the path of the arrow, which hissed as it flew. At that moment Pi Yun, a servant of Shiqi Niangniang, happened to be at the foot of Kulou Shan (Skeleton Hill), in front of the cave of his mistress. The arrow pierced his throat and he fell dead, bathed in his blood. Shiqi Niangniang came out of her cave, and examining the arrow found that it bore the inscription: "Arrow which shakes the heavens." She knew that it must have come from Chentang Guan, where the magic bow was kept.

The goddess mounted her blue phoenix, flew over the fort, seized Li Jing and carried him to her cave. There she made him kneel before her. She reminded him how she had protected him so that he might gain honour and glory on earth before he attained to immortality.

"And this is how you show your gratitude – by killing my servant!"

Li Jing swore that he was innocent; but the tell-tale arrow was there, and it could only have come from the fortress. Li Jing begged the goddess to set him free so that he might find the culprit and bring him to her. "If I cannot find him," he added, "you may take my life."

Once again Nezha frankly admitted his deed to his father and followed him to the cave of Shiqi Niangniang. When he reached the entrance the second servant reproached him with the crime, immediately after which Nezha struck him with a heavy blow. Shiqi Niangniang, infuriated, threw herself at Nezha, sword in hand; one after the other she wrenched from him his bracelet and magic trousers.

Deprived of his magic weapons, Nezha fled to his master, Taiyi Zhenren. The goddess followed and demanded that he be put to death. A terrible conflict ensued between the two champions, until Taiyi Zhenren hurled his globe of nine fire-dragons into the air. This fell on Shiqi Niangniang, enveloping her in a whirlwind of flame. When it had passed they saw that she had changed into stone.

"Now you are safe," said Taiyi Zhenren to Nezha, "but return quickly, for the Four Dragon kings have laid their accusation before Yu Huang, and they are going to carry off your parents. Follow my advice, and you will rescue your parents from their misfortune."

On his return Nezha found the Four Dragon-kings on the point of carrying off his parents. "It is I," he said, "who killed Ao Ping and I who should pay the penalty. Why are you molesting my parents? I am about to return to them what I received from them. Will it satisfy you?"

Long Wang agreed, so Nezha took a sword and before their eyes cut off an arm, sliced open his stomach and fell unconscious. His soul, carried on the wind, went straight to the cave of Taiyi Zhenren, while his mother busied herself with burying his body.

"Your home is not here," said his master to him; "return to Chentang Guan, and beg your mother to build a temple on Cuiping Shan. Incense will be burned to you for three years, at the end of which time you will be reincarnated."

During the night, while his mother was in a deep sleep, Nezha appeared to her in a dream and said: "My mother, pity me; since my death, my soul, separated from my body, wanders about without a home. Build me, I pray you, a temple on Cuiping Shan, that I may be reincarnated." His mother awoke in tears and related her vision to Li Ching, who reproached her for her blind attachment to her unnatural son – the cause of so much disaster.

For five or six nights the son appeared to his mother, each time repeating his request. The last time he added: "Do not forget that by nature I am ferocious; if you refuse my request evil will befall you."

His mother then sent builders to the mountain to construct a temple to Nezha, and his image was set up in it. Miracles were not wanting, and the number of pilgrims who visited the shrine increased daily.

One day Li Jing was passing this mountain with a troop of his soldiers. He saw the roads crowded with pilgrims of both sexes. "Where are these people going?" he asked. "For six months past," he was told, "the spirit of the temple on this mountain has continued to perform miracles. People come from far and near to worship him."

"What is the name of this spirit?" inquired Li Ching. "Nezha," they replied. "Nezha!" exclaimed the father. "I will go and see him myself." In a rage Li Jing entered the temple and examined the statue, which was the image of his son. By its side were images of two of his servants. He took his whip and began to beat the statue, cursing it all the while. "It is not enough, apparently, for you to have been a source of disaster to us," he said; "but even after your death you must deceive the multitude." He whipped the statue until it fell to pieces; he then kicked over the images of the servants, and went back, telling the people not to worship so wicked a man, the shame and ruin of his family. By his orders the temple was burnt to the ground.

When he reached Chentang Guan his wife came to him but he received her coldly. "You gave birth to that cursed son," he said, "who has been the plague of our lives, and after his death you build him a temple in which he deceives the people. Do you wish to have me disgraced? If I were to be accused at Court of having instituted the worship of false gods, would not my destruction be certain? I have burned the temple, and intend that that shall settle the matter once and for all; if ever you think of rebuilding it I will break off all relations with you."

At the time of his father's visit Nezha was absent from the temple. On his return he found only its smoking remnants. "Who has demolished my temple?" he asked. "Li Ching," the spirits of his servants replied. "In doing this he has exceeded his powers," said Nezha. "I gave him back the substance I received from him; why did he come with violence to break up my image? I will have nothing more to do with him."

Nezha's soul had already begun to be spiritualized. So he decided to go to Taiyi Zhenren and beg for his help. "The worship given to you there," replied the Taoist, "had nothing in it that should have offended your father; it did not concern him. He was in the wrong. Before long Jiang Ziya will descend to inaugurate the new dynasty, and since you must throw in your lot with him I will find a way to help you."

Taiyi Zhenren had two water lily stalks and three lotus leaves brought to him. He spread these on the ground in the form of a human being and placed the soul of Nezha in this lotus skeleton, uttering a magic spell as he worked. There emerged a new Nezha full of life, with a fresh complexion, purple lips and keen glance, who was sixteen feet tall. "Follow me to my peach garden," said Taiyi Zhenren, "and I will give you your weapons." He handed him a sharp fiery spear and two wind-and-fire wheels which, placed under his feet, served as a vehicle. A brick of gold in a panther-skin bag completed his magic armament. The new warrior, after thanking his master, mounted his wind-and-fire wheels and returned to Chentang Guan.

Li Jing was informed that his son Nezha had returned and was threatening vengeance. So he took his weapons, mounted his horse and went to meet him. They joined in battle, but Li Jing was soon overcome and compelled to flee. Nezha pursued his father, but as he was on the point of overtaking him Li Ching's second son, Mucha, came on the scene. Mucha criticized his brother for his unfilial conduct.

"Li Jing is no longer my father," replied Nezha. "I gave him back my substance; why did he burn my temple and smash up my image?"

Mucha prepared to defend his father, but took a blow to his back from the golden brick. He fell, unconscious. Nezha then resumed his pursuit of Li Ching.

His strength exhausted and in danger of falling into the hands of his enemy, Li Jing drew his sword and was about to kill himself. "Stop!" cried a Taoist priest. "Come into my cave, and I will protect you."

When Nezha arrived he could not see Li Ching. He demanded his surrender from the Taoist. But he had to do with one stronger than himself, no less a being than Wenzhu Tianzun, whom Taiyi Zhenren had sent in order that Nezha might receive a lesson. The Taoist, with the aid of his magic weapon, seized Nezha, and in a moment he found a gold ring fastened round his neck, two chains on his feet, and he was bound to a pillar of gold.

At this moment, as if by accident, Taiyi Zhenren appeared on the scene. His master had Nezha brought before Wenzhu Tianzun and Li Ching, and advised him to live at peace with his father. But he also rebuked the father for having burned the temple on Cuiping Shan. This done, he ordered Li Jing to go home and Nezha to return to his cave. The latter, overflowing with anger and with his heart full of vengeance, started again in pursuit of Li Ching, swearing that he would punish him. But the Taoist reappeared and prepared to protect Li Ching.

Nezha, bristling like a savage cat, threw himself at his enemy and tried to pierce him with his spear. At that moment a white lotus flower emerged from the Taoist's mouth and arrested the course of the weapon. As Nezha continued to threaten him, the Taoist drew a mysterious object from his sleeve which rose in the air and, falling at the feet of Nezha, enveloped him in flames. Then Nezha prayed for mercy. The Taoist exacted from him three separate promises: to live in harmony with his father, to recognize and address him as his father, and to throw himself at his (the Taoist's) feet, to indicate his reconciliation with himself.

After this act of reconciliation had been performed, Wenzhu Tianzun told Li Jing that he should leave his official post to become an Immortal. That he should place his services at the disposal of the new Zhou dynasty, shortly to come into power. In order to ensure that their reconciliation should last forever and to place it beyond Nezha's power to seek revenge, he gave Li Jing the wonderful object that had caused Nezha's feet to have been burned, and which had been the means of bringing him into subjection. It was a golden pagoda, which became the characteristic weapon of Li Ching, and gave rise to his nickname, Li the Pagoda-bearer. Finally, Yu Huang appointed him Generalissimo of the Twenty-Six Celestial Officers, Grand Marshal of the Skies, and Guardian of the Gate of Heaven.

A BATTLE OF THE GODS

It is thought that during the wars that preceded the accession of the Zhou dynasty in 1122 BCE, a multitude of demigod Buddhas and Immortals took part on one side or the other some fighting for the old dynasty, some for the new. They were wonderful creatures, gifted with marvellous powers. They could change their form at will, multiply their heads and limbs, become invisible, and create – by simply uttering a word – terrible monsters who bit and destroyed, or sent forth poisonous gases, or emitted flames from their nostrils. In these battles there is much lightning, thunder, flight of fire dragons, dark clouds that vomit burning hails of murderous weapons; swords, spears, and arrows fall from the sky on to the heads of the combatants; the earth trembles and the pillars of Heaven shake.

One of these gifted warriors was Chunti, a Taoist of the Western Paradise, who appeared on the scene when the armies of the rival dynasties were facing each other. Kong Xuan was gallantly holding the pass of the Jinchi Ling; Jiang Ziya was trying to take it by assault – so far without success.

Chunti's mission was to take Kong Xuan to the abode of the blessed, his wisdom and general progress having now reached the required degree of perfection. This was a means of breaking down the invincible resistance of this powerful enemy and at the same time of rewarding his brilliant talents.

But Kong Xuan did not approve of this plan and a fight took place between the two champions. At one moment Chunti was seized by a luminous bow and carried into the air. While enveloped in a cloud of fire he appeared with eighteen arms and twenty-four heads, holding in each hand a powerful talisman.

He put a silk cord round Kong Xuan's neck, touched him with his wand and forced him to reassume his original form of a red one-eyed peacock. Chunti sat himself on the peacock's back and it flew across the sky, carrying its saviour and master to the Western Paradise. Brilliantly variegated clouds marked its track through space.

On the disappearance of its defender, the pass of Jinchi Ling was captured and the village of Jiepai Guan was reached. This place was the fort of the enemy's forces. It was defended by a host of genii and Immortals, the most distinguished among them being the Taoist Tongtian Jiaozhu, whose especially effective charms had so far kept the fort secure against every attempt on it.

Laozi himself had descended from dwelling in happiness, together with Yuanshi Tianzun and Jieyin Dao ren, to take part in the siege. But the town had four gates and these heavenly rulers were only three in number. So Chunti was recalled, and each member of the quartet was given the task of capturing one of the gates.

Chunti's duty was to take the Jueh Xian Men, defended by Tongtian Jiaozhu. The warriors who had tried to enter the town by this gate had all paid for their temerity with their lives. The moment each had crossed the threshold a clap of thunder had resounded, and a mysterious sword, moving with lightning speed, had slain him.

As Chunti advanced at the head of his warriors terrible lightning filled the air and the mysterious sword descended like a thunderbolt on his head. But Chunti held up his Seven-Precious Branch. Thousands of lotus flowers emerged from it, which formed an impenetrable barrier and stopped the sword in its fall. This and the other gates were then forced, and a grand assault was now directed against the chief defender of the town.

Tongtian Jiaozhu, riding his ox and surrounded by his warriors, for the last time risked the chance of war and bravely faced his four terrible adversaries. With his sword held high, he threw himself on Jieyin Dao ren, whose only weapon was his fly whisk. But there emerged from this a five-coloured lotus flower, which stopped the sword thrust. While Laozi struck the hero with his staff, Yuanshi Tianzun warded off the terrible sword.

Chunti now called for the spiritual peacock to help. He took the form of a warrior with twenty-four heads and eighteen arms. His mysterious weapons surrounded Tongtian Jiaozhu, and Laozi struck the hero so hard that fire came out from his eyes, nose and mouth. Unable to ward off the assaults of his adversaries, he next received a blow from Chunti's magic wand, which felled him. He took flight in a whirlwind of dust.

The defenders now offered no further resistance. Yuanshi Tianzun thanked Chunti for the valuable assistance he had given in the capture of the village. Afterwards the gods returned to their palace in the Western Heaven.

But Tongtian Jiaozhu swore to have his revenge. He called to the spirits of the twenty-eight constellations for help, and marched to attack Wu Wang's army. The honour of the victory that followed belonged to Chunti, who disarmed both the Immortal Wu Yun and Tongtian Jiaozhu.

Wu Yun, armed with his magic sword, attacked Chunti; but the latter opened his mouth and a blue lotus flower came out and stopped the blows aimed at him. Other thrusts were met by similar miracles.

"Why continue so useless a fight?" said Chunti at last. "Abandon the cause of the Shang and come with me to the Western Paradise. I came to save you, and you must not compel me to make you resume your original form."

An insulting flow of words was the reply; again the magic sword descended like lightning, and again the stroke was averted by a timely lotus flower. Chunti now waved his wand and the magic sword was broken to bits, with only the handle remaining in Wu Yun's hand.

Mad with rage, Wu Yun seized his club and tried to fell his enemy. But Chunti summoned a disciple, who appeared with a bamboo pole. This he thrust out like a fishing rod, and on a hook at the end of the line attached to the pole dangled a large golden-bearded turtle. This was the Immortal Wu Yun, now in his original form of a spiritual turtle. The disciple sat himself on its back, and both disappeared into space, returning to the Western Heavens.

To conquer Tongtian Jiaozhu was more difficult, but after a long fight Chunti waved his Wand of the Seven Treasures and broke his adversary's sword. The latter, disarmed and vanquished, disappeared in a cloud of dust. Chunti did not trouble to pursue him. The battle was won.

A disciple of Tongtian Jiaozhu, Pilu Xian, 'the Immortal P'i-lu,' seeing his master beaten in two successive engagements, left the battlefield and followed Chunti to the Western Paradise, to become a Buddha. He is known as Pilu Fo, one of the principal gods of Buddhism.

Chunti's festival is celebrated on the sixth day of the third moon. He is generally shown with eight hands and three faces one of the latter being that of a pig.

THE CASTING OF THE GREAT BELL

In every province of China there is a legend relating to the casting of the great bell swung in the bell tower of the chief city. These legends are curiously identical in almost every detail. This is the story of the one found in Beijing.

It was in the reign of Yongle, the third monarch of the Ming dynasty, that Beijing first became the capital of China. Till that period the 'Son of Heaven' had held his Court at Nanjing, and Beijing had been of relatively little note. Now, however, on being honoured by the 'Sacred Presence,' stately buildings sprang up in all directions for the Emperor and his courtiers. Clever men from all parts of the Empire were attracted to the capital, sure of lucrative employment. About this time the Drum Tower and the Bell Tower were built; both of them as 'lookout' and 'alarm' towers. The Drum Tower was furnished with a massive drum, which it still possesses. It was of such a size that the thunder of its tones might be heard all over the city, the sound being almost enough to waken the dead.

The Bell Tower had been completed sometime before attempts were made to cast a bell proportionate to the size of the building. Eventually Yung Lo ordered Guan Yu, a mandarin who was skilled in casting guns, to cast a bell the sound of which should be heard in every part of the city. Guan Yu immediately set to work. He secured the services of a great number of experienced workmen and collected huge quantities of material. Months passed before it was announced to the Emperor that everything was ready for the casting. A day was appointed when the Emperor, surrounded by a crowd of courtiers and preceded by the Court musicians, went to witness the ceremony. At a given signal, and to the crash of music, the melted metal rushed into the mould prepared for it. The Emperor and his Court then left, leaving Guan Yu and his subordinates to wait for the metal to cool, which would tell of failure or success.

At last the metal was cool enough to detach the mould from it. Guan Yu, breathless with trepidation, rushed to inspect it but to his horror found it to be honeycombed in many places. This was reported to the Emperor, who was naturally annoyed at the expenditure of so much time, labour and money with such an unsatisfactory result. However, he ordered Guan Yu to try again.

The mandarin was quick to obey and, thinking the failure of the first attempt must have resulted from some oversight or omission on his part, he watched every detail with care and attention, fully determined that nothing should go wrong with this second casting.

After months of labour the mould was prepared again. The metal was poured into it but again with the same result. Guan Yu was worried, not only at the loss of his reputation but also at the certain loss of the Emperor's favour. When Yung Lo heard of this second failure he was very angry, and at once ordered Guan Yu into his presence. The Emperor told him he would give him a third and final chance. But if he did not succeed this time he would behead him. Guan Yu went home in despair, asking himself what crime he or any of his ancestors could have committed to have justified this disaster.

Now Guan Yu had an only daughter, about sixteen years of age, and, having no sons, the whole of his love was centred in this girl. He had hopes of perpetuating his name and fame through her marriage to some deserving young nobleman. She was truly worthy of being loved. She had almond shaped eyes, like the autumn waves, which, sparkling and dancing in the sun, seemed to leap up in joy to kiss the fragrant reeds that grow on the rivers' banks, yet of such transparency that one's form could be seen in their liquid depths as if reflected in a mirror. These were surrounded by long silken lashes – now drooping in coy modesty, before rising in youthful happiness and disclosing the laughing eyes concealed beneath them. Eyebrows like the willow leaf; cheeks of snowy whiteness, yet tinged with the gentlest colouring of the rose; teeth like pearls of the finest water were seen peeping from between half-open lips, so luscious and juicy that they resembled two cherries; hair of the jettest black and of the silkiest texture. Her form was such as poets love to describe; there was grace and ease in every movement; she appeared to glide rather than walk. Add to her other charms that she was skilful in writing poetry, excellent in embroidery and unequalled in the execution of her household duties, and we have just a brief description of Ke'ai, the beautiful daughter of Guan Yu.

Easy to see how Guan Tu loved his beautiful child. She returned his love with all the enthusiasm of her affectionate nature; often cheering him with her innocent joyfulness when he returned from his daily work wearied or angry. Seeing him now return with despair, she tenderly asked him the cause, hoping to be the means of alleviating it. When her father told her of his failures and of the Emperor's threat she exclaimed: "Oh, my father, be comforted! Heaven will not always be so unrelenting. Are we not told that 'out of evil comes good'? These two failures will only enhance the glory of your eventual success, for success this time must crown your efforts. I am only a girl and cannot assist you but with my prayers; these I will daily and hourly offer up for your success; and the prayers of a daughter for a loved parent must be heard." Somewhat soothed by the sweet words of Ke'ai, Guan Yu devoted himself to his task with renewed energy, Ke'ai meanwhile constantly praying for him and attending to his needs when he returned home. One day it occurred to the girl to go to a celebrated astrologer to find out the cause of these failures and to ask what could be done to stop them happening again. It was here she learned that the next casting would also be a disappointment if the blood of a maiden was not mixed with the ingredients. She returned home full of horror at this information, but inwardly resolving to sacrifice herself rather than allow her father to fail. The day for the casting finally came and Ke'ai asked her father to allow her to witness the ceremony and "to delight in his success," as she laughingly said. Guan Yu gave his consent and, accompanied by several servants, she took up a position near the mould.

Everything was prepared as before. An immense concourse assembled to witness the third and final casting, which was to result either in honour or degradation and death for Guan Yu. A dead silence prevailed through the vast crowd as the melted metal once again rushed to its destination. This was broken by a shriek and a cry, "For my father!" and Ke'ai was seen to throw herself headlong into the seething, hissing metal. One of her servants attempted to seize her but only succeeded in grasping one of her shoes, which came off in his hand. The father was frantic and had to be kept by force from following her lead. He was taken home a raving maniac. But the prediction of the astrologer was fulfilled, for, on uncovering the bell after it had cooled, it was found to be perfect. Not a trace of Ke'ai was to be seen; the blood of a maiden had indeed been infused with the ingredients.

After a time the bell was suspended by order of the Emperor. There were high expectations to hear it rung for the first time. The Emperor himself was present. The bell was struck and the deep tone of its sonorous boom was heard far and wide. This indeed was a triumph! Here was a bell surpassing in size and sound any other that had ever been cast! But – and the surrounding crowds were horrified as they listened – the heavy boom of the bell was followed by a low wailing sound like the agonized cry of a woman, and the word hsieh (shoe) was distinctly heard. To this day the bell, each time it is rung, after every boom appears to utter the word 'hsieh,' and people when they hear it shudder and say, "There's poor Ke'ai's voice calling for her shoe."

THE CURSED TEMPLE

The reign of Chongzhen, the last monarch of the Ming dynasty, was troubled both by internal quarrels and by wars. He was constantly threatened by Tartar hordes, though these were generally beaten back by the celebrated general Wu Sangui. The country was in a constant state of anarchy and confusion, being overrun by bands of marauding rebels; indeed, so bold did these become under a chief named Li

Zicheng that they actually marched on the capital with the intention of placing their leader on the Dragon Throne. Chongzhen, on hearing this startling news, with no one that he could trust in such an emergency (as Wu Sangui was absent on an expedition against the Tartars), was at his wits' end. The insurgents were almost in sight of Beijing, and at any moment might arrive. Rebellion threatened in the city itself. If he went out boldly to attack the oncoming rebels his own troops might go over to the enemy, or deliver him into their hands; if he stayed in the city the people would probably open the gates to the rebels.

In such dire straits he resolved to go to the San Guan Miao, an imperial temple situated near the Chaoyang Men, and ask the gods what he should do. He would decide his fate by 'drawing the slip.' If he drew a long slip, this would be a good omen and he would boldly march out to meet the rebels, confident of victory; if a middle length one, he would remain quietly in the palace and passively wait for whatever might happen; but if he should unfortunately draw a short one he would take his own life rather than suffer death at the hands of the rebels.

On arriving at the temple, in the presence of the high officers of his Court, the sacrifices were offered up and the incense burnt, previous to drawing the slip on which hung the destiny of an empire. Meanwhile Chongzhen remained on his knees in prayer. At the end of the sacrificial ceremony the tube containing the bamboo fortune-telling sticks was placed in the Emperor's hand by one of the priests. His courtiers and the attendant priests stood round breathless in suspense, watching him as he swayed the tube backwards and forwards. Finally one fell to the ground. There was a deadly silence as it was raised by a priest and handed to the Emperor. It was a short one! Dismay fell on everyone present, no one daring to break the painful, horrible silence.

After a pause the Emperor, with a cry of rage and despair, threw the slip to the ground exclaiming: "May this temple built by my ancestors evermore be accursed! From this time on may every suppliant be denied what he entreats, as I have been! Those who come in sorrow, may that sorrow be doubled; in happiness, may that happiness be changed to misery; in hope, may they meet despair; in health, sickness; in the pride of life and strength, death! I, Chongzhen, the last of the Mings, curse it!"

Without another word he left, followed by his courtiers. He went at once to the palace and went straight to the apartments of the Empress. The next morning he and his Empress were found suspended from a tree on Prospect Hill. 'In their death they were not divided.'

The scenes that followed; how the rebels took possession of the city and were driven out again by the Chinese general, assisted by the Tartars; how the Tartars finally succeeded in establishing the Manchu dynasty, are all matters of history. The words used by the Emperor at the temple were prophetic; he was the last of the Mings. The tree on which the monarch of a mighty Empire closed his career and brought the Ming dynasty to an end was ordered to be surrounded with chains; it still exists, and is still in chains. Upward of two hundred and seventy years have passed since that time, yet the temple is standing as of old; but the halls that at one time were crowded with worshippers are now silent, no one ever venturing to worship there; it is the home of the fox and the bat. People at night pass it shudderingly – "It is the cursed temple!"

THE MANIAC'S MITE

An interesting story is told of a lady named Chen, who was a Buddhist nun celebrated for her virtue and austerity. Between the years 1628 and 1643 she left her nunnery near Weihai city and set out on a long journey in order to collect subscriptions for casting a new image of the Buddha.

She wandered through Shandong and Zhili and finally reached Beijing, and there – subscription book in hand – she stationed herself at the great south gate in order to take money from those who wished to lay treasures for themselves in the Western Heaven. The first passer-by who took any notice of her was a friendly maniac. His dress was made of coloured shreds and patches and his general appearance was wild and uncouth. "Whither away, nun?" he asked. She explained that she was collecting subscriptions for the casting of a great image of Buddha, and had come all the way from Shandong. "Throughout my life," remarked the madman, "I was ever a generous giver." So, taking the nun's subscription book, he headed a page with his own name (in very large characters) and the amount subscribed. The amount in question was two cash, equivalent to a small fraction of a penny. He then handed over two small coins and went on his way.

In course of time the nun returned to Weihaiwei with her subscriptions, and the work of casting the image was begun. When the time had come for the process of smelting, it was observed that the copper remained hard and intractable. Again and again the furnace was fed with fuel, but the shapeless mass of metal remained firm as a rock. The head workman, who was a man of vast experience, volunteered an explanation of the mystery. "An offering of great value must be missing," he said. "Let the collection book be examined so that we can see whose subscription has been withheld." The nun, who was standing by, immediately produced the madman's money, which on account of its minute value she had not taken the trouble to hand over. "There is one cash," she said, "and there is another. Certainly, the offering of these must have been an act of the highest merit and the giver must be a holy man who will someday attain Buddhahood." As she said this she threw the two cash into the midst of the cauldron. Great bubbles rose and burst, the metal melted and ran like the sap from a tree, clear as flowing water, and in a few moments the work was accomplished and the new Buddha successfully cast.

THE UNNATURAL PEOPLE

Leaving behind the countless gods, goddesses, immortals, heroes and saints, we turn now to some unusual myths surrounding the curious people supposed to inhabit the regions on the maps represented on the nine tripod vases of the Great Yu, first emperor of the Hsia dynasty.

The Pygmies

The pygmies inhabit many mountainous regions of the Empire, but are few in number. They are less than nine inches tall, but are well formed. They live in thatched houses that resemble ants' nests. When they walk out they go in companies of from six to ten, joining hands in a line for mutual protection against birds that might carry them away, or other creatures that might attack them. Their tone of voice is too low to be distinguished by an ordinary human ear. They occupy themselves in working in wood, gold, silver and precious stones, but a small proportion are tillers of the soil. They wear red clothing. The sexes are distinguishable by a slight beard on the men and long tresses on the women, the latter in some cases reaching four to five inches in length. Their heads are unduly large, being quite out of proportion to their small bodies. A husband and wife usually go about hand in hand.

The story goes that a Hakka charcoal burner once found three of the children playing in his tobacco box. He kept them there and afterward, when he was showing them to a friend, he laughed and drops of saliva flew from his mouth and shot two of them dead. He then begged his friend to take the third and put it in a place of safety before he should laugh again. His friend attempted to lift it from the box, but it died on being touched.

The Giants

In the Country of the Giants the people are fifty feet tall. Their footprints are six feet in length. Their teeth are like those of a saw. Their fingernails resemble hooked claws, while their diet consists wholly of uncooked animal food. Their eyebrows are of such length as to protrude from the front of the carts on which they ride, large though it is necessary for these vehicles to be. Their bodies are covered with long black hair resembling that of the bear. They live to the advanced age of eighteen thousand years. Though cannibals, they never eat members of their own tribe, confining their indulgence in human flesh, specifically to enemies taken in battle. Their country extends some thousands of miles along certain mountain ranges in North Eastern Asia, in the passes of which they have strong iron gates, easy to close but difficult to open. For this reason, though their neighbours maintain large standing armies, they have so far never been conquered.

The Headless People

The Headless People inhabit the Long Sheep range, to which their ancestors were banished in the remote past for an offence against the gods. One of the said ancestors had entered into a controversy with the rulers of the heavens, and they in their anger had transformed his two breasts into eyes and his navel into a mouth. They removed his head, leaving him without nose and ears, thereby cutting him off from smell and sound. They then banished him to the Long Sheep Mountains, where with a shield and axe, the only weapons given to the people of the Headless Country, he and his posterity were compelled to defend themselves from their enemies and provide their subsistence. This, however, does not in the least seem to have affected their tempers, as their bodies are wreathed in perpetual smiles, except when they flourish their war-like weapons on the approach of an enemy. They are not without understanding, because, according to Chinese notions of physiology, "their bellies are full of wisdom."

The Armless People

In the Mountains of the Sun and Moon, which are in the Centre of the Great Waste, are the people who have no arms, but whose legs instead grow out of their shoulders. They pick flowers with their toes. They bow by raising the body horizontal with the shoulders, so turning the face to the ground.

The Long-Armed and Long-Legged People

The Long-armed People are about thirty feet tall, their arms reaching from the shoulders to the ground. Once when a company of explorers was passing through the country that borders on the Eastern Sea they inquired of an old man if he knew whether or not there were people dwelling beyond the waters. He replied that a cloth garment, in fashion and texture not unlike that of a Chinese coat, with sleeves thirty feet in length, had been found in the sea. The explorers fitted out an expedition and the discovery of the Long-armed Country was the result.

The natives subsist for the most part on fish, which they obtain by wading in the water and taking the fish with their hands instead of with hooks or nets.

The arms of the Long-legged People are of a normal length, the legs are developed to a length corresponding to that of the arms of the Long-armed People.

The country of the latter borders on that of the Long-legs. The habits and food of the two are similar. The difference in their physical structure makes them of mutual assistance, those with the long arms being able to take the shellfish of the shallow waters, while those with the long legs take the surface fish from the deeper localities. The two therefore gather a harvest otherwise unobtainable.

The One-Eyed People and Others

A little to the east of the Country of the Long-legs are to be found the One-eyed People. They have only one eye, rather larger than the ordinary human eye, placed in the centre of the forehead, directly above the nose. Other clans or families have but one arm and one leg, some having a right arm and left leg, others a left arm and right leg, while others have both on the same side and go in pairs, like shoes. Another species not only has one arm and one leg, but is of such fashion as to have just one eye, one nostril and beard on only one side of the face, there being as it were rights and lefts. The two in reality are one, for it is in this way that they pair. The Long-eared People resemble Chinese in all except their ears. They live in the far West among mountains and in caves. Their pendant, flabby ears extend to the ground and would impede their feet in walking if they did not support them on their hands. They are sensitive to the faintest sound. Still another people in this region are distinguished by having six toes on each foot.

The Feathered People and Others

The Feathered People are very tall and are covered with fluffy down. They have wings in place of arms and can even fly short distances. On the points of the wings are claws, which serve as hands. Their noses are like beaks. Gentle and timid, they do not leave their own country. They have good voices and like to sing ballads. If a man wishes to visit this people he must go far to the south-east and then inquire. There is also the Land of the People with Three Faces, who live in the centre of the Great Waste and never die; the Land of the Three-heads, east of the K'un-lun Mountains; the Three-body Country, the inhabitants of which have one head with three bodies, three arms and only two legs; and yet another where the people have square heads, broad shoulders and three legs, and the stones on the land are all gold and jade.

The People of the Punctured Bodies

Another community is said to be composed of people who have holes through their chests. They can be carried about on a pole put through the orifice, or may be comfortably hung on a peg. They sometimes string themselves on a rope and walk out in file. They are harmless people. They eat snakes that they kill with bows and arrows. They live for a very long time.

The Women's Kingdom

The Women's Kingdom, the country inhabited exclusively by women, is said to be surrounded by a sea of less density than ordinary water, so that ships sink on approaching the shores. It has been reached only by boats carried there in whirlwinds, and only a few of those wrecked on its rocks have survived and returned to tell of its wonders. The women have houses, gardens and shops.

Instead of money they use gems, perforated and strung like beads. They reproduce their kind by sleeping where the south wind blows over them.

The Land of the Flying Cart

Situated to the north of the Plain of Great Joy, the Land of the Flying Cart joins the Country of the One-armed People on the south west and that of the Three-bodied People on the south east. The inhabitants have only one arm and an additional large eye in the centre of the forehead, making three eyes in all. Their carts, though wheeled, do not run along the ground. Instead they chase each other in mid-air as gracefully as a flock of swallows. The vehicles have a kind of winged framework at each end, and the one-armed occupants, each grasping a flag, talk and laugh one to another in great delight during what might be called their aerial recreation were it not for the fact that it seems to be their sole occupation.

The Expectant Wife

A curious legend is told regarding a solitary, weird figure which stands out from a hill top in the pass called Shaohsing Xia, in Guangdong Province. This point of the pass is called Longmen, or Dragon's Mouth, and the hill the Husband-expecting Hill. The figure itself, which is called the Expectant Wife, resembles that of a woman. Her bent head and figure down to the waist are very lifelike.

The story, widely known in this and the neighbouring province, goes as follows. Centuries ago a certain poor woman was left by her husband, who went on a journey into Guangxi, close by, but in those days considered a wild and distant region, full of dangers. He promised to return in three years. The time went slowly and sadly past, for she dearly loved her husband, but he never appeared. He, an ungrateful and unfaithful spouse, had fallen in love with a fair one in Guangxi, a sorceress or witch, who threw a spell over him and charmed him to his destruction, turning him into stone. To this day his figure may be seen standing near a cave close by the river that is known by the name of the Detained Man Cave.

The wife, broken by grief at her husband's failure to return, was likewise turned into a stone, and it is said that a supernatural power will one day bring the couple to life again and reward the ever-faithful wife.

The Wild Men

The wild beasts of the mountain have a king. He is a wild man, with long, thick locks, fiery red in colour. His body is covered with hair. He is very strong: with a single blow of his huge fist, he can break large rocks to pieces; he can also pull up the trees of the forest by the root. His flesh is as hard as iron and is invulnerable to the thrusts of knife, spear or sword. He rides on a tiger when he leaves his home; he rules over the wolves, leopards and tigers, and governs all their affairs. Many other wild men, like him in appearance, live in these mountains, but on account of his great strength he alone is king. These wild men kill and eat all human beings they meet. Other hill tribes live in terror of meeting them. Indeed, who of all these mountain people would have been left alive had not some men, craftier than the wild men, devised a means of overpowering these fierce savages?

This is the method referred to: On leaving his home the herb gatherer of the mountains arms himself with two large hollow bamboo tubes, which he slips over his wrists and arms. He also carries a jar of very strong wine. When he meets one of the wild men he stands still and allows the giant to grasp him by the arm. As the giant holds him fast, as he supposes, in his firm grasp, he quietly and slowly withdraws one arm from the bamboo cuff, and, taking the pot of wine from the other hand, quickly pours it down the throat of the stooping giant, whose mouth is wide open with laughter at the thought of having captured his victim so easily. The potent wine acts at once, causing the victim to drop to the ground in a dead sleep. Then the herb-gatherer can kill him with a thrust through the heart, or leave the drunken tyrant to sleep off the effect of the wine, while he returns to his work of collecting the health-restoring herbs. Because of this the numbers of these wild men became less and less, until at the present time when now just a few remain.

The Rong Zu

The final tale in this collection is about why the people of the Rong Zu have heads of dogs. It is thought that the wave of conquest that swept from north to south in the earliest periods of Chinese history left on its way, like small islands in the ocean, certain remnants of aboriginal tribes which survived and continued to exist despite the sustained hostile attitude of the flood of foreign settlers around them.

Not many miles inland from the city of Fuzhou, up in the mountainous country, there was once the settlement of one of these tribes. It was that of the Rong Zu, the members of which wore a large and peculiar headgear constructed of bamboo splints resting on a peg inserted in the chignon at the back of the head. The weight of the structure in front was counterbalanced by a pad, serving as a weight, attached to the end of the splints, which projected as far down as the middle of the shoulders. This framework was covered by a scarf of red cloth which, when not rolled up, concealed the whole head and face. The following legend explains the origin of this unusual headdress.

In early times the Chief of a Chinese tribe was at war with the Chief of another tribe who came to attack his territory from the west. The Western Chief so badly defeated the Chinese army that none of the generals or soldiers could be persuaded to renew hostilities and try to drive the enemy back to his own country. This distressed the Chinese Chief very much. As a last resort he issued a proclamation promising his daughter in marriage to anyone who would bring him the head of his enemy, the Chief of the West.

The people in the palace talked a great deal of this promise made by the Chief, and their conversation was listened to by a fine large white dog belonging to one of the generals. This dog, having thought about the matter, waited until midnight and then crept over to the tent of the enemy Chief. The latter, as well as his guard, was asleep; or, if the guard was not, the dog succeeded in avoiding him in the darkness. Entering the tent, the dog gnawed through the Chief's neck and carried his head off in his mouth. At dawn he placed it at the Chinese Chief's feet and waited for his reward. The Chief was soon able to verify the fact that his enemy had been slain, for the headless body had caused so much distress in the hostile army that it had already begun to retreat from Chinese territory.

The dog then reminded the Chief of his promise and asked for his daughter's hand in marriage. "But how," said the Chief, "can I possibly marry my daughter to a dog?" "Well," replied the dog, "will you agree to her marrying me if I change myself into a man?" This seemed a safe promise to make and so the Chief agreed. The dog then stipulated that he should be placed under a large bell and that no one should move it or look into it for a period of 280 days.

This was done, and for 279 days the bell remained unmoved, but on the 280th day the Chief could not restrain his curiosity any longer, and tilting up the bell saw that the dog had changed into a man all except his head, the last day being required to complete the transformation. However, the spell was now broken and the result was a man with a dog's head. Since it was the Chief's fault that, through his over-inquisitiveness, the dog could not altogether become a man, he was obliged to keep his promise. The wedding duly took place, the bridegroom's head being veiled for the occasion by a red scarf.

Unfortunately the fruit of the union took more after their father than their mother and they had exceedingly ugly faces. They were therefore obliged to continue to wear the head-covering adopted by their father at the marriage ceremony. This became so much an integral part of the tribal costume that not only has it been worn ever since by their descendants, but a change of headgear has become synonymous with a change of husbands or a divorce. One account says that at the original bridal ceremony the bride wore the red scarf to prevent her seeing her husband's ugly features, and that is why the headdress is worn by the women and not by the men, or more generally by the former than the latter, though others say that it was originally worn by the ugly children of both sexes.

This legend explains the dog worship of the Rong Zu, which now consists of four clans, with a separate surname (Lei shi, Zhong shi, Lang shi, and Pan shi) to each, has a language of its own, and does not intermarry with the natives. At about the time of the old Chinese New Year (somewhere in February) they paint a large figure of a dog on a screen and worship it, saying it is their ancestor who was victorious over the Western invader.

A GLOSSARY OF
MYTH & FOLKLORE

Aaru Heavenly paradise where the blessed go after death.

Ab Heart or mind.

Abiku (Yoruba) Person predestined to die. Also known as ogbanje.

Absál Nurse to Saláman, who died after their brief love affair.

Achilles The son of Peleus and the sea-nymph Thetis, who distinguished himself in the Trojan War. He was made almost immortal by his mother, who dipped him in the River Styx, and he was invincible except for a portion of his heel which remained out of the water.

Acropolis Citadel in a Greek city.

Adad-Ea Ferryman to Ut-Napishtim, who carried Gilgamesh to visit his ancestor.

Adapa Son of Ea and a wise sage.

Adar God of the sun, who is worshipped primarily in Nippur.

Aditi Sky goddess and mother of the gods.

Adityas Vishnu, children of Aditi, including Indra, Mitra, Rudra, Tvashtar, Varuna and Vishnu.

Aeneas The son of Anchises and the goddess Aphrodite, reared by a nymph. He led the Dardanian troops in the Trojan War According to legend, he became the founder of Rome.

Aengus Óg Son of Dagda and Boann (a woman said to have given the Boyne river its name), Aengus is the Irish god of love whose stronghold is reputed to have been at New Grange. The famous tale 'Dream of Aengus' tells of how he fell in love with a maiden he had dreamt of. He eventually discovered that she was to be found at the Lake of the Dragon's Mouth in Co. Tipperary, but that she lived every alternate year in the form of a swan. Aengus thus plunged into the lake transforming himself also into the shape of a swan. Then the two flew back together to his palace on the Boyne where they lived out their days as guardians of would-be lovers.

Aesir Northern gods who made their home in Asgard; there are twelve in number.

Afrásiyáb Son of Poshang, king of Túrán, who led an army against the ruling shah Nauder. Afrásiyáb became ruler of Persia on defeating Nauder.

Afterlife Life after death or paradise, reached only by the process of preserving the body from decay through embalming and preparing it for reincarnation.

Agamemnon A famous King of Mycenae. He married Helen of Sparta's sister Clytemnestra. When Paris abducted Helen, beginning the Trojan War, Menelaus called on Agamemnon to raise the Greek troops. He had to sacrifice his daughter Iphigenia in order to get a fair wind to travel to Troy.

Agastya A rishi (sage). Leads hermits to Rama.

Agemo (Yoruba) A chameleon who aided Olorun in outwitting Olokun, who was angry at him for letting Obatala create life on her lands without her permission. Agemo outwitted Olokun by changing colour, letting her think that he and Olorun were better cloth dyers than she was. She admitted defeat and there was peace between the gods once again.

Aghasur A dragon sent by Kans to destroy Krishna.

Aghríras Son of Poshang and brother of Afrásiyáb, who was killed by his brother.

Agni The god of fire.

Agora Greek marketplace.

Ahura-Mazda Supreme god of the Persians, god of the sky. Similar to the Hindu god Varuna.

Ajax Ajax the Greater was the bravest, after Achilles, of all warriors at Troy, fighting Hector in single combat and distinguishing himself in the Battle of the Ships. He was not chosen as the bravest warrior and eventually went mad.

Ajax of Locris Another warrior at Troy. When Troy was captured, he committed the ultimate sacrilege by seizing Cassandra from her sanctuary with the Palladium.

Aje (Igbo) Goddess of the earth and the underworld.

Aje (Yoruba) Goddess of the River Niger, daughter of Yemoja.

Akhet Season of the year when the River Nile traditionally flooded.

Akkadian Person of the first Mesopotamian empire, centred in Akkad.

Akwán Diw An evil spirit who appeared as a wild ass in the court of Kai-khosráu. Rustem fought and defeated the demon, presenting its head to Kai-khosráu.

Alba Irish and Scottish Gaelic word for Scotland.

Alberich King of the dwarfs.

Alcinous King of the Phaeacians.

Alf-heim Home of the elves, ruled by Frey.

All Hallowmass All Saints' Day.

Allfather Another name for Odin; Yggdrasill was created by Allfather.

Alsvider Steed of the moon (Mani) chariot.

Alsvin Steed of the sun (Sol) chariot.

Amado Outer panelling of a dwelling, usually made of wood.

Ama-no-uzume Goddess of the dawn, meditation and the arts, who showed courage when faced with a giant who scared the other deities, including Ninigi. Also known as Uzume.

Amaterasu Goddess of the sun and daughter of Izanagi after Izanami's death; she became ruler of the High Plains of Heaven on her father's withdrawal from the world. Sister of Tsuki-yomi and Susanoo.

Ambalika Daughter of the king of Benares.

Ambika Daughter of the king of Benares.

Ambrosia Food of the gods.

Amemet Eater of the dead, monster who devoured the souls of the unworthy.

Amen Original creator deity.

Amen-Ra A being created from the fusion of Ra and Osiris. He champions the poor and those in trouble. Similar to the Greek god Zeus.

Ananda Disciple of Buddha.

Anansi One of the most popular African animal myths, Anansi the spider is a clever and shrewd character who outwits his fellow animals to get his own way. He is an entertaining but morally dubious character. Many African countries tell Anansi stories.

Ananta Thousand-headed snake that sprang from Balarama's mouth, Vishnu's attendant, serpent of infinite time.

Andhrímnir Cook at Valhalla.

Andvaranaut Ring of Andvari, the King of the dwarfs.

Angada Son of Vali, one of the monkey host.

Anger-Chamber Room designated for an angry queen.

Angurboda Loki's first wife, and the mother of Hel, Fenris and Jormungander.

Aniruddha Son of Pradyumna.

Anjana Mother of Hanuman.

Anunnaki Great spirits or gods of Earth.

Ansar God of the sky and father of Ea and Anu. Brother-husband to Kishar. Also known as Anshar or Asshur.

Anshumat A mighty chariot fighter.

Anu God of the sky and lord of heaven, son of Ansar and Kishar.

Anubis Guider of souls and ruler of the underworld before Osiris; he was one of the divinities who brought Osiris back to life. He is portrayed as a canid, African wolf or jackal.

Apep Serpent and emblem of chaos.

Apollo One of the twelve Olympian gods, son of Zeus and Leto. He is attributed with being the god of plague, music, song and prophecy.

Apsaras Dancing girls of Indra's court and heavenly nymphs.

Apsu Primeval domain of fresh water, originally part of Tiawath with whom he mated to have Mummu. The term is also used for the abyss from which creation came.

Aquila The divine eagle.

Arachne A Lydian woman with great skill in weaving. She was challenged in a competition by the jealous Athene who destroyed her work and when she killed herself, turned her into a spider destined to weave for eternity.

Aralu Goddess of the underworld, also known as Eres-ki-Gal. Married to Nergal.

Ares God of War, 'gold-changer of corpses', and the son of Zeus and Hera.

Argonauts Heroes who sailed with Jason on the ship Argo to fetch the golden fleece from Colchis.

Ariki A high chief, a leader, a master, a lord.

Arjuna The third of the Pandavas.

Aroha Affection, love.

Artemis The virgin goddess of the chase, attributed with being the moon goddess and the primitive mother-goddess. She was daughter of Zeus and Leto.

Arundhati The Northern Crown.

Asamanja Son of Sagara.

Asclepius God of healing who often took the form of a snake. He is the son of Apollo by Coronis.

Asgard Home of the gods, at one root of Yggdrasill.

Ashvatthaman Son of Drona.

Ashvins Twin horsemen, sons of the sun, benevolent gods and related to the divine.

Ashwapati Uncle of Bharata and Satrughna.

Asipû Wizard.

Asopus The god of the River Asopus.

Assagai Spear, usually made from hardwood tipped with iron and used in battle.

Astrolabe Instrument for making astronomical measurements.

Asuras Titans, demons, and enemies of the gods with magical powers.

Atef crown White crown made up of the Hedjet, the white crown of Upper Egypt, and red feathers.

Atem The first creator-deity, he is also thought to be the finisher of the world. Also known as Tem.

Athene Virgin warrior-goddess, born from the forehead of Zeus when he swallowed his wife Metis. Plays a key role in the travels of Odysseus, and Perseus.

Atlatl Spear-thrower.

Atua A supernatural being, a god.

Atua-toko A small carved stick, the symbol of the god whom it represents. It was stuck in the ground whilst holding incantations to its presiding god.

Augeas King of Elis, one of the Argonauts.

Augsburg Tyr's city.

Avalon Legendary island where Excalibur was created and where Arthur went to recover from his wounds. It is said he will return from Avalon one day to reclaim his kingdom.

Ba Dead person or soul. Also known as ka.

Bairn Little child, also called bairnie.

Balarama Brother of Krishna.

Balder Son of Frigga; his murder causes Ragnarok. Also spelled as Baldur.

Bali Brother of Sugriva and one of the five great monkeys in the *Ramayana*.

Balor The evil, one-eyed King of the Fomorians and also grandfather of Lugh of the Long Arm. It was prophesied that Balor would one day be slain by his own grandson so he locked his daughter away on a remote island where he intended that she would never fall pregnant. But Cian, father of Lugh, managed to reach the island disguised as a woman, and Balor's daughter eventually bore him a child. During the second battle of Mag Tured (or Moytura), Balor was killed by Lugh who slung a stone into his giant eye.

Ban King of Benwick, father of Lancelot and brother of King Bors.

Bannock Flat loaf of bread, typically of oat or barley, usually cooked on a griddle.

Banshee Mythical spirit, usually female, who bears tales of imminent death. They often deliver the news by wailing or keening outside homes. Spelled *bean sí* in Gaelic.

Bard Traditionally a storyteller, poet or music composer whose work often focused on legends.

Barû Seer.

Basswood Any of several North American linden trees with a soft light-coloured wood.

Bastet Goddess of love, fertility and sex and a solar deity. She is often portrayed with the head of a cat.

Bateta (Yoruba) The first human, created alongside Hanna by the Toad and reshaped into human form by the Moon.

Bau Goddess of humankind and the sick, and known as the 'divine physician'. Daughter of Anu.

Bawn Fortified enclosure surrounding a castle.

Beaver Largest rodent in the United States of America, held in high esteem by Native American people. Although a land mammal, it spends a great deal of time in water and has a dense waterproof fur coat to protect it from harsh weather conditions.

Behula Daughter of Saha.

Bel Name for the god En-lil, the word is also used as a title meaning 'lord'.

Belus Deity who helped form the heavens and earth and created animals and celestial beings. Similar to Zeus in Greek mythology.

Benten Goddess of the sea and one of the Seven Divinities of Luck. Also referred to as the goddess of love, beauty and eloquence and as being the personification of wisdom.

Bere Barley.

Berossus Priest of Bel who wrote a history of Babylon.

Berserker Norse warrior who fights with a frenzied rage.

Bestla Giant mother of Aesir's mortal element.

Bhadra A mighty elephant.

Bhagavati Shiva's wife, also known as Parvati.

Bhagiratha Son of Dilipa.

Bharadhwaja Father of Drona and a hermit.

Bharata One of Dasharatha's four sons.

Bhaumasur A demon, slain by Krishna.

Bhima The second of the Pandavas.

Bhimasha King of Rajagriha and disciple of Buddha.

Bier Frame on which a coffin or dead body is placed before being carried to the grave.

Bifrost Rainbow bridge presided over by Heimdall.

Big-Belly One of Ravana's monsters.

Bilskirnir Thor's palace.

Bodach The term means 'old man'. The Highlanders believed that the Bodach crept down chimneys in order to steal naughty children. In other territories, he was a spirit who warned of death.

Bodkin Large, blunt needle used for threading strips of cloth or tape through cloth; short pointed dagger or blade.

Boer Person of Dutch origin who settled in southern Africa in the late seventeenth century. The term means 'farmer'. Boer people are often called Afrikaners.

Bogle Ghost or phantom; goblin-like creature.

Boliaun Ragwort, a weed with ragged leaves.

Book of the Dead Book for the dead, thought to be written by Thoth, texts from which were written on papyrus and buried with the dead, or carved on the walls of tombs, pyramids or sarcophagi.

Bors King of Gaul and brother of King Ban.

Bothy Small cottage or hut.

Brahma Creator of the world, mythical origin of colour (caste).

Brahmadatta King of Benares.

Brahman Member of the highest Hindu caste, traditionally a priest.

Bran In Scottish legend, Bran is the great hunting hound of Fionn Mac Chumail. In Irish mythology, he is a great hero.

Branstock Giant oak tree in the Volsung's hall; Odin placed a sword in it and challenged the guests of a wedding to withdraw it.

Brave Young warrior of Native American descent, sometimes also referred to as a 'buck'.

Bree Thin broth or soup.

Breidablik Balder's palace.

Brigit Scottish saint or spirit associated with the coming of spring.

Brisingamen Freyia's necklace.

Britomartis A Cretan goddess, also known as Dictynna.

Brocéliande Legendary enchanted forest and the supposed burial place of Merlin.

Brokki Dwarf who makes a deal with Loki, and who makes Miolnir, Draupnir and Gulinbursti.

Brollachan A shapeless spirit of unknown origin. One of the most frightening in Scottish mythology, it spoke only two words, 'Myself' and 'Thyself', taking the shape of whatever it sat upon.

Brownie A household spirit or creature which took the form of a small man (usually hideously ugly) who undertakes household chores, and mill or farm work, in exchange for a bowl of milk.

Brugh Borough or town.

Brunhilde A Valkyrie found by Sigurd.

Buddha Founder of buddhism, Gautama, avatar of Vishnu in Hinduism.

Buddhism Buddhism arrived in China in the first century BCE via the silk trading route from India and Central Asia. Its founder was Guatama Siddhartha (the Buddha), a religious teacher in northern India. Buddhist doctrine declared that by destroying the causes of all suffering, mankind could attain perfect enlightenment. The religion encouraged a new respect for all living things and brought with it the idea of reincarnation; i.e. that the soul returns to the earth after death in another form, dictated by the individual's behaviour in his previous life. By the fourth century, Buddhism was the dominant religion in China, retaining its powerful influence over the nation until the mid-ninth century.

Buffalo A type of wild ox, once widely scattered over the Great Plains of North America. Also known as a 'bison', the buffalo was an important food source for Native American tribes and its hide was also used in the construction of tepees and to make clothing. The buffalo was also sometimes revered as a totem animal, i.e. venerated as a direct ancestor of the tribesmen, and its skull used in ceremonial fashion.

Bull of Apis Sacred bull, thought to be the son of Hathor.

Bulu Sacrificial rite.

Bundles, sacred These bundles contained various venerated objects of the tribe, believed to have supernatural powers. Custody or ownership of the bundle was never lightly entered upon, but involved the learning of endless songs and ritual dances.

Bushel Unit of measurement, usually used for agricultural products or food.

Bushi Warrior.

Byre Barn for keeping cattle.

Byrny Coat of mail.

Cacique King or prince.

Cailleach Bheur A witch with a blue face who represents winter. When she is reborn each autumn, snow falls. She is mother of the god of youth (Angus mac Og).

Calabash Gourd from the calabash tree, commonly used as a bottle.

Calchas The seer of Mycenae who accompanied the Greek fleet to Troy. It was his prophecy which stated that Troy would never be taken without the aid of Achilles.

Calpulli Village house, or group or clan of families.

Calumet Ceremonial pipe used by Native Americans.

Calypso A nymph who lived on the island of Ogygia.

Camaxtli Tlascalan god of war and the chase, similar to Huitzilopochtli.

Camelot King Arthur's castle and centre of his realm.

Caoineag A banshee.

Caravanserai Traveller's inn, traditionally found in Asia or North Africa.

Carle Term for a man, often old; peasant.

Cat A black cat has great mythological significance, is often the bearer of bad luck, a symbol of black magic, and the familiar of a witch. Cats were also the totem for many tribes.

Cath Sith A fairy cat who was believed to be a witch transformed.

Cazi Magical person or influence.

Ceasg A Scottish mermaid with the body of a maiden and the tail of a salmon.

Ceilidh Party.

Cerberus The three-headed dog who guarded the entrance to the Underworld.

Chalchiuhtlicue Goddess of water and the sick or newborn, and wife of Tlaloc. She is often symbolized as a small frog.

Changeling A fairy substitute-child left by fairies in place of a human child they have stolen.

Channa Guatama's charioteer.

Chaos A state from which the universe was created – caused by fire and ice meeting.

Charon The ferryman of the dead who carries souls across the River Styx to Hades.

Charybdis *See* Scylla and Charybdis.

Chicomecohuatl Chief goddess of maize and one of a group of deities called Centeotl, who care for all aspects of agriculture.

Chicomoztoc Legendary mountain and place of origin of the Aztecs. The name means 'seven caves'.

Chinawezi Primordial serpent.

A GLOSSARY OF MYTH & FOLKLORE

Chinvat Bridge Bridge of the Gatherer, which the souls of the righteous cross to reach Mount Alborz or the world of the dead. Unworthy beings who try to cross Chinvat Bridge fall or are dragged into a place of eternal punishment.

Chitambaram Sacred city of Shiva's dance.

Chrysaor Son of Poseidon and Medusa, born from the severed neck of Medusa when Perseus beheaded her.

Chryseis Daughter of Chryses who was taken by Agamemnon in the battle of Troy.

Chullasubhadda Wife of Buddha-elect (Sumedha).

Chunda A good smith who entertains Buddha.

Churl Mean or unkind person.

Circe An enchantress and the daughter of Helius. She lived on the island of Aeaea with the power to change men to beasts.

Citlalpol The Mexican name for Venus, or the Great Star, and one of the only stars they worshipped. Also known as Tlauizcalpantecutli, or Lord of the Dawn.

Cleobis and Biton Two men of Argos who dragged the wagon carrying their mother, priestess of Hera, from Argos to the sanctuary.

Clio Muse of history and prophecy.

Clytemnestra Daughter of Tyndareus, sister of Helen, who married Agamemnon but deserted him when he sacrificed Iphigenia, their daughter, at the beginning of the Trojan War.

Coatepetl Mythical mountain, known as the 'serpent mountain'.

Coatl Serpent.

Coatlicue Earth mother and celestial goddess, she gave birth to Huitzilopochtli and his sister, Coyolxauhqui, and the moon and stars.

Codex Ancient book, often a list with pages folded into a zigzag pattern.

Confucius (Kong Fuzi) Regarded as China's greatest sage and ethical teacher, Confucius (551–479 BCE) was not especially revered during his lifetime and had a small following of some three thousand people. After the Burning of the Books in 213 BCE, interest in his philosophies became widespread. Confucius believed that mankind was essentially good, but argued for a highly structured society, presided over by a strong central government which would set the highest moral standards. The individual's sense of duty and obligation, he argued, would play a vital role in maintaining a well-run state.

Coracle Small, round boat, similar to a canoe. Also known as curragh or currach.

Coyolxauhqui Goddess of the moon and sister to Huitzilopochtli, she was decapitated by her brother after trying to kill their mother.

Creel Large basket made of wicker, usually used for fish.

Crodhmara Fairy cattle.

Cronan Musical humming, thought to resemble a cat purring or the drone of bagpipes.

Crow Usually associated with battle and death, but many mythological figures take this form.

Cu Sith A great fairy dog, usually green and oversized.

Cubit Ancient measurement, equal to the approximate length of a forearm.

Cuculain Irish warrior and hero. Also known as Cuchulainn.

Cutty Girl.

Cyclopes One-eyed giants who were imprisoned in Tartarus by Uranus and Cronus, but released by Zeus, for whom they made thunderbolts. Also a tribe of pastoralists who live without laws, and on, whenever possible, human flesh.

Daedalus Descendant of the Athenian King Erechtheus and son of Eupalamus. He killed his nephew and apprentice. Famed for constructing the labyrinth to house the Minotaur, in which he was later imprisoned. He constructed wings for himself and his son to make their escape.

Dagda One of the principal gods of the Tuatha De Danann, the father and chief, the Celtic equivalent of Zeus. He was the god reputed to have led the People of Dana in their successful conquest of the Fir Bolg.

Dagon God of fish and fertility; he is sometimes described as a sea-monster or chthonic god.

Daikoku God of wealth and one of the gods of luck.

Daimyō Powerful lord or magnate.

Daksha The chief Prajapati.

Dana Also known as Danu, a goddess worshipped from antiquity by the Celts and considered to be the ancestor of the Tuatha De Danann.

Danae Daughter of Acrisius, King of Argos. Acrisius trapped her in a cave when he was warned that his grandson would be the cause of his ultimate death. Zeus came to her and Perseus was born.

Danaids The fifty daughters of Danaus of Argos, by ten mothers.

Daoine Sidhe The people of the Hollow Hills, or Otherworld.

Dardanus Son of Zeus and Electra, daughter of Atlas.

Dasharatha A Manu amongst men, King of Koshala, father of Santa.

Deianeira Daughter of Oeneus, who married Heracles after he won her in a battle with the River Achelous.

Deirdre A beautiful woman doomed to cause the deaths of three Irish heroes and bring war to the whole country. After a soothsayer prophesied her fate, Deidre's father hid her away from the world to prevent it. However, fate finds its way and the events come to pass before Deidre eventually commits suicide to remain with her love.

Demeter Goddess of agriculture and nutrition, whose name means earth mother. She is the mother of Persephone.

Demophoon Son of King Celeus of Eleusis, who was nursed by Demeter and then dropped in the fire when she tried to make him immortal.

Dervish Member of a religious order, often Sufi, known for their wild dancing and whirling.

Desire The god of love.

Deva A god other than the supreme God.

Devadatta Buddha's cousin, plots evil against Buddha.

Dhrishtadyumna Twin brother of Draupadi, slays Drona.

Dibarra God of plague. Also a demonic character or evil spirit.

Dik-dik Dwarf antelope native to eastern and southern Africa.

Dilipa Son of Anshumat, father of Bhagiratha.

Dionysus The god of wine, vegetation and the life force, and of ecstasy. He was considered to be outside the Greek pantheon, and generally thought to have begun life as a mortal.

Dioscuri Castor and Polydeuces, the twin sons of Zeus and Leda, who are important deities.

Distaff Tool used when spinning which holds the wool or flax and keeps the fibres from tangling.

Divan Privy council.

Divots Turfs.

Dog The dog is a symbol of humanity, and usually has a role helping the hero of the myth or legend. Fionn's Bran and Grey Dog are two examples of wild beasts transformed to become invaluable servants.

Dōshin Government official.

Dossal Ornamental altar cloth.

Doughty Persistent and brave person.

Dragon Important animal in Japanese culture, symbolizing power, wealth, luck and success.

Draiglin' Hogney Ogre.

Draupadi Daughter of Drupada.

Draupnir Odin's famous ring, fashioned by Brokki.

Drona A Brahma, son of the great sage Bharadwaja.

Druid An ancient order of Celtic priests held in high esteem who flourished in the pre-Christian era. The word 'druid' is derived from an ancient Celtic one meaning 'very knowledgeable'. These individuals were believed to have mystical powers and in ancient Irish literature possess the ability to conjure up magical charms, to create tempests, to curse and debilitate their enemies and to perform as soothsayers to the royal courts.

Drupada King of the Panchalas.

Dryads Nymphs of the trees.

Dun A stronghold or royal abode surrounded by an earthen wall.

Durga Goddess, wife of Shiva.

Durk Knife. Also spelled as dirk.

Duryodhana One of Drona's pupils.

Dvalin Dwarf visited by Loki; also the name for the stag on Yggdrasill.

Dwarfie Stone Prehistoric tomb or boulder.

Dwarfs Fairies and black elves are called dwarfs.

Dwarkanath The Lord of Dwaraka; Krishna.

Dyumatsena King of the Shalwas and father of Satyavan.

Ea God of water, light and wisdom, and one of the creator deities. He brought arts and civilization to humankind. Also known as Oannes and Nudimmud.

Eabani Hero originally created by Aruru to defeat Gilgamesh, the two became friends and destroyed Khumbaba together. He personifies the natural world.

Each Uisge The mythical water-horse which haunts lochs and appears in various forms.

Ebisu One of the gods of luck. He is also the god of labour and fishermen.

Echo A nymph who was punished by Hera for her endless stories told to distract Hera from Zeus's infidelity.

Ector King Arthur's foster father, who raised Arthur to protect him.

Edda Collection of prose and poetic myths and stories from the Norsemen.

Eight Immortals Three of these are reputed to be historical: Han Zhongli, born in Shaanxi, who rose to become a Marshal of the Empire in 21 BCE. Chang Kuo-Lao, who lived in the seventh to eighth century CE, and Lu Dongbin, who was born in 755 CE.

Einheriear Odin's guests at Valhalla.

Eisa Loki's daughter.

Ekake (Ibani) Person of great intelligence, which means 'tortoise'. Also known as Mbai (Igbo).

Ekalavya Son of the king of the Nishadas.

Electra Daughter of Agamemnon and Clytemnestra.

Eleusis A town in which the cult of Demeter is centred.

Elf Sigmund is buried by an elf; there are light and dark elves (the latter called dwarfs).

Elokos (Central African) Imps of dwarf-demons who eat human flesh.

Elpenor The youngest of Odysseus's crew who fell from the roof of Circe's house on Aeaea and visited with Odysseus at Hades.

Elysium The home of the blessed dead.

Emain Macha The capital of ancient Ulster.

Emma Dai-o King of hell and judge of the dead.

En-lil God of the lower world, storms and mist, who held sway over the ghostly animistic spirits, which at his bidding might pose as the friends or enemies of men. Also known as Bel.

Eos Goddess of the dawn and sister of the sun and moon.

Erichthonius A child born of the semen spilled when Hephaestus tried to rape Athene on the Acropolis.

Eridu The home of Ea and one of the two major cities of Babylonian civilization.

Erin Term for Ireland, originally spelled Éirinn.

Erirogho Magical mixture made from the ashes of the dead.

Eros God of Love, the son of Aphrodite.

Erpa Hereditary chief.

Erysichthon A Thessalian who cut down a grove sacred to Demeter, who punished him with eternal hunger.

Eshu (Yoruba) God of mischief. He also tests people's characters and controls law enforcement.

Eteocles Son of Oedipus.

Eumaeus Swineherd of Odysseus's family at Ithaca.

Euphemus A son of Poseidon who could walk on water. He sailed with the Argonauts.

Europa Daughter of King Agenor of Tyre, who was taken by Zeus to Crete.

Eurydice A Thracian nymph married to Orpheus.

Excalibur The magical sword given to Arthur by the Lady of the Lake. In some versions of the myths, Excalibur is also the sword that the young Arthur pulls from the stone to become king.

Fabulist Person who composes or tells fables.

Fafnir Shape-changer who kills his father and becomes a dragon to guard the family jewels. Slain by Sigurd.

Fairy The word is derived from 'Fays' which means Fates. They are immortal, with the gift of prophecy and of music, and their role changes according to the origin of the myth. They were often considered to be little people, with enormous propensity for mischief, but they are central to many myths and legends, with important powers.

Faro (Mali, Guinea) God of the sky.

Fates In Greek mythology, daughters of Zeus and Themis, who spin the thread of a mortal's life and cut it when his time is due. Called Norns in Viking mythology.

Fenris A wild wolf, who is the son of Loki. He roams the earth after Ragnarok.

Ferhad Sculptor who fell in love with Shireen, the wife of Khosru, and undertook a seemingly impossible task to clear a passage through the mountain of Beysitoun and join the rivers in return for winning Shireen's hand.

Fialar Red cock of Valhalla.

Fianna/Fenians The word 'fianna' was used in early times to describe young warrior-hunters. These youths evolved under the leadership of Finn Mac Cumaill as a highly skilled band of military men who took up service with various kings throughout Ireland.

Filheim Land of mist, at the end of one of Yggdrasill's roots.

Fingal Another name for Fionn Mac Chumail, used after MacPherson's Ossian in the eighteenth century.

Fionn Mac Chumail Irish and Scottish warrior, with great powers of fairness and wisdom. He is known not for physical strength but for knowledge, sense of justice, generosity and canny instinct. He had two hounds, which were later discovered to be his nephews transformed. He became head of the Fianna, or Féinn, fighting the enemies of Ireland and Scotland. He was the father of Oisin (also called Ossian, or other derivatives), and father or grandfather of Osgar.

Fir Bolg One of the ancient, pre-Gaelic peoples of Ireland who were reputed to have worshipped the god Bulga, meaning god of lighting. They are thought to have colonized Ireland around 1970 BCE, after the death of Nemed and to have reigned for a short period of thirty-seven years before their defeat by the Tuatha De Danann.

Fir Chlis Nimble men or merry dancers, who are the souls of fallen angels.

Flitch Side of salted and cured bacon.

Folkvang Freyia's palace.

Fomorians A race of monstrous beings, popularly conceived as sea-pirates with some supernatural characteristics who opposed the earliest settlers in Ireland, including the Nemedians and the Tuatha De Danann.

Frey Comes to Asgard with Freyia as a hostage following the war between the Aesir and the Vanir.

Freyia Comes to Asgard with Frey as a hostage following the war between the Aesir and the Vanir. Goddess of beauty and love.

Frigga Odin's wife and mother of gods; she is goddess of the earth.

Fuath Evil spirits which lived in or near the water.

Fulla Frigga's maidservant.

Furies Creatures born from the blood of Cronus, guarding the greatest sinners of the Underworld. Their power lay in their ability to drive mortals mad. Snakes writhed in their hair and around their waists.

Furoshiki Cloths used to wrap things.

Gae Bolg Cuchulainn alone learned the use of this weapon from the woman-warrior, Scathach and with it he slew his own son Connla and his closest friend, Ferdia. Gae Bolg translates as 'harpoon-like javelin' and the deadly weapon was reported to have been created by Bulga, the god of lighting.

Gaea Goddess of Earth, born from Chaos, and the mother of Uranus and Pontus. Also spelled as Gaia.

Gage Object of value presented to a challenger to symbolize good faith.

Galahad Knight of the Round Table, who took up the search for the Holy Grail. Son of Lancelot, Galahad is considered the purest and most perfect knight.

Galatea Daughter of Nereus and Doris, a sea-nymph loved by Polyphemus, the Cyclops.

Gandhari Mother of Duryodhana.

Gandharvas Demi-gods and musicians.

Gandjharva Musical ministrants of the upper air.

Ganesha Elephant-headed god of scribes and son of Shiva.

Ganges Sacred river personified by the goddess Ganga, wife of Shiva and daughter of the mount Himalaya.

Gareth of Orkney King Arthur's nephew and knight of the Round Table.

Garm Hel's hound.

Garuda King of the birds and mount Vishnu, the divine bird, attendant of Narayana.

Gautama Son of Suddhodana and also known as Siddhartha.

Gawain Nephew of King Arthur and knight of the Round Table, he is best known for his adventure with the Green Knight, who challenges one of Arthur's knights to cut off his head, but only if he agrees to be beheaded in turn in a year and a day, if the Green Knight survives. Gawain beheads the Green Knight, who simply replaces his head. At the appointed time, they meet, and the Green Knight swings his axe but merely nicks Gawain's skin instead of beheading him.

Geisha Performance artist or entertainer, usually female.

Geri Odin's wolf.

Ghommid (Yoruba) Term for mythological creatures such as goblins or ogres.

Giallar Bridge in Filheim.

Giallarhorn Heimdall's trumpet – the final call signifies Ragnarok.

Giants In Greek mythology, a race of beings born from Gaea, grown from the blood that dropped from the castrated Uranus. Usually represent evil in Viking mythology.

Gilgamesh King of Erech known as a half-human, half-god hero similar to the Greek Heracles, and often listed with the gods. He is the personification of the sun and is protected by the god Shamash, who in some texts is described as his father. He is also portrayed as an evil tyrant at times.

Gillie Someone who works for a Scottish chief, usually as an attendant or servant; guide for fishing or hunting parties.

Gladheim Where the twelve deities of Asgard hold their thrones. Also called Gladsheim.

Gled Bird of prey.

Golden Fleece Fleece of the ram sent by Poseidon to substitute for Phrixus when his father was going to sacrifice him. The Argonauts went in search of the fleece.

Goodman Man of the house.

Goodwife Woman of the house.

Gopis Lovers of the young Krishna and milkmaids.

Gorgon One of the three sisters, including Medusa, whose frightening looks could turn mortals to stone.

Graces Daughters of Aphrodite by Zeus.

Gramercy Expression of surprise or strong feeling.

Great Head The Iroquois believed in the existence of a curious being known as Great Head, a creature with an enormous head poised on slender legs.

Great Spirit The name given to the Creator of all life, as well as the term used to describe the omnipotent force of the Creator existing in every living thing.

Great-Flank One of Ravana's monsters.

Green Knight A knight dressed all in green and with green hair and skin who challenged one of Arthur's knights to strike him a blow with an axe and that, if he survived, he would return to behead the knight in a year and a day. He turned out to be Lord Bertilak and was under an enchantment cast by Morgan le Fay to test Arthur's knights.

Gruagach Mythical creature, often a giant or ogre similar to a wild man of the woods. The term can also refer to other mythical creatures such as brownies or fairies. As a brownie, he is usually dressed in red or green as opposed to the traditional brown. He has great power to enchant the hapless, or to help mortals who are worthy (usually heroes). He often appears to challenge a boy-hero, during his period of education.

Gudea High priest of Lagash, known to be a patron of the arts and a writer himself.

Guebre Religion founded by Zoroaster, the Persian prophet.

Gugumatz Creator god who, with Huracan, formed the sky, earth and everything on it.

Guha King of Nishadha.

Guidewife Woman.

Guinevere Wife of King Arthur; she is often portrayed as a virtuous lady and wife, but is perhaps best known for having a love affair with Lancelot, one of Arthur's friends and knights of the Round Table. Her name is also spelled Guenever.

Gulistan *Rose Garden*, written by the poet Sa'di

Gungnir Odin's spear, made of Yggdrasill wood, and the tip fashioned by Dvalin.

Gylfi A wandering king to whom the Eddas are narrated.

Haab Mayan solar calendar that consisted of eighteen twenty-day months.

Hades One of the three sons of Cronus; brother of Poseidon and Zeus. Hades is King of the Underworld, which is also known as the House of Hades.

Haere-mai Maori phrase meaning 'come here, welcome.'

Haere-mai-ra, me o tatou mate Maori phrase meaning 'come here, that I may sorrow with you.'

Haere-ra Maori phrase meaning 'goodbye, go, farewell.'

Haji Muslim pilgrim who has been to Mecca.

Hakama Traditional Japanese clothing, worn on the bottom half of the body.

Hanuman General of the monkey people.

Harakiri Suicide, usually by cutting or stabbing the abdomen. Also known as seppuku.

Hari-Hara Shiva and Vishnu as one god.

Harmonia Daughter of Ares and Aphrodite, wife of Cadmus.

Hatamoto High-ranking samurai.

Hathor Great cosmic mother and patroness of lovers. She is portrayed as a cow.

Hati The wolf who pursues the sun and moon.

Hatshepsut Second female pharaoh.

Hauberk Armour to protect the neck and shoulders, sometimes a full-length coat of mail.

Hector Eldest son of King Priam who defended Troy from the Greeks. He was killed by Achilles.

Hecuba The second wife of Priam, King of Troy. She was turned into a dog after Troy was lost.

Heimdall White god who guards the Bifrost bridge.

Hel Goddess of death and Loki's daughter. Also known as Hela.

Helen Daughter of Leda and Tyndareus, King of Sparta, and the most beautiful woman in the world. She was responsible for starting the Trojan War.

Heliopolis City in modern-day Cairo, known as the City of the Sun and the central place of worship of Ra. Also known as Anu.

Helius The sun, son of Hyperion and Theia.

Henwife Witch.

Hephaestus or **Hephaistos** The Smith of Heaven.

Hera A Mycenaean palace goddess, married to Zeus.

Heracles An important Greek hero, the son of Zeus and Alcmena. His name means 'Glory of Hera'. He performed twelve labours for King Eurystheus, and later became a god.

Hermes The conductor of souls of the dead to Hades, and god of trickery and of trade. He acts as messenger to the gods.

Hermod Son of Frigga and Odin who travelled to see Hel in order to reclaim Balder for Asgard.

Hero and Leander Hero was a priestess of Aphrodite, loved by Leander, a young man of Abydos. He drowned trying to see her.

Hestia Goddess of the hearth, daughter of Cronus and Rhea.

Hieroglyphs Type of writing that combines symbols and pictures, usually cut into tombs or rocks, or written on papyrus.

Himalaya Great mountain and range, father of Parvati.

Hiordis Wife of Sigmund and mother of Sigurd.

Hoderi A fisher and son of Okuninushi.

Hodur Balder's blind twin; known as the personification of darkness.

Hoenir Also called Vili; produced the first humans with Odin and Loki, and was one of the triad responsible for the creation of the world.

Hōichi the Earless A biwa hōshi, a blind storyteller who played the biwa or lute. Also a priest.

Holger Danske Legendary Viking warrior who is thought to never die. He sleeps until he is needed by his people and then he will rise to protect them.

Homayi Phoenix.

Hoodie Mythical creature which often appears as a crow.

Hoori A hunter and son of Okuninushi.

Horus God of the sky and kinship, son of Isis and Osiris. He captained the boat that carried Ra across the sky. He is depicted with the head of a falcon.

Hotei One of the gods of luck. He also personifies humour and contentment.

Houlet Owl.

Houri Beautiful virgin from paradise.

Hrim-faxi Steed of the night.

Hubris Presumptuous behaviour which causes the wrath of the gods to be brought on to mortals.

Hueytozoztli Festival dedicated to Tlaloc and, at times, Chicomecohuatl or other deities. Also the fourth month of the Aztec calendar.

Hugin Odin's raven.

Huitzilopochtli   God of war and the sun, also connected with the summer and crops; one of the principal Aztec deities. He was born a full-grown adult to save his mother, Coatlicue, from the jealousy of his sister, Coyolxauhqui, who tried to kill Coatlicue. The Mars of the Aztec gods. In some origin stories he is one of four offspring of Ometeotl and Omecihuatl.

Hurley   A traditional Irish game played with sticks and balls, quite similar to hockey.

Hurons   A tribe of Iroquois stock, originally one people with the Iroquois.

Huveane   (Pedi, Venda) Creator of humankind, who made a baby from clay into which he breathed life. He is known as the High God or Great God. He is also known as a trickster god.

Hymir   Giant who fishes with Thor and is drowned by him.

Iambe   Daughter of Pan and Echo, servant to King Celeus of Eleusis and Metaeira.

Icarus   Son of Daedalus, who plunged to his death after escaping from the labyrinth.

Ichneumon   Mongoose.

Idunn   Guardian of the youth-giving apples.

Ifa   (Yoruba) God of wisdom and divination. Also the term for a Yoruban religion.

Ife   (Yoruba) The place Obatala first arrived on Earth and took for his home.

Igigi   Great spirits or gods of Heaven and the sky.

Igraine   Wife of the duke of Tintagel, enemy of Uther Pendragon, who marries Uther when her first husband dies. She is King Arthur's mother.

Ile (Yoruba) Goddess of the earth.

Imhetep High priest and wise sage. He is sometimes thought to be the son of Ptah.

Imam Person who leads prayers in a mosque.

Imana (Banyarwanda) Creator or sky god.

In The male principle who, joined with Yo, the female side, brought about creation and the first gods. In and Yo correspond to the Chinese Yang and Yin.

Inari God of rice, fertility, agriculture and, later, the fox god. Inari has both good and evil attributes but is often presented as an evil trickster.

Indra The King of Heaven.

Indrajit Son of Ravana.

Indrasen Daughter of Nala and Damayanti.

Indrasena Son of Nala and Damayanti.

Inundation Annual flooding of the River Nile.

Iphigenia The eldest daughter of Agamemnon and Clytemnestra who was sacrificed to appease Artemis and obtain a fair wind for Troy.

Iris Messenger of the gods who took the form of a rainbow.

Iseult Princess of Ireland and niece of the Morholt. She falls in love with Tristan after consuming a love potion but is forced to marry King Mark of Cornwall.

Ishtar Goddess of love, beauty, justice and war, especially in Ninevah, and earth mother who symbolizes fertility. Married to Tammuz, she is similar to the Greek goddess Aphrodite. Ishtar is sometimes known as Innana or Irnina.

Isis Goddess of the Nile and the moon, sister-wife of Osiris. She and her son, Horus, are sometimes thought of in a similar way to Mary and Jesus. She was one of the most worshipped female

Egyptian deities and was instrumental in returning Osiris to life after he was killed by his brother, Set.

Istakbál Deputation of warriors.

Izanagi Deity and brother-husband to Izanami, who together created the Japanese islands from the Floating Bridge of Heaven. Their offspring populated Japan.

Izanami Deity and sister-wife of Izanagi, creator of Japan. Their children include Amaterasu, Tsuki-yomi and Susanoo.

Jade It was believed that jade emerged from the mountains as a liquid which then solidified after ten thousand years to become a precious hard stone, green in colour. If the correct herbs were added to it, it could return to its liquid state and when swallowed increase the individual's chances of immortality.

Jambavan A noble monkey.

Jason Son of Aeson, King of Iolcus and leader of the voyage of the Argonauts.

Jatayu King of all the eagle-tribes.

Jesseraunt Flexible coat of armour or mail.

Jimmo Legendary first emperor of Japan. He is thought to be descended from Hoori, while other tales claim him to be descended from Amaterasu through her grandson, Ninigi.

Jizo God of little children and the god who calms the troubled sea.

Jord Daughter of Nott; wife of Odin.

Jormungander The world serpent; son of Loki. Legends tell that when his tail is removed from his mouth, Ragnarok has arrived.

Jorō Geisha who also worked as a prostitute.

Jotunheim Home of the giants.

Ju Ju tree Deciduous tree that produces edible fruit.

Jurasindhu A rakshasa, father-in-law of Kans.

Jyeshtha Goddess of bad luck.

Ka Life power or soul. Also known as ba.

Kai-káús Son of Kai-kobád. He led an army to invade Mázinderán, home of the demon-sorcerers, after being persuaded by a demon. Known for his ambitious schemes, he later tried to reach Heaven by trapping eagles to fly him there on his throne.

Kaikeyi Mother of Bharata, one of Dasharatha's three wives.

Kai-khosrau Son of Saiawúsh, who killed Afrásiyáb in revenge for the death of his father.

Kai-kobád Descendant of Feridún, he was selected by Zál to lead an army against Afrásiyáb. Their powerful army, led by Zál and Rustem, drove back Afrásiyáb's army, who then agreed to peace.

Kailyard Kitchen garden or small plot, usually used for growing vegetables.

Kali The Black, wife of Shiva.

Kalindi Daughter of the sun, wife of Krishna.

Kaliya A poisonous hydra that lived in the jamna.

Kalki Incarnation of Vishnu yet to come.

Kalnagini Serpent who kills Lakshmindara.

Kal-Purush The Time-man, Bengali name for Orion.

Kaluda A disciple of Buddha.

Kalunga-ngombe (Mbundu) Death, also depicted as the king of the netherworld.

Kama God of desire.

Kamadeva Desire, the god of love.

Kami Spirits, deities or forces of nature.

Kamund Lasso.

Kans King of Mathura, son of Ugrasena and Pavandrekha.

Kanva Father of Shakuntala.

Kappa River goblin with the body of a tortoise and the head of an ape. Kappa love to challenge human beings to single combat.

Karakia Invocation, ceremony, prayer.

Karna Pupil of Drona.

Kaross Blanket or rug, also worn as a traditional garment. It is often made from the skins of animals which have been sewn together.

Kasbu A period of twenty-four hours.

Kashyapa One of Dasharatha's counsellors.

Kauravas or Kurus Sons of Dhritarashtra, pupils of Drona.

Kaushalya Mother of Rama, one of Dasharatha's three wives.

Kay Son of Ector and adopted brother to King Arthur, he becomes one of Arthur's knights of the Round Table.

Keb God of the earth and father of Osiris and Isis, married to Nut. Keb is identified with Kronos, the Greek god of time.

Kehua Spirit, ghost.

Kelpie Another word for each uisge, the water-horse.

Ken Know.

Keres Black-winged demons or daughters of the night.

Keshini Wife of Sagara.

Khalif Leader.

Khara Younger brother of Ravana.

Khepera God who represents the rising sun. He is portrayed as a scarab. Also known as Nebertcher.

Kher-heb Priest and magician who officiated over rituals and ceremonies.

Khnemu God of the source of the Nile and one of the original Egyptian deities. He is thought to be the creator of children and of other gods. He is portrayed as a ram.

Khosru King and husband to Shireen, daughter of Maurice, the Greek Emperor. He was murdered by his own son, who wanted his kingdom and his wife.

Khumbaba Monster and guardian of the goddess Irnina, a form of the goddess Ishtar. Khumbaba is likened to the Greek gorgon.

Kia-ora Welcome, good luck. A greeting.

Kiboko Hippopotamus.

Kikinu Soul.

Kimbanda (Mbundu) Doctor.

Kimono Traditional Japanese clothing, similar to a robe.

King Arthur Legendary king of Britain who plucked the magical sword from the stone, marking him as the heir of Uther Pendragon and 'true king' of Britain. He and his knights of the Round Table defended Britain from the Saxons and had many adventures, including searching for the Holy Grail. Finally wounded in battle, he left Britain for the mythical Avalon, vowing to one day return to reclaim his kingdom.

Kingu Tiawath's husband, a god and warrior who she promised would rule Heaven once he helped her defeat the 'gods of light'. He was killed by Merodach who used his blood to make clay, from which he formed the first humans. In some tales, Kingu is Tiawath's son as well as her consort.

Kinnaras Human birds with musical instruments under their wings.

Kinyamkela (Zaramo) Ghost of a child.

Kirk Church, usually a term for Church of Scotland churches.

Kirtle One-piece garment, similar to a tunic, which was worn by men or women.

Kis Solar deity, usually depicted as an eagle.

Kishar Earth mother and sister-wife to Anshar.

Kist Trunk or large chest.

Kitamba (Mbundu) Chief who made his whole village go into mourning when his head-wife, Queen Muhongo, died. He also pledged that no one should speak or eat until she was returned to him.

Knowe Knoll or hillock.

Kojiki One of two myth-histories of Japan, along with the *Nihon Shoki*.

Ko-no-Hana Goddess of Mount Fuji, princess and wife of Ninigi.

Kore 'Maiden', another name for Persephone.

Kraal Traditional rural African village, usually consisting of huts surrounded by a fence or wall. Also an animal enclosure.

Krishna The Dark one, worshipped as an incarnation of Vishnu.

Kui-see Edible root.

Kumara Son of Shiva and Paravati, slays demon Taraka.

Kumbha-karna Ravana's brother.

Kunti Mother of the Pandavas.

Kura Red. The sacred colour of the Maori.

Kusha or Kusi One of Sita's two sons.

Kvasir Clever warrior and colleague of Odin. He was responsible for finally outwitting Loki.

Kwannon Goddess of mercy.

Labyrinth A prison built at Knossos for the Minotaur by Daedalus.

Lady of the Lake Enchantress who presents Arthur with Excalibur.

Laertes King of Ithaca and father of Odysseus.

Laestrygonians Savage giants encountered by Odysseus on his travels.

Laili In love with Majnun but unable to marry him, she was given to the prince, Ibn Salam, to marry. When he died, she escaped and found Majnun, but they could not be legally married. The couple died of grief and were buried together. Also known as Laila.

Laird Person who owns a significant estate in Scotland.

Lakshmana Brother of Rama and his companion in exile.

Lakshmi Consort of Vishnu and a goddess of beauty and good fortune.

Lakshmindara Son of Chand resurrected by Manasa Devi.

Lancelot Knight of the Round Table. Lancelot was raised by the Lady of the Lake. While he went on many quests, he is perhaps best known for his affair with Guinevere, King Arthur's wife.

Land of Light One of the names for the realm of the fairies. If a piece of metal welded by human hands is put in the doorway to their land, the door cannot close. The door to this realm is only open at night, and usually at a full moon.

Lang syne The days of old.

Lao Tzu (Laozi) The ancient Taoist philosopher thought to have been born in 571 BCE a contemporary of Confucius with whom, it is said, he discussed the tenets of Tao. Lao Tzu was an advocate of simple rural existence and looked to the Yellow Emperor and Shun as models of efficient government. His philosophies were recorded in the Tao Te Ching. Legends surrounding his birth suggest that he emerged from the left-hand side of his mother's body, with white hair and a long white beard, after a confinement lasting eighty years.

Laocoon A Trojan wiseman who predicted that the wooden horse contained Greek soldiers.

Laomedon The King of Troy who hired Apollo and Poseidon to build the impregnable walls of Troy.

Lava Son of Sita.

Leda Daughter of the King of Aetolia, who married Tyndareus. Helen and Clytemnestra were her daughters.

Legba (Dahomey) Youngest offspring of Mawu-Lisa. He was given the gift of all languages. It was through him that humans could converse with the gods.

Leman Lover.

Leprechaun Mythical creature from Irish folk tales who often appears as a mischievous and sometimes drunken old man.

Lethe One of the four rivers of the Underworld, also called the River of Forgetfulness.

Lif The female survivor of Ragnarok.

Lifthrasir The male survivor of Ragnarok.

Lil Demon.

Liongo (Swahili) Warrior and hero.

Lofty mountain Home of Ahura-Mazda.

Logi Utgard-loki's cook.

Loki God of fire and mischief-maker of Asgard; he eventually brings about Ragnarok. Also spelled as Loptur.

Lotus-Eaters A race of people who live a dazed, drugged existence, the result of eating the lotus flower.

Ma'at State of order meaning truth, order or justice. Personified by the goddess Ma'at, who was Thoth's consort.

Macha There are thought to be several different Machas who appear in quite a number of ancient Irish stories. For the purposes of this book, however, the Macha referred to is the wife of Crunnchu. The story unfolds that after her husband had boasted of her great athletic ability to the King, she was subsequently forced to run against his horses in spite of the fact that she was heavily pregnant. Macha died giving birth to her twin babies and with her dying breath she cursed Ulster for nine generations, proclaiming that it would suffer the weakness of a woman in childbirth in times of great stress. This curse had its most disastrous effect when Medb of Connacht invaded Ulster with her great army.

Machi-bugyō Senior official or magistrate, usually samurai.

Macuilxochitl God of art, dance and games, and the patron of luck in gaming. His name means 'source of flowers' or 'prince of flowers'. Also known as Xochipilli, meaning 'five-flower'.

Madake Weapon used for whipping, made of bamboo.

Maduma Taro tuber.

Mag Muirthemne Cuchulainn's inheritance. A plain extending from River Boyne to the mountain range of Cualgne, close to Emain Macha in Ulster.

Magni Thor's son.

Mahaparshwa One of Ravana's generals.

Maharaksha Son of Khara, slain at Lanka.

Mahasubhadda Wife of Buddha-select (Sumedha).

Majnun Son of a chief, who fell in love with Laili and followed her tribe through the desert, becoming mad with love until they were briefly reunited before dying.

Makaras Mythical fish-reptiles of the sea.

Makoma (Senna) Folk hero who defeated five mighty giants.

Mana Power, authority, prestige, influence, sanctity, luck.

Manasa Devi Goddess of snakes, daughter of Shiva by a mortal woman.

Manasha Goddess of snakes.

Mandavya Daughter of Kushadhwaja.

Man-Devourer One of Ravana's monsters.

Mandodari Wife of Ravana.

Mandrake Poisonous plant from the nightshade family which has hallucinogenic and hypnotic qualities if ingested. Its roots resemble the human form and it has supposedly magical qualities.

Mani The moon.

Manitto Broad term used to describe the supernatural or a potent spirit among the Algonquins, the Iroquois and the Sioux.

Man-Slayer One of Ravana's counsellors.

Manthara Kaikeyi's evil nurse, who plots Rama's ruin.

Mantle Cloak or shawl.

Manu Lawgiver.

Manu Mythical mountain on which the sun sets.

Mara The evil one, tempts Gautama.

Markandeya One of Dasharatha's counsellors.

Mashu Mountain of the Sunset, which lies between Earth and the underworld. Guarded by scorpion-men.

Matali Sakra's charioteer.

Mawu-Lisa (Dahomey) Twin offspring of Nana Baluka. Mawu (female) and Lisa (male) are often joined to form one being. Their own offspring populated the world.

Mbai (Igbo) Person of great intelligence, also known as Ekake (Ibani), which means 'tortoise'.

Medea Witch and priestess of Hecate, daughter of Aeetes and sister of Circe. She helped Jason in his quest for the Golden Fleece.

Medusa One of the three Gorgons whose head had the power to turn onlookers to stone.

Melpomene One of the muses, and mother of the Sirens.

Menaka One of the most beautiful dancers in Heaven.

Menat Amulet, usually worn for protection.

Mendicant Beggar.

Menelaus King of Sparta, brother of Agamemnon. Married Helen and called war against Troy when she eloped with Paris.

Menthu Lord of Thebes and god of war. He is portrayed as a hawk or falcon.

Mere-pounamu A native weapon made of a rare green stone.

Merlin Wizard and advisor to King Arthur. He is thought to be the son of a human female and an incubus (male demon). He brought about Arthur's birth and ascension to king, then acted as his mentor.

Merodach God who battled Tiawath and defeated her by cutting out her heart and dividing her corpse into two pieces. He used these pieces to divide the upper and lower waters once controlled by Tiawath, making a dwelling for the gods of light. He also created humankind. Also known as Marduk.

Merrow Mythical mermaid-like creature, often depicted with an enchanted cap called a cohuleen driuth which allows it to travel between land and the depths of the sea. Also known as murúch.

Metaneira Wife of Celeus, King of Eleusis, who hired Demeter in disguise as her nurse.

Metztli Goddess of the moon, her name means 'lady of the night'. Also known as Yohualtictl.

Michabo Also known as Manobozho, or the Great Hare, the principal deity of the Algonquins, maker and preserver of the earth, sun and moon.

Mictlan God of the dead and ruler of the underworld. He was married to Mictecaciuatl and is often represented as a bat. He is also the Aztec lord of Hades. Also known as Mictlantecutli. Mictlan is also the name for the underworld.

Midgard Dwelling place of humans (Earth).

Midsummer A time when fairies dance and claim human victims.

Mihrab Father of Rúdábeh and descendant of Zohák, the serpent-king.

Milesians A group of iron-age invaders led by the sons of Mil, who arrived in Ireland from Spain around 500 BCE and overcame the Tuatha De Danann.

Mimir God of the ocean. His head guards a well; reincarnated after Ragnarok.

Minos King of Crete, son of Zeus and Europa. He was considered to have been the ruler of a sea empire.

Minotaur A creature born of the union between Pasiphae and a Cretan Bull.

Minúchihr King who lives to be one hundred and twenty years old. Father of Nauder.

Miolnir *See* Mjolnir.

Mithra God of the sun and light in Iran, protector of truth and guardian of pastures and cattle. Alo known as Mitra in Hindu mythology and Mithras in Roman mythology.

Mixcoatl God of the chase or the hunt. Sometimes depicted as the god of air and thunder, he introduced fire to humankind. His name means 'cloud serpent'.

Mjolnir Hammer belonging to the Norse god of thunder, which is used as a fearsome weapon which always returns to Thor's hand, and as an instrument of consecration.

Mnoatia Forest spirits.

Moccasins One-piece shoes made of soft leather, especially deerskin.

Modi Thor's son.

Moly A magical plant given to Odysseus by Hermes as protection against Circe's powers.

Montezuma Great emperor who consolidated the Aztec Empire.

Mordred Bastard son of King Arthur and Morgawse, Queen of Orkney, who, unknown to Arthur, was his half-sister. Mordred becomes one of King Arthur's knights of the Round Table before betraying and fatally wounding Arthur, causing him to leave Britain for Avalon.

Morgan le Fay Enchantress and half-sister to King Arthur, Morgan was an apprentice of Merlin's. She is generally depicted as benevolent, yet did pit herself against Arthur and his knights on occasion. She escorts Arthur on his final journey to Avalon. Also known as Morgain le Fay.

Morholt The knight sent to Cornwall to force King Mark to pay tribute to Ireland. He is killed by Tristan.

Morongoe the brave (Lesotho) Man who was turned into a snake by evil spirits because Tau was jealous that he had married the beautiful Mokete, the chief's daughter. Morongoe was returned to human form after his son, Tsietse, returned him to their family.

Mosima (Bapedi) The underworld or abyss.

Mount Fuji Highest mountain in Japan, on the island of Honshū.

Mount Kunlun This mountain features in many Chinese legends as the home of the great emperors on Earth. It is written in the *Shanghaijing* (*The Classic of Mountains and Seas*) that this towering structure measured no less than 3300 miles in circumference and 4000 miles in height. It acted both as a central pillar to support the heavens, and as a gateway between Heaven and Earth.

Moving Finger Expression for taking responsibility for one's life and actions, which cannot be undone.

Moytura Translated as the 'Plain of Weeping', Mag Tured, or Moytura, was where the Tuatha De Danann fought two of their most significant battles.

Mua An old-time Polynesian god.

Muezzin Person who performs the Muslim call to prayer.

Mugalana A disciple of Buddha.

Muilearteach The Cailleach Bheur of the water, who appears as a witch or a sea-serpent. On land she grew larger and stronger by fire.

Mul-lil God of Nippur, who took the form of a gazelle.

Muloyi Sorcerer, also called mulaki, murozi, ndozi or ndoki.

Mummu Son of Tiawath and Apsu. He formed a trinity with them to battle the gods. Also known as Moumis. In some tales, Mummu is also Merodach, who eventually destroyed Tiawath.

Munin Odin's raven.

Murile (Chaga) Man who dug up a taro tuber that resembled his baby brother, which turned into a living boy. His mother killed the baby when she saw Murile was starving himself to feed it.

Murtough Mac Erca King who ruled Ireland when many of its people – including his wife and family – were converting to Christianity. He remained a pagan.

Muses Goddesses of poetry and song, daughters of Zeus and Mnemosyne.

Musha Expression, often of surprise.

Muskrat North American beaver-like, amphibious rodent.

Muspell Home of fire, and the fire-giants.

Mwidzilo Taboo which, if broken, can cause death.

Nabu God of writing and wisdom. Also known as Nebo. Thought to be the son of Merodach.

Nahua Ancient Mexicans.

Nakula Pandava twin skilled in horsemanship.

Nala One of the monkey host, son of Vishvakarma.

Nana Baluka (Dahomey) Mother of all creation. She gave birth to an androgynous being with two faces. The female face was Mawu, who controlled the night and lands to the west. The male face was Lisa and he controlled the day and the east.

Nanahuatl Also known as Nanauatzin. Presided over skin diseases and known as Leprous, which in Nahua meant 'divine'.

Nandi Shiva's bull.

Nanna Balder's wife.

Nannar God of the moon and patron of the city of Ur.

Naram-Sin Son or ancestor of Sargon and king of the Four Zones or Quarters of Babylon.

Narcissus Son of the River Cephisus. He fell in love with himself and died as a result.

Narve Son of Loki.

Nataraja Manifestation of Shiva, Lord of the Dance.

Natron Preservative used in embalming, mined from the Natron Valley in Egypt.

Nauder Son of Minúchihr, who became king on his death and was tyrannical and hated until Sám begged him to follow in the footsteps of his ancestors.

Nausicaa Daughter of Alcinous, King of Phaeacia, who fell in love with Odysseus.

Nebuchadnezzar Famous king of Babylon. Also known as Nebuchadrezzar.

Necromancy Communicating with the dead.

Nectar Drink of the gods.

Neith Goddess of hunting, fate and war. Neith is sometimes known as the creator of the universe.

Nemesis Goddess of retribution and daughter of night.

Neoptolemus Son of Achilles and Deidameia, he came to Troy at the end of the war to wear his father's armour. He sacrificed Polyxena at the tomb of Achilles.

Nephthys Goddess of the air, night and the dead. Sister of Isis and sister-wife to Seth, she is also the mother of Anubis.

Nereids Sea-nymphs who are the daughters of Nereus and Doris. Thetis, mother of Achilles, was a Nereid.

Nergal God of death and patron god of Cuthah, which was often known as a burial place. He is also known as the god of fire. Married to Aralu, the goddess of the underworld.

Nestor Wise King of Pylus, who led the ships to Troy with Agamemnon and Menelaus.

Neta Daughter of Shiva, friend of Manasa.

Ngai (Gikuyu) Creator god.

Ngaka (Lesotho) Witch doctor.

Niflheim The underworld In Norse mythology, ruled over by Hel.

Night Daughter of Norvi.

Nikumbha One of Ravana's generals.

Nila One of the monkey host, son of Agni.

Nin-Girsu God of fertility and war, patron god of Girsu. Also known as Shul-gur.

Ninigi Grandson of Amaterasu, Ninigi came to Earth bringing rice and order to found the Imperial family. He is known as the August Grandchild.

Niord God of the sea; marries Skadi.

Nippur The home of En-lil and one of the two major cities of Babylonian civilization.

Nirig God of war and storms, and son of Bel. Also known as Enu-Restu.

Nirvana Transcendent state and the final goal of Buddhism.

Nis Mythological creature, similar to a brownie or goblin, usually harmless or even friendly, but can be easily offended. They are often associated with Christmas or the winter solstice.

Noatun Niord's home.

Noisy-Throat One of Ravana's counsellors.

Noondah (Zanzibar) Cannibalistic cat which attacked and killed animals and humans.

Norns The fates and protectors of Yggdrasill. Many believe them to be the same as the Valkyries.

Norvi Father of the night.

Nott Goddess of night.

Nsasak bird Small bird who became chief of all small birds after winning a competition to go without food for seven days. The

Nsasak bird beat the Odudu bird by sneaking out of his home to feed.

Nüwa The Goddess Nüwa, who in some versions of the Creation myths is the sole creator of mankind, and in other tales is associated with the God Fuxi, also a great benefactor of the human race. Some accounts represent Fuxi as the brother of Nüwa, but others describe the pair as lovers who lie together to create the very first human beings. Fuxi is also considered to be the first of the Chinese emperors of mythical times who reigned from 2953 to 2838 BCE.

Nuada The first king of the Tuatha De Danann in Ireland, who lost an arm in the first battle of Moytura against the Fomorians. He became known as 'Nuada of the Silver Hand' when Diancecht, the great physician of the Tuatha De Danann, replaced his hand with a silver one after the battle.

Nunda (Swahili, East Africa) Slayer that took the form of a cat and grew so big that it consumed everyone in the town except the sultan's wife, who locked herself away. Her son, Mohammed, killed Nunda and cut open its leg, setting free everyone Nunda had eaten.

Nut Goddess of the sky, stars and astronomy. Sister-wife of Keb and mother of Osiris, Isis, Set and Nephthys. She often appears in the form of a cow.

Nyame (Ashanti) God of the sky, who sees and knows everything.

Nymphs Minor female deities associated with particular parts of the land and sea.

Obassi Osaw (Ekoi) Creator god with his twin, Obassi Nsi. Originally, Obassi Osaw ruled the skies while Obassi Nsi ruled the Earth.

Obatala (Yoruba) Creator of humankind. He climbed down a golden chain from the sky to the earth, then a watery abyss, and formed land and humankind. When Olorun heard of his success, he created the sun for Obatala and his creations.

Oberon Fairy king.

Odin Allfather and king of all gods, he is known for travelling the nine worlds in disguise and recognized only by his single eye; dies at Ragnarok.

Oduduwa (Yoruba) Divine king of Ile-Ife, the holy city of Yoruba.

Odur Freyia's husband.

Odysseus Greek hero, son of Laertes and Anticleia, who was renowned for his cunning, the master behind the victory at Troy, and known for his long voyage home.

Oedipus Son of Leius, King of Thebes and Jocasta. Became King of Thebes and married his mother.

Ogdoad Group of eight deities who were formed into four male-female couples who joined to create the gods and the world.

Ogham One of the earliest known forms of Irish writing, originally used to inscribe upright pillar stones.

Oiran Courtesan.

Oisin Also called Ossian (particularly by James Macpherson who wrote a set of Gaelic Romances about this character, supposedly garnered from oral tradition). Ossian was the son of Fionn and Sadbh, and had various brothers, according to different legends. He was a man of great wisdom, became immortal for many centuries, but in the end he became mad.

Ojibwe Another name for the Chippewa, a tribe of Algonquin stock.

Okuninushi Deity and descendant of Susanoo, who married Suseri-hime, Susanoo's daughter, without his consent. Susanoo tried to kill him many times but did not succeed and eventually forgave Okuninushi. He is sometimes thought to be the son or grandson of Susanoo.

Olokun (Yoruba) Most powerful goddess who ruled the seas and marshes. When Obatala created Earth in her domain, other gods began to divide it up between them. Angered at their presumption, she caused a great flood to destroy the land.

Olorun (Yoruba) Supreme god and ruler of the sky. He sees and controls everything, but others, such as Obatala, carry out the work for him. Also known as Olodumare.

Olympia Zeus's home in Elis.

Olympus The highest mountain in Greece and the ancient home of the gods.

Omecihuatl Female half of the first being, combined with Ometeotl. Together they are the lords of duality or lords of the two sexes. Also known as Ometecutli and Omeciuatl or Tonacatecutli and Tonacaciuatl. Their offspring were Xipe Totec, Huitzilopochtli, Quetzalcoatl and Tezcatlipoca.

Ometeotl Male half of the first being, combined with Omecihuatl.

Ometochtli Collective name for the pulque-gods or drink-gods. These gods were often associated with rabbits as they were thought to be senseless creatures.

Onygate Anyway.

Opening of the Mouth Ceremony in which mummies or statues were prayed over and anointed with incense before their mouths were opened, allowing them to eat and drink in the afterlife.

Oracle The response of a god or priest to a request for advice – also a prophecy; the place where such advice was sought; the person or thing from whom such advice was sought.

Oranyan (Yoruba) Youngest grandson of King Oduduwa, who later became king himself.

Orestes Son of Agamemnon and Clytemnestra who escaped following Agamemnon's murder to King Strophius. He later returned to Argos to murder his mother and avenge the death of his father.

Orpheus Thracian singer and poet, son of Oeagrus and a Muse. Married Eurydice and when she died tried to retrieve her from the Underworld.

Orunmila (Yoruba) Eldest son of Olorun, he helped Obatala create land and humanity, which he then rescued after Olokun flooded the lands. He has the power to see the future.

Osiris God of fertility, the afterlife and death. Thought to be the first of the pharaohs. He was murdered by his brother, Set, after which he was conjured back to life by Isis, Anubis and others before becoming lord of the afterworld. Married to Isis, who was also his sister.

Otherworld The world of deities and spirits, also known as the Land of Promise, or the Land of Eternal Youth, a place of everlasting life where all earthly dreams come to be fulfilled.

Owuo (Krachi, West Africa) Giant who personifies death. He causes a person to die every time he blinks his eye.

Palamedes Hero of Nauplia, believed to have created part of the ancient Greek alphabet. He tricked Odysseus into joining the fleet setting out for Troy by placing the infant Telemachus in the path of his plough.

Palermo Stone Stone carved with hieroglyphs, which came from the Royal Annals of ancient Egypt and contains a list of the kings of Egypt from the first to the early fifth dynasties.

Palfrey Docile and light horse, often used by women.

Palladium Wooden image of Athene, created by her as a monument to her friend Pallas who she accidentally killed. While in Troy it protected the city from invaders.

Pallas Athene's best friend, whom she killed.

Pan God of Arcadia, half-goat and half-man. Son of Hermes. He is connected with fertility, masturbation and sexual drive. He is also associated with music, particularly his pipes, and with laughter.

Pangu Some ancient writers suggest that this God is the offspring of the opposing forces of nature, the yin and the yang. The yin (female) is associated with the cold and darkness of the earth, while the yang (male) is associated with the sun and the warmth of the heavens. 'Pan' means 'shell of an egg' and 'Gu' means 'to secure' or 'to achieve'. Pangu came into existence so that he might create order from chaos.

Pandareus Cretan King killed by the gods for stealing the shrine of Zeus.

Pandavas Alternative name for sons of Pandu, pupils of Drona.

Pandora The first woman, created by the gods, to punish man for Prometheus's theft of fire. Her dowry was a box full of powerful evil.

Papyrus Paper-like material made from the pith of the papyrus plant, first manufactured in Egypt. Used as a type of paper as well as for making mats, rope and sandals.

Paramahamsa The supreme swan.

Parashurama Human incarnation of Vishnu, 'Rama with an axe'.

Paris Handsome son of Priam and Hecuba of Troy, who was left for dead on Mount Ida but raised by shepherds. Was reclaimed by his family, then brought them shame and caused the Trojan War by eloping with Helen.

Parsa Holy man. Also known as a zahid.

Parvati Consort of Shiva and daughter of Himalaya.

Passion Wife of desire.

Pavanarekha Wife of Ugrasena, mother of Kans.

Peerie Folk Fairy or little folk.

Pegasus The winged horse born from the severed neck of Medusa.

Peggin Wooden vessel with a handle, often shaped like a tub and used for drinking.

Peleus Father of Achilles. He married Antigone, caused her death, and then became King of Phthia. Saved from death himself by Jason and the Argonauts. Married Thetis, a sea nymph.

Penelope The long-suffering but equally clever wife of Odysseus who managed to keep at bay suitors who longed for Ithaca while Odysseus was at the Trojan War and on his ten-year voyage home.

Pentangle Pentagram or five-pointed star.

Pentecost Christian festival held on the seventh Sunday after Easter. It celebrates the holy spirit descending on the disciples after Jesus's ascension.

Percivale Knight of the Round Table and original seeker of the Holy Grail.

Persephone Daughter of Zeus and Demeter who was raped by Hades and forced to live in the Underworld as his queen for three months of every year.

Perseus Son of Danae, who was made pregnant by Zeus. He fought the Gorgons and brought home the head of Medusa. He eventually founded the city of Mycenae and married Andromeda.

Pesh Kef Spooned blade used in the Opening the Mouth ceremony.

Phaeacia The Kingdom of Alcinous on which Odysseus landed after a shipwreck which claimed the last of his men as he left Calypso's island.

Pharaoh King or ruler of Egypt.

Philoctetes Malian hero, son of Poeas, received Heracles's bow and arrows as a gift when he lit the great hero's pyre on Mount Oeta. He was involved in the last part of the Trojan War, killing Paris.

Philtre Magic potion, usually a love potion.

Pibroch Bagpipe music.

Pintura Native manuscript or painting.

Pipiltin Noble class of the Aztecs.

Pismire Ant.

Piu-piu Short mat made from flax leaves and neatly decorated.

Po Gloom, darkness, the lower world.

Polyphemus A Cyclops, but a son of Poseidon. He fell in love with Galatea, but she spurned him. He was blinded by Odysseus.

Polyxena Daughter of Priam and Hecuba of Troy. She was sacrificed on the grave of Achilles by Neoptolemus.

Pooka Mythical creature with the ability to shapeshift. Often appears as a horse, but also as a bull, dog or in human form, and has the ability to talk. Also known as púca.

Popol Vuh Sacred 'book of counsel' of the Quiché or K'iche' Maya people.

Poseidon God of the sea, and of sweet waters. Also the god of earthquakes. His is brother to Zeus and Hades, who divided the earth between them.

Pradyumna Son of Krishna and Rukmini.

Prahasta (Long-Hand) One of Ravana's generals.

Prajapati Creator of the universe, father of the gods, demons and all creatures, later known as Brahma.

Priam King of Troy, married to Hecuba, who bore him Hector, Paris, Helenus, Cassandra, Polyxena, Deiphobus and Troilus. He was murdered by Neoptolemus.

Pritha Mother of Karna and of the Pandavas.

Prithivi Consort of Dyaus and goddess of the earth.

Proetus King of Argos, son of Abas.

Prometheus A Titan, son of Iapetus and Themus. He was champion of mortal men, which he created from clay. He stole fire from the gods and was universally hated by them.

Prose Edda Collection of Norse myths and poems, thought to have been compiled in the 1200s by Icelandic historian Snorri Sturluson.

Proteus The old man of the sea who watched Poseidon's seals.

Psyche A beautiful nymph who was the secret wife of Eros, against the wishes of his mother Aphrodite, who sent Psyche to perform many tasks in hope of causing her death. She eventually married Eros and was allowed to become partly immortal.

Ptah Creator god and deity of Memphis who was married to Sekhmet. Ptah built the boats to carry the souls of the dead to the afterlife.

Puddock Frog.

Pulque Alcoholic drink made from fermented agave.

Purusha The cosmic man, he was sacrificed and his dismembered body became all the parts of the cosmos, including the four classes of society.

Purvey To provide or supply.

Pushkara Nala's brother.

Pushpaka Rama's chariot.

Putana A rakshasi.

Pygmalion A sculptor who was so lonely he carved a statue of a beautiful woman, and eventually fell in love with it. Aphrodite brought the image to life.

Quauhtli Eagle.

Quern Hand mill used for grinding corn.

Quetzalcoatl Deity and god of wind. He is represented as a feathered or plumed serpent and is usually a wise and benevolent god. Offspring of Ometeotl and Omecihuatl, he is also known as Kukulkan.

Ra God of the sun, ruling male deity of Egypt whose name means 'sole creator'.

Radha The principal mistress of Krishna.

Ragnarok The end of the world.

Rahula Son of Siddhartha and Yashodhara.

Raiden God of thunder. He traditionally has a fierce and demonic appearance.

Rakshasas Demons and devils.

Ram of Mendes Sacred symbol of fatherhood and fertility.

Rama or **Ramachandra** A prince and hero of the *Ramayana*, worshipped as an incarnation of Vishnu.

Ra-Molo (Lesotho) Father of fire, a chief who ruled by fear. When trying to kill his brother, Tau the lion, he was turned into a monster with the head of a sheep and the body of a snake.

Rangatira Chief, warrior, gentleman.

Regin A blacksmith who educated Sigurd.

Reinga The spirit land, the home of the dead.

Reservations Tracts of land allocated to the Native American people by the United States Government with the purpose of bringing the many separate tribes under state control.

Rewati Daughter of Raja, marries Balarama.

Rhadha Wife of Adiratha, a gopi of Brindaban and lover of Krishna.

Rhea Mother of the Olympian gods. Cronus ate each of her children, but she concealed Zeus and gave Cronus a swaddled rock in his place.

Rill Small stream.

Rimu (Chaga) Monster known to feed off human flesh, which sometimes takes the form of a werewolf.

Rishis Sacrificial priests associated with the devas in Swarga.

Rituparna King of Ayodhya.

Rohini The wife of Vasudeva, mother of Balarama and Subhadra, and carer of the young Krishna. Another Rohini is a goddess and consort of Chandra.

Rōnin Samurai whose master had died or fallen out of favour.

Rubáiyát Collection of poems written by Omar Khayyám.

Rúdábeh Wife of Zál and mother of Rustem.

Rudra Lord of Beasts and disease, later evolved into Shiva.

Rukma Rukmini's eldest brother.

Rustem Son of Zál and Rúdábeh, he was a brave and mighty warrior who undertook seven labours to travel to Mázinderán to rescue Kai-káús. Once there, he defeated the White Demon and rescued Kai-káús. He rode the fabled stallion Rakhsh and is also known as Rustam.

Ryō Traditional gold currency.

Sabdh Mother of Ossian, or Oisin.

Sabitu Goddess of the sea.

Sagara King of Ayodhya.

Sahadeva Pandava twin skilled in swordsmanship.

Sahib diwan Lord high treasurer or chief royal executive.

Saiawúsh Son of Kai-káús, who was put through trial by fire when Sudaveh, Kai-káús's wife, told him that Saiawúsh had taken advantage of her. His innocence was proven when the fire did not harm him. He was eventually killed by Afrásiyáb.

Saithe Blessed.

Sajara (Mali) God of rainbows. He takes the form of a multi-coloured serpent.

Sake Japanese rice wine.

Sakuni Cousin of Duryodhana.

Salam Greeting or salutation.

Saláman Son of the Shah of Yunan, who fell in love with Absál, his nurse. She died after they had a brief love affair and he returned to his father.

Salmali tree Cotton tree.

Salmon A symbol of great wisdom, around which many Scottish legends revolve.

Sám Mighty warrior who fought and won many battles. Father of Zál and grandfather to Rustem.

Sambu Son of Krishna.

Sampati Elder brother of Jatayu.

Samurai Noblemen who were part of the military in medieval Japan.

Sanehat Member of the royal bodyguard.

Sango (Yoruba) God of war and thunder.

Sangu (Mozambique) Goddess who protects pregnant women, depicted as a hippopotamus.

Santa Daughter of Dasharatha.

Sarapis Composite deity of Apis and Osiris, sometimes known as Serapis. Thought to be created to unify Greek and Egyptian citizens under the Greek pharaoh Ptolemy.

Sarasvati The tongue of Rama.

Sarcophagus Stone coffin.

Sargon of Akkad Raised by Akki, a husbandman, after being hidden at birth. Sargon became King of Assyria and a great hero. He founded the first library in Babylon. Similar to King Arthur or Perseus.

Sarsar Harsh, whistling wind.

Sasabonsam (Ashanti) Forest ogre.

Sassun Scottish word for England.

Sati Daughter of Daksha and Prasuti, first wife of Shiva.

Satrughna One of Dasharatha's four sons.

Satyavan Truth speaker, husband of Savitri.

Satyavati A fisher-maid, wife of Bhishma's father, Shamtanu.

Satyrs Elemental spirits which took great pleasure in chasing nymphs. They had horns, a hairy body and cloven hooves.

Saumanasa A mighty elephant.

Scamander River running across the Trojan plain, and father of Teucer.

Scarab Dung beetle, often used as a symbol of the immortal human soul and regeneration.

Scylla and Charybdis Scylla was a monster who lived on a rock of the same name in the Straits of Messina, devouring sailors. Charybdis was a whirlpool in the Straits which was supposedly inhabited by the hateful daughter of Poseidon.

Seal Often believed that seals were fallen angels. Many families are descended from seals, some of which had webbed hands or feet. Some seals were the children of sea-kings who had become enchanted (selkies).

Seelie-Court The court of the Fairies, who travelled around their realm. They were usually fair to humans, doling out punishment that was morally sound, but they were quick to avenge insults to fairies.

Segu (Swahili, East Africa) Guide who informs humans where honey can be found.

Sekhmet Solar deity who led the pharaohs in war. She is goddess of healing and was sent by Ra to destroy humanity when people turned against the sun god. She is portrayed with the head of a lion.

Selene Moon-goddess, daughter of Hyperion and Theia. She was seduced by Pan, but loved Endymion.

Selkie Mythical creature which is seal-like when in water but can shed its skin to take on human form when on land.

Seneschal Steward of a royal or noble household.

Sensei Teacher.

Seriyut A disciple of Buddha.

Sessrymnir Freyia's home.

Set God of chaos and evil, brother of Osiris, who killed him by tricking him into getting into a chest, which he then threw in the Nile, before cutting Osiris's body into fourteen separate pieces. Also known as Seth.

Sgeulachd Stories.

Sháhnámeh *The Book of Kings* written by Ferdowsi, one of the world's longest epic poems, which describes the mythology and history of the Persian Empire.

Shaikh Respected religious man.

Shaivas or Shaivites Worshippers of Shiva.

Shakti Power or wife of a god and Shiva's consort as his feminine aspect.

Shaman Also known as the 'Medicine Men' of Native American tribes, it is the shaman's role to cultivate communication with the spirit world. They are endowed with knowledge of all healing herbs, and learn to diagnose and cure disease. They are believed to foretell the future, find lost property and have power over animals, plants and stones.

Shamash God of the sun and protector of Gilgamesh, the great Babylonian hero. Known as the son of Sin, the moon god, he is also portrayed as a judge of good and evil.

Shamtanu Father of Bhishma.

Shankara A great magician, friend of Chand Sadagar.

Shashti The Sixth, goddess who protects children and women in childbirth.

Sheen Beautiful and enchanted woman who casts a spell on Murtough, King of Ireland, causing him to fall in love with her and cast out his family. He dies at her hands, half burned and half drowned, but she then dies of grief as she returns his love. Sheen is known by many names, including Storm, Sigh and Rough Wind.

Shesh A serpent that takes human birth through Devaki.

Shi-en Fairy dwelling.

Shinto Indigenous religion of Japan, from the pre-sixth century to the present day.

Shireen Married to Khosru. Her beauty meant that she was desired by many, including Khosru's own son by his previous marriage. She killed herself rather than give in to her stepson.

Shitala The Cool One and goddess of smallpox.

Shiva One of the two great gods of post-Vedic Hinduism with Vishnu.

Shogun Military ruler or overlord.

Shoji Sliding door, usually a lattice screen of paper.

Shu God of the air and half of the first divine couple created by Atem. Brother and husband to Tefnut, father to Keb and Nut.

Shubistán Household.

Shudra One of the four fundamental colours (caste).

Shuttle Part of a machine used for spinning cloth, used for passing weft threads between warp threads.

Siddhas Musical ministrants of the upper air.

Sif Thor's wife; known for her beautiful hair.

Sigi Son of Odin.

Sigmund Warrior able to pull the sword from Branstock in the Volsung's hall.

Signy Volsung's daughter.

Sigurd Son of Sigmund, and bearer of his sword. Slays Fafnir the dragon.

Sigyn Loki's faithful wife.

Símúrgh Griffin, an animal with the body of a lion and the head and wings of an eagle. Known to hold great wisdom. Also called a symurgh.

Sin God of the moon, worshipped primarily in Ur.

Sindri Dwarf who worked with Brokki to fashion gifts for the gods; commissioned by Loki.

Sirens Sea nymphs who are half-bird, half-woman, whose song lures hapless sailors to their death.

Sisyphus King of Ephrya and a trickster who outwitted Autolycus. He was one of the greatest sinners in Hades.

Sita Daughter of the earth, adopted by Janaka, wife of Rama.

Skadi Goddess of winter and the wife of Niord for a short time.

Skanda Six-headed son of Shiva and a warrior god.

Skraeling Person native to Canada and Greenland. The name was given to them by Viking settlers and can be translated as 'barbarian'.

Skrymir Giant who battled against Thor.

Sleipnir Odin's steed.

Sluagh The host of the dead, seen fighting in the sky and heard by mortals.

Smote Struck with a heavy blow.

Sohráb Son of Rustem and Tahmineh, Sohráb was slain in battle by his own father, who killed him by mistake.

Sol The sun-maiden.

Soma A god and a drug, the elixir of life.

Somerled Lord of the Isles, and legendary ancestor of the Clan MacDonald.

Soothsayer Someone with the ability to predict or see the future, by the use of magic, special knowledge or intuition. Known as seanagal in Scottish myths.

Squaw A Native American woman or wife (now offensive).

Squint-Eye One of Ramana's monsters.

Squire Shield- or armour-bearer of a knight.

Srutakirti Daughter of Kushadhwaja.

Stirabout Porridge made by stirring oatmeal into boiling milk or water.

Stone Giants A malignant race of stone beings whom the Iroquois believed invaded their territory, threatening the Confederation of the Five Nations. These fierce and hostile creatures lived off human flesh and were intent on exterminating the human race.

Stoorworm A great water monster which frequented lochs. When it thrust its great body from the sea, it could engulf islands and whole ships. Its appearance prophesied devastation.

Stot Bullock.

Styx River in Arcadia and one of the four rivers in the Underworld. Charon ferried dead souls across it into Hades, and Achilles was dipped into it to make him immortal.

Subrahmanian Son of Shiva, a mountain deity.

Sugriva The chief of the five great monkeys in the *Ramayana*.

Sukanya The wife of Chyavana.

Suman Son of Asamanja.

Sumantra A noble Brahman.

Sumati Wife of Sagara.

Sumedha A righteous Brahman who dwelt in the city of Amara.

Sumitra One of Dasharatha's three wives, mother of Lakshmana and Satrughna.

Suniti Mother of Dhruva.

Suparshwa One of Ravana's counsellors.

Supranakha A rakshasi, sister of Ravana.

Surabhi The wish-bestowing cow.

Surcoat Loose robe, traditionally worn over armour.

Surtr Fire-giant who eventually destroys the world at Ragnarok.

Surya God of the sun.

Susanoo God of the storm. He is depicted as a contradictory character with both good and bad characteristics. He was banished from Heaven after trying to kill his sister, Amaterasu.

Sushena A monkey chief.

Svasud Father of summer.

Swarga An Olympian paradise, where all wishes and desires are gratified.

Sweating A ritual customarily associated with spiritual purification and prayer practised by most tribes throughout North America prior to sacred ceremonies or vision quests. Steam was produced within a 'sweat lodge', a low, dome-shaped hut, by sprinkling water on heated stones.

Syrinx An Arcadian nymph who was the object of Pan's love.

Tablet of Destinies Cuneiform clay tablet on which the fates were written. Tiawath had given this to Kingu, but it was taken by Merodach when he defeated them. The storm god Zu later stole it for himself.

Taiaha A weapon made of wood.

Tailtiu One of the most famous royal residences of ancient Ireland. Possibly also a goddess linked to this site.

Tall One of Ravana's counsellors.

Tammuz Solar deity of Eridu who, with Gishzida, guards the gates of Heaven. Protector of Anu.

Tamsil Example or guidance.

Tangi Funeral, dirge. Assembly to cry over the dead.

Taniwha Sea monster, water spirit.

Tantalus Son of Zeus who told the secrets of the gods to mortals and stole their nectar and ambrosia. He was condemned to eternal torture in Hades, where he was tempted by food and water but allowed to partake of neither.

Taoism Taoism (or Daoism) came into being at roughly the same time as Confucianism, although its tenets were radically different and were largely founded on the philosophies of Lao Tzu (Laozi). While Confucius argued for a system of state discipline, Taoism strongly favoured self-discipline and looked upon nature as the architect of essential laws. A newer form of Taoism evolved after the Burning of the Books, placing great emphasis on spirit worship and pacification of the gods.

Tapu Sacred, supernatural possession of power. Involves spiritual rules and restrictions.

Tara Also known as Temair, the Hill of Tara was the popular seat of the ancient High-Kings of Ireland from the earliest times to the sixth century. Located in Co. Meath, it was also the place where great noblemen and chieftains congregated during wartime, or for significant events.

Tara Sugriva's wife.

Tartarus Dark region, below Hades.

Tau (Lesotho) Brother to Ra-Molo, depicted as a lion.

Taua War party.

Tefnut Goddess of water and rain. Married to Shu, who was also her brother. She, like Sekhmet, is portrayed with the head of a lion. Also known as Tefenet.

Telegonus Son of Odysseus and Circe. He was allegedly responsible for his father's death.

Telemachus Son of Odysseus and Penelope who was aided by Athene in helping his mother to keep away the suitors in Odysseus's absence.

Temu The evening form of Ra, the Sun god.

Tengu Goblin or gnome, often depicted as bird-like. A powerful fighter with weapons.

Tenochtitlán Capital city of the Aztecs, founded around 1350 CE and the site of the 'Great Temple'. Now Mexico City.

Teo-Amoxtli Divine book.

Teocalli Great temple built in Tenochtitlán, now Mexico City.

Teotleco Festival of the Coming of the Gods; also the twelfth month of the Aztec calendar.

Tepee A conical-shaped dwelling constructed of buffalo hide stretched over lodge-poles. Mostly used by Native American tribes living on the plains.

Tepeyollotl God of caves, desert places and earthquakes, whose name means 'heart of the mountain'. He is depicted as a jaguar, often leaping at the sun. Also known as Tepeolotlec.

Tepitoton Household gods.

Tereus King of Daulis who married Procne, daughter of Pandion King of Athens. He fell in love with Philomela, raped her and cut out her tongue.

Tezcatlipoca Supreme deity and Lord of the Smoking Mirror. He was also patron of royalty and warriors. Invented human sacrifice to the gods. Offspring of Ometeotl and Omecihuatl, he is known as the Jupiter of the Aztec gods.

Thalia Muse of pastoral poetry and comedy.

Theia Goddess of many names, and mother of the sun.

Theseus Son of King Aegeus of Athens. A cycle of legends has been woven around his travels and life.

Thetis Chief of the Nereids loved by both Zeus and Poseidon. They married her to a mortal, Peleus, and their child was Achilles. She tried to make him immortal by dipping him in the River Styx.

Thialfi Thor's servant, taken when his peasant father unwittingly harms Thor's goat.

Thiassi Giant and father of Skadi, he tricked Loki into bringing Idunn to him. Thrymheim is his kingdom.

Thomas the Rhymer Also called 'True Thomas', he was Thomas of Ercledoune, who lived in the thirteenth century. He met with the Queen of Elfland, and visited her country, was given clothes and a tongue that could tell no lie. He was also given the gift of prophecy, and many of his predictions were proven true.

Thor God of thunder and of war (with Tyr). Known for his huge size, and red hair and beard. Carries the hammer Miolnir. Slays Jormungander at Ragnarok.

Thoth God of the moon. Invented the arts and sciences and regulated the seasons. He is portrayed with the head of an ibis or a baboon.

Three-Heads One of Ravana's monsters.

Thrud Thor's daughter.

Thrudheim Thor's realm. Also called Thrudvang.

Thunder-Tooth Leader of the rakshasas at the siege of Lanka.

Tiawath Primeval dark ocean or abyss, Tiawath is also a monster and evil deity of the deep. She took the form of a dragon or sea serpent and battled the gods of light for supremacy over all living beings. She was eventually defeated by Merodach, who used her body to create Heaven and Earth.

Tiglath-Pileser I King of Assyria, who made it a leading power for centuries.

Tiki   First man created, a figure carved of wood, or other representation of man.

Tirawa   The name given to the Great Creator (*see* Great Spirit) by the Pawnee tribe who believed that four direct paths led from his house in the sky to the four semi-cardinal points: north-east, north-west, south-east and south-west.

Tiresias   A Theban who was given the gift of prophecy by Zeus. He was blinded for seeing Athene bathing. He continued to use his prophetic talents after his death, advising Odysseus.

Tirfing   Sword made by dwarves which was cursed to kill every time it was drawn, be the cause of three great atrocities, and kill Suaforlami (Odin's grandson), for whom it was made.

Tisamenus   Son of Orestes, who inherited the Kingdom of Argos and Sparta.

Titania   Queen of the fairies.

Tlaloc   God of rain and fertility, so important to the people, because he ensured a good harvest, that the Aztec heaven or paradise was named Tlalocan in his honour.

Tlazolteotl   Goddess of ordure, filth and vice. Also known as the earth-goddess or Tlaelquani, meaning 'filth-eater'. She acted as a confessor of sins or wrongdoings.

Tohu-mate   Omen of death.

Tohunga   A priest; a possessor of supernatural powers.

Toltec   Civilization that preceded the Aztecs.

Tomahawk   Hatchet with a stone or iron head used in war or hunting.

Tonalamatl   Record of the Aztec calendar, which was recorded in books made from bark paper.

Tonalpohualli   Aztec calendar composed of twenty thirteen-day weeks called trecenas.

Totec Solar deity known as Our Great Chief.

Totemism System of belief in which people share a relationship with a spirit animal or natural being with whom they interact. Examples include Ea, who is represented by a fish.

Toxilmolpilia The binding up of the years.

Tristan Nephew of King Mark of Cornwall, who travels to Ireland to bring Iseult back to marry his uncle. On the way, he and Iseult consume a love potion and fall madly in love before their story ends tragically.

Triton A sea-god, and son of Poseidon and Amphitrite. He led the Argonauts to the sea from Lake Tritonis.

Trojan War War waged by the Greeks against Troy, in order to reclaim Menelaus's wife Helen, who had eloped with the Trojan prince Paris. Many important heroes took part, and form the basis of many legends and myths.

Troll Unfriendly mythological creature of varying size and strength. Usually dwells in mountainous areas, among rocks or caves.

Truage Tribute or pledge of peace or truth, usually made on payment of a tax.

Tsuki-yomi God of the moon, brother of Amaterasu and Susanoo.

Tuat The other world or land of the dead.

Tupuna Ancestor.

Tvashtar Craftsman of the gods.

Tyndareus King of Sparta, perhaps the son of Perseus's daughter Grogphone. Expelled from Sparta but restored by Heracles. Married Leda and fathered Helen and Clytemnestra, among others.

Tyr Son of Frigga and the god of war (with Thor). Eventually kills Garm at Ragnarok.

Tzompantli Pyramid of Skulls.

Uayeb The five unlucky days of the Mayan calendar, which were believed to be when demons from the underworld could reach Earth. People would often avoid leaving their houses on uayeb days.

Ubaaner Magician, whose name meant 'splitter of stones', who created a wax crocodile that came to life to swallow up the man who was trying to seduce his wife.

Uile Bheist Mythical creature, usually some form of wild beast.

Uisneach A hill formation between Mullingar and Athlone said to mark the centre of Ireland.

uKqili (Zulu) Creator god.

Uller God of winter, whom Skadi eventually marries.

Ulster Cycle Compilation of folk tales and legends telling of the Ulaids, people from the northeast of Ireland, now named Ulster. Also known as the *Uliad Cycle*, it is one of four Irish cycles of mythology.

Unseelie Court An unholy court comprising a kind of fairies, antagonistic to humans. They took the form of a kind of Sluagh, and shot humans and animals with elf-shots.

Urd One of the Norns.

Urien King of Gore, husband of Morgan le Fey and father to Yvain.

Urmila Second daughter of Janaka.

Usha Wife of Aniruddha, daughter of Vanasur.

Ushas Goddess of the dawn.

Utgard-loki King of the giants. Tricked Thor.

Uther Pendragon King of England in sub-Roman Britain; father of King Arthur.

Utixo (Hottentot) Creator god.

Ut-Napishtim Ancestor of Gilgamesh, whom Gilgamesh sought out to discover how to prevent death. Similar to Noah in that he was sent a vision warning him of a great deluge. He built an ark in seven days, filling it with his family, possessions and all kinds of animals.

Uz Deity symbolized by a goat.

Vach Goddess of speech.

Vajrahanu One of Ravana's generals.

Vala Another name for Norns.

Valfreya Another name for Freyia.

Valhalla Odin's hall for the celebrated dead warriors chosen by the Valkyries.

Vali The cruel brother of Sugriva, dethroned by Rama.

Valkyries Odin's attendants, led by Freyia. Chose dead warriors to live at Valhalla. Also spelled as Valkyrs.

Vamadeva One of Dasharatha's priests.

Vanaheim Home of the Vanir.

Vanir Race of gods in conflict with the Aesir; they are gods of the sea and wind.

Varuna Ancient god of the sky and cosmos, later, god of the waters.

Vasishtha One of Dasharatha's priests.

Vassal Person under the protection of a feudal lord.

Vasudev Descendant of Yadu, husband of Rohini and Devaki, father of Krishna.

Vasudeva A name of Narayana or Vishnu.

Vavasor Vassal or tenant of a baron or lord who himself has vassals.

Vedic Mantras, hymns.

Vernandi One of the Norns.

Vichitravirya Bhishma's half-brother.

Vidar Slays Fenris.

Vidura Friend of the Pandavas.

Vigrid The plain where the final battle is held.

Vijaya Karna's bow.

Vikramaditya A king identified with Chandragupta II.

Vintail Moveable front of a helmet.

Virabhadra A demon that sprang from Shiva's lock of hair.

Viradha A fierce rakshasa, seizes Sita, slain by Rama.

Virupaksha The elephant who bears the whole world.

Vishnu The Preserver, Vedic sun god and one of the two great gods of post-Vedic Hinduism.

Vision Quest A sacred ceremony undergone by Native Americans to establish communication with the spirit set to direct them in life. The quest lasted up to four days and nights and was preceded by a period of solitary fasting and prayer.

Vivasvat The sun.

Vizier High-ranking official or adviser. Also known as vizir or vazir.

Volsung Family of great warriors about whom a great saga was spun.

Vrishadarbha King of Benares.

Vrishasena Son of Karna, slain by Arjuna.

Vyasa Chief of the royal chaplains.

Wairua Spirit, soul.

Wanjiru (Kikuyu) Maiden who was sacrificed by her village to appease the gods and make it rain after years of drought.

Weighing of the Heart Procedure carried out after death to assess whether the deceased was free from sin. If the deceased's heart weighed less than the feather of Ma'at, they would join Osiris in the Fields of Peace.

Whare Hut made of fern stems tied together with flax and vines, and roofed in with raupo (reeds).

White Demon Protector of Mázinderán. He prevented Kai-káús and his army from invading.

Withy Thin twig or branch which is very flexible and strong.

Wolverine Large mammal of the musteline family with dark, very thick, water-resistant fur, inhabiting the forests of North America and Eurasia.

Wroth Angry.

Wyrd One of the Norns.

Xanthus & Balius Horses of Achilles, immortal offspring of Zephyrus the west wind. A gift to Achilles's father Peleus.

Xipe Totec High priest and son of Ometeotl and Omecihuatl. Also known as the god of the seasons.

Xiupohualli Solar year, composed of eighteen twenty-day months. Also spelt Xiuhpōhualli.

Yadu A prince of the Lunar dynasty.

Yakshas Same as rakshasas.

Yakunin Government official.

Yama God of Death, king of the dead and son of the sun.

Yamato Take Legendary warrior and prince. Also known as Yamato Takeru.

Yashiki Residence or estate, usually of a daimyō.

Yasoda Wife of Nand.

Yemaya (Yoruba) Wife of Obatala.

Yemoja (Yoruba) Goddess of water and protector of women.

Yggdrasill The World Ash, holding up the Nine Worlds. Does not fall at Ragnarok.

Ymir Giant created from fire and ice; his body created the world.

Yo The female principle who, joined with In, the male side, brought about creation and the first gods. In and Yo correspond to the Chinese Yang and Yin.

Yomi The underworld.

Yudhishthira The eldest of the Pandavas, a great soldier.

Yuki-Onna The Snow-Bride or Lady of the Snow, who represents death.

Yvain Son of Morgan le Fay and knight of the Round Table, who goes on chivalric quests with a lion he rescued from a dragon.

Zahid Holy man.

Zál Son of Sám, who was born with pure white hair. Sám abandoned Zál, who was raised by the Símúrgh, or griffins. Zal became a great warrior, second only to his son, Rustem. Also known as Ním-rúz and Dustán.

Zephyr Gentle breeze.

Zeus King of gods, god of sky, weather, thunder, lightning, home, hearth and hospitality. He plays an important role as the voice of justice, arbitrator between man and gods, and among them. Married to Hera, but lover of dozens of others.

Zohák Serpent-king and figure of evil. Father of Mihrab.

Zu God of the storm, who took the form of a huge bird. Similar to the Persian símúrgh.

Zukin Head covering.

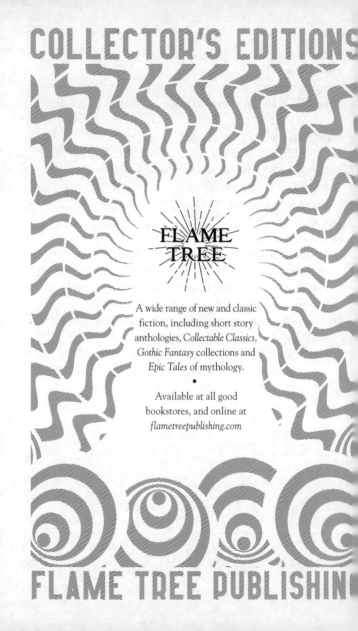